'A compulsive, heart-stopping read! Characters so real you feel you might bump into them. A bone-chiller of a book that you won't forget' **Sam Blake**

'An eighteen-year-old murder mystery makes for a gripping and highly atmospheric page-turner' **Andrea Carter**

'Superbly crafted – a gripping thriller, but also a sensitive and insightful portrayal of guilt and grief. It's both beautifully written and nerve-shreddingly tense' **Jane Casey**

'Sharp with emotional depth. The portrayal of life as an influencer, curated for "likes" and full of secrets, feels disturbingly real and painfully resonant. Perdue delivers brilliant, intricate and suspenseful storytelling' **Amanda Cassidy**

'A complex mystery that takes in the secrets of families and relationships, and how we never know what goes on behind closed doors. A contemporary white-knuckle ride that I could not look away from until the shocking end' **Edel Coffey**

'Start reading Gill Perdue now, and thank me later'
Claire Coughlan

'An all-too-believable look behind the glossy world of the social media influencer – both a satisfying mystery and a new twist on the traditional police duo' **Sinéad Crowley**

'Her propulsive narrative and perfect plotting make this Gill Perdue's best book yet – grabs you from the very first page and it won't let go' **Michelle Dunne**

'A cautionary tale of the slippery world of social media where the curated life masks another world entirely. Lyrical, clever, tense and deliciously dark' **Rory Egan**

'I loved every word. It combines a detective duo to root for and believe in, and a fresh and current mystery that builds to a stunning and atmospheric climax' **C. M. Ewan**

'I absolutely loved it. So tightly plotted with great characters – even one I myself wanted to kill! Had me on tenterhooks throughout' **Patricia Gibney**

'Richly compelling characters and a plot that keeps the pages turning' **Rosemary Hennigan**

'A dark, unsettling mystery. Gill Perdue's ability to capture relationship dynamics is rivalled only by her skill at creating nail-biting tension' **Amy Jordan**

'Utterly, UTTERLY magnificent – great writing, gorgeous characterization and such a plot! I'm awarding it 13/10 on my QWJ* scale (*Queasy with Jealousy That I Didn't Write It)' **Marian Keyes**

'Her best book yet . . . [it has] empathy and drama, and a thrill of a second ending' **Catherine Kirwan**

'High stakes, secrecy and betrayal, with such terrific dynamism between characters. I raced through it' **L. V. Matthews**

'A twisty, intriguing, clever crime thriller. Gill Perdue's characters are so well drawn, with the setting which is a fabulous character in itself. It's beautifully written, the author's empathy shining through' **Michelle McDonagh**

'Propulsive and engaging . . . such authentic, believable characters you won't want to say goodbye' **Fiona McPhillips**

'Perdue has a real way of seeing into people's minds and hearts, and she's not afraid of the dark' **Kitty Murphy**

'Sharp, savvy, twisty, modern . . . gets you in the gut – I loved it!' **Vicki Notaro**

'Gill Perdue is firmly taking her place among the best of women crime writers' **Liz Nugent**

'Masterfully written with a heart-thumping climax' **Tina Orr Munro**

'So completely gripping that by the time I reached the final chapters you would have had to tear the book from my cold dead hands. Told with delicacy and real understanding and perfectly paced, this is one of the best crime novels I've read in ages' **Karen Perry**

'Brilliant. Nobody does the combination of police procedural paired with the slow-burn of a sinister domestic thriller like Gill Perdue. An absolute page-turner' **Jo Spain**

The Night I Killed Him

GILL PERDUE

SANDYCOVE

an imprint of

PENGUIN BOOKS

SANDYCOVE

UK | USA | Canada | Ireland | Australia
India | New Zealand | South Africa

Sandycove is part of the Penguin Random House group of companies
whose addresses can be found at global.penguinrandomhouse.com

Penguin Random House UK,
One Embassy Gardens, 8 Viaduct Gardens, London SW11 7BW

penguin.co.uk

Penguin
Random House
UK

First published 2025

001

Copyright © Gill Perdue, 2025

The moral right of the author has been asserted

Set in 13.5/16pt Garamond MT Std
Typeset by Jouve (UK), Milton Keynes
Printed and bound in Great Britain by Clays Ltd, Elcograf S.p.A.

The authorized representative in the EEA is Penguin Random House Ireland,
Morrison Chambers, 32 Nassau Street, Dublin DO2 YH68

A CIP catalogue record for this book is available from the British Library

ISBN: 978–1–844–88681–4

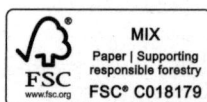

For the RNLI and all those
who risk their lives to save others.

Fear and Guilt are the only enemies of man.

—Elisabeth Kübler-Ross

The last fragment of rope, barely a strand, perishes, consumed by a microscopic marine organism with an unpronounceable name – if it even has a name. As it does, the body begins to rise, no longer tethered in its dark water-coffin.

It rises from the ocean floor face down, limbs hanging, arms spread like a blessing – a water angel. Fragments of sea-rotted fabric are borne away in the currents to be nibbled by curious fish.

The belt of rope sways, umbilical – in the vast, marine womb.

The boy is going home.

Thursday

I

Laura

The text comes in just as I'm finishing up the first lecture of the morning. I feel the vibration but ignore it. Well done, I tell myself. Progress. Time was when I would have been compelled to check it even with thirty pairs of eyes on me, or maybe only twenty-nine – manspreading guy at the end of the second row has been on his phone for the last ten, his meaty right thigh pressing up against the hapless red-haired girl sitting beside him. She looks flushed and uncomfortable, failing in an effort to look as though she hasn't noticed.

'So, basically, these are the interview techniques you will need, the ones you will come to rely on in your day-to-day work. We're not – repeat, not – looking for a natural inter-view guided by your intuition,' I say, stepping down off the low podium and making my way towards Manspreader. I stand in front of him; he's in my peripheral vision, but I direct my gaze above him, up towards the back row.

'The problem with so-called natural interviews is that they're useless. They elicit less information than what's potentially available, but worse – sometimes they actually entice the witness to provide incorrect evidence.'

The outside of my left knee is so close to his I can feel a faint heat.

'Not so with the science-based approach,' I continue. There's a flicker of light beneath the bag that's propped on his lap. Then a shift in his shoulders as he hides the phone. He looks up at me.

'Science-based approaches have been shown to elicit more witness information in more cases, without – and this is the most important part – without distorting the witness's memory.'

I turn, making sure I knock against his knee as I do so. Two can play at that game. Not too hard though – *Dial down the rage, Laura. It was a long time ago. It will never happen again.*

'And next week, we'll be looking at memory.'

I even make myself wait while they file out past me on their way to the coffee break, many of them smiling their thanks. That's the thing with guards, I suppose. Basically, they're hardwired to communicate, to interact. But there are always exceptions. Manspreader makes his way out without a word, his eyes locked on to a distant point in the corridor. Niamh's voice in my head says *little bollix*, and I have to hide my smile.

Her text – because of course it was her – asks if I can get back to Dublin by two thirty, or three at the latest.

There's a body. We're up. Will fill you in. Call when you're on the road.

'So do we have an ID?' I merge on to the motorway, adjusting the visor to deflect the midday sun. The drive will take the best part of two and a half hours and I could do without being blinded the whole way.

'Still not certain, but it's looking like Max Fitzgerald. MisPer – Dún Laoghaire, from, like eighteen years ago?'

I nod, a vague memory of the name and the case beginning to filter through my mind.

'Something about a twenty-first birthday?'

'Yeah, that's right – here, wait.' She begins reading.

6

'This from the portal: Gardaí are seeking – blah blah – tracing the whereabouts of twenty-one-year-old Max Fitzgerald from Dún Laoghaire, who has been missing since 1 June 2007. He is described as being 6 feet 01 inches in height, of strong build with fair hair. He was wearing a black "tuxedo"-type suit, with a monogrammed black leather belt, a white shirt and black bow tie. Max was last seen at Corrig Point Yacht Club in Dún Laoghaire at approximately 10.30 p.m.

'They found remains washed up near Howth – a belt that fits the bill. And a cufflink,' says Niamh. 'He's with Parminter now – we'll get DNA results later.'

State pathologist Dr Parminter – or Dr Death as he's known in the unit – is the crucial first phase of every investigation. I picture him hunched over the body on his slab, his Italian suit hidden under the gown, scavenging for clues like a vulture picking over a corpse. If ever a person's appearance suited the job, it's Parminter's.

'The decay must have been desperate,' I say, shivering at the thought of the poor boy – only twenty-one when he disappeared – underwater all those years. Surely he was reduced to bare bones. 'How could they—'

She cuts me off. 'Parminter is wetting himself in excitement. He was preserved in mud or silt or something. So he's actually in quite good nick.'

'Wow – like one of those bog bodies?'

'Well, no – because he's only been gone about eighteen years. But, I suppose, yeah. Well preserved, if that's what you meant.'

She waits. And I know she can't resist it.

'Kind of like yourself. What with your advanced age an' all.'

I'm turning forty in three weeks. Here we go.

'You're relentless,' I say, 'I'll give you that. Never miss an opportunity—'

'In fairness, you know I've only got your best interests at heart.' I can hear the laughter in her voice. 'Exposure therapy, or whatever it's called – it helps you get ready for it. The big four oh. So you'll be prepared.'

I concentrate on overtaking a tractor. The sun has gone in and, in the distance, blue-black rain clouds huddle. I think of the boy – young man – Max Fitzgerald.

'Does Parminter – do they reckon he's been dead since that night? Like he wasn't, you know, hiding out or in the UK or—'

'Living under an assumed name in wherever the feck? No. The photo – ah – you'll see.'

Her voice is flat. So she's seen photos.

'We've to talk to the sister later on. You know who that is, right?' Something niggles – wealth, fame – but no name appears.

'Should I?'

'Well, yeah, if you're on Instagram or like – if you ever read a magazine. The sister is Gemma – as in—'

She says something I can't make out.

'What?'

'She's massive on Insta, Twitter, TikTok, what have you – you must have heard of her?' More crackling. 'Gemma Fitzgerald? Calls herself Gemstone, I think.'

'I'll ask Alva,' I say, knowing that my half-sister will be up on all this. Nine years makes a difference. 'I never check my Instagram.'

'Jeekers! There's a shocker!' She laughs. 'Annieway – no matter. They'll send someone from Family Liaison when they know for definite. We don't have to break it to her. Look, you'll have to come into the unit first, okay? Cig wants a word. Then we'll head out to Dún Laoghaire together. We'll just gather a bit of info, yeah?'

8

Shit. I add another four hours to the time I'm likely to make it home to Matt and the kids – as well as the overnight I've already had. I feel the lurch of guilt, but I squash it down. They love their dad and he's – go on, admit it, Laura – he's better with them than you are. And now we've Alva living with us it means that there's no juggling with babysitters and childminders. She's taken compassionate leave from her job so she's around to help out when she's not with her – our – dad, and the various playdates and the after-school club take up the rest. And Matt. Good old Matt.

'Oh, okay. Why us? Is she not—'

'Yeah – she is – Corrig Point is her local station. But they contacted us – you, really. There's a statement from the girl in 2007, when it happened – when he went missing. They want your expert input.'

A beat of silence while she waits. And I wonder about the interview: 2007 pre-dates the role of specialist victim interviewer.

'What age was she when—'

'Sixteen.'

And like that, I'm in. What did they get out of her back then? Who conducted the interview? Who took the statement? What can she remember now, eighteen years later?

'Okay. I'll be another hour and a half – it's going to lash,' I say. 'See you in the big shmoke.' I do my best impression of Niamh's accent. I imagine her pained expression.

'God, that was embarrassing,' she says, ending the call.

The road unspools ahead of me, bounded on either side with chequerboard fields, like rugs spread over the Tipperary landscape. Ancient and timeless. I check my rear-view mirror in preparation for overtaking the battered Nissan ahead of me. And my heart lurches – the body reacting before the

9

brain has time to engage. Because in the rear-view mirror I see a van driven by a man in his thirties – heavy-set, scowling. It's the van I see everywhere, not every day but – face it, Laura – you've never had an entire week without thinking you've seen it. I carry him with me, that bastard who raped me when I was nineteen. I carry him in spite of years of therapy. In spite of doing the job I do, where I lock away people like him every bloody day. So why do I still feel his weight, his panting roughness? Why can I still see his entitled, ignorant smirk?

I make myself look again before putting the boot down to overtake. The guy in the van is a young man – as opposed to over fifty, which is how old he'd have to be by now. And the van registration is 2022. So, yeah – of course it's not him. Tell that to my subconscious.

2

Niamh

I hand her a coffee as soon as she walks in the door.

'Thanks,' she breathes. 'Lifesaver.'

She moves towards the desk, shrugging off her green suit jacket. For days when she's lecturing on the SVI training course Laura alternates between this new green trouser suit and one in a brutal shade of brown. But I know from my fashion training back in the days when I was seeing Amber that the sludgier the colour, the more expensive the brand. Or maybe that was only that particular season.

'Were they not all ordering drinks and snacks off you?' I point towards the jacket. 'In your fecking shamrock Aer Lingus uniform?'

'Piss off.' She grins, placing her coffee on the desk and moving to sit. 'Piss right off.'

'Ah-ah.' I shake my head. 'Cig's expecting us – as in, right now. Five minutes ago.'

'Damn,' she says, putting the jacket back on. She takes a quick gulp of coffee, wincing at the temperature, then leaves the cup on the corner of the desk. She smooths her dark hair behind her ears, straightens the waistband of the trousers – I mean, green trousers, plain weird – and grabs her briefcase.

'Bring the coffee, for feck's sake!' I yell. 'I paid for that!'

She shakes her head. Even now, she wouldn't want to be casually sipping a coffee in front of Cig.

'I'll have it after. Come on.'

The corridor linking the SVI office to the main unit is long and narrow with doors opening off on either side the whole way along. I can't help it.

'On board this aircraft there are six emergency exits, two doors at the rear of the cabin, left and right' – I turn to face her – 'two doors at the front of the cabin—'

A bear-like growl emerges from Cig's office, the last door on the right. Shit. I reckoned without his supersonic hearing. Plus, you'd expect the door to be closed – he's been in foul humour, with me in particular, for weeks. They're decorating, and his door sign is hanging drunkenly askew. *D. McNeil Detective Inspector* is perpendicular to the floor. I resist the urge to straighten it. Best say nothing. Maybe he'll blame Laura for the noise.

'There you are,' he says, his frown tightening to a scowl. If it wasn't for the scowl, I'd have added, *No shit, Sherlock.* We stand to attention. He really doesn't look well. His eyes are pouchy – in fact, his whole face is sort of saggy.

'Cig,' nods Laura. I do the same.

A file is open in front of him – one of the old ones in the speckly grey stiffened paper. My nose itches. I can smell the mildew from where I'm standing three feet away.

'This is from O'Riordan in Corrig Point,' he says. 'Stuff on the sister from way back – even before the lad disappeared. Look, I'm not going to go through this with ye now.' He sighs, looking up and shuffling the yellowed foolscap pages into a bundle. 'Ye can do it in the car.'

He pats the outside of the folder then slides it and some other pages into a large, battered envelope.

'But ye can expect a fair amount of rírá on this one for certain. This case was huge when it happened. It was all over the telly, the papers. You – ye're both too young to remember, but yeah – huge.'

'Thanks, Cig,' says Laura, taking hold of the envelope.

'She lives in the family home with the husband and kid—'

'There's a kid?' says Laura, exactly at the same time as I go: 'There's a husband?' Cig's head swivels slowly – an old bull looking over a gate. Waiting.

'The husband, Conleth O'Hara – not sure what he does. Involved in a sailing charity thing. Online presence – check him out. Kid is a boy – Ferdia. He's four.'

'Does she know we're coming out to talk to her?'

'Yeah. Garda Killeen will probably be there still. She's the family liaison officer from Corrig Point,' he says, reading the name from a Post-it on the desk. 'And you'll link up with your former colleague – McCarthy is based there now. Sergeant McCarthy. He'll keep ye in the loop.'

McArsey? Great! I know I gave him a hard time – and I know he's decent underneath all the shite – I mean, he was prepared to take a bullet for us and all – but he's still a preening, prissy goody-goody. Can't say I'd been missing having him around. I sigh. A thought strikes me.

'She didn't have to identify the body, did she? Holy God, that'd be shite—'

'No,' Cig interrupts. 'The belt or something matches the description from way back. Still – look—' A crease of irritation crumples his features. He's so impatient I don't know how he ever made inspector. 'Go on. O'Riordan is SIO on this; ye're reporting to him. I told him I can spare ye for a day or two. So ye're on TT. Now get cracking.'

I consider asking him how long the temporary transfer is for, because 'a day or two' is a bit vague. But then I catch Laura's frown.

We get cracking. I drive so Laura can go through the file, shaking her head and sighing before she's even turned the page.

'What?'

13

'She was already on the books from way back.' She spreads the pages across her lap, smoothing creased paper. 'Shoplifting – just petty stuff, drunk and disorderly – they had to bring her home more than once, cautioned—'

'All because of the brother?' I interrupt her flow. Laura flips back a page.

'Well, yeah – but like I said – some of it was way back. And then there was an overdose,' says Laura. 'That same year. Alcohol and painkillers.'

'Copycat after Max?' I speculate.

She says nothing. She's shaking her head at some photographs pinned to the sheets.

'What?'

It takes a fair amount to silence her. Laura's seen it all. We both have. Maybe it's the mammy thing. She denies it, but I know she's been more affected by stuff since having Katie – it can't be easy keeping it at a distance.

'What is it?'

She shakes her head, closing the file abruptly.

'You'll see later.' She sighs. 'Poor kid. She was on a major self-destruct mission, by the looks of it.' She pats the file. 'And the suicide attempt was before the brother died.'

3

Gemma

I make myself breathe — three in, three out. The garda watches me while I make tea. I can feel it, though my back is turned. Three seconds for the in breath, three to exhale through pursed lips, a downward draught. I turn to face her, setting the cups down on the table, and her ponytail swings forward as she leans to add the milk, glossy red waves bouncing. It strikes me that her hair is too cheerful for her job description.

I don't think she's a follower, though she's trying not to stare. I'll give her that. Her eyes keep sliding away from the cup of tea to the wall of photographs behind me. I consider telling her it was Conleth's idea to do a celebrity wall, but that seems petty. Her eyes skim the photos left to right, like she's reading code.

'Wimbledon,' she says, tilting her head with a little nod of appreciation. 'Is that Centre Court?'

'Yeah,' I say, 'but only the quarter finals.'

God, that sounds stupid.

'And is that Ryan Tubridy? Holding your little boy?'

I don't need to look to know what photo she means. Conleth again — I was mortified. Interrupting Tubs over his quiet coffee on the seafront. But he was right. He knows what works. Over seven hundred likes on a slow morning.

'Look, I'm — I don't need to be babysat,' I say, ignoring her question. Breathe in, two, three. I just want her gone. We've exhausted all the small talk – she's been here the guts of an hour and the tea is a follow-up to the glass of water. My voice is shaky. The less she gets to hear it, the better.

Four missed calls on my phone this morning meant that it was Conleth who answered the door to her and brought her downstairs, eyeing me over the top of her head.

'This is Garda Killeen. She's the family liaison garda from Corrig Point station,' he'd said. 'She's here to talk to you about Max.'

'Max,' I'd whispered. 'Oh.'

And my heart pounded in my chest as the dark moths swirled, rising from the depths. I swallow a gulp of tea, tasting metal. I'm carved in ice. I check the time.

Conleth had left us then, saying he'd do the pick-up from school, although I told him that I could easily ask Penny.

'Of course I'll get him,' he said, with a broad smile, which the garda returned. 'No need for us to trouble Penny.'

He's not that keen on Penny. She has twin boys, Eli and Jude, in Ferdia's class, and a big house set back from the road, on one of those Edwardian squares. I'm not sure why he doesn't like her, because he usually likes good-looking women. It could be that she tends to focus on me anytime we meet up and she doesn't make an effort for him, for anyone. 'I'm not big into the whole people-pleasing thing,' she told me when we first met. 'But I won't bullshit you – and I can help out with your little guy anytime.'

God! I need to see Ferdia. To have him barrel into me, all elbows and knees and grubby hands, hugging me around the neck. To feel myself loved, needed. I can endure anything if he's safe. In my son's eyes, I'm something. Something good.

I struggle to refocus. 'I'm fine, honestly. I can look after myself until he – sorry, I can't remember who – what did you say the detective's name was? The guy coming to talk to me?'

She studies me, her gaze travelling to my hands, which are clasped around the mug. I relax my grip.

'It's Detective Garda Laura Shaw – she's from Seskin West, and' – she gives a wry smile – 'it'll be more than my job is worth if I head off before she arrives. You – I mean, it's a deeply shocking experience, you know? Finding out this – this kind of n—'

She was going to say *news*. Yes – I suppose it is. Family tragedy is news.

'Information,' she amends.

There's a ring of the doorbell, and our eyes meet.

'That could be her,' she says, getting to her feet. 'I'll go.'

She takes the two flights of stairs up to the hall at a sprint. Obviously she doesn't want to keep Detective Shaw waiting. I hear raised voices and the slam of the door. Of course, I think, moving to look out the window. They're here already. A little flock of reporters, flapping and bickering like the seagulls wheeling overhead. How do they know what's happening before I do? I'd better post something.

@gemstone: Today, Gardaí have confirmed that the missing person appeal for my brother, Max Fitzgerald, who went missing from Dún Laoghaire in June 2007, has been stood down.
Incredibly grateful to An Garda Síochána for finding my big bro after all these years.
Rest in peace, Max –

No – that's too religious. And I should say something about privacy.

Incredibly grateful to An Garda Síochána for finding my beloved big brother at long last. Thank you for understanding our request for privacy at this time.

#A safe harbour for Max.

Wasn't that safe a harbour, was it? I try to ignore that voice. Three in. I will take this darkness to my grave. Three out.

I hit post as Garda Killeen enters the kitchen, her phone in her hand.

'Journalist. I've sent for someone to clear them,' she says and, finally, instead of envy, something like sympathy mists her eyes. 'I don't know how you stand it.'

I shrug, allowing the sigh to escape. Then I add a smile to counteract the resting bitch face. Conleth says I look like a hag unless I'm actually smiling. People-pleasing is part of my DNA. Now.

'Thank you. It's grand. Part of the job.'

@missymurfi: Oh my God, Gemma! Saw the guards at your house. The guards are our friends.

@nolimitsgrl: Hope this will bring closure. And the answers you seek.

@marymary2: The same as @nolimitsgrl. It's heart-breaking, but I hope it brings you peace.

@missymurfi: We're all here for you, Gemma. We are your friends. May your brother rest in peace.

4

Laura

We arrive just in time to see the squad car pulling up in front of the towering four-storey mansion and two uniforms getting out. We wait while they herd the reporters from the footpath to the strip of grass which separates the terrace from the lower road. Nelson Terrace is set high above this road, behind iron railings, a long row of tall Georgian houses facing the sea.

Niamh pulls in and cuts the engine.

'Roysh?' she says, in Southside tones. 'Jaysus, I wouldn't mind living here!'

I can't summon a smile. I'm still thinking about the photos, imagining if that was Katie in just a few years. Imagining the pain of Max's parents: one child missing, one destroying herself. And then I remember Niamh hasn't seen the file yet. The skinny teenage arms marked by scars – scars on top of scars – purple cuts and black bruises, cigarette burns.

Cameras click and flash as we get out of the car and I struggle to file the images away.

'As opposed to your mansion in the exclusive south-city suburb of Ranelagh?' I quip, clicking the car lock with the fob. 'You fell on your feet there with Dorothy.'

Niamh's face softens at the mention of her landlady – the terrifyingly tweedy elderly Dorothy, ninety-two years and still going strong. Dorothy set up her own pharmacy in the fifties and ran it for over four decades – at a time when professional women were a rarity, never mind one who ran her own business. She went on to be pharmacist/agony-aunt-cum-GP-cum-therapist for generations of families in the area – and now landlady to Niamh, who lives in her annexe.

'Ah, fair dues.' Niamh grins. 'Dorothy's pure sound. Not gonna argue with you on that.'

We stride through a barrage of questions:

'Any results from the autopsy yet, detectives?'

'Is it definitely Max?'

'Why did it take so long to locate the body?'

'Why did Max commit suicide?'

Confidential information leaked to the press already. Perfect.

I bite back the urge to tell that ignorant idiot that the phrase is *die by suicide*. That it's not a crime someone 'commits'. Not in the way he understands it anyway. Instead, we ignore the yells of the reporters and sprint up the front steps. Midway up, to my left I glimpse a flash of long blonde hair, a blue cardigan through the basement window. Niamh sees me clock Gemma. She nods.

'She posted a couple of minutes ago,' she says. 'First thing we do is get her to switch off the phone, right?'

The FLO – Killeen – lets us in without us having to ring the bell. She seems happy to hand over, but there's no chance to talk in private. Gemma – immaculate, ice-blonde, tiny and beautiful – waits at the top of the stairs. She stares, then blinks. Like one of those china dolls – and about the same size. She offers a slim, chilly hand. I take it, suppressing a shiver.

5

Gemma

They say their names but, immediately, I forget. I'm so bad at taking in new information. Already I don't know which one is which. Conleth says I don't listen. I'm trying to work on this.

'Sure, why would you care what the little people are called? It's up to them to remember your name,' he teases. I've told him I'm not like that. That's not why I can't remember. I tell him I actually do wish I could remember names, but he just does that thing where he walks away or moves on to something else, like he knows me better than I know myself. Like he knows things about me that I don't know. And that's true.

'Sorry.' I look at the shorter one who takes the chair closer to me. She'd said something.

'It's okay – I was just—'

'What's your name again?' I blurt. 'I didn't quite catch it.'

She turns towards me, and her jaw-skimming bob swings. Breathe, I tell myself. Concentrate. I focus on her outfit – the suit is great – I reckon it's by that company that uses recycled fabrics. The Portuguese one.

'I'm Detective Shaw – Laura,' she says. She pauses, allowing the other one to speak – tall, with long, honeyed hair. I wonder is it two shades of highlights, maybe caramel highlights and—

'I'm Niamh,' she says, her voice softer than I expected.

'Laura.' I say. 'Niamh.'

I've got this. Two. Three. I can do it. For Ferdia. For Max.

'Look, this is just an informal chat,' says Laura. 'While we wait for Dr Parminter's official results. We're from Seskin West, but we're working with the team from Corrig Point on this case. You spoke to the senior investigating officer, Detective Inspector Alan O'Riordan, I believe?'

She's going way too fast. I'm so bad at names.

'I can't remember the name – sorry. But yes, I got a call and then the – Garda, um – Killeen came and—'

'Right,' she says. 'Of course. Look – would you like to sit down?'

She indicates the chair, and I sit. 'We wanted to tell you in person – that the body they found this morning – we're ninety-nine per cent certain that it's Max.'

Max. Such a short name. Three little letters. One syllable. Like 'die'. And 'sad'. And 'bro' – my big bro. *Maxattacks* – our chanting challenge. He always won races. But I won the staring matches. They were my department. The chasing games, when he and Conleth would chase me in the back garden when they got home from school or sailing club, I never had a hope. But Max was kind. I realize that now. He'd pretend to trip over his lace or knock his knee against the steps that led into the upper bit of the garden. And that would give me time to clamber into the wooden treehouse. Kinder than Conleth, who didn't like to be beaten by a nine year-old kid. Conleth would follow me all the way into the treehouse. He'd poke my arm, or my bony chest – 'Gotcha.'

Later, he said it's because I drove him crazy, even then. But Max – poor Max. Maxattacks.

'Gemma?' Her voice – the taller one. Niamh. It comes from far away. Like she's – like I'm down a well, and she's leaning over the edge, and she's calling to me. But the words are so far away. Max.

'Sorry. Yes. I understand. You're sure it's him?' They could be wrong. It could be a mistake. The other one puts her hand on my arm. She leans in as she squeezes.

'Unfortunately – yes. We're sure it's Max.'

'Oh! And now – what will happen next?' And I need them to be talking and explaining because my heart hammers and their voices are so faint and I can't believe that now, today – after all this time. Today is the day. 'Like, when – oh my God! Poor Max! After all this time!'

Laura nods quick little nods of sympathy.

'We're going to take it one step at a time, Gemma. And just so you know, there's quite a bit of red tape, and procedures to follow when' – she pauses, inhales – 'when something like this happens.'

But I'm not listening. I'm remembering my big brother. Max was so young. Just twenty-one. And I'm so much older than he ever got to be – more than a decade older. I'm thirty-four. He's twenty-one. But in my head he's always my big brother, five years older. 'Five years older, but Gemma's bolder,' he'd chant, teasing – enjoying my flares of temper. When I had a temper. When I was real. That girl is an echo of a memory. Like a dream.

'There will be an inquiry first. And then they'll release the body in due course,' she's saying. 'For the funeral.'

I mirror the fast little head nods that Laura's doing. 'Yes, yes, of course,' I whisper. 'A funeral. Of course. I understand.'

'In due course,' she repeats the phrase, and I repeat the nods. 'But for now, all we want to do this evening,' says Laura, 'is go over a few facts.'

I draw my cardigan across my chest, allowing her hand to slip from my arm. Sustainable cashmere. Crashed the website with the number of orders. The softness makes me want to cry. I get loads of questions every time I wear it in photos.

'Where did you find him?' I know it's a non-sequitur, but I need to know. She checks something in her file.

'Apparently, the recent neap tide, combined with that storm—'

'Storm Lucy,' interjects Niamh. Go me. Remembering both their names.

'Caused massive tidal surges which washed him up on Drumleck Point. It's in Howth.'

'Oh.'

I think of that girl he dated. She lived in Howth. Michelle. I remember thinking she looked French, like her name. I should invite her as well.

I see them exchange a look. I shake my head.

'I'm sorry,' I say. 'I was thinking – I was thinking about Howth. Sorry.' Let's say that's what I was thinking about.

'That's quite all right,' Niamh says, and her voice is so kind. 'They – we don't know for certain the trajectory, you know, or how he came to end up there. We'll be talking to a tidal expert, and they're doing – ah – analysis. Tests. But—'

Now Laura sits forward. She looks at Niamh and it occurs to me that she's deciding whether or not to reveal something.

Don't hold back, Laura. I can take it.

'It's likely he was – his body was somewhere very deep. It could have remained undisturbed all this time.'

Yes. Poor Max. All those years buried deep. I'm sorry, Max.

And all that he could see, see, see,

Was the bottom of the deep blue sea, sea, sea.

And the dark.

Although Max wasn't scared of the dark, not like me. We camped in the back garden once – it was freezing when I woke in the middle of the night and the sunny afternoon had been gobbled up by the dark and the night noises. A smell of compost and wet grass hung in the air, and I was terrified. I wanted to go inside to my warm bed, and I shook Max to make him bring me inside. The thought of opening the zip, of padding across the spiders and slugs and the wet grass, of maybe finding the back door locked – it was too much for me. But he was just a teenage boy of what? He must have been about fifteen then. He was so deeply asleep I just couldn't wake him. He mumbled something and stuck his hand out of the sleeping bag like he was offering a Christmas cracker. He held my hand all night. And his hand was surprisingly soft. And warm. And I held his mumbled sentences – *Go to sleep. I'm here* – I held them like a precious stone.

But I can't think like that.

She's still talking. Get a grip. Breathe. Christ – I need a drink.

'So the body is—' She hesitates, and I'm skewered by her pity. It stings. I don't deserve it. 'Actually, it's well preserved.'

I freeze. What does she mean?

'Great,' I say, though I know that's not right. Well preserved? But he – how can that be? He's been gone for so long. And I'm on my feet before I can stop myself. 'I'm sorry – but it's been such a shock – I—' It's all I can do not to sprint. And I despise myself, because I'm barely holding it together.

'Gin?' I slosh some into a glass and top it up with another slosh from a can of flat tonic, then swig it down. I keep my back turned so I don't have to see their reaction. It takes less than ten seconds, but the gin hits my empty stomach and I could cry with relief.

'He was – the body was preserved in deep mud,' says Laura. 'So Dr Parminter will have a good chance of finding out—'

She stops. And I can feel them both watching me, and I don't dare turn around. There's a body – an actual body – which means there could be evidence. Even now.

'Finding out what?' My voice is brittle. It clangs. I take another swig.

'What happened to your brother. How he died.'

A look passes between them, and I'm jealous. They're friends, you can see it between them, like they're listening to the same song – they don't even have to speak. And a baby voice – that same voice, that whining, pathetic victim that lives inside my brain – she goes, *I want a friend like that.* But you need honesty to get a friend like that. Even Penny – the kindest, sweetest friend ever – she literally only knows the half of it.

Niamh settles her face into a harmless smile. She's pretty, with wide green eyes and a generous mouth. No Botox. No fillers. Outdoor-girl vibes.

'But isn't it certain – sorry, I didn't mean—' I pause, struggling for calm. 'What I meant to say was, didn't you say he drowned?' I continue, my voice tilting up valley-girl at the end.

'Yes, but perhaps there were other factors involved, you know?'

She's watching me closely. In a gentler voice, she goes on. 'Perhaps he'd taken drugs, or some medication – perhaps he even slipped and fell. An accident.'

'So, it might not have been suicide?' I say, and I'm careful with my voice and I hold my glass of double gin very steady.

'We don't know yet,' says Laura, glancing at her.

Oh, but we do, Laura. We do.

And I won't think about that. Instead, I wonder when they will release the body. Poor Max. I'm – I'll be glad to have a body to put in a coffin. I imagine the coffin being carried up the aisle of the church on the shoulders of the men. It will be all those guys from the yacht club. And Conleth. Of course.

And Conleth will walk slowly, although Max's twenty-one-year-old body – or what's left of it – is probably half the weight of Conleth's thirty-nine-year-old heft. But they'll all walk slowly out of respect.

And I know it won't be like this, but I picture seawater spilling out of the coffin and down over their shoulders, particles of tiny shells and slivers of seaweed trickling on to the red tiles.

And then I nearly gasp out loud because I almost thought the phrase *buried at sea*. I almost said that he should be buried at sea.

But he's been there. Done that. That's the problem. He's no longer buried at sea. I'm sorry, Max. Your eternal rest disturbed. The sea churned you up and spat you out. No rest for Maxattacks. I'm so sorry.

6

Laura

She's wound so tight I can nearly hear the vibrations in the air. And I should know. It takes one to know one. She's processing information, her mind racing behind that beautiful mask of a face. But her fingers are white-bone clenched around the glass and her jaw is rigid. I need to get her to relax. We'll get nothing like this.

I point towards one of the photos on the wall. A toddler of about three – who must be Ferdia – is standing in a sandbox clutching a bright red and blue digger toy, an expression of delight plastered on his face.

'What's your little boy's name? He's gorgeous.' And he is – he's wearing those wraparound glasses they use for kids – the sturdy ones. His are bright blue and his eyes look huge through the thick lenses. He's fair, like his mum.

She unclenches – less than I'd hoped, but still. A genuine smile lights her features.

'Ferdia—' Her head tilts as she looks at the picture. She walks to the wall of photos and takes it down, bringing it over to the table and finally pulling out a chair to sit on.

'That was his third birthday. We gave him the sandpit and the digger. It's hilarious – he absolutely loves it. He's obsessed with it still. Brings it everywhere. Treats it like a doll, but Conleth—' She stops.

I'm on the verge of telling her about Noah, that he's the same age. That, in fact, I think we even have that same digger

29

toy. But something holds me back. I wonder why she stopped speaking.

'He's so cute!' Niamh is grinning. 'I love his glasses.'

Gemma shoots her a suspicious look, her face closing down once more. Niamh rows back.

'I'm not winding you up – sorry. Did that sound rude? Jaysus, sorry, I meant I actually love when little kids have those. You know, the whole Harry Potter brainbox—'

'Stop digging, Niamh.' I look over at Gemma. 'She's not usually such a—'

Gemma is smiling now. She looks down at the photo, which she's cradling in two hands as though it was the child himself.

'He – yeah, he still has to wear them. He has astigmatism, you know?'

'Oh God.' Niamh is crimson. She pulls at the collar of her shirt as though releasing the heat. If she was older, I'd be thinking hot flush. Gemma breaks into a shy smile.

'No, you're right. He does look like a little nerd. He really does.'

She places the photo on the kitchen table and smooths back a swathe of platinum blonde that had swung forward.

'He saved my life, that little nerd.'

And I feel that I've just witnessed something important. A glimpse into the real woman. Because every word of that sentence is true. She means it. And I know exactly what she means.

7

Niamh

'So, basically—' Gemma gets to her feet and rehangs the photo, her fingers trembling. Shock? Or maybe she's on medication?

'Sorry. I mean, what I'm wondering is, like, what happens now?'

There's a faint buzzing sound, and she takes her phone from her pocket and reads a message as she sits back down, clutching the phone like a holy relic. She's a bit calmer: Laura was right to get her chatting about the kid. Her focus is entirely on the phone though, her two thumbs scrolling and clicking at warp fecking speed. I catch eyes with Laura and she hesitates, then places her palms flat on the table, giving a couple of taps, like a call to attention. On cue, Gemma looks up.

'Sorry, you know I' – she tilts the phone and Laura cranes forward to read it – 'I have to post regularly, especially at a time like this.'

'Surely your fans – followers – will understand if you take some time off?' Laura's brows are stitched together in puzzlement. Or fake puzzlement – it's basically disapproval.

'Oh yes, of course they would. I mean, I've already asked for privacy. It's not like they harass me or anything. It's—' She clicks out of the app and puts the phone back in the pocket of her cardi. 'They're – well, most of them anyway – they're so kind and supportive. They're more like friends.'

I look down at my own phone, where I've just searched

her on Insta: 180k followers. That's a lot of friends. Over a thousand posts – mostly fashion, lifestyle, make-up, but lots of Ferdia and places they visit, kids' clothes and stuff.

'Sure, I can imagine,' I say, although I'm not sure I can. 'Tell us a bit about the job, like, how often would you post? Are there ever days when you literally post nothing?' The thought of having to be 'on' and visible all the time the way she seems to be, it'd bring me out in a rash. I'd rather stick pins in my eyes.

'Like, I saw your post about Ferdia's first day at school.'

A shadow crosses Gemma's face.

I go on: 'I mean, I'm not – this is not a criticism – but I thought all mammies would like to keep that day – days like that – I mean, maybe you'd want to just keep it for yourself? Like, what if he bawled his head off?'

She shrinks down in the chair, gathering the cardigan across herself with rail-thin arms. The tremor is back.

'In fairness, they're the cutest photos!'

I'm gushing to make amends. She's bloody touchy. 'The one where he's looking back at you over his shoulder, like he's checking you're still watching? Jaysus! It'd break your heart.'

'Thanks.' She gives a rueful smile. 'Yes, well, I didn't post anything after that because he came running back, and actually, he did start crying his eyes out then. Conleth was—' She breaks off at the sound of a door slamming and feet tramping down the stairs.

'They're back now,' she says, her voice breathy, urgent. 'As you can hear. So, I mean' – she glances at her watch – 'is there anything else that has to be done today? I'll have to get Ferdia his tea.'

I start packing up, but slowly. Laura's taking her time too.

'Slow down!' A male voice. 'You'll trip. Mummy's in there. You don't have to—'

'Mummy!'.

A thin blond kid launches himself on to her like a bloody lemur in a raincoat. In a nanosecond he's on her hip, burrowing into her like he wants to hide in her armpit. His hands clasp around her neck, the little fingers poking through her blonde hair.

'You didn't pick me up, even though you promised! You breaked your promise! You know you did. And you should never, never break your promise. I had to sit on the blue chair outside the Oifig and I was crying.'

Gemma reaches around the back of her head and peels one hand away, kissing his fingers, rubbing the tip of her nose against his. Her face is transformed. And his cheeks are flushed, the blond curls that look so cute in the photos matted. A streak of dried silver trails on to his upper lip as though his nose has been running. Behind the specs, his eyes are tear-stained. She hugs him to her more closely.

'I'm sorry, love,' she whispers. 'I didn't break my promise. I – it was an accident. I had to have a meeting with – with . . .' Her voice trails away.

The shed in human form that must be Conleth O'Hara reaches across to ruffle the child's hair with a giant bear-paw hand.

'Daddy came and got you though – dah-dah!' He makes a superhero sound, eyes creasing above a big grin.

Gemma extracts Ferdia from the puffa bodywarmer (Timberland, I reckon. A replica of Daddy's) and places it on the back of one of the chairs.

'Conleth—'

He holds the raze-the-room smile, positive energy rolling off him in waves. A good-looking bloke, if you're into that. Charismatic.

'This is—'

'I'm Detective Garda Laura Shaw,' says Laura, stepping forward.

'And I'm Niamh Darmody,' I finish. 'You must be—'

'He's Daddy,' says Ferdia, burying his face in Gemma's hair when we all laugh.

'So it's definite? It's definitely his—' Conleth's smile fades and he mouths the word *body?* over the top of the child's head, a concerned expression shadowing his even features.

'Yes,' says Laura. 'Dr Parminter is doing the PM later this evening.'

He sets down the sports bag he's been holding and walks over to Gemma, placing his arm around her shoulders in a gesture of protection. It'd make a perfect family photo. They're literally picture perfect. He leans in to kiss the side of her face.

'We're more or less finished for today,' Laura says, giving me the nod. I take out my card and offer it to Gemma. But it's Conleth who leans forward to take it, placing it carefully on the table.

'My number's on that, and the office. If there's anything you want to talk about. If – if you need a chat even, don't hesitate to call. And Garda Killeen, your family liaison officer, she'll be in touch about coming in.'

'There's no way Gemma's going in there.' Conleth peels his arm from around her shoulders and steps forward, lowering his voice. 'Surely you're not asking her to identify the – I mean—'

Laura's voice glides over his.

'No need. Although, depending on the condition of the remains, it might be something you'd like to do? But it doesn't have to be decided now. We're ninety-nine per cent sure already. There were articles—' I fill in the blanks.

'There was a belt – with a monogram. And cufflinks.

34

Between that and the DNA we have on file, it won't be necessary for you to do the identification, no.'

He returns into position beside his wife, and now she sags against him, strands of platinum drifting over his sweater. He hugs her closer, planting another kiss on the top of her head, then lets go and accompanies us to the door.

'Thank you for your time, guards.' He nods. 'We so appreciate it.'

8

Gemma

Ferdia's too exhausted to eat much of his dinner, but Conleth lets it go. Ferdia clambers down from his chair, making towards the latest 'nest' he's made for his digger in the centre of the bean bag.

'Go inside and play,' Conleth says, looking up from his phone. 'It's grown-up time now.'

'But I want—'

'Now means now, Ferdia.' Conleth's voice is flat. He's tired too.

'Daddy and I need our grown-up time. I'll come in in a few minutes,' I soothe, handing him the toy. 'We'll watch something before Bedtime Cuddles.'

Bedtime Cuddles is a regular feature on my Insta. Conleth recommends I put it up three or four times a week, though we get a shot of it every night. It was Sally's idea. Sally's his new PA and she's in charge of media for the company.

Bedtime Cuddles is actually a great idea – it's a family selfie shot with Ferdia in his pyjamas and the two of us on the sofa beside him, usually with a picture book. My followers love it, and we get sent loads of great books and sleepwear suggestions, so that's another debt of gratitude to Sally. She's been amazing in the office too, sorting the filing system and bookkeeping as well as the advertising. And she's one of those smiley, positive people who makes you feel better about the world.

'Good boy,' I say, waiting for him to leave. He plods into the den clutching his digger and I wait for the sound of the TV, anxiously scanning the kitchen to see if I've missed anything. I take in the gleaming surfaces, the polished chrome and stone. There's no sign of the supper party we hosted last night which saw Conleth elated after our guests – top senior counsel and her surgeon husband, Fiona and Sam – committed to sponsoring four places on this summer's sailing course. With Ferdia in the den there's no danger of interruptions, no sign of the usual noise and chaos of living with children.

But this is different. And I can't read his mood. They've found Max and I'm – it's like I'm all psyched up. A part of me wants to say, *Thank God*, as though I didn't know where he was for the last eighteen years. Maybe I've been faking so long I've started to believe my own lies.

He watches me in silence. And I can feel myself beginning to panic. So instead, I talk about Ferdia.

'Was he upset when you picked him up? He looks like he was crying. I'm sorry. Penny had offered – you didn't have to—'

Conleth stands abruptly and starts taking food out of the fridge, his back to me. He puts out the Tupperware containers featured the day before yesterday from the 2Tired2Cook chain – three different pestos that I'd posted on Monday evening. Over a thousand likes.

'It will have to be pasta,' he says, closing the fridge door.

'I'm sorry, I didn't get time—' He holds up his hand to stop me and the words die away.

'Why would I do that? Ask a stranger to pick up our kid? How would that look?' *She's not a stranger*, I want to say. Penny is the closest thing to a friend that I have. But I say nothing. I know how important it is to him to be there for Ferdia, to be a good dad. He thinks we should manage ourselves.

'Thanks,' I whisper. He nods, appeased.

'He was grand,' Conleth carries on, taking a jar of olives from the cupboard. He sits down and leans back in the chair. 'The tears are not because I was, like, twenty seconds late. They were put on because he didn't want to go swimming.'

Oh no! I'd forgotten the swimming lesson. I usually bring him straight from school on a Thursday. He needs me there.

Now Conleth pats the table and gets to his feet again.

'So, I'll cook something,' he says, 'and give you a bit of a rest.' And it's like his bad mood this morning – it's like it never happened. He's full-on supportive husband. And he's so kind when he's like this that I doubt myself. He cares. He looks after me. It's the flip side of his obsession.

How can he even think of eating? I'm sick to my stomach. I spot the open bottle of white wine in the door of the fridge.

'Will we have a glass of wine? I could do with one,' I say, trying to make my voice light – brave.

He glances at me then, pointedly, at the empty glass by the sink from earlier.

'A chaser, is it?' He smiles. 'Did you start before or after the guards arrived? And don't forget there was that cappuccino with Penny earlier.' He laughs, to take the sting out of his words. 'Someone's gone over their calorie budget today.'

I don't tell him that it was a flat white, not a cappuccino, and I try not to react. He's only teasing. And he's actually trying to help, because we've been trying not to have wine during the week. But – thank God – he takes the wine from the fridge and two glasses from the cupboard. He pours wine into both. The smaller one, he passes to me. He looks at me, daring me to comment, but I say nothing. He's only messing.

'Was he okay at swimming?' I say instead. 'You didn't force him, did you, Conleth? Usually, he does it. He's very good when I bring him. But I—'

'Relax, would you? Listen to yourself. No. I didn't force him.' He stresses the word 'force'. 'I explained to him that we would see Mummy *after* he did his lesson. And because he understood that there was no negotiation and no wheedling and whining was going to work on *me* – because of that, he was in the water with the others in two seconds flat. I mean, they still allow him his armbands, which seems like a complete waste of time to me. But I let that go.'

I can picture Ferdia at the side of the pool, shivering, still wearing the glasses. He can't see a thing without them. Each session, it takes him longer than everyone else to get in. It's like he gets more, not less, fearful with every passing week.

'You want him to be able to swim, don't you?' Conleth says, emptying the rest of the bottle into his glass. 'The most important of all life skills. He jumped in, actually. He had a great time.'

He jumped in? He must have been desperate to get home to me. He usually clutches the ladder and backs into the water step by step with Hazel, the swimming coach, directly behind him. The thought of him, his pale trembling body and his little brave face as he leapt into the water, it's like a crack in my heart. But I drop the subject.

'What do I say to the gardaí, Conleth?' I whisper. 'There'll be an inquiry, they said. What if – what do I tell them?'

He drains the rest of his wine glass in two gulps, and I sip mine.

'There's nothing *to* tell them. Nothing. Another missing person case solved. A tragedy. A tragic suicide. You arrange for a cremation followed by a – maybe something at the club. Then we bring the ashes out on the boat and scatter them. All of us, as a family.'

His expression is thoughtful and I know he's visualizing it like a movie. The photos in the media. He'll probably want me to do a reel. He'll certainly post on the MaxSpirit site. He drums his fingers on the table. Neither of us mention the fact that since Max, I'll do almost anything to avoid going out in a boat. Though I've been trying to work on this – to surprise him. Dad sold *Corrig Cailín* after Max, and that was the end of sailing for him. The new boat is named for the charity set up in my brother's memory – *MaxSpirit*, Conleth called her. It – she's a Dutch make, I think. This is where Conleth spends all his free time. When he's not doing lessons with the kids who are booked in from all over the country – some even come from the US – he'll be out with sailing buddies or private investors. The company is a registered charity, so people get tax breaks if they support it.

'Your brother has been missing for eighteen years,' he says, 'and now he's been found.'

He nods towards my phone.

'Write a post. You know the type of thing. Final chapter. You're glad that your beloved brother can be laid to rest at last, that's your message – something like that. Contact Sally if you get stuck. End of.'

I inhale, but the words I was going to say die on my tongue. Because I don't think it's the end of anything. It's just the beginning.

9

Laura

I pull up outside the house just as the digital display changes to 21:21 and cut the engine. A narrow slice of blueish light escapes from between the curtains of Katie's bedroom window. The new nightlight. She's obsessed with it – a moving-in gift from Alva. It's a solar-powered light in the shape of a cloud with a smiley face. I thought she'd find it babyish, but she adores it. It charges on the windowsill during the day – if one of us remembers to set it in the right position – and then you can leave it on one particular colour or set it so that the rotating plate changes. Katie decided that was too stressful, which had Niamh snorting with laughter when I told her.

'Glad to see the mania is making it to the next generation,' was the comment. But actually – cue more mummy guilt – she likes the blue because she knows about the flashing blue light on my car and she wants to be like me, with her own special blue light. The familiar disappointment of missing the goodnight kiss settles on me like a sodden blanket. I told Matt this morning I'd be back by six latest, so I reckon there'll be a bit of eyerolling. I did message him from the unit when we got back, saying it'd be another half-hour as we were waiting for the PM results. That was almost two hours ago.

I'd told Niamh to head on home to Dorothy, and that I'd wait to hear from Parminter. She'd been yawning non-stop, which is not like her. So I'd written up the notes from the meeting with Gemma and shuffled through the piles of paper until I found the transcript of her original statement. But before I could start into it, word came in of the delay with the PM results, which meant there was no point in hanging around. Apparently, because it's rare to find a body so well preserved after all this time, Parminter wants to get another expert in on the case. I packed up, yawning myself, and headed straight home.

I sigh, listening to the engine ticking in the dark of the cul-de-sac. One of the streetlamps has been broken for weeks, and that's all it takes to give it a run-down, neglected look. I feel like I'm on a stake-out. I can't be seen.

How alike all our houses are, with their squares of yellow light oozing from behind curtains and blinds. The little front gardens that couldn't be more than two metres square, with our low-maintenance borders, our pebbles, our slabs of granite. It calms me, that thought. I want life to be like that – calm and ordered.

I should move. But instead, I sit watching. I want to be transported, like in *Star Trek*. I want to be beamed from here in the quiet car directly into my bed, into the darkness and silence. I grit my teeth. We're still getting used to having another adult in the house – and Alva's lovely. She's into cooking, so we've been treated to Ottolenghi and Jamie Oliver recipes and loads of tasty dishes. Niamh was raving about her last weekend after the feast of food she'd pre-pared. She kept telling Alva that instead of paying us rent, we should be paying her for the services of a personal chef.

'We're not actually charging her, you know,' I'd said later, irked by the slagging. And I suppose I was frustrated as well. Why are families so complicated? It's one thing to cut your dad out of your life, but what about his blameless children, your half-siblings? I wanted to hate them – as a teenager, when Mum was still alive – sure. It was easy. It was black and white. Mum was the innocent party. Dad walked out. He'd been unfaithful with someone else, even before he got together with Charlie.

But somewhere, at some stage, the lines became blurred. He was already separated when Charlie met him. And she was always friendly to us. She even sent me a card when Mum died – and they'd all signed it. I can still remember Seán's childish handwriting. He must have been about eight. And then, when I used to be on Facebook, there'd be a message or a like from one of them – usually Alva. She seems to be the most outgoing. I suppose they kept an eye on my life in the way I tracked theirs. Christenings and birthdays got a thumbs-up or a smiley emoji. Which is more honest than what I used to do, which was just look at their photos, but not comment.

Then, two months ago, Alva direct-messaged me on Instagram, telling me that her dad (and mine, but neither of us say that) is being treated in Beaumont for a brain tumour. She wanted to know if she could stay for a few weeks while he got his treatment. Charlie has rented a room nearby, but it's minuscule. Áine's away in London still and Seán somewhere in Scotland.

And so I find myself in the middle of a big family thing. There's even a WhatsApp group for updates. Cian is talking about coming over from Canada.

And in the middle of all that chaos and concern, the operations, the treatment, the photos of Dad – a dad I don't recognize, vulnerable and shrunken in the hospital bed – in the middle of it all is the single glaring fact. I still haven't spoken to him. Not since the day he walked out.

Friday

10

Niamh

I concentrate on the screen as opposed to the grey-white waxy form on the slab, praying I don't boke. I'm between McArsey and Laura, both of them with their freaking school prefect faces on. Jaysus! How many of these did Laura sit through feeling like this? I nudge her with my shoulder and she tilts her head to listen, not wanting to get caught chatting while Parminter is in full flight.

'What?' she hisses.

'Nothing,' I hiss back. 'I just don't see why this – why we have to be here at the freaking crack of dawn! It's a done deal, isn't it? He drowned. Why do *we* need to know about the fecking state of the tissue?' She gives me a quizzical look, opening her mouth as though she's going to speak, then closing it.

'It's important.' She turns back to the scene, frowning. We're sitting in the viewing gallery, along with a fair crowd. As Cig predicted, there's huge interest. Everyone above a certain age seems to remember the case. And poor dead Max lies on his back, his face exposed, the rest of him covered in a sheet. Thank Christ. Not sure I could stomach a full view of him. Not when I'm feeling like this. Meanwhile, Parminter and Fallon are pacing between the trolley and the laptop. Interesting that Fallon has been called in – the top expert in plant forensics. She's helped us out on more than one occasion. One of the mortuary assistants – don't know his name,

47

but he's a lanky streel – flitting between the pair of them and the dead boy. And yeah, he is a boy. Somehow, he still has strands of nineties heavy-fringed hair plastered to his grey-tinged skull.

'How in the hell is he so well preserved?' I hiss. Now it's McArsey's turn to give me the look.

'He's about to tell us, Darmody.'

He raises his thumb and forefinger to his lips and mimes a little twisting action like a freaking national schoolteacher miming *Ciúnas*. Jaysus! The rage surges. Hormones. I try to dial down the urge to punch him.

But it's Dr Fallon – Danni – who speaks first. I could listen to her all day, I think. She's soft-spoken, but there's a steely edge. And her face is a bit the same, heart-shaped and pretty, but the eyes – the gaze is fixed and strong. You don't mess with her, I'd say.

'The remains were discovered washed ashore near Drumleck Point in Howth, but this is not where he died or, indeed, where he has been. We can now put together a picture of where this man – where Max has been in the intervening time since his disappearance. Firstly, I draw your attention to this.'

She pulls the sheet up from his feet until it's just above the waist, and there's a pure gasp from the crowd. A freaking collective gasp. Because tied around Max's waist, half embedded in the crumbling cheese-like stuff that is part flesh, part rags, is what looks like a chunk of blue nylon rope.

Danni waits for the whispers to subside. The visual on the screen changes to a close-up of the rope with blobs of the grey-white substance clumped on it.

'This is a fragment of nylon rope – a synthetic polymer – the type often used in boating, camping, rock climbing, sailing, et cetera. Even though nylon is durable and resistant to abrasion, one of its weaknesses is its low performance in water. It absorbs water, and here, you'll see that the rest of the rope is gone.'

With her gloved hand, she raises the end of the rope, then lets it fall back.

'But what we do know from marks on the flesh is that this rope was tied fully around the victim's — the deceased's — waist.'

'Did she just say "victim"?'

Laura turns to me, eyes wide. 'She did. Ssh.'

'And an important side note here' — she points to another close-up; this time it's some kind of fungus or mould growing on the fibres of the rope — 'this is red algae, or Rhodophyta, a type of algae that grows in the deeper parts of the ocean. So, everything is telling us that this body lay at a depth of perhaps fifty metres, before a storm surge or freak current swept him ashore in Howth. Storm Lucy is the likely culprit.'

She pauses, and a silence takes hold. I find myself wondering if she's a mother. She looks as though she's touched by the story. But who wouldn't be? God, these fecking hormones have me in flitters! Or could it be — I swallow down the lump in my throat. Seriously, was I just about to cry?

'At this point, I'll hand over to my learned colleague, Dr Parminter,' she says, breaking the silence. She steps back.

'Thank you, Dr Fallon.' Parminter steps carefully towards the body, moving like an ancient heron. Gently, as though not wishing to wake him up, he draws the sheet up another few centimetres, revealing more of the abdomen. 'Now some of you may be wondering about the excellent, ah — condition — of the body.'

He looks up, as though waiting for an answer. Beside me, McArsey nods as though, yes, he was wondering exactly that.

49

'I refer you to my paper on the subject of adipocere,' he says, 'as I don't wish to burden you with details at this point.'

This is greeted with a bit of rustling movement. Parminter does like to give a bit of a show.

'Adipocere is sometimes called grave wax, or corpse wax. It's formed under a variety of conditions, but submersion in water is important for the processes involved. What happens is that as the adipose tissue in the body decomposes it is transformed into glycerin and free fatty acids.'

He waits for just a moment, before mercifully putting it in English.

'In other words, it's a soapy, wax-like substance that is formed when bacteria break down a person's body fat. It forms a firm' – and here, he presses on the unyielding stomach area of the corpse – 'you can see that it's solid. We have, in effect, a firm and very, ah, stable cast of the soft tissues that would otherwise undergo putrefaction.'

This is bonkers stuff.

'Is he saying we have, like, a wax mould of the body?' I hiss.

Laura doesn't answer.

'Studies – recent studies of adipocere formation – have shown that it occurs rapidly in cold water, although it can form in other circumstances. But here, we have a classic case of adipocere formation. It's most often seen in corpses that have been submerged in water for a long period of time, for example bodies recovered from shipwrecks or plane crashes in the ocean.'

Now, his long, gloved fingers catch hold of the edge of the sheet with the precision of a ballerina holding her skirts, and he pulls the whole thing off Max's body, handing it to the waiting assistant.

There are full-on gasps and excited talk.

Even McArsey can't control himself. 'Holy God!'

A close-up of a stab wound to the boy's chest appears on the screen.

'From this evidence,' says Parminter, steepling his fingers and peering over them, 'we can conclude that Max died from a stab incision of approximately three centimetres in depth, which entered the third intercostal space to the left of the sternum.'

He's quiet for a moment as we absorb this. 'For clarity, what this means is that the victim died from a stab wound to the heart and it is almost certain that he entered the water post-mortem.' He opens his steepled hands and spreads them wide, indicating the body and the fragments of rope. 'Most likely, the body was weighted with something, tied around the torso.'

'And is there any way he could have inflicted this wound himself?' Laura can't help herself – she blurts the question. Fallon and Parminter exchange glances.

'We don't believe so. From the depth and angle of the wound, it appears that the killer was positioned above the victim, enabling them to' – he mimes a stabbing action – 'strike downwards. Interestingly, we also discovered a small metal fragment embedded in the bone.'

He steps back, removing his glasses and momentarily pinching the skin at the bridge of his nose. On the screen, another close-up photograph appears.

'We will be conducting a complete PMCT later today – that is, post-mortem computed tomography – but even here, our preliminary CT image of the sternum reveals a fragment of metal has become lodged in the left sternoclavicular joint.'

There's absolute silence while we study the image – a tiny speck of metal. Parminter turns to look at us with the air of a college lecturer setting an assignment.

'You're looking for a right-handed assailant, I believe.'

I try not to snort out loud. That's all he's got for us? A right-handed killer?

'Dr Parminter, you said that from the angle of the injury, the killer was positioned above the victim? Would this mean that we're looking for someone taller than Max – who at over six foot was not exactly short?' I've kind of blurted this question out, and Laura gives me a glare. It's like school in here – you have to put your hand up and wait your turn.

His head swivels in my direction and I swallow my nervous giggle. 'So, like a bloke? Or a tall woman?'

'Yes and no,' he replies. 'If killer and victim were upright at the time of the stabbing, it's likely that the killer would be a few centimetres taller. However' – his head swivels to take in the rest of the gallery – 'if the victim was prone, then a smaller person could have inflicted this wound in the same manner. Indeed, if the victim was seated and the assailant standing' – his bony shoulders finish the sentence with a slow-motion shrug – 'the result could be the same.'

Laura looks up from her notes, a question on her lips.

'And, sorry if this is an obvious question, Dr Parminter, but you mentioned a fragment caught in the bone. Does this mean that if we can find the murder weapon, if we find the knife, will we be able to match it to the wound – to this – to the image there?'

Parminter nods, the tiniest of smiles curving his thin lips. He's always liked her – the head-girl vibe she gives off.

'Precisely. And though this is a magnified image, it should just be visible to the naked eye. You understand, it is often the hard tissues that best record and preserve the impression of the weapon. Indeed, in a case like this, though we are indeed fortunate to have a body in such, ah, excellent condition after so long, if you can find the murder weapon – if you can find the blade – then it will fit with all the satisfaction of a completed jigsaw puzzle.'

His gaze sweeps the room, and he rests his slender, blue-gloved hand on the shoulder of the dead boy.

'Sorry,' I blurt, a wave of nausea rising from my stomach. I get to my feet, scrambling past Laura on my way to the bathroom.

@unatracey5: OMG Gemma, heard the news! Sending love.

@nolimitsgrl: Do the guards know what happened?

@missymurfi: I am so worried about you @gemstone. Do you need anything?

@gemstone: Thank you for your concern.

@theirishmammy: I couldn't believe it.

@nolimitsgrl: Are they contacting the original investigation team?

@unatracey5: They'll have to.

@annahanna: Are you okay?

@missymurfi: I could babysit your little boy if you like? My mam says I'm really great with kids. You can DM me if you need anything.

11

Gemma

The sympathy of Múinteoir Derval at the classroom door nearly undoes me. She even breaks into English once Ferdia has gone on into the room, weighed down by his schoolbag, which, I realize too late, has his digger stuffed inside.

'We're so sorry for your loss,' she'd said, her hand reaching to clasp my forearm, fixing me with a look of such genuine sympathy, I felt almost – I wanted to shut my eyes and dissolve.

'You're so brave to come to school, you know?'

Her eyes tracked the huddle of reporters who line the road opposite, waiting for me to come back out. 'But for what it's worth, even though I'm sure it's really, really difficult, I think you did the right thing.'

I'm so glad Ferdia has her as his teacher – she's kind. You can see it.

People are real, Gemma. Some people are not acting and they're not fake, no matter what he says. And they don't want anything. Derval is one of them.

'Thanks so much, Derval.' I meet her gaze, willing myself not to fall apart.

'Will it be you or Daidí collecting?'

'Oh God! That reminds me. I'm so sorry about yesterday.'

'Sure, don't be ridiculous! Not a problem at all.'

And I'd begun wittering something about one of us collecting, that it might be Conleth or I might get one of the other mums, clearly not on top of the situation. The full extent of the morning's plan had been to get Ferdia into school.

'Carry on as normal,' Conleth had said. 'There's nothing to fuss about. Just get Ferdia into school, come back and check in.'

Of course. He's right. He'd turned away from me then, looking out into the front yard. From there, we get a view of the stone steps, the little park – although it's just a square of grass bounded by trees – and beyond that, the sea. That strip of sea – grey or green or blue – harsh like cold steel or glittering in silver shreds of light, always there. Taunting me, haunting me.

When I was pregnant, sick and exhausted, we did a series of reels called 'Pregnant on the Pier'. And loads of mums with bumps would join me to walk the pier. It was a huge success for us financially, and for the brand. But I was weak – the morning sickness was terrible and Conleth didn't want me putting on too much weight. So I couldn't fill up on carbs, which seemed to be all I wanted to eat. Toast – just a slice of toast and marmalade – what I wouldn't have given for that.

'You'll thank me afterwards,' he'd said. 'French doctors put their pregnant clients on a diet.'

And he was right. That's the thing. He just always seems to know so much about everything. And I didn't want to walk the pier, because I knew I looked desperate. The vomiting had made my face gaunt and the hormones had me flushed-looking with bad skin.

'I just want to hide away for a while,' I'd said, dreaming of a little cottage on the side of a mountain or something, miles away from people. 'With just me and – you, of course – and the baby. We could move somewhere quiet?'

'People would kill to live your life,' he'd said, 'you muppet!

Coastal Southside Dublin, the best of everything is on your doorstep. Why do you think you've so many followers? The brand – and you are a brand, for God's sake – the brand is based here. You think they'd be following the Happy shagging Pear if they came from a sinkhole estate on the side of a dump?'

I was so sorry I'd spoken – he was really annoyed. 'People don't follow you because they like you, Gemma. They're not your friends – how many times do I have to tell you that? It's not you. It's not about you and they're not your friends. And what about MaxSpirit?'

He meant the foundation – the charity – as opposed to the boat.

'I – I didn't mean – it's just, you know my followers are incredibly loyal. They would follow me, I know they would.'

And he'd reached across like he was going to brush something off me, but instead he brought his thumb and finger together and flicked the skin of my cheek with a little smacking sting.

'Muppet.' He shook his head. 'Leave the business end of things to me, hmm?'

And he smiled fondly and I wondered if I'd imagined the sting. Sometimes it's like that – over before it's begun.

'We're not moving. What would it say about your brother? What caring sister would pack up and leave? What if Max came home and you weren't there?'

And I didn't say it. That we both knew that Max was never coming home.

He taps the side of his forehead.

'You've got to think about the optics. What would it look like if you gave up on Max and moved somewhere else? When you're at National Missing Persons Day and you're in the photos with the president or whatever, it won't look good if you're all, *Oh, I don't live in Dún Laoghaire now. I'm moving on and I don't care any more.*

And I say nothing. I'm thinking of the day that I dread more than any other – National Missing Persons Day – when we all come together and we listen to the pure voices of a school choir and the musicians, and to the politicians, the experts in forensics and the grief counsellors. We hold hands, and I despise myself – if it's possible – even more than my regular daily self-hatred. We cry together, myself and Linda, holding hands. Linda's gorgeous daughter Nadia is missing since 2005, and I'm the age she would be now. Linda holds my hand and squeezes it, and she says things like *Hope springs eternal* or *Never give up*. And we hug, so I can hide my lying, treacherous, imposter's face. The brave mothers, sisters, daughters, fathers and brothers, sons and grandparents, united in the unrelenting horror of the not knowing what happened to our loved ones. Except I know. I know, and I'm to blame, and I despise myself.

And then he'd ruffled my hair.

'Your roots are showing,' he'd said. 'You should sort that. I'll leave out the Visa card in the morning.'

Before I headed home, I spoke to the reporters. Gave them the *Sorry, lads, nothing to see* talk. *Privacy at this time.* And thankfully, it seems to have done the trick and they trickled away. And now, I'm walking the two blocks back towards our terrace, with that song going round and round in my head.

> *Three sailors went to sea, sea, sea,*
> *To see what they could see, see, see,*
> *But all that they could see, see, see,*
> *Was the bottom of the deep blue sea, sea, sea.*

I remember the game we played along with it – you did it

with a partner and you did these actions, like a salute or some-thing. And you hit your knees and elbows and it got faster and faster. Nola – the name of my then best buddy – she always beat me. She was so smart, but I used to get muddled up. Even then, not much older than Ferdia is now, I was in the shadow of golden Max. Because, of course, everywhere I went, everyone remembered my big brother who had gone before. Long before he – he was already winning sailboat races before he left primary school. From the age of eleven or twelve he and Conleth were sailing in regattas and cham-pionships. They'd come home after Mum collected them from the club, both of them windchapped and sunburned, starving after the day out on the water, ready to regale Dad (if he was home) with the stories of their triumphs.

By contrast, and to everyone's disappointment, even though I learned the basics of how to swim, I had no real love of it. And definitely no desire to start sailing out on open water. I shivered on the pier, refusing to get into the dinghy at my first (and last) sailing camp. Nola had told me that they made you capsize it, and I was terrified.

But watching Ferdia at his swimming lessons has inspired me this past year. He's so brave. He makes me realize the importance of challenging yourself. I want them both to be proud of me – Conleth and Ferdia. And if the sea is going to be part of my son's life – and it looks like there's no doubt about that – then I'm going to have to come to terms with it. All of it. So, in secret – while Conleth's at work and Ferdia's in school, for the past five months I've been doing a weekly swimming lesson – it comes up as a gym class for payments, so Conleth doesn't suspect. The water is warm, and I'm not out of my depth and, bit by bit, I'm improving. I get a few strokes closer to the stepladder each week.

Without meaning to, I've walked to Seapoint beach.

There's a fresh breeze whipping iced peaks across the water and carrying the clinking sound of cables and steel along with it. Maybe I did mean to walk here. Because I'm hoping that Conleth will have left by the time I get back. I can't think straight when he's there. I barely slept last night, even though I was in the bed, and when I did, Max was in my dreams. His blue T-shirt with the sunrise logo, his tanned, bare feet on the side of the dock. I could identify him from his feet alone. And the birthmark on his left calf. His blue eyes studied mine, like he was trying to figure something out. I woke time and again throughout the night.

Now, I stand on the top step, watching the swimmers, listening to the shrieks of the gulls. Four people are in the water and there's a huddled pair trying to dress themselves under the dryrobes. How are they not frozen? It's only May. But they're clearly having fun, the swimmers squealing and splashing each other. I realize too late that I must be staring, because one of the dryrobed women turns and waves at me. It's Penny.

She shouts something, but it's lost on the wind. I raise my hand in farewell, then take a quick photo of the bay. For the brand. Or for Conleth – even if I don't post, it'll show that I was thinking about it. Today, the sea is a warm green shade, the bathers' outfits bright flashes of colour against it.

Morning dip for the brave. Blessed to live by the sea.

Grateful that Max can finally be laid to rest.

#ThinkingOfYou

#MissingPersonsDay

#BlessedbyNature

#Seaswimming

#Placetobelong

#CoastalLife

Conleth says it'll all be over by this time next week. What if he's wrong?

12

Niamh

After a cup of scalding tea from the garage, I'm right again – for now. The Corrig Point desk sergeant is on a call when I arrive, but he lets me through with a head nod and a stubby pointing finger telling me where to find her – in a poky room at the end of the corridor which seems to double as a stationery cupboard. Cutbacks. When I come in she's rummaging through a sheaf of pages, setting them into different piles.

'Are you feeling any better?' she says, scanning my face.

'Grand,' I lie. The nausea is definitely lurking. Though it's too early to test. Six more days.

'Look at this,' she says, obviously eager to get into it. 'I've had a quick look through these statements – mostly from people who were at the party. Most say the same thing – that they remember seeing Max around the time of the speeches, but after that, it's as if he just vanished. This one, though,' she shakes her head. 'The sister's –' she exhales an irritated sigh, 'it's dated 2 June 2007 – so that's the next day. They must have got the whole family in. But here – you need to see it. It's—' She slides the sheet closer. 'I mean – bloody hell. It's a joke!'

There's silence while she waits for me to get the gist of it. I get about three lines in before I'm seized by the urge to crumple it into a heap.

'What the hell? What sixteen-year-old talks like that? Oh

my God! It must have been a freaking picnic of leading questions!' I read on a few more lines.

'"At approximately 22:30 hours, I left the party. I then decided to walk the half-kilometre to my home, where I went to bed and fell asleep. The following morning my mother woke me and informed me that Max was missing" – I mean, lads! Are we expected to believe that those were her words?'

'I know. That's what I thought,' she says. 'The statement was taken by Nolan.'

'You'd think they would have found a ban garda.' I layer on the irony. *Ban garda* is what they used to call female guards, back when that was a novelty. Woman garda, like, what's that about? We didn't call the male guards man garda, did we?

Laura is shaking her head.

'I don't know – you'd think they could have found someone – but that's the way it was before the SVI programme. Like, whoever had a reputation for being good with children could have been tasked with getting the statement. Maybe Nolan was a bit of a family man? I mean, he's not bad. But do you know what? One thing was weird. He's made a note here that she kept on asking if she was in trouble. A couple of times.'

She looks back at the page, her finger tracing the notes.

'He's circled the words "in trouble", but it seems like he didn't pursue it.'

'She was a kid.' I shrug. 'And her mam was probably in the room with her when she was making the statement. Is there any mention of drugs or anything? Could it be that?'

Laura shakes her head.

'Nothing here so far.'

We look at each other.

'Well, that's a bit of a car crash.'

She nods.

'And from that, we get this.' She begins reading the statement from the start.

'"On the evening of 1 June 2007, I attended a birthday party for my brother Max at Corrig Point Yacht Club. The party commenced at approximately 20:00 hours. My brother was enjoying himself with family and friends. There were speeches and a cake was presented, but I had begun feeling unwell. I did not feel well enough to attend the dancing and I made my way outside following the speeches to get some air."'

She looks up.

'And then we're back to "At approximately 22:30 hours, I left the party."'

A sigh.

'Okay. Well, let's start with her – Gemma. Let's get her in for a chat – or maybe we should call to the house?' she says, closing the file and reaching behind her neck with both hands, pressing to relieve the tension.

'The house, yeah? It might keep her calm. She's fair wired.'

A click as she releases some muscle in her bony little neck.

'Feck's sake! State of you! Tough morning at the gym?'

She splutters a half-laugh.

'Yeah, gym before a Parminter session? I don't think so. Although maybe that's what I should have done, right enough. Another week of membership gone to waste.'

'Well, at least it's not your money.'

'Oh, stop! Now I feel even worse! Poor Justy!'

Laura's mother-in-law – Justina Flynn, now retired, but formerly a senior partner in top Dublin law firm Stonehouse Flynn Mortimer – looms, sinewy and scary, between us.

'Ah, she's only doing her best, and it's a great present, you have to admit. The billionaire's gym, they call it.'

Laura laughs.

63

'Yeah, but it's a good thing I'm not easily offended. She handed me the voucher and told me she was giving it to me in advance, so I'd have time to get in shape for *the big day*.'

'What big day? Ye're married to her son already! Anyway, she means well. That's what we'll say.'

'Right. Oh—' She breaks off as McArsey comes in. 'Sarge.' She nods a greeting.

I mumble something – it seems I find it difficult to call him by his new title. What am I, twelve? But he doesn't notice.

'Good. You're both here,' he says. 'Darmody, are you all right? You rushed out of Parminter's place like a scalded cat.'

I feel myself flush. 'I, ah – had to leave abruptly. Something I ate.'

'Poor you.' McCarthy's sympathy is genuine. Can't fault him. But he's a bubbling pot of suppressed excitement, so it's on to the next thing.

'Good. You're recovered. Right. Briefing in the incident room in five.' He does a military-grade about-turn. 'There's a big crowd,' he says. 'This is huge.'

We carefully do not catch each other's eyes. Now would not be a good time to tell her.

13

Gemma

'Gemma! Wait up, Gemma!'

My heart lurches at the sound of running feet. Extreme reactions – another gift that constant lying gives you. Just for a second, I'd thought it was one of the detectives coming to arrest me.

But it's only Penny, doing her best to catch up with me but finding it hard to run with the long dryrobe flapping and sort of lolloping along in a pair of oversize slipper boots. I stop, willing myself to be calm. But my heart is pounding in my chest. Could I have said something? That time when she and I got chatting at the school social evening. I'd had way too much to drink – I knew Conleth couldn't say anything with everyone there. If he knew how long the two of us were talking he'd be raging. I'm not meant to be on my own with people. And it's laughable because that would never happen. I've barely any friends. Our friends are his friends. So there's no danger that's ever going to happen. My lies are a solid wall between me and the world.

I release the breath I've been holding. She's probably just going to offer to help or something. She doesn't know. Nobody knows.

She reaches me and leans forward, catching her breath.

'Christ! You walk fast!'

'Do I?'

I didn't know that. Usually, I'm the one running to catch

up with Conleth. Straightening up, she pushes a tangled hank of hair behind her ear and pats her chest, still panting.

'Yes. But that's fine – sorry. Here.' She takes my arm and steers me to one of the benches overlooking the bay. Behind us, the usual Friday-morning traffic snakes along the coast road, but in front of us there's only sea, the chimneys and, in the distance, grey as the sky above it, Howth.

'Can we sit for a second?' she says, pulling the dryrobe tighter.

'Sure, or—'

Why is my brain so slow? Should I be inviting her for a coffee or something? I could say she called in. 'Would you like – do you want to come to mine? I'll make us coffee? Pay you back for all the ones you've stood me?'

'Not a bit! Don't be daft! You've enough on your plate. I thought you'd ring – why didn't you ring me? You must be worn out with it all.'

She pushes her dark hair away from her mouth, where it had been blown by the wind. Up close, I can see the freckles scattered across her nose and cheeks. She has sand caught in her eyelashes. I don't think I've ever seen someone so real.

'Let me help,' she's saying. 'What can I do?'

And I can't answer that. Because what I want to do is bury my face in the darkness of her dryrobe and I want her to hug me the way a mum would – a mum whose life you hadn't destroyed.

'Ferdia can come back to mine today, after school? I'll pick him up. You must be—'

She shakes her head, like she's getting rid of something. She leans forward and peers at my face and I realize I've still got the sunglasses on and she's trying to see through them.

'Look, no bullshit, okay? Let's agree on no bullshit between us. I was going to tell you this anyway. I've been meaning to

66

tell you for ages, but I can never get you alone, haha. But anyway, I know a little bit of what you're going through. Nothing – obviously nothing as bad as the years you've endured – I mean, the years when you didn't know where he was and everything. That must have been devastating. So I'm not claiming to know what that must be like. But—' She looks away from me, out to sea, but she's now holding my elbow against her side and it's a firm grip.

'I had an older sister, Helen,' she says to the Poolbeg towers. 'She died of an overdose. No – correction.' Her chin trembles the tiniest amount, and she bites down on her bottom lip to stop it. 'Who killed herself when she was twenty-five.'

She turns to look at me square on and, without knowing what I'm doing, I'm taking off my sunglasses and I can tell by the stinging in my nose that tears are coming. Tears that will match the ones that shimmer, waiting to spill, from her eyes.

'No time for bullshit when death is around, is there?' She grins and her tears fall. She wipes them away impatiently. 'This is not about me. This is about you. And I know you – well, you seem to be very together. I mean, when I see you at school, and I hear about your media stuff, like, you're amazing. But all of that – that's, if you don't mind me saying, that's absolute shite.'

And she laughs and, oh my God, I can feel a sob building inside me and it wants to burst out, and I try to squash it and I make this weird snort thing and I feel my nose start to run. So I try to turn it into a laugh and I look down, and I'm frantic, trying to find a tissue, but all I have is the plastic wrapper. And Penny is still laughing. She lets go of my hand and rummages in the pocket of the dryrobe and pulls out a roll – a whole roll of toilet paper.

'There,' she says, unrolling about twenty squares and

67

passing it to me. 'And now that I've insulted your profession and ruined your peace and quiet – well, what I was saying and all I was meaning to tell you was this: I know how tough this is. So, why don't you let me pick up Ferdia after school today? My two will be ecstatic, and he'll be grand. Okay?'

I'm dabbing my eyes and I'm breathing. I'm doing the breath where it's like you channel it into a stream, to keep you calm. The lump hasn't gone, but it's subsided.

'Oh, it's grand—'

'Again, at the risk of ruining our beautiful friendship, no more bullshit. Okay? I know you're about to say that you're fine and' – she shakes her head, pressing her lips together in a grin like she's thinking of insulting things to say but not letting them out – 'but just for a second, consider the offer. It's what, almost ten o'clock now? I can do the pick-up, give them a bit of lunch, they can play on the slide in the park, then a bit of TV.' She pauses, gives me a bit of side-eye. 'Just half an hour? Then they can trash the house a bit, mill a bit more food or whatever, draw a picture, and before you know it, it's half four or five and you can come and collect? Or we'll walk up to you?'

She waits.

'Think of it. It's Friday. He doesn't have any after-school stuff, does he?'

He doesn't, but I'm feeling guilty because I didn't get him yesterday and I'm worried about what Conleth will say. But he doesn't need to know. I can collect him before Conleth gets back. And then I remember that Ferdia has his digger with him and there's a big covered sandpit in that park that he loves to play in, and I know he'll be grand. Plus, he's in awe of Eli and Jude – the way they swagger around the place like a pair of Texan ranch hands. If she takes him, that's more than seven hours to get myself together.

'That's decided then,' says Penny. 'You have my number, don't you? In the WhatsApp group? Now go back to bed or go and clean your perfect house or whatever it is you need to do. See you later.'

She gives my arm a final squeeze and stands. 'This is good, because it'll make me actually cook some decent food for their lunch.'

And she's gone. And it's like being ten years old, watching the big girls in the playground. I'm in awe.

14

Laura

Sergeant Senan McCarthy was not wrong. A loud burble of conversation swells into the hallway to greet us before we even reach the incident room. It stops abruptly as we enter and Niamh glances over her shoulder to see if the super or Cig is behind us. She clearly doesn't consider Senan worthy of the silence.

I raise an eyebrow. McCarthy clutches his folder and clipboard like a shield and, in fairness, as Niamh would say, the silence does last until he reaches the front. He motions for us to wait and, obediently, we take the nearest free chairs at the back and sit. There's easily twenty people crammed in here, a mix of uniforms and non. I organize the statements into a neater pile on my lap, declining Niamh's offer of help.

While McCarthy does his introduction, I scan the room. It's not a bad set-up, as far as I can see. Given that stations are closing on a daily basis, you're lucky to get a Portakabin and a handful of uniform. But this is going to be different, clearly. I spot Tara, the IRC who I met earlier, but beyond her and Senan there's no one I recognize. And no sign of their cig yet.

'Okay, people,' says McCarthy. 'Cig is on his way, but before he joins us I'd like to introduce you to SVI detectives Laura Shaw and Niamh Darmody, who are with us on temporary transfer from Seskin West. They'll be on the team investigating the murder of Max Fitzgerald, and in particular, they'll be studying statements and transcripts of interviews conducted at the time.'

He holds out a hand towards us like a talent-show host introducing the next act, and there's a cringey moment as Niamh and I hold tight smiles in place. Surely he'll leave it at that. Unfortunately not.

'I had the great pleasure of working with these outstanding officers during the Clonchapel siege some time ago.' Clonchapel siege? Good God! Nobody calls it that.

He pats his shoulder regretfully, semaphore for *where I took a bullet.* 'Their help was crucial.'

And now I can't stop myself glancing at Niamh, though I know it's risky. Our 'help'? I don't know where to start. She's gone crimson, though I don't know if it's rage or embarrassment.

Mercifully, deliverance is on hand. The door swings open, and O'Riordan comes in, brisk and to the point. It's like someone pressed fast forward. He's in his mid-fifties, heavy-set and red-cheeked. Like our cig, he looks jaded. He nods at McCarthy, effectively dismissing him.

'This was the biggest MisPer of the decade,' he says. 'And I know some of you will remember it. I certainly do, though I was even greener than some of you, and that's saying something.'

Unlike McCarthy's attempts at humour, this little aside gets a bigger laugh than it deserves. And unlike poor McCarthy, O'Riordan doesn't wait for the reaction.

'Max Fitzgerald was a national superstar by the time he was twenty. The Olympic hope – the golden boy.'

A pause as he looks at the wall of photos already posted up on the board showing Max and Conleth on podiums and stages clutching trophies and medals – smiling. 'Both of them were, I suppose, but Max was like, like – Brad Pitt, if you all still know who he is?' Another burst of laughter. 'Yeah, Max was the golden boy. Here in Dún Laoghaire, and throughout the sailing community, everyone knew the Fitzgeralds. Nationally, everyone knew Max. The papers were full of it. *Yacht club's Olympic dream turns to nightmare*, *Tragic twenty-first at Corrig Point*, and all that. I remember there was even talk at the time that it was a kidnapping.'

He taps the desk.

'But after the PM results this morning, I think we can safely assume it wasn't.' He looks down at something on the page.

'For operational reasons, by which I mean so we can get a bit of a head start, we're not going public yet – *yet* – about the murder. There'll be no mention of the stab wound. Nothing about the body being weighed down. For the *Six One* news tonight, they can have the fact that a body has been identified, that it's Max Fitzgerald who disappeared – give the last-seen date, et cetera. Let them know we're setting up an investigation team and seeking information. Can we get the helpline number operational by this evening?' This last question is addressed to Tara, who nods assent.

'Grand. And have you had a chance to look at the statements yet, Detective Shaw? By the way, yourself and Darmody are very welcome here at Corrig Point.'

He gestures for me to come forward. I join him at the top of the room, aware of the curious stares. Maybe the Clonchapel siege is bigger news than I thought.

'Yes, thanks, Cig. We – we've had a preliminary look at the sister's, Gemma Fitzgerald's, statement. Now, it being 2007, this was before the introduction of the SVI programme, so some of the questions are – were – perhaps less open-ended than would be the norm nowadays.'

They're all waiting for more.

72

'The statement was taken by a DI Gerard Nolan, who has since passed away, I believe.'

I look to see if there are any glints of recognition. The way it is in the guards, we could easily have a son or daughter of Nolan sitting among us. 'And he—'

Okay, how to make this sound diplomatic? Especially because the man is dead.

'What I mean to say is that Gemma's statement doesn't tell us much. Likewise, the one from Max's parents. His mother remembers seeing him dancing – well, she said he was "horsing around" on the dance floor. Fitzgerald senior said the same thing. And we haven't begun going through the remaining statements yet.'

'I see. Thank you. That's a start. All right,' says O'Riordan, turning towards Tara again. 'Anything further on the possessions recovered on the body?'

She nods.

'Yes, Cig. There was a single gold cufflink and a leather belt with a monogram of his initials. Still being tested, but they've sent photos in the meantime.'

Before O'Riordan can continue, McCarthy interrupts.

'And just so you know, Cig, the Water Unit have invited me to accompany them – you see, not to brag, heh heh, but I have my Advanced Powerboat Coxswain training – so we're going to have a look at Drumleck Point, the spot where he washed up. And Dr Fallon is to get back to me about a possible dive location, although that's a long shot. Because the algae on the rope suggests—'

General embarrassment curdles the air and O'Riordan's smile seems to be through gritted teeth. 'Wonderful. Let me know the findings.'

Niamh leans in to whisper.

'He's got his swimming badge too. Bet you didn't know that.'

I ssh her.

'Right,' says O'Riordan, 'to continue. Dr Parminter concluded that Max was stabbed in the chest, causing death. The body was then weighted and dumped in the sea. Now Dr Fallon's findings with the algae suggest that Max's body remained at a spot at least fifty metres deep before he washed up in Howth.'

He waits for this to sink in, nodding with satisfaction as a burly guy who's sitting near the window raises a finger to say something.

'Yes, Detective Bourke. You're going to tell us that—'

Bourke grins.

'That Dún Laoghaire harbour is nowhere near that deep. And that you'd have to go miles out in Dublin Bay to—'

'Exactly,' says O'Riordan, pointing to the map showing the tides between Ireland and the UK in varying shades of blue, dotted with directional arrows. He traces a line with his finger from Dún Laoghaire harbour out into Dublin Bay and continuing towards Howth. He turns. 'So, we need to talk to tide experts. How did the body get washed out that far? Was there an unusually high tide or a neap tide or whatever on the night of 1 June?' He scratches his head in a cartoon parody of puzzlement.

'And the big questions. Why would someone kill Max? Had he pissed someone off? Had he got into something he couldn't handle? Who stood to gain with him being out of the picture? Next question: where was he killed? And the most important questions of all: who killed him, and where is the murder weapon?'

Now he leans back against the desk, looking weary.

'Right. Bourke, I want you to get hold of Nolan's notes on the case. You could work with Shaw and Darmody on that?'

Bourke nods. 'Nolan was nothing if not thorough.'

74

O'Riordan pushes himself off his perch on the edge of the table with a sudden surge of energy. He barks orders and, in the space of five minutes, he's got someone looking into CCTV footage and phone records. Max's phone was never found. Another person is tasked with the tide information, looking into Max's parents' family finances, into the charity which was set up after Max's disappearance. A suitably nerdy-looking bloke gets the job of searching the computer records on file from 2007. The same guy will investigate Gemma's influencer career. Bourke says he'll look into the search that was conducted at the time, including the RNLI help and the records from the security hut beside the marina.

O'Riordan turns to the bank of photos showing Max with his trophies, Max on his boat with Conleth by his side, Max with his parents, Max at his debs.

'Okay, house to house and boat to boat as well, yeah? Let's jog a few memories, right? Where were they on the night in question? What did they hear? See? All that. Let's get on it. There's gonna be a bloody big spotlight shining on Corrig Point until we get some answers. And all we have at the moment is a shedload of questions.'

O'Riordan dismisses us and the group begins dispersing in clusters while he starts making his way in our direction. I just have time to elbow Niamh before he's standing in front of us, a big smile on his face.

'Shaw and Darmody,' he says, 'I've heard great things about you.' There's an awkward pause. 'Oh yes,' he contin-ues. 'I'm thinking I might extend your TT for a couple of months. That'll give McNeil something to moan about, not that he needs encouragement. Sure, he's always moaning, that fella. Isn't that right?'

He waits.

'No comment,' grins Niamh.

'Haha!' He bursts out laughing. 'Good answer.'

He moves to let a group out the door, then turns back to us, his expression serious.

'I mean it, though. Your reputation precedes you.' A nod. 'I want you fully involved in this investigation, as operational detectives. The SVI stuff – the statements – you said yourself, I don't think they have much for us. Get to it. You can start with Bourke at the yacht club.'

15

Gemma

'I'm just going through for a short visit today,' I say, lowering my mask so the receptionist can see who I am. Seaview House is still insisting on visitors wearing masks indoors – the continued gifts of Covid. 'In the garden.'

'Oh, of course, Gemma.' She smiles the tinged-with-sadness smile which means that she's heard as well.

'Thanks.'

I pass through the dining room, where there's a small group of women playing a card game, and out the sliding doors into the courtyard. There's a sheltered corner under a wooden awning which has become 'our' place.

I've come to tell him about Max but, now that I'm here, I can't seem to find the words. And I wonder what's the point? What's to be gained by telling him that his only son, his favourite child – his golden boy – has been declared dead once and for all?

None of it makes sense. So what if they've found the body of my brother? Is there any way in which he benefits by knowing that Max is dead? For the past eighteen years, those years my parents spent searching and wondering and hoping, before Mum died of grief – because I've no doubt that the grief over the loss of her son put her in an early grave – for years we've lived with this. Mum died in 2014, seven years after Max disappeared. *Disappeared.* That's how I trained myself to think of it. And he did disappear.

And for Dad, the dementia was a kindness. Not at first. At first, he was scared, and confused, realizing that bits of his life were being stolen from him. But, as he went further into it, maybe – maybe the worst of the pain became hidden? Maybe he is spared the first waking thought, the last conscious thought – the one-word trigger of pain that is Max. It'd be good if one of us was.

Even in the worst of his confusion, the mention of Max's name lit him up like a match. Like someone flicked a switch in his brain. They say some people light up a room and, yeah, a glow followed Max wherever he went. My golden brother.

I sometimes bring Ferdia on these visits. The distraction is good. But this has to be done on my own. I have to – I need to – tell him. Maybe I won't go through with it. Maybe I'll start to talk about Max and – I don't know.

I see Dad hunched in the chair, his fingers scrolling the folds of the blanket. I long to reach over and cover his hand with mine, but I can't. That distance – always between us.

'Hi, Dad. It's a lovely day,' I say, though it's not really. There's a bit of chill on the breeze, and heavy clouds hang over the silty grey water. The storm that delivered Max to us must have stirred up mud and grit from the depths of the ocean. The water has a brownish tinge. It looks dirty.

'Do you remember me, Dad?' I whisper, because I know you're not supposed to do that. To set him memory tests, to quiz him.

He smiles the empty smile again. His standard response to that one – 'Sure, no one could forget you' – and I can't help smiling at him, at his genius confabulation. But along with the smile, the sting. Because this is public Dad. With the witty quip and the apt aside. This is John Fitzgerald, property magnate, builder, developer, investor. Former commodore of Corrig Point Yacht Club. This is Dad at his best.

'Dad, that's good. Because you remember me and you remember Max, don't you?'

And it's like I've stung him. I watch the smile melt from his features; his gaze slides away from mine and he seems to deflate. He looks at his lap, at his hands – frozen now, the fabric bunched together – like he's choking on something.

'Max and Gemma,' he whispers, shaking his head. And his knuckles are white with the strength of his grasp on the blanket when he lifts his gaze to mine, and I feel a crater gouged into my chest. I feel like – my heart – like someone pulled apart my ribcage and reached in to grab my lying, diseased and withered excuse for a heart. The skin on his face is cross-hatched by countless hours out on the open water, the cheeks and eyes sunken into themselves. This is a face ready for death. But the watery eyes find mine and I see a look of such naked hope and love that it seems reality is present between us, just for an instant.

'They found Max,' I say, and before I even draw breath to continue, before I begin to formulate how I will tell him the terrible news, I know with certainty that I'm not going to.

I look towards the doorway, where a group of nurses are chatting, then over my shoulder at the card-playing team. I lean forward. I picture myself taking his hands in mine and bringing them to my lips.

'They found Max,' I repeat, and I want to lift the knuckles to my mouth and lay a kiss on each bony ridge.

'Yes?'

'Yes.' I nod, and his smile begins to spread and so I smile too, because they did find Max. That is true. And then – then I see it all. He's standing on the deck of his beloved 49er against a massive orange sunset, his face in shadow. And I see the guards – for some reason, it's the detectives from yesterday, Laura and Niamh – and they're in a speedboat coming out to him. They cut the engine and their boat draws up level with Max's. And the boats are bobbing in the sunset. And Niamh leans over to catch on to the – the shroud, I think it's called – so the two boats are right beside each other, and he grins that grin. And his teeth are white in the evening light.

'And – and—'

And now, I see so much hope and joy in Dad's expression I can hardly bear it.

'But – b-but he was gone?' says Dad. 'He was gone for so long?' And the tears trickle down his withered cheek, and that makes me cry.

'He was, he was. Oh, Dad! Don't cry,' I say, and we both cry. And I'm so sad that, even in his dementia, he remembers that pain. 'Please don't cry, Dad.' I can't bear it. The pain I've caused. 'He – he got into trouble on the boat – but he's fine now, Dad. He's fine.'

He is. He's sitting on the garda boat, or maybe it's the RNLI rescue boat. That would make more sense. That's better. They searched all over, that whole month after he disappeared. The coastguard and the RNLI volunteers. The yacht club – the three yacht clubs.

And I know that this is – these are the fantasies – the dreams I never allowed myself. Max is all right. My father has been delivered from the living nightmare. The events of June 2007 never happened.

'He says – he's going to come in to visit you soon,' I whisper. And I picture him drawing up a chair, and it'll be Max's tanned hand on Dad's knee. Dad is nodding like that makes sense. Sailing is exhausting. There's no way you'd be up to visit a nursing home after a day out on the boat. Even I know that.

'Tomorrow,' he says, and the tone in which he says it is certain. 'Tomorrow. Oh, Max.' He leans against the back of the chair, exhaling a long, luxurious sigh. 'He's home. Thank you. Thank you, Gemma. You're a good girl.'

I choke the sob before it's fully formed.

16

Laura

'Do you sail yourself?' Niamh's voice is innocent enough but, even so, I glance over to see if she's slagging the broad and burly Detective Garda Stephen Bourke – or if her question is genuine. We're at the back of Corrig Point Yacht Club – to meet up with Christy Walsh, who did caretaking and night security duties for the club at the time. He's going to show us around.

'No,' he says. 'I'm more of a GAA man.' I suppress a smile. Maybe he's the one slagging her?

'Sound. And how are you enjoying working with our auld pal McCarthy?'

'We were fortunate enough to work with him for – how long would it be, Niamh?' I say, willing her not to get into anything she can't get out of. 'About a couple of years, in your case?'

She takes the hint. Backs down.

'I heard. The "Clonchapel siege", no less! Ah, he's not bad at all, considering he's, you know – from Tipp,' Stephen quips. He's definitely taking the piss.

'Feck off,' says Niamh, grinning.

He doesn't reply, and we draw level with a weatherbeaten elderly man wearing about three fleeces standing at the wrought-iron security gate.

'You must be Christy,' says Bourke.

'I must. I am.' Christy smiles a piratical grin as we

introduce ourselves. 'Stand back now,' he says. 'This place is like Fort Knox.' He spreads his fingers across a black box set at shoulder height to the right of the gate, and presses.

'Digital recognition pad,' he says over his shoulder as the gate swings open. 'But back in 2007 you got in with a key-card.' He smiles. 'We thought they were the height of high tech.'

'Pretty swish for 2007,' says Niamh.

'Were you working here then?' I have my notebook ready to get a bit more info, but Christy is already shaking his head.

'I was, yes, but not that night. Jim Dunphy was on duty, God rest him. I know he gave a statement at the time, and your lot took the diary and all the keycard stuff.'

That answers that then, I think. My expression must betray my disappointment, because Christy leans in towards me, so close I get the whiff of his fried breakfast – the sausages anyway.

'But I'll head back to the hut now and see if there's anything ye could have missed. The place hasn't been cleaned in twenty years, so you never know.'

'Thanks, Christy,' says Stephen. Christy shrugs away the thanks.

'I'll be in the hut if you need me,' he says, snapping the poppers of his fleeces closed against the breeze.

We stand in a line, looking at the marina, which is laid out in a grid shape with maybe a dozen boats berthed either side of long pontoons. Then we start walking, following Stephen past rows of shining steel and chrome, smooth fibreglass, complex arrangements of ropes and levers, the tall masts soaring skywards, wires and guy ropes sounding in the breeze.

He stops in front of a beautiful sailing craft and waits for us to catch up. The yacht is long and narrow with two blue lines just above the waterline and a selection of tall poles,

83

masts, and what must be the sails, in a heavy blue fabric, neatly furled. Stephen checks the name, nods.

'*MaxSpirit* herself. The not-so-shabby Hallberg-Rassy.'

'Jaysus,' from Niamh.

'Indeed,' Stephen grins.

'So this is the boat belonging to Conleth O'Hara now, the one from the charity?' says Niamh. Stephen nods. 'And is this also where the Fitzgerald boat was kept – er, moored – at the time?'

'Yes. The *Corrig Cailín* was berthed here. It was sold a few months after Max disappeared. Max's parents – John and Vandra Fitzgerald – never sailed again.'

He walks slowly along the side of the craft, then stops.

'This was where they found his shoes.'

The boat is tied to the dock – coils of nylon and a thicker, whitish rope which looks like it's made of a more natural fibre.

'There are photographs back at the incident room – you'll see. I've looked out the exhibits log. But yeah.' He looks down at the wooden planking beneath his feet. 'They were found the next morning, sitting here neatly like he'd stepped out of them.'

I continue on down the walkway, turning right, passing the stern. Right next to *MaxSpirit* is a similar craft – or maybe it's not that similar at all. Perhaps they're hugely different boats and I'm just going on the colour. This one is white as well, with bright orange and purple lettering both on the stern and near the prow: *Wave Princess*. I continue walking along the rows of beautiful boats, soothed by the beauty and wealth on display as much as by the lapping sounds of the water. I breathe a deep breath.

I've been so much better in recent months. That's one good thing about surviving your nightmares – you make it out the other side. You're triumphant. For months now, I've been free of compulsions. I can sit downstairs and watch a movie with Matt without checking the kids. I've let Katie go on playdates – she goes with other mothers in their cars – or with Alva. Both Matt and Katie love having her around. When she brought them to Rathmines the other day, I enjoyed the peace – well, I used the time to clean the windows and, sure, there were intrusive thoughts. But even so. For me, this is groundbreaking stuff. But still there's always the fear that I'll slip again. It's like I have the fear of the fear coming back. And when you're seized by that terror, there's nothing like it. That's when the world is a storm of risk, chaos, and noise – so much noise. But here in the marina, among thousands – no, millions – of euros' worth of boats and equipment, it's possible to feel protected, cocooned by wealth.

The boats' names speak of bright mornings and whole days spent having fun. I picture light splintering into silver chips on the water, suntanned children racing about in bright T-shirts. I can almost hear their voices – the families, friends, the sailing buddies.

Knot on Duty, Shelly Swelly, Sea & Tonic, Catching Rays.

This is how some people live, I remind myself. They work and then they play. It's possible to believe in a world like this, where nothing bad ever happens. I remember, suddenly, that Matt did sailing camps during the summer holidays when he was a kid. I can't remember which yacht club. Maybe it was even this one, Corrig Point. I'll check with him later.

'Can you see yourself on deck, sipping your G&T?' laughs Niamh, drawing level with me. 'I can picture Matt doing the whole captain thing, can you?'

I smile.

'I was just remembering that he did some sailing when he

was a kid, actually. I think Dermot was quite keen. I'll ask him what he remembers.'

She nods, zipping up her jacket against a sudden gust.

'Maybe ye should try it – family outing?'

And I know she's only making conversation, but I wish she hadn't said that. Because as soon as I think of the kids on the boat, I picture Noah falling overboard. I see him running to catch Katie and he slips or gets his foot caught in the rope and over he goes. And she's distraught. She jumps in to save him. And they're both drowning. I remind myself to breathe. I do the beginning of the tapping sequence. *It's only a thought. Thoughts aren't real*, I tell myself.

'Sorry,' says Niamh, reaching to squeeze my arm. 'It's—'

'I know.' I exhale, calmer already. 'It's grand.' And it is. You're never 'over' OCD, but you can learn to manage it, and that's what I'm doing.

'Ongoing process.' I smile.

Stephen joins us, phone in hand.

'So, McArsey was just—' He stops himself. Niamh whirls around, grinning.

'I fecking knew it!' She laughs.

'Sarge has a bit more info for us.' He grins.

As we turn away from the marina and head back towards the town, I test myself. I picture me signing them up for classes, zipping up their little lifejackets. Zipping up my own. Couldn't I go with them?

Yeah. I'm not there yet.

17

Laura

'I'm drawing a picture for Grandad,' Katie announces, 'to make him better. He says he'll put it up over his bed.'

I finish putting my stuff away, delighted at the calm scene in my kitchen. It's just past seven, Alva has the kids in pjs already, something's in the oven, there's a bottle of white open, and Matt's car is in the drive.

'I could get used to this.' I grin at Alva. 'Thanks.'

'Heard the news,' she says, her voice sympathetic. 'Reckoned you'd be happy not to have to cook.'

She tucks her hair behind her ear, and something about the movement reminds me of Mum, which is ridiculous, seeing as how we only share DNA from our father. She's slim, a couple of centimetres taller than I am, and, I realize, she's reminding me of myself. Not sure how I feel about that. Noah comes pelting out from the sitting room and clambers up me like I'm a tree, shattering the peace.

'Mummeeeee,' he yells, grabbing my face in his hands and planting cold, wet kisses on my cheek. His hands are sticky and I'm pretty sure he's full of sugar energy – but it's Friday and I don't have to be in till midday tomorrow, so I can have a bit of a lie-in and still get in early to get to grip with the files.

'Ah, they're great kids.' She smiles. 'And I didn't cook. Just heating up a chicken casserole.'

She hands me a glass of wine and I plonk down on the chair, snuggling Noah on my lap.

'You brought the kids to Justy and Dermot?' I say, passing a piece of paper and some crayons to Noah so he can draw too. Alva busies herself putting the wine bottle back in the fridge. I can't see her face.

'Not Gran-PA! Gran-DAD,' says Katie. 'Our other gran-dad, Mummy! Your daddy.' She shakes her head at me, like I'm a waste of space. 'We went to see him and we were really helpful, and—'

'And we had to be really QUIET!' yells Noah. 'Because there's sick people there and sick people sleep all the time.'

He pulls my face to make me look at him. 'And I was whispering, and he said we are the best grandkids in the galaxy and we had Jelly Babies.'

I don't trust myself to speak. Alva sits down at the far side of the table, her gaze flickering from mine to the worn wood.

'And he was crying a bit,' Noah says, turning back to his picture, 'because – because he's sick. But then I showed him my racing car and he said, "Amaze-bombs."'

'And I drew him a picture and it was – he said that was amaze-bombs too,' Katie butts in, not to be outdone.

The word stuns. Because that's what he used to say. *Amaze-bombs, kiddos.* And why does memory work like this? Something you didn't even know you knew – a phrase from the past, from a different life – comes back, bringing with it the whole scene – or a part-remembered scene. I remember scratchy flip-up seats, and a huge bag of sweets, and coloured lights – and sitting between Mum and Dad, and the excitement! We were at the panto.

'I'm sorry,' whispers Alva. 'They – they wanted to come and—'

I look at her and, just for a second, it's like we're in the interview room and I'm leaving her to stew. I know I should answer her, put her out of her misery. I should say

88

something like, *It's okay, I'm glad you made that decision.* Instead, I keep looking at her and my face is blank. She knows that was not the deal. The deal was that she could stay in our spare room for a few weeks, months, whatever, so she could visit him in the hospice. I have no animosity towards her, or Áine or Seán. I don't even have anything against Charlie. She – she's nothing to me, or not even that – that sounds mean. I've nothing against the woman my father married after Mum. And I've nothing against their kids. I'm happy to help, and I know it's not easy watching someone you love die. But there's a line I'm not crossing, and she knows that. I don't trust myself to speak because the words that come out – I can't be responsible for them.

He was *my* dad. He was my dad first. He was my dad and that was who he was and that was his job and that was all he had to be – a dad to me and Cian. And he was such fun. That was the thing – he made us laugh and he sang funny songs. He sang 'On Top of Spaghetti' and the other one – the one about the dog. Bingo. *There was a farmer had a dog, and Bingo was its name-oh.*

But all of it was fake because he left us. And he left our mum, and she was so brave. She did it all on her own, and he just disappeared off to the other end of the country like we were nothing. And he shacked up – and I should be horrified with myself for sounding like an auld one disapproving – okay. Okay. He married Charlie and she was younger and prettier than our mum and then he started over. With you. You and your twin and your brother. And he made it like you were his real family and we were just a mistake. Like a trial run that he made a mess of.

I don't say any of these words and, even though the stony silence is cruel, it's better than saying those words. Because you can't take them back.

I'm so angry.

Matt comes into the kitchen, grinning. He's fresh from the shower and he looks so happy. Oblivious, he goes to the fridge and takes out the bottle.

'Top-up, anyone?'

Alva is sweet and utterly genuine. I know she didn't mean to interfere, and I know she means well. And I can't really blame her for not knowing the strength of my feelings when I've never – not once – spoken to her about Dad or told her how I really feel. She thinks her mum married a separated man who had moved away from his family years before. And maybe it's best if that's what she continues to think. And maybe he – the serial womanizer – maybe he was faithful to Charlie. People change – people can change. It's a possibility. So, I sat there in my own kitchen letting my half-sister serve up the supper, with my excited kids clambering over her, delighted with their afternoon's entertainment, already planning their next visit.

'I'm so sorry,' she'd mouthed quietly, anxiety tracing her features, ageing her. Niamh says the twins are a bit like me but 'with less bitterness and disappointment around the eyes'.

'I should have thought of that, Laura. I should have known that you'd want to be the one to introduce them.'

As if that's what I minded.

So, I smiled and said that no, I was glad she'd been the one to do it. And yeah, maybe I actually am glad. They're so happy. How are kids born happy, with all that goodness and love inside them? Ready to lavish it left, right and centre? And how – what do you have to do to hang on to that?

Matt had caught my gaze then. He gave the tiniest of winks.

'Cheers to the chef,' he grinned, toasting Alva. 'Great improvements on the culinary front since you've moved in.' He attempted a bit of footsie under the table with me.

'You're funny,' I said. But I can't help the smile.

We headed to bed early, leaving Alva watching the *Late Late Show* and sending texts.

That was over an hour ago. I just can't sleep. I'm lying like I'm carved on a tombstone, staring at the fingers of orange streetlight poking through the curtains. I'm trying not to wake Matt, but I'm pretty sure he's not asleep. There's a listening quality to the silence.

The mattress dips as he turns on his side so he's facing me. I should turn towards him. They say marriages live or die on the approaches ignored. He's trying, Laura. So turn the fuck over and take his hand. I turn over.

'Dorm chat,' he says, his teeth white in the dark. 'Good girl.'

He reaches to push back the hair which has covered my face, tucking it behind my ear gently. *It's not his fault, Laura.* I summon a smile.

'I can't talk about it—'

My hands are clasped in fists, like an angry prayer. He pulls the top fist towards his face, uncurling my fingers one by one, kissing the tips.

'She means well,' he whispers, mildly. 'And the kids were delighted. Is that so bad?'

And I know he's right. I know the kids were thrilled that they got to meet their other grandad. And I know – I know all too well about his charm and how easy it is, how skilled he is, probably even now – he could always make you laugh. He could make you love him. He made you laugh and he made you love him. And then he just walked off. And now—

'He's dying, Matt.'

'Exactly,' Matt whispers back. 'You only have one dad –
and he's—'

'He wasn't a dad to me – or, he walked away from that job,'
I hiss, angry tears falling now. 'He might have been a dad to
Alva, but before that, with us, he got tired of being our dad,
and he left us. You – you've no idea, Matt.'

Matt pulls my hands against his chest and I feel his beating
heart.

'Sssh. I know I haven't a clue. You're right. And it's okay to
be sad.'

'I'm not sad! I'm – don't turn it into sadness. Don't let him
off the hook. I'm so angry with him.'

And I hold tight to the anger because it's all I have. And
it's better than the sadness. Less scary. I followed him around
like a shadow when I was little. I cried when he went away on
business trips. I lived for his praise. And the chasm when he
left was so vast and so dark and so scary that I filled it with
rage. Layers of anger. Why were we not enough for him?

@unatracey5: Hope you're bearing up all right @gemstone. Thinking of you.
@marymary2: Can we do anything?
@missymurfi: I said that too @marymary2. I live locally and am always here to help.
@annahanna: ♡
@yes2wine: Heard the news bulletin. Will spread the word down here in Wexford. May be people who remember that night.
@ingridanne: ♡ 🙏
@theirishmammy: DM if you need anything. Right behind you, Gemma.

Saturday

18

Gemma

'What am I meant to do, Conleth?' I'm speaking quietly, aware that Ferdia might hear the conversation over the noise of the wind. We're making our way to the Roger Casement statue on the new jetty, and the place is hopping with weekend walkers. Above us, people are sitting out in the café, the place unrecognizable from the run-down building which used to house the Dún Laoghaire baths. One or two recognize me and give me a sad smile. Nobody asks for a selfie. I spot Lesley – *Superfan Les,* as Conleth would say – the most loyal and visible of my followers, lurking beneath a parasol on the corner table. Bizarrely, I'm sort of comforted to see her. Conleth calls her my stalker, and we do end up bumping into her more times than random chance can account for. She's wearing the cropped hoody I'd featured in March. She sees me looking and bends to check her phone, embarrassed. I move so Conleth can't see her. He'll only say something about her size.

'Why are they saying it's suspicious? That guard – the family liaison person – she couldn't tell me anything. What – it's only a matter of time till they—'

'Not now.' His glare shuts down that line of talk. 'Here, give me your phone.' Then, louder, to Ferdia, 'You two walk on down to the seat there. I'll take some photos.' Conleth takes the phone out of my hand, flapping his hand to indicate that we're to do what he says.

'Are you not coming, Daddy?'

And the sight of Ferdia looking up at him through the thick glasses, his cheeks purple with the fresh wind, silver lines running from his nose to his upper lip, clutching the digger against his chest – it's heartbreaking. I can't go to prison! I can't leave him alone. I – I pull at Conleth's sleeve to get him to look at his son. But he's scrolling through my phone. There's nothing incriminating. And I've bought nothing at all since the Teddy's ice-cream for the boys last week.

'Con, please?'

He looks up, and I tilt my head towards Ferdia, blinking, pleading. 'All he wants is a bit of attention.'

As if to prove me right, Ferdia moves to grab the edge of his father's jacket.

'You come too, Daddy,' he says, and Conleth is irritated by the two of us pulling at him while he's concentrating. I know he doesn't intend what happens next. He's never deliberately hurt Ferdia. But he struggles to hold his patience – it's not easy for him. But now Conleth pulls away sharply and the movement knocks the digger out of Ferdia's grip and it tumbles to the ground with a loud cracking sound. And we watch as it bounces and breaks into three pieces – trailer, main body and front loader. Ferdia's face is chalked in shock. I scurry to pick up the pieces, fake smile frozen in place.

'Don't worry,' I whisper. Why am I whispering? 'I'll mend it, Ferdie.'

In my peripheral vision, I see Lesley's shocked face, her hand flying to cover the round 'O' of her mouth.

Ferdia keeps hold of the body of the digger, pressing it to his heart, bending to kiss it. 'Is he dead?' he says, looking up.

And the worst thing is, he doesn't cry. I kneel to hug him, the digger jabbing against both of our chests. I cradle the back of his head and speak into his ear.

'No, he can be fixed. I'll fix him.'

Conleth sighs. And I wait, my heart pounding, willing Ferdia not to make a fuss, not to start crying. The slightest whinge from Ferdia is like lighting a fuse. A guy passes us, his baby strapped to his chest. Insurance. Thank God. And Lesley is still watching. Conleth waits till he's gone.

'It's time you stopped carrying that around anyway. You're too big for that nonsense. Now.' He beckons for me to stand.

'Mummy needs to post some photos,' he says in a hearty voice. 'So, behave yourself. You want to be a helpful boy, don't you?'

Now? I think. But he's clearly decided that I must. I know he's stressed too – neither of us slept last night. And I know, with a weariness that fills my soul, that it's all my fault. That I have brought this on us. That even though I sometimes hate what he has become, I'm responsible for it. And that, without him, I wouldn't have Ferdia, I wouldn't have this life. Conleth sorted out the mess I had made of my life before it had even begun. My own father would have disowned me. I can't even think about Mum. To think that she held her little boy – that she went through all this with Max, and me – and that she went through a mother's worst nightmare – losing a child. All because of me. And she lost both of us. Of course she did. After Max died, the chasm between me and my parents was like a crack in the earth's crust. I stood on one side and watched them shrivel, waste and die.

I wished I was dead for so long. And Mum and Dad were the same. We were like zombies, going through the motions of being alive. Conleth was the only person strong enough to be with us. By that stage, his parents had died and we were his second family – but sometimes I wish he *had* just left us alone.

I'd be dead by now. I know that. *And would that be so bad?* I drop the thought like a shard of broken glass. Only Conleth held it all together. And he's strict, yes – unforgiving, I suppose. But it's like he says: without him, I'd be dead. And then I found out I was pregnant. And I know he wasn't happy about it, but we made the best of it. It was the only time – the only time I ever, ever stood up to him. This is a prison of my own making. My husband lost his best friend that night. And his Olympic dream. But we're bound together, Conleth, me and Ferdia, in a lie – my lie.

And so I take a tissue from my pocket, wipe Ferdia's pink nose and hold him close.

'Come on, brave boy,' I say. 'We'll walk to the seat and watch the swimmers.'

My son's hand is small and cold in mine as we walk along the jetty. And I know it will make a poignant photo. And I'm torn – because this is real. The sadness is so real. It's more than a photograph. But it's a commodity too. I'm the tragic little sis. *Heartbroken Gemma waits for her big brother. Saddened sis sets up sailing club in brother's memory.* And every year, at the Missing Persons Event at the Áras, it's *Grief-stricken Gemma mourns another year.*

And when Conleth set up MaxSpirit it really felt like we were doing something good. For over ten years, he's run sailing lessons and trips for kids who would otherwise never get a chance to sail. They're out every weekend – every day in the summer. He brings in thousands in sponsorship. He's making a difference.

But nothing can change the facts. Max is dead. And I don't think his spirit lives on in the sailing club. I try not to think about his spirit. I don't even believe – I don't know – sometimes I see glimpses of him in Ferdia, especially when he smiles. But that's not some mystical spirit living on – that's science. That's DNA.

Ferdia is still clutching his broken digger. I hold his hand tight in case he trips. He often trips. He was born prematurely, at twenty-nine weeks. After a night I've scrubbed from my memory. I will not go there.

I look back over my shoulder. Conleth is scrolling through my phone. A surge of panic rips through me – I always check my texts before handing it over in the morning. Did I delete Penny's text about the swimming? When I picked up Ferdia yesterday, she said it was still going to happen.

'I can't, Penny, I'm just – I'm a mess.'

'Can't equals won't,' she'd replied, glancing at the boys. 'And if you're a mess, which by the way is completely normal with something like this, then it's the perfect time. All the more reason to do it. You owe it to them, to your son,' she said. 'You live in a swimmer's paradise.' She gestured towards the view, Dún Laoghaire bay laid out in front of us. 'You've no excuse. And I'm going to help you.'

Meet you on the beach Monday after drop-off, her text read.

She said she'd get me into the sea, that the sea is way easier than the pool. She said she'd have me sea-swimming in three days. And I'd agreed – for Conleth, for Ferdia, for Penny, but mostly for Max. Surely I can do that for him. It would be one thing to be proud of.

We make our way as a family, holding hands – poignant. Touching. And as we go up the steps towards the café I notice the bloodstains – old and brownish grey – that track someone's progress from the jetty to the main road. Probably someone who simply grazed themselves on a rock while barefoot on the stony beach. But I shiver. It seems like a sign of something worse.

19

Laura

I stifle a yawn, annoyed with myself for my inability to switch off last night, fed up with my repetitive thought processes. Niamh tilts her head, mouthing, 'You okay?' I nod. We're sitting in the incident room, in the same seats as before – it seems that all garda stations and schools are the same. You stick to your desk unless the teacher moves you. On the whiteboard, there's the grainy image from the CT scan showing the nicked bone, along with photos of the items recovered with Max's body – a monogrammed belt and a cufflink.

O'Riordan clicks to a close-up.

'Max was stabbed in the chest at an angle which caused the blade to nick the bone and leave a fragment embedded. The murder weapon, if it can be found, will have a matching nick out of it.' He pauses. 'Although I'm aware that it could have been sitting on the bottom of the seabed for the past eighteen years.'

He looks back at his notes. 'And it could still be there now. It hasn't been decided yet if we're going to do a search of the harbour' – another pause – 'although no doubt, Sergeant McCarthy, you'd be in like Flynn if we need you to do a dive.'

There's laughter, and McCarthy laughs too – not sure whether he's being made fun of. Nothing changes, it seems.

'And our bookman – bookwoman, rather – tells me we've had a lot of activity on the hotline, which is good.'

'Any sightings?' This from a uniformed guard sitting to my left.

'So far, no. People recall the speeches and the cake. The crowd moved freely around the interior and exterior of the club. We have people who attended the party saying' – he consults his notepad – 'Max was in great form that night and everyone loved him. Or, and take your pick' – a wry smile – 'Max was clearly depressed that night and anxious about the Olympics.'

Tara indicates that she's got something for us and comes forward.

'We're still sifting through these emails and voice messages. But in terms of actual sightings, there's nothing to go on. Security footage from the clubhouse was confined to the main entrance. That's at the front, and we've nothing at all from the rear. The only record we have of him digitally is that he used his keycard for the gate into the marina.'

'Do we have a time for that?' Niamh asks.

Tara checks the notes. 'Just after 10.15 p.m.'

Which means Max left the party after the speeches.

'Hang on, though.' She turns a page. 'There's two entries of Max's keycard. The keycard was used twice.'

'What time is the second entry?' I say. 'Or is that him leaving?'

Tara shakes her head.

'You don't need the card to leave,' she says. 'So those times – the second time he enters is 10.42 p.m. – both of those are him, Max.'

She looks up.

'Okay, so we know that Max's card is used to enter the marina – twice – for some reason. He leaves the party and enters the marina. He comes back. Then he repeats this and what – vanishes into thin air?' O'Riordan scans the room for answers.

103

'Well, does he come back though?' says Niamh. 'Because nobody saw him.' She shrugs. 'So maybe he doesn't go back to the club, he goes somewhere else?' She frowns. 'Nah, we're forgetting something, lads. We're forgetting that someone killed him and made it look like he disappeared. So—'

I'm nodding.

'So what if someone else was there with him? Three of us got in the gate there yesterday. So let's say he's with someone else. This person, they kill him, hide the body. And they leave the shoes to make it look like, you know, here ends the trail?' I add.

'Or someone follows him a bit later,' Stephen interjects.

'How did they get in though?' This from Niamh. 'Without a keycard?'

'And why?' says Tara. 'Who would want to kill him?' she says simply.

'What else did ye get at the club yesterday?' says O'Riordan, looking at Stephen.

'Yeah, we spoke to Christy and had a look around. The security guard on duty at the time has since died, but Christy said he'd seen nothing that night.'

He checks his notes.

'Shaw checked that statement.' He pauses, and I nod in agreement. 'And look, it seems clear that it was a celebratory night. Christy implied that his colleague from the security hut, Jim Dunphy, might have enjoyed a bit of a quiet drink and, eh, a nap of an evening, so he noticed nothing. We went into the club, and it's possible to sneak out unseen, even now. There's this half-door behind the bar. It's still there. No cameras on it. It's sort of cut into the window and wall. You could sneak out that way without being noticed.'

'And you said something about the Olympics?' I shake my

head. 'I've yet to see that mentioned in the statements. Who was it who said that? Did that come in through the hotline?'

Tara looks down at her notes.

'Yes, a Carol-Ann Skehan. She's – she's semi-retired now. Apparently, she was the sailing coach. I've a number for her.'

'Great, thanks.'

'Okay, can someone check that, please? And Darmody, Shaw, can you also re-interview the sister as a matter of urgency?'

'Yes, Cig. And we'll speak to the husband. As Max's best friend and sailing partner, presumably he was there at the party, although we've no statement from him.'

'Okay. And Bourke' – O'Riordan gives Stephen a nod – 'what about Nolan – Garda Nolan's files? He was SIO at the time. Have you got his notes yet?'

Stephen leans to whisper a comment to an older guard sitting beside him; grizzled and grubby, he reminds me of a farm collie. He shakes his head.

'Poor old Nolan had barely cleared his desk before he, ah, passed. There might be stuff – eh, you know, waiting to be filed. You know how it is.'

I do know: boxes of papers, bags of evidence waiting, piling up in drawers and plastic bags in dusty corners of evidence rooms. Not enough manpower to input the info digitally. I nod in sympathy, hoping that this will work in our favour. A box of papers, maybe.

Murmurs of sympathy ripple through the room. Something about the quality of the sympathy alerts me. 'What actually happened?'

'He was on a fishing trip,' says the older guard. 'Solo. Boat capsized about a mile out of Bullock Harbour and he – hypothermia got him in the end. He'd a lifejacket and all. But—' He exhales a smoker's wheeze. 'Nothing to be done. By the time they reached him, he was a goner.'

20

Niamh

There's something up. We're like sisters. In fact, I reckon I can read her better than I can read Siobhán. Her voice is just that bit flat, there's a sort of rigid set to her shoulders. We're back in the stationery cupboard, going through the statements – Gemma's in particular, because we're calling down to interview her later on. I know better than to ask Laura outright what's the matter. She gathers the sheaf of pages between her fingers, tapping them on the surface of the table to get them level.

'How's the little gang at home?' I push the packet of crackers towards her, but she shakes her head. 'Are they pissed off with you working on a Saturday?'

'Oh, yeah – no. Actually, it's better to leave Matt to it on Saturdays.' She shrugs. 'He brings them to the park, then up to Nutgrove. I've given up trying to make sure, you know, that he remembers everything.'

'I'd say that's a relief for him.' I grin. 'He's probably been counting down the days till you lighten the bejaysus up and let him off! That helicopter parenting thing – not good.'

'Shut up,' she says, in a half-hearted way.

'So the kids are fine, and the handsome hubby is fine—' I leave it open-ended, demonstrating my excellent interviewing technique.

'Ah, look. It's stuff at home – with Alva. You know, I've told you about my dad—'

'Yeah. You have. How's he doing? What's going on?'

She shrugs, begins patting the loose sheets back into the file, not making eye contact. I spot the tell-tale redness around her thumbnail. She's back at the picking.

'She – Alva brought the kids in to meet him. Yesterday. In the hospice.'

'Without asking you?'

Now she looks at me. Directly.

'Yes! I know! Oh my God, thank you for that! And look – I'm just – I just feel a bit ambushed is all. But it's fine. It's fine now.'

She shakes her head.

'Well, she should have asked you,' I say. 'But what's done is done. How did it go?'

Her eyes flood with tears suddenly, and oh, for feck's sake, so do mine. That and the prickling in my freaking armpits. Hormones are bastards.

'Thanks for saying that, Niamh. You always – that's – that's all I needed to hear. It went okay.' She smiles a watery smile. 'They had a great time actually.'

I busy myself fixing imaginary lint on my shirt so she doesn't see the tears, but not before she looks at me strangely. She inhales as if to say something but thinks better of it. Both of us hiding stuff.

'Come on,' she says. 'Let's see what we get from the little sister.'

21

Gemma

I'm still shaking, though we pretended it was just a chat. It's not like you see on the TV. I was expecting them to bring me into the station – into a little room with all this recording equipment and a big mirror where they're watching you. But they came to the house and Niamh played with Ferdia while Laura asked the questions. But I felt their connection, like they can talk without words. And Conleth had said to play it cool, but I talked and talked in a torrent of words. All that stuff from when we were kids. Why did I have to even mention it at all? It's the way she listens – Laura. I couldn't help filling in the silence. It was such a relief to see them out the door, to hear their car drive off. To delay the inevitable.

And so I go to visit Dad. It calms me, although he's pretty much asleep. He always says he listens with his eyes closed, so it will have to do. My head is thumping, still. One of the care assistants brought a blanket and lit the outdoor heater, even though it's May. She was worried I'd get cold. They really are so kind. I make a note to do a post about them in the coming days. If I – if I'm still here.

Because they know. They know Max didn't kill himself, that he didn't drown accidentally. As soon as they told me about the rope and the weight, my hands turned to ice and I had to put them in my pockets to hide the shake. I hadn't a clue. I'd never – I'd never once thought that through. Not once. Why did they have to tell me? Now it's all I can see. I picture him and rope is winding around and around him, like he's in a cocoon. But he won't be emerging from his rope cocoon. *Maxattacks* no more. And Conleth said to keep my answers short, and I really tried. I shut my mouth and I sat on my trembling hands. They said we'd talk again soon.

Dad's head dips. It could be sleepiness, or it could be surprise at the mention of his son's name. And I hate seeing him like this, shrunken and weak. He'd been a giant of a man, his tanned forearms like tree trunks. Max was tall – an inch taller than Dad – and all the sailing meant that he was strong too. The way they looked at him, my parents – and not just them, his friends too. Girls – even Conleth, sometimes. People drank him in. You'd catch them looking at him like he was a movie star, with a kind of hunger.

My childhood memories are a jumble of outdoor scenes, with trailers and boats, ropes being flung over roof racks, massive heavy carryalls in which sails were folded away. I stood on slipways and in harbours watching and listening to the cries and the clangs and the heavy thumps of sailing gear being hauled about. Dad would be directing, shouting orders, back-slapping and tapping against the hull signifying a job well done. I've seen him lift anchors, haul engines, load boxes, veins bulging at his temples, tendons like ropes. This man can barely lift his own head.

'When Max comes back, we – we'll go out in the boat. Would you like that?'

I lean closer, bending to try and see his features, conjuring up what I can't see – the eyes crinkled with love and delight – because of what I'm telling him. And I know I shouldn't, but there's no one to overhear, and what harm does it do, so I carry on. If you're going to lie, lie properly. Lie big.

'Yes, that's right, Dad. After my swim yesterday – did I tell you, I go swimming now? Well, I do. I do, can you believe it?

And I went out with Max yesterday. For real. In the harbour.' And his mouth moves; I think I see it move. So I carry on. If I'm going to reinvent myself, I'll do it properly. 'In the 49er! It was – it was a race. I know! Imagine. Me! In a boat! I was in the 49er.'

And he doesn't challenge that, though the idea of me in any boat – let alone a 49er, sprinting like a flash across the water, the crew leaning out dangling in mid-air – it's preposterous. But I – I can't stop myself. I don't want to. I don't want to think about the rope around my poor big brother. I want to believe this, and Dad is nodding vigorously, like he believes it. And so the truth doesn't matter. This is a new truth.

I summon Max's love for the 49er. He adored it like it was a living thing. He couldn't wait to get out sailing each morning, impressive when you think that he was a teenager, peak age for lying in bed in the mornings. School holidays meant he'd be out on the water before eight. The name of the boat comes from its hull length of 4.99 metres. I remember Max explaining it to me, about how the top of the mast is square so the upper main sail can twist and flatten out, making it have a faster gust response. Gust response. Main, jib, spinnaker. Onshore wind. Offshore wind. Which one is better? I rack my brains to remember the sailing terms – the phrases they used, the commentary after races, the jokes, the slang.

'We lost a bit of speed after – I mean, the conditions were really difficult, Dad. You know, big waves and, eh, poor visibility, but, but then the wind got up and we gained speed. We got to – um, thirty knots.' I look over my shoulder, aware that my voice is creeping up and up in volume.

'And Max said I did great,' I whisper, and I'm filled with such a flood of warmth at that idea. Once, he did say that. I remember now. He was trying to zip up a kitbag and it was stuffed to bursting, so the zip wouldn't close. So he squashed the two sides in and told me to pull up the zip, and it was like magic. My big brother needed me, and he made it so I could help him. I pulled so hard that I nearly reefed the metal off, but I did it. And Max ruffled my hair.

And when he lost stuff – he was always losing things: his locker key from the club, his wallet, his pocketknife, favourite pens – I would go looking in the kitchen cupboards and down the side of the car and in jacket pockets, and I always found them for him.

'Good woman, Gemstone,' he'd laugh.

There's no stopping me now. And I don't care about the truth any more. I've left it far behind. This fiction is the best thing I've ever done.

'I crewed for Max, Dad.'

And it's so quiet that I wonder if I've gone too far. I wait for him to make eye contact, to fix me with his cold blue stare, that stare I'm so familiar with – the one where it seemed he was waiting for me to be a better daughter. Less of a disappointment. More like Max. I wait for him to say, 'Enough of your nonsense, Gemma.'

But he doesn't.

The 49er is a double-handed high-performance dinghy. The helm is the one who makes the tactical decisions and steers the boat. That used to be Max, while Conleth crewed for him. The crew is the guy who controls the sails. There isn't a chance in hell that I could ever, ever be the crew. Or the helm.

But Dad says nothing. And in the dim evening light, I think I see the faintest smile.

'Max said I did great.'

He nods. 'You did great,' whispers Dad.

22

Niamh

'Come on.' I nudge her. 'We can talk more in the car. Will I write up the notes for today, let you get back home?'

She starts the engine and manoeuvres on to the road, glancing over her shoulder at me.

'Ah no, I can't ask you to do that, Niamh. You're tired.'

'Sure who isn't? Don't be daft. You've to get things sorted, you know? What do you think you'll do about – about Alva and the kids visiting, you know, the hospice?'

I see her swallow, like she's squashing down words. Her jaw clenches.

'Look,' I say, biting the bullet. 'Tell me to piss off if you want, if I'm overstepping, but – but is there any harm? Really? Is there any harm in your kids meeting your dad?'

'Piss off,' she says, politely.

I can't help laughing.

'That was brutal! That was the most rubbish "Piss off" I ever heard.'

She has the decency to look a bit ashamed.

'Yeah, well. I don't have the luxury of telling everyone to piss off. It's not the same coming from me.'

She's not wrong there.

'This is true. You've kind of cornered the market on passive-aggressive uptight bitch, in fairness.'

She indicates and exits the roundabout on to the motorway, picking up speed.

'I'll – I'll see how I feel later. Alva said she'd babysit, so Matt and I are going out for dinner.'

I'm nodding. 'Good plan. Get a schlepp of wine into you and see how you feel. What harm?'

'It's not the harm.' She sighs. 'It's the can of worms. Already, Katie's asking why I'm not visiting. And I don't know what to tell her.'

'Fair enough,' I say, knowing full well that I've said enough for now. She'll decide in her own time. She can't be pushed. Nothing with Laura can ever be forced. She'll shut me out completely if I say more.

'So, what about little sister Gemma? Is it just me or is there something very off about her? Like, all that stuff about the brother – and then when you asked her if she sailed and she said the bit about being the first Fitzgerald in generations who didn't even complete a sailing course.'

'Yes, yes.' Laura's tone changes completely. 'I thought so too. Definitely, there's something odd about her. The stuff about "Am I in trouble?" and – don't you think she was jumpy? I mean, for someone who has had what, eighteen years, to accept this loss. Or, not jumpy, exactly. Just kind of – terrified. I don't know. She seems fearful, doesn't she? But what do you reckon? Are you liking her as a suspect? Kills her brother out of – take your pick: jealousy, sibling rivalry?'

She changes lanes and slows down ready to exit, eyes on the road ahead.

'Too soon to say.' I shake my head. 'I mean, she was sixteen and half his size, like. And why? But yeah, incredibly jumpy and wound up to ninety. That's for sure. And she seemed genuinely shocked to hear about the weight and the rope, didn't she?' I ask her, remembering how Gemma had looked when we told her. Her hand had jerked towards her mouth, but not in time to stifle the gasp.

113

'Yeah, I thought so,' says Laura. 'You?'

'Yeah, definitely. No way was that put on. And she fessed up about being out of it that night, didn't she?'

Laura glances at me.

'Exactly! She did. And do you know what I wondered? What did her parents do about that? I mean, you're hosting a party and your sixteen-year-old gets blind drunk. I mean, you'd think as a parent, if your teenager gets plastered, well, wouldn't you maybe march her home or, you know, keep an eye on her in case she—'

'Chokes on her own puke,' I finish. 'Or passes out into an alcohol coma. Yeah. But instead, they let her go home alone and then – like they mustn't even have checked on her?'

I think about the risks. People die from alcohol poisoning. People choke on their vomit.

'In the GAA club, you know, we have a rule. We look out for each other. Someone holds your hair if you're puking and pats your back. It's an unwritten rule. They bring you home in a taxi or call your mam if they think she'll be sound and not flip her lid.'

'Yeah.' Laura's voice is thoughtful. We drive in under the barrier and she parks. Then switches off the engine.

'Yeah,' she repeats. 'I did think that was strange. And she strikes me as very lonely – and it sounds like she was lonely back then, doesn't it?'

'But it does tie in with the statement?'

'You mean the statement Nolan invented?' Her voice is scathing.

'Well, yes,' I admit. 'But one thing I thought was weird – she said nothing about the husband in the statement, there's no mention of Conleth. Isn't that right? But today, she's all "He saved my life" and, I dunno – it could be me – maybe my radar is off, but there's something fishy about him. Is he too good to be true? All that "He saved my life" stuff, where's that coming from and do we believe it?'

Laura looks thoughtful. 'Yeah, I noticed that too. I'm going to see if there could be more statements put away somewhere though, because we've nothing for him. Zero. I've asked Senan to have another look.'

'Sergeant Senan to you.'

Laura rolls her eyes.

'You could be a sergeant too, Niamh.'

She busies herself reaching into the back to get her laptop and bag, not making eye contact.

'So, you know?'

'What? That you aced your sergeant exam? Yes indeed, of course I know that. Everyone knows. Well done, you.' She smiles, opening the car door and putting one leg out, then turning back to look at me, squarely.

'And I also know that, as far as Cig is concerned, you're basically the Chosen One, his anointed heir. You do realize that, don't you?'

My reply – *what about us?* – fades before I utter it.

If I go on with this – even if I get a good ranking in the psychometric exam, and even if I pass the interview – is this what I want? I'll be deployed somewhere else. I'd be back in uniform, based in a station. No more partnership with Laura. Is that what I want? Especially now?

Monday

23

Gemma

'It's the ingratitude I can't take.' He sighs. I say nothing, not wanting to raise the stakes. Not wanting to wake Ferdia. It's past one in the morning and Conleth's lying on his back in the centre of the bed watching me to make sure I don't cheat by holding on to the doorjamb. I'm shivering with exhaustion, but I've to kneel where he can see me, in the doorway of the bathroom until he says I can go to bed. Although I'll be sleeping on the floor tonight, because he's thrown my pillow off. The marble tiles are harsh under my knees and already I'm swaying, my right knee actually creaking. I know from experience this can take hours. There's no way he's letting me sleep yet.

'What's wrong with showing gratitude, huh?' He thumbs through images on my phone, checking today's posts. 'When I think of all I've done for you – kept your secrets, lied for you, helped you build your business, looked after you and your parents, this house, our son – and for what? Not a whit of gratitude. And worst of all – no loyalty. It's the disloyalty that hurts the most. The fact that you'd rather spend time with Penny.'

He's always at his worst when I've hurt his feelings. It's like a child's tantrum.

'Conleth, no, I—' He lifts an index finger, it's barely a twitch – but it tells me that it's not my turn to speak.

'I mean, is it me? Have you fallen out of love with me,

119

hmm?' He sighs and – God, please no – sits up and swings his legs over the side of the bed.

'Or maybe you never loved me and I'm the fool. Maybe all I ever was to you was a fix-it man.' He walks towards me in just his boxers and T-shirt. Stops in front of me so my head is level with his crotch. 'Is that it? You had to stick with me because of what you did. Is that it, Gem*stone*?'

'Con, I'm sorry. I am grateful – you know I am.' Maybe I can still reach him. Make him understand. But he leans over to take hold of my hair and begins winding it once, twice, around his wrist. It's not hurting – yet. My legs start trembling.

'Gem*stone* is right. Dense as a stone and hard as hell. You're a hard wagon, Gemma. And you're incapable of loyalty.'

He jerks his hand, and my head knocks against the wooden door surround.

'I – it's not like that, Con. I swear.' I'm gabbling, desperate to end this, furious with myself and absolutely petrified he'll wake Ferdia. I didn't dose him up with anything tonight. Sometimes when – when Conleth's in really bad form, I give Ferdia that cough medicine that knocks him out, and I hate myself for drugging my child. But I'd hate it more if Ferd got dragged into this.

Two thin lines crease down the sides of Conleth's mouth, like a puppet's jaw. He's paranoid, I tell myself. It's an illness. He doesn't mean it – and I don't know if it's because I was with Penny, or because I told him about the interview, and what the guards had said about Max – about his – his body being tied up and weighted.

'I was just scared, that's all. I – I – it was just you hadn't told me about it, and when the guards said it—'

'How do you think the body stayed underwater till now?'

120

he says. 'By magic? I had to wrap a rope around my best friend's body and tie him to the spare anchor. It was bloody awful. I cleaned up your mess that night. I've dedicated my life to cleaning up your mess, Gemma. And what do I get?'

He stands facing me with his legs apart, arms folded, hands bunched into fists under his biceps. Like he's ready to enter a boxing ring. He tenses his abs, and four ridges of muscle appear. He's reflected in the mirror behind me, I realize, and he gives himself a nod of approval before walking closer.

'Might as well get what I paid for.'

And afterwards he shoves me aside. He gets into bed and switches off the light, while I shiver, still on my knees. The bed creaks. He hears me begin to move.

'Did I say you could get up?'

He laughs as though this is a game we play.

'Count to a hundred – no – three hundred. Then go to your bed.'

And that's what I do. Pathetic. I wait. And I actually count. I hear him punch the pillow a couple of times, then settle into silence. At the count of three hundred, I fold my feet underneath myself, grabbing the doorjamb, and struggle to stand. It's like I'm over eighty. I tiptoe to the wardrobe and take out my long puffa coat – it was a big hit last year. Then, as quietly as I can – exactly as if I was his dog, I stretch out at the foot of the bed. On the floor.

All night, I semi-doze, thinking of Max – the boy who loved the sea, who was more at home in water than on land. I wish he was alive, to play with Ferdie, to have a coffee and chat with me as grown-ups. And Conleth is not in that picture. I think of the rope and I see it around Max's narrow, boyish hips. And though I know I shouldn't, I wish the rope was wound around Conleth from his head to his feet. And I wish the anchor was dragging him down and down beneath the waves.

And maybe I do eventually sleep, because I have a dream about Max. I see us both together, sinking to the bottom of the sea to where Ferdie is waiting. Max and I hold hands, and Max closes his eyes. He holds a finger to his lips. *Sssh. Max-attacks the bottom of the sea. Max and Gem and little Ferdie.*

I jerk awake again. The floor is rock hard underneath this rug and I can't stand it any more. A strand of daylight hangs below the windowsill. Gingerly, so as not to wake Conleth, I sit up. Every part of me is aching. On my hands and knees, I shuffle over to the laundry basket and grab some clothes, then I inch my way out of the bedroom and into the hallway.

My heart is thumping. As I wait for the kettle to boil it feels like my blood is copying the boiling water and I can't tell if the sound is in my head or outside of me. Through the kitchen window it's a camouflage of navy, blue and green, but beyond the trees, past the dark trunks and the blackness of the iron railings, there's a sliver of icy blue – sky or sea.

I said I'd meet Penny at six thirty down on the beach. Just the two of us. I told her not to text to remind me, that I'd be there.

'We'll take it as it comes,' she'd said. 'Okay? We'll find out what it's like to be in the sea – even just standing. That's all.'

Unspoken objections raced through my brain. Panicked questions. What if I pass out? What if a huge wave comes and—

'Don't overthink it,' she'd said. 'Look, if you don't actually throw up, we'll count it a success, okay?'

She's so chilled. Maybe it goes with the territory. She used to work for the state, but she gave up the full-time job when she had the twins. Now she does private counselling and life-coaching. I wonder if it's the work that makes her so calm and accepting, or if you're drawn to that work because it's in your nature.

Maybe I – for the millionth time, I think about telling her. About him. About Max.

Except, if I did, what is she supposed to do with that information? It would put her in the position where she has to report it. I can't do that to her – and I can't escape. Conleth's made it perfectly clear what would happen if I try to leave.

'You're not going anywhere with our son,' he's told me. 'And if you leave without him, I wouldn't hesitate. It'd be a mercy killing.'

24

Gemma

I had no one to confide in. After Max was gone my parents were bereft – we couldn't be in the same room together. We drifted through the shuttered house, insubstantial as sea mist. I don't remember much of the early months, though I know it was a hot summer because I sweltered in jeans and Max's blue hoody. I refused to take it off. I slept in it, pulling the hood up and the sleeves down over my wrists so I could keep his scent near, so I couldn't see the veins beckoning. From outside, the shouts of children and gulls mingled as Dún Laoghaire batted her lashes and swished her skirts, living up to her Victorian seaside vibe. In summer, the town is a state of mind. A statement of intent. Bursts of music and laughter from the People's Park, honking car horns, happy screams. A multicoloured snake of humanity queuing for Teddy's ice-cream, curly-haired blond dogs prancing and pulling against their leads. Bright boats, white sails, stripes and surf. Laughter, motorbikes and noisy exhausts. Flowers and market stalls in People's Park. The scent of freshly brewed coffee overlaid with the cloying smell of burnt sugar. Vibrant Dún Laoghaire living it up while the Fitzgeralds withered and died.

And – and then. And then the searches stopped and the news bulletins died down, and everything went back to being the same. The air grew chill and every day was windier than the last. Families walked the pier in bundles of Trespass, North Face and Patagonia.

And there was no routine for the new season. No Max-led schedule of races and bags of kit and loading the boat up on the trailer to bring him off to lakes and bays and competitions to win more trophies. Nothing on the calendar. It all fell away. My parents were left with little old lying me. And Mum would look at me, and it was like her eyes had hands reaching out to my heart, like she wanted to reach inside me and find the soft part and – I don't know what she wanted. Maybe she thought we'd hug and cry and the pain would be shared and eased. But that couldn't happen. Because I'd destroyed our lives and I couldn't speak. I couldn't tell. And every day that passed coated another layer of lies on to me.

I began cutting the lies out slice by slice. The sharp sting as it bit into flesh was like someone arriving on the doorstep and ringing the bell. *Yoohoo? Only me, the black-handled knife. Oh, come in, come in.* And you push it in further, and the hairs on your neck stand up and the goosepimples rise – and then it comes – blood and relief, relief. Relief.

And when that stopped working, I began starving the lies into submission. And I shrank myself until I looked like a little girl again – the girl I had been. Max's little sister. And when you're hungry – really hungry – a kind of peace comes over you. It feels like when you're going to fall asleep. A drifting I-don't-care-if-I-die peace.

Back then, Conleth was everything to me. He stayed over, and he tried to make it normal with my parents. That's the thing about manners. When he was with them, social etiquette still ruled. It was as normal as Mum and Dad could manage. They spoke to him. They even tried to encourage him to get back sailing. Dad offered to sponsor him. They would have given him Max's boat. But he couldn't face it. The 49er was sold. Then *Corrig Cailín*.

And Conleth's eyes would seek mine, and he'd give a little nod with his face closed and his lips pressed together. I knew what it meant. We had a secret – a bad, bad secret. But it was ours and it bound us together, and I couldn't believe all he'd done for me. What he'd lost for me.

And I forgot about the time when we were kids and he found me in the treehouse and pushed me down on the chipboard floor full of splinters. And he knelt on top of me with his knees pressing the thin skin of my skinny inner arms down so I couldn't move, and I shouted for Max or Mum or anyone, and Conleth just grinned. His head blocked the light from the small window and I twisted and thrashed, trying to flip my lower body upwards, trying to kick him, or knee him, or find a way out. But all I could feel were the little splinters poking into my shoulders and the back of my head with every move I made.

How he'd scrunched his mouth together, sucking his cheeks in against his teeth, rolling his mouth round and around, gathering saliva. I yelled, and he clamped his hand over my mouth and I scrunched my eyes closed and held my breath, because I knew what he was going to do.

The spit, when it landed on my forehead, was warm and wet. It smelt of the cheesy crisps he'd been eating. 'Don't be a crybaby,' he'd laughed, jumping up and making his way through the hatch on to the little wooden ladder. 'I'm only messing.'

There was a cruelty in Conleth which I'd always known. Now, I knew I deserved it.

And then things changed between us. And when it became clear that the sea was not going to give up its dead and when all the searches had faded away, I began to fall apart in earnest. Conleth could always get weed – and I started there. And days went by and turned into weeks where I didn't get up until three or four, and only then, if my parents were out, to smoke. And I made a trail of circular burns, like stepping stones for an elf, to walk along my arms, my wrists, the back of my hand. And I shrank more and more. I hung around the town getting shitfaced. It was Dad who picked me up from the Garda station when I got caught shoplifting, and Mum who opened the door to find a squad car outside with me, drunk, in the back. By November of that year, when I'd had my stomach pumped and narrowly avoided liver failure, they'd had enough. They called a halt and I was sent to boarding school.

And I couldn't get drugs, or cigarettes, or knives there. But I could starve. And the irony – oh my God, the irony. Because the thinner I got, the higher my social status. The more I starved myself, the more popular I became. It's addictive. And things turned around, and even Conleth looked at me differently. Everyone did. And let's face it – that was what kickstarted my career. When you're a size six with blonde hair, people don't care about your tortured soul. Your rotten core. The rift in your heart caused by your own evil.

That detective – Laura – she has a way of looking at you and waiting, and you feel like – it's like trying to pick your way across the ice. She asks a question, maybe a seemingly innocent question, but you don't trust yourself to answer it in case it falls away and – whoosh! You've cracked through the solid surface and you're sinking and it can't be stopped. Up close, there are threads of greenish gold in the iris of her eyes, like an owl. They're clever eyes.

And I told her about the sailing. Or, in my case, the not sailing. I told her I was the first Fitzgerald in five generations who couldn't swim or sail.

And she waited with her head tilted, like she was listening

to a sound I couldn't hear. And for the first time ever – I mean, I always thought this was my fault, something I brought on myself by my own weakness – she gave it a name.

'It's a phobia,' she said. 'Sounds like it, anyway. And phobias – well, they don't get better on their own.'

And that's when they'd told me about Max's body being tied up and sunk with a weight. And Laura watched me absorb that information. She watched as the fact of Max's murder rose between us like a tidal wave and I began to fall apart in earnest.

In school, when I was little, the teacher read us a legend about this king who had massive donkey ears. Nobody knew about them. He hid them under his crown. So, every time he got a haircut, the king had the barber killed, because if the barber blabbed his secret, everyone would laugh and have no respect for him.

So, one day this new barber promised the king that he'd never tell. I think in the story his mother talked to the king, and pleaded and begged. The barber swore he'd never say a word to anyone, and so this time, the king let him off.

But the secret burned and burned inside the barber. He had to tell. It hurt him so much that he whispered it to a tree. He reckoned that it wasn't telling a person. He just told a tree.

And then it all fell apart, because someone made a harp out of the wood of the tree and the king invited the harpist to play at a banquet in the castle. But when the harp started to play, it sang, 'The king has donkey's ears.' I can't remember how it ended. All I remember is thinking he shouldn't have told the tree. That was stupid. The whole point of a secret is you don't tell anyone.

This is too big a secret.

I'm going to get into the cold, cold sea. I'm going to let it shove me and batter me and drag me across the sharp stones. I'm going to not care that my blood turns to ice and my lungs freeze to the point of collapse. Because I've got to tell. I'm going to scream it into the uncaring dark waves.

25

Gemma

My heart starts pounding the moment I step into the water, and I don't want to make a noise, but my mouth opens and I'm taking these little shallow breaths. Penny is striding ahead of me.

'Come on, come on! Delaying makes it worse. Come on. Pretend it's the pool. Just keep stepping forwards, we're going to stop just there.' She points to a spot a few metres further out, where the water is smooth and blue. I'm in up to my ankles, my shins, my knees. Penny sees my panic and steps closer, waving her hand for me to take it. She's nodding. I grip her chilled hand in mine.

'Well done! That's the worst bit – the bare skin!' I try to return her smile. She'd lent me a wetsuit – a shortie, she called it – and as I keep walking, feeling the water rise past my thighs, to my waist, I realize I'm chanting under my breath, *It's okay. It's okay.*

'There's a really sandy bit there,' grins Penny. 'See where I'm pointing? Come on!'

And I hold her hand, biting down the panic that's threatening to rise. I think of brave people, people who keep going when life should have shattered them into a thousand pieces. People like Penny, like that amazing couple who set up Laura-Lynn Children's Hospice – *Come on, Gemma. You can do this.*

And when the water is past my waist, Penny lets go of my hand and floats backwards in the water, kicking her feet to move lazily into the blue patch.

'You're doing it, Gemma,' she laughs. 'The worst is over. Muscle memory will take care of the rest.'

And I fix my eyes on hers and I'm so tired of being a lie and a fake. I'm so ashamed of myself for never having challenged myself. I've never done anything I'm proud of. And I take a breath and I bend my knees, scrunching my eyes closed too, and down I go. Down until I feel the water close over me and some trickles down the neck of the shortie, but it's okay, because I'm doing it.

'You're amazing,' says Penny ten minutes later, turning to grin over her shoulder at me. 'Full body immersion!' She takes the coffee from the young barista and passes it to me. 'Did you see her, Tom?'

She turns back to me. 'Be nice to him.' She smiles. 'He's a local – plus, he makes the best coffee. And we only have him for a few weeks in the summer before the competitions start. Are you not going out this morning, Tom? Don't you have a competition coming up? When are you and Alex off?'

The dark-haired young man grins under the barrage of questions, and his face, weatherbeaten like a surfer's or a sailor's, creases into a grin as he closes the till. Penny has that effect on everyone.

'Not till later on today, but yeah, at the moment we try to get out on the water early, at least four days a week. The first big race is in July,' he says. 'We'll be in Portugal.'

'What do you race?'

As I watch him, time rewinds and I think of my brother, and I know how he'll answer.

'49ers,' he grins. 'When my studies allow.'

'He's a baby lawyer,' laughed Penny, her voice lilting in a 'Fancy that!' tone.

Tom shakes his head, throwing two chocolates into a

paper bag, folding it closed and handing it to Penny. 'On the house.'

He turns back to me. 'Fair play.' He gestures towards the sea.

'Tha—thanks,' I say, through chattering teeth.

'Cheers!' grins Penny, steering me towards the bench and away from the tin coffee truck. 'Thanks, Tom. I'll get you next time.'

We sit on the bench sipping our coffees and I can almost believe in a good world. He won't check on me – not this early. For now, for this moment, I just enjoy sitting beside a friend in the early-morning sunshine. My stomach growls as the chocolate hits, and the sun dries the damp ends of my hair that have emerged from the swim cap.

'This is the life,' says Penny. She hesitates a beat before continuing. 'Sorry – I know you're sad, and I'm not belittling that. But what you did there was just brilliant. Open water, Gem! You've cracked it!'

She blows on her coffee to cool it, nodding towards the expanse of sea spread like a shawl in front of us.

'I'm not going to lie. I wasn't sure you'd be up for it – especially with that part where there's a shelf. But you smashed it, Gemma.'

And I feel a flare inside, the tiniest little spark of some-thing so small, you couldn't even call it happiness, or pride or anything. But I know what it's not. It's not despair and it's not shame. It's not crippling guilt and it's not self-loathing.

I'd stood on the cold, shifting stones and I was shaking from my frozen toes to my hunched shoulders. But I walked out into the water, even beyond the shelf of sand and shale to where Penny stood up to her chest, her arms outstretched. She twiddled her fingers. 'Come on! You can do it!'

I fixed my gaze on her face and I stepped, then another

step, then another. Shivers chased along my spine and I could feel my heart high up in my throat.

A sailor went to sea, sea, sea.

And I made it out to her, and she grabbed my hands and we bounced like girls in a playground. And for the briefest of moments, I didn't hate myself.

'Right.' Penny takes my empty cup and inserts it in hers. 'It's almost ten past seven. The kids will be running rings around Malachy already, so I'd better get back home. See you at the gate?'

I tighten the drawstring of my hood against the breeze, although it's already shaping up to be a bright May morning. Penny grabs my shoulder and squeezes.

'That was amazing! You should be so proud of yourself, Gem. Same time tomorrow? We'll have you swimming the harbour by the end of the week.'

And it's as though she takes the sunlight with her. I turn in the opposite direction, cross the road and let myself in the side door. There's no sun in the passage and I'm shivering when I get into the kitchen. Conleth and Ferdia are having breakfast. Ferdia is kneeling up on the chair so he can reach, instead of using the booster seat I got him. Conleth insists on him sitting at the table and goes mad if he comes home and finds evidence of us eating on the sofa in front of the TV. I see he's parked the broken digger on the seat beside him. My shoulders constrict immediately.

'Oh, hi, you two.' I aim for Penny's tone. Fake it.

'Mummy!' squeals Ferdia, dropping his spoon into the cereal bowl with a clatter and reaching up for me to lift him.

'He was looking for you,' says Conleth, his tone disappointed. 'Ah-ah!' he snaps at Ferdia, the way you'd speak to a dog. 'Finish your breakfast.'

Ferdia sits back and picks up his spoon. I move to stand

behind him, giving his shoulders a little squeeze and kissing the top of his head.

'Good boy,' I whisper in his ear.

'Where were you?' Conleth studies me, and I know he's taking in the baggy tracksuit and lack of make-up. I shake my head.

'I just went for a walk. I couldn't sleep.'

He frowns.

'You didn't take your phone. What if I wanted to reach you?'

'Sorry, I – I forgot,' I say, not wanting to admit the fear. To say it out loud means it exists.

'I see,' he says, disbelieving. 'Who were you with?'

I hesitate – and it's the hesitation that does it.

'Don't tell me – let me guess, you were with her – your best friend.' *Best friend* sounds derisory, the way he says it.

'We just went for a walk.'

His smile is incredulous. His eyes rove over my face and I have to tell myself I did nothing wrong.

'And you didn't think to ask me? Dumped me – your husband – for your friend.'

He slaps the table in front of Ferdia, and he jumps. 'What do you make of that, Ferd? Your mother ditched the two of us. She could've invited us for a walk on the beach, but no – she had a better offer.'

Ferdia blinks rapidly, unsure of the response required. He looks at me guiltily. My eyes drift to the bowl in front of him.

Conleth spots the movement. He swipes the bowl and pours the remains of milk and cereal down the sink.

'I'm very disappointed in you both,' he says, frowning at Ferdia, whose eyes immediately fill with tears. 'And no snacks for Mummy either, because she's been naughty too.'

He grins, and I know he wants me to respond.

I say nothing. Instead, I see him floating face down in a wide, wide ocean. His lungs filling, filling.

Suddenly, he tires of the exchange. He gulps a mouthful of coffee.

'You should maybe do a meditation today.'

There's a pause in which he's considering what I could sell. 'Talk to them about self-care,' he's thinking aloud. 'Yes. How about the Libertine yoga gear and the meditation candles?'

There's a lurch of something inside me – nothing big. Nothing scary. The explosive equivalent of a bubble bursting in a glass of Coke. Nothing bigger than that. But still.

'Maybe I shouldn't post today,' I say, and my chin is trembling like a living creature. 'You know, se—sell stuff?'

I never do this. The silence yawns.

'I was actually thinking of your welfare,' he says. 'Not the brand. You're the one who mentioned selling.'

He stands and puts his mug on top of the dishwasher, then he walks over to Ferdia's chair. He points at the digger, fastened together with bits of ribbon.

'Throw that away,' he says. 'It's just a broken lump of plastic.' Ferdia grabs the digger, clutching it to his chest.

26

Laura

I'm glad to see Niamh looking a bit more rested. We agreed we'd both take Sunday off, and maybe she got a good break, because her colour is better. She declines a pre-interview coffee though, which is not like her, and it's just after nine thirty-five when we walk into the office of MaxSpirit. Conleth is winding up a phone call. Or maybe he winds it up because he sees us coming in. He strikes me as a man who wants to do the right thing. Then again, he hasn't exactly covered himself in glory, making us come down here for the interview. Senan says he left messages for him on Saturday but there was no response.

The office is a sort of combination of sunroom and changing area at the back of Corrig Point Yacht Club. It consists of a reception desk and a small waiting area clustered around a central table on which various sailing magazines and brochures sit in neat, shiny piles. Behind the desk, an enormous photograph dominates the space. It shows a 49er, and its two-man crew, presumably Max and Conleth, in full sail – the boat cresting the waves in bright sunshine, carving a path through turquoise water laced with white frills. Both boys are angled half out of the boat at forty-five degrees, Conleth seeming to float in mid-air, Max leaning back, holding what must be the tiller. In the distance, specks of white signify similar craft and, beyond them, a line of golden sand in the distance. The other walls of the cabin have smaller photographs, all showing groups of children out on the water in dinghies and various small boats, red-cheeked and grinning, the picture of happiness.

Conleth waits for us to scan the room, a smile hovering at the edges of his mouth.

'Ladies?' he says eventually. 'Apologies that you had to come here. I would have come to you.'

Niamh and I lock eyes for a second. *Ladies.*

'Not a problem,' I say, though I thought Senan had tried calling him. 'We can talk here.'

Niamh moves closer to the wall.

'Is that the two of ye?' Niamh says, pointing to the photo. 'Back in the day.'

He sighs.

'It is. Certainly. That's us.' His voice is heavy with regret. 'That was in 2006 – San Francisco. We won everything.'

'Fair play,' says Niamh.

'So,' he says, 'what can I do for you? Would you like tea or coffee? I'm afraid Sally's not in today.' He waves vaguely in the direction of a glass-doored office, presumably Sally's. A huge cut-glass vase of roses in shades of red, pink and peach tower over her desk, casting a shadow across glossy leather-bound folders and a crystal paperweight.

'She's off at a media course, but I can certainly rustle up a cup of tea – or we could go into the club or—'

He pauses as though embarrassed at his garrulousness, and it's hard not to take to him. He's trying. I sit and take out my notebook.

'Sally?' Niamh waits, pen at the ready.

'My PA.'

'Thank you. And does Sally have a surname?'

'Oh, yes. Sorry. It's Gibson. She does four days a week.'

'We don't need anything, thanks. We were just hoping

you'd have time to answer a few questions,' I say. 'If you're not busy.'

'Of course. I'll help in any way I can.'

He comes out from behind the desk and moves to sit opposite. 'Is this a formal interview?'

'This is just you helping us with our enquiries,' says Niamh. 'If you're happy to do so.'

'Absolutely, I'm – of course.'

Earlier we'd agreed that Niamh would lead on this one. So I take notes and listen.

'Well, the first thing is, we wanted to get a bit of information about that night – the night Max disappeared. And we noticed that there seems to be no statement from you. Did you make a statement?'

He thinks, brow furrowed.

'Would it be something I'd know for certain? I mean, apologies – that sounds idiotic. What I mean to say is that I spoke to various gardaí at the time – every two minutes someone was asking us questions – but if you're asking did I make a formal statement, then—'

'You'd know,' Niamh interrupts, 'because you'd sign it. It's a signed document.'

He looks perplexed.

'Then no is the answer. I – well – I think the reason might be that in those early days after he went missing, I went out searching for him every single day. Loads of us did. So, I might have been, you know, hard to catch? Or rather, pin down.'

'Tell me a bit about the searches,' says Niamh, and I breathe a sigh of relief. We're taught to elicit as much information as possible by our questions. It's exactly what I teach in the garda college: Tell, Explain, Describe. If you can engage your witness, so that he or she is actively involved in thinking about the accident or the event, it's worth a thousand direct questions which have one-word answers. You don't ask what colour the assailant's shirt was. You ask them to describe what he was wearing. You don't let them compose a story – because stories are unreliable. Especially ones with a beginning, middle, end. Stories are fiction. You leap in, looking for details – in the cracks. In the parts where it makes no sense.

'Oh God,' he says, and his face compresses into itself. 'From the moment we heard he was missing we didn't let up. I think I was the first one out. We checked everywhere. Half the sailors in Dún Laoghaire – from everywhere – we went out every day for weeks, it seemed. The RNLI searched too – the inshore and offshore boats, the garda sub-aqua unit, as it was then – they did searches in the harbour, but there was nothing.' He sighs.

'In the 49er?' Niamh nods in the direction of the photo.

'No – no – God, no. You couldn't search in a 49er. Far too small. No, I went in the Fitzgerald boat, sometimes alone, sometimes with John. His boat was more suitable. But lots of the club members were out. I mean, everyone wanted to help. Everyone was devastated at the thought of, you know—'

Niamh waits. She does the nodding and a quiet 'uh-hum?'

When he says nothing, she inserts, 'You know?'

'Well, the suicide, I suppose I mean. We were all devastated to think that he might want to—'

We wait in silence.

'Kill himself.'

'Do you think that's what he did?' Niamh's voice is kind, understanding.

'I do, actually,' he says. 'Although I heard that you're now treating his death as suspicious?'

139

Niamh makes no reply, and silence stretches. He picks up a gold pen from where it lay in the fold of his desk diary, spinning it over end to end between his fingers. The burnished metal has been engraved in diamond-shaped facets. They glint in the light. A narrow strip of plain gold bears a name in cursive script.

'Max's favourite pen,' he says sadly, replacing it on the desk. 'I mean, look, it seems to me that—' He turns his palms upwards. 'Nothing else makes sense.'

'You two were close? Best friends?' Niamh sits forward. His eyes flick quickly to hers, then back to his hands.

'Yes. Yes, we were.'

'And ye were all set for the Olympics, is that right? Can you tell me a bit about that?'

He studies his hands, turning them over slowly one at a time, like he's examining them. The action seems slightly staged, rehearsed almost.

'Well, yes, we were on track to compete in 2008, in Beijing.' He looks up.

'Go on,' says Niamh.

He places both hands on his knees and his shoulders hunch forward.

'Look,' he says. 'I – I suppose I should have said this at the time, but when Max went missing, well, it seemed unnecessary, you know?'

'What was unnecessary?'

He compresses his lips and the movement causes a rigid line of muscle to twitch in his jaw.

'We had just run into difficulties, you see. There's all sorts of testing and formalities that have to be gone through long before the Olympics, you know? You have to provide clean samples long before the competition itself. And, well, something had come up which meant that the Olympic Committee were about to withdraw their offer. We were ruled out, before we even got started. Max was devastated, of course, and he—'

He lifts his hands on to his fingertips, then replaces them.

'But that information wasn't – that wasn't widely known at the time,' he says. 'And I didn't want, well, to be honest, I didn't want people to know. Especially if Max had, you know, harmed himself. I wanted to preserve his reputation. For him, for his parents – for the whole family.'

He leans back in the chair, folding his arms across his chest.

'It seemed the least I could do for him. He – well, I'm sure Gemma has told you. He was the golden boy.'

'I'm not sure I see,' Niamh says. 'Why was the Olympic Committee going to withdraw your offer – what happened there?'

His face closes down.

'Not my offer,' he says. 'It – it's just that they weren't going to offer anything to Max.'

He turns to look at me and I pause in what I'm writing.

'I suppose it will all have to come out now, anyway.' He sighs. 'And at least his mother never knew. That's got to be a blessing.'

He directs his words at me now, watching as I write.

'Max hadn't been able to provide a clean sample – you know, a sample that was clear of any banned substances.'

'What kind of banned substances?' Niamh looks up sharply. 'I thought that was, like, swimmers and cyclists. I didn't know it applied to, eh, athletes like yourselves.'

He winces, as if the memory causes pain.

'Look, it gives me no pleasure to, you know, speak ill of – Max was my best friend. But in answer to your question, banned substances refers to all drugs – medications and stuff. Including, ah, recreational drugs.'

Niamh waits.

'And Max never sent in a sample at all. He knew he couldn't, because he'd been taking – I mean, just recreationally and, look, he was young.' A sigh. 'And it was all going to come out. Failure to provide a sample is as bad – almost as bad – as a tainted sample. So it would have come out about his cocaine use and I suppose for Max, for his family, maybe it was, maybe he found the prospect unbearable. And, you see, it didn't just affect him.'

He gestures to the photograph.

'We'd sailed together for years, since we were schoolboys. You – you probably don't realize, but the relationship between helm and crew, it's like a marriage. You know one another's thoughts, you anticipate one another's every move, you literally breathe in tandem. And it can't be replicated with someone else. So' – he's shaking his head, looking at the picture – 'when Max shattered his Olympic dream, he believed he'd shattered mine too.'

'And did he?'

'I suppose, yes – for the 49ers. Or for the 2008 Olympics, at any rate. But I like to think our friendship could have withstood that test.'

He picks a piece of lint off his chinos. He nods, looking from Niamh and back to me. 'But we'll never know. And, as it was, that dream ended anyway. But if you're asking me if he could have killed himself, then, definitely. Max was nothing if not impetuous. I see it in his sister too. I believe he killed himself.'

This comment hangs in the silence.

'I see,' says Niamh. 'You know we found a rope around his body, which we believe had been weighted with something?'

'Yes,' he says, continuing the nod. 'I heard. Gemma told me. Is that why you're treating it as suspicious?'

Niamh says nothing and I know she's thinking, *No, it'll be the bit of metal embedded in his chest that makes it suspicious.* That and the fact that he was found several miles from the harbour.

'It does seem strange,' she says. 'A strange decision for a sailor. I mean, if he wanted to kill himself, why wouldn't he go out in the boat or just swim out to sea until he died of exposure? Why tie a – block or something around himself and step into the harbour?'

'People fill their pockets with stones,' muses Conleth. 'So they sink.'

'Yes,' Niamh says, 'and people tie weights around bodies so they're never found.'

He says nothing, and I let Niamh's comment sit. We have a rhythm: some days we're absolutely in sync and some days we're not. But today it's working.

'Let's go back. What can you tell me about that night, the night Max disappeared? What were your movements?'

He inhales noisily, his lips pressed together. Something about the line of his jaw, the glint of stubble where he must have missed a bit when shaving, I feel a sort of lurch of fear. Triggered. That's what they call it. The smallest thing can take me back to that night and to the panicked feeling of a bigger, heavier, stronger and crueller human being pinning you in place, taking what he wants. My gut is telling me something. Niamh steps in.

'Were you at the party?' she says.

'Yes,' he says. 'Of course I was at the party. We were close friends. Best friends.'

'And when was the last time you saw him?'

He looks up towards the ceiling, shaking his head.

'I really can't remember. You know how difficult it is, I'm sure – after all this time and, well – we were just kids, you know? There was drink involved – the champagne was flowing.'

'You must have been asked that afterwards, surely?' I butt in. 'I mean, presumably his parents – everyone – must have been asking each other what happened and who'd seen him last?'

'Of course! Absolutely! But I couldn't help them. I remember the speeches and the dancing. And then poor Gemma – I mean, she was absolutely hammered, and I didn't want her to get in trouble with her folks, so I walked her home.'

He tilts his head, concern playing across the lines of his brow. 'She was very upset. I escorted her home.'

I see Niamh write something, and I know we're both thinking of Gemma's original statement, in which there's no mention of Conleth.

'And then what? What time was this?'

'Not late – ten thirty or so? I saw her into the house, she said she was okay, and I – well, I left at that point.'

'Okay,' I say. 'You escorted your friend's little sister home and saw her into the house and she went to bed?'

'That's it, yes.'

'So you didn't see her into her bedroom?' I say, mildly. 'I suppose – well, no, help me out here. How come you didn't, you know, bring her inside and make her drink a glass of water or something? I mean, how drunk was she?'

He doesn't like this. It doesn't suit the gallant role he's given himself.

'Look, I can't remember,' he says. 'She probably told me to go – she was, she's very independent – spirited. She probably told me to piss off. And so I did.'

Spirited and independent, I think. Two words less likely to be applied to Gemma Fitzgerald you couldn't find. She's as insubstantial as air. A beautiful wisp of something. I find it hard to believe she's made of flesh and blood. That she gave birth to Ferdia.

144

'And then what? Where did you go after that?' Niamh is pressing on.

'Back to the yacht club,' he says, shaking his head regretfully. 'Where I proceeded to, you know, drink more than was good for me and' – a shrug and a self-deprecating grin – 'you know, party hard.'

'And what time would this have been?' Niamh flicks back through the notes.

'Well, I can't say exactly. I mean, you know? But it was after I saw Gemma home, so – I don't know, fifteen minutes later? About ten forty-five, eleven?'

'And were you seen when you went back? Is there anyone to corroborate this version?'

He looks affronted.

'Well, yes! Of course I was seen and, if you must know, I'm not proud of myself, because I – well, I actually don't remember this with a great deal of clarity, but in my defence, I was young. And it was a party. But there would be people who would remember – ah – might remember. Because I may have – ah – behaved, em, inappropriately.'

Niamh sets down her pen and leans back in the chair, as if readying herself to watch a show.

'Go on.' She smiles. 'You behaved inappropriately how?'

27

Gemma

Penny's house is like something from a children's storybook. Thick white walls, sash windows, a riot of spring flowers leaning in to nuzzle your legs as you walk up the narrow path to the yellow front door. I ring the bell before I can change my mind. There's a long wait, and then the door opens.

'Gem! What – come in.'

She closes the door and ushers me ahead of her.

'Go through to the kitchen. I was just making soup for—'

I stand at her kitchen counter, rubbing the surface of the wood, feeling its warmth.

'What is it?' she says, reading my face. 'Has something happened?'

I go to speak, and my mouth opens, but nothing comes out. Penny comes towards me, she pulls out the nearest chair and kind of presses me into it.

'Sit,' she says, grabbing a mug and filling it with coffee from the cafetière which was out on the table. 'Still warm.'

From where I sit, I can see a wall of photographs. Two girls – Penny and Helen, it must be, because Penny hasn't really changed. They're in matching dungarees and at the gap-toothed stage, on bikes, on a beach, with an adult group at a restaurant. There's a wedding photo, with Penny and Helen as bridesmaids. And that's it. My eyes flit from one to the next and back again, looking for clues, for signs of what is to come. Is destiny visible? Is there any way the photos predict tragedy? There's a photo of them squashed in a booth where their faces are pressed against each other's and they're wearing crazy hats, and I look to see if I can see Helen's despair. Or Penny's concern. And I hate myself.

'She – she looks so lovely,' I say, and the tears I've been holding in for hours and days and weeks and months and years – a lifetime's worth of tears start to flow down my cheeks.

'She was,' says Penny, pulling her chair to face me and sitting so close our knees are touching. 'She really was.'

'And I – I want – I need to tell you – I'm just so, so sorry.' I'm babbling. 'I'm so sorry about it. I never knew.'

'Of course,' she soothes. 'I know – sure, you of all people, I know you understand.'

'But that's not it! That's not it! I do understand, but I – oh my God! I don't know if I can do this. How do you – I mean, how do you keep going? How—' I break off, waiting like a child as she peels off squares of kitchen roll and passes them to me.

'The guilt is the worst thing of all,' she says without looking at me. 'That's the hardest thing to cope with. You ask yourself if you could have done anything differently. If you'd taken that phone call, replied to that message, not gone out that day' – she passes me another square – 'you wonder if it was this comment or that, if she'd misunderstood something or overheard something, if you pushed her away. If you – if I somehow betrayed her by moving away.'

She folds a square over and over, until it won't fold any further. She looks directly at me.

'The guilt is normal, Gemma. Unfortunately, the human brain seems, I don't know' – she shakes her head – 'kind of primed for guilt. Regret and guilt – they corrode your brain in the months afterwards. And if you don't find a way to live with it, they'll destroy you too.'

147

'How do you live with it?' My voice is barely a whisper.

'How does anyone live with loss?' she says. 'You just keep living. There's no alternative, is there? I try to think of it like she was caught in a storm, like an electrical storm in her brain, inside her mind, where we couldn't reach her. Helen couldn't fight it. And my parents, the rest of us, we couldn't fight it either. There's nothing we could have said or done once she was in the eye of that storm. Nothing. And for Helen, the only way she could escape was—' She gives a small shrug, and I'm distracted by the necklace she wears, which I see now is composed of three little gold shapes – a P, an H and a heart shape dislodging from the nook of her collarbone and tumbling on to her chest, where it glints in the light. 'She escaped by ending her life.'

A smile cracks her face, and it's as though she's summoned a memory – something warm – from deep within.

'She was incredibly stubborn. Really. I try to take comfort from that. She knew we loved her – we adored her, all of us. And she knew it. But she – to her, this was a rational decision. She was still determined to end her life. She succeeded.'

The smile fades and she reaches to take hold of my hand.

'You can't blame yourself any longer, Gem. You can't live like that. Not when you've lived so long with the torment of not knowing. Enough.'

A burst of birdsong pierces the silence and it sounds like it's spilling its soul. And I want to spill out my soul in a garden of flowers like the blackbird. But my secrets are dark and I am poisoned by them. There's no garden of flowers – there's that – the flower that lures in living creatures – the flytrap. Venus flytrap.

I want to tell her what I did – how I killed my poor big brother who held my hand when I was scared, who tried so hard to teach me not to fear the water, who made time for me when he was at college.

I take my hand from hers. I'm not worthy of her comfort.

'I'm so sorry,' I whisper. And I shake my head and the trap closes around the words. Because I can't tell Penny and I can't tell Laura or Niamh or I'll be sent away, and I won't see Ferdia and I can't bear it.

Penny reaches for my hand again, but I hold it back against myself. I think I will die of shame if she touches me with kindness.

'I'm so sorry about Helen,' I sob.

'Ssh,' she's saying, and she hugs me. 'It's going to be okay.'

But it's never going to be okay. If I can't tell Penny and I can't tell the guards and I can't protect Ferdia, I may as well be dead. And I wonder if we would get to see Max. If I – if I brought Ferdia with me and we'd be together always at the bottom of *the deep blue sea, sea, sea.*

28

Gemma

'Are you sure you're okay?' says Albertina, the nurse from Portugal. Albertina. When Dad moved here five years ago, hers was the first name he learned.

'Thanks, Albertina. I'll – I'll be fine. I won't stay long – I've to collect Ferdia.'

She notices my tear-stained face but says nothing.

'Okay, but if you want to come inside, sit in the chapel or anything?'

I shake my head, not trusting myself to speak. It's the kindness that does it. Albertina presses my shoulder – a little squeeze like you'd squeeze a lemon. I pat her hand on my shoulder. She does a sort of goodbye squeeze and walks away.

I don't know why I'm here. But I need to be – I need to be in his presence. Especially now, if time is running out. A lurch of terror grabs me in the throat. I'll be taken away – locked in a cell. I won't be able to come here to visit. And Ferdia – no Ferdia. I can't bear it.

'Gemma?' Albertina's voice startles me. She's at the doorway, miming a cup of tea gesture. I shake my head.

'No, thanks, I'm fine.'

And I talk to Dad, though he says nothing. And it's strange, because even though I know it's a pack of lies, the comfort of being able to tell Dad these things, it sort of filters them.

Yes, they're lies, but they're better than all the other lies. These are lies we want to believe. And who's to say? Who gets to be in charge of the truths or lies you believe? Believe what you want. What you need.

If I could have spoken like this to Mum – oh my God, it fills me with such longing to think of that. Mum died in the cold light of truth. No. Mum died in the middle of the bleakest lie. The one where she thought her son had chosen to leave us – to kill himself. She lived long enough to torment herself with all the things she wished she'd said and done. Death by a thousand cuts of despair.

I'm sorry, Mum. I am so, so sorry.

'Do you remember when Max and Conleth won silver in Lanzarote?' I say, because I know that's a story the boys loved to tell. Though, at nineteen, they were hardly boys any more. 'They sprinted out of the start line – it looked like they were going to win. Do you remember?'

And I talk about the swell – the massive swell and the 'fluky' breeze. That's what Max had christened it. And the Austrian team powered ahead, laughing, but Conleth and Max kept going, trying to climb waves taller than skyscrapers, struggling to control their craft as it plunged downwards. They never caught up – but they beat everyone else.

And that night, later, when Mum, Dad and Max toasted the silver medal in the bar, Conleth came to find me. I don't tell Dad this part.

He found me sitting on an upturned surfboard abandoned near the shoreline. He said I shouldn't be hiding. He said he couldn't wait any longer – that I was driving him crazy. He said it was my fault for leading him on. And I believed it. Back then, I could believe it. I was fourteen. We walked away from the lights, the noise, to the dark part of the beach. Behind us, the party continued on the patio, with everyone singing and dancing, bass thumping. He tilted one of the giant beach umbrellas back until it toppled on to the sand,

and he pulled me into it so we were hidden. He kissed me, his hand squashing my face like he was squeezing a sponge, and his fingers pressed my cheeks against the side of my nose so I couldn't breathe, but I said nothing. I thought it was my naivety. I thought that's how grown-ups kissed.

He'd kissed me before, of course – it began the year I went to secondary school. A kiss of greeting that was just a shade too close to my mouth. Or his hand moved further down my back in the hug, pressing me against him. But I couldn't say anything about it. A strange distance had come between us – he wasn't like a brother any more. The thumps and shoves, the casual assaults of childhood where there were no helicopter parents, no witnesses – they all faded away as I changed. Nola was ahead of me in bras and periods. It was Nola who told me what bra to get and what brand of tampons hurt least.

And it was Nola who, on seeing the love bite on my neck, told me I should tell Mum. 'What the hell, Gemma? He's too old. That's just weird. Tell your mum.'

And I fell out with Nola then. I accused her of being jealous.

'Jesus! How childish can you be?' she'd spluttered. 'He's way too old for you. He's using you, for Christ's sake.'

And all I heard was her jealousy – because I'd done things she hadn't. I was on my way to becoming a woman, I thought. And no way would I tell Mum, because she'd put a stop to it. And anyway, I felt like finally I could join the little gang. It wouldn't be just Max and Conleth, now it'd be me and Conleth. And I felt a strange power over my brother, like I could be more to Conleth than him. Maybe. Eventually.

And always, Conleth found time to be with me. He practically lived at our house anyway, even before his parents died. Conleth's dad was a wizard with engines, and back then, he'd often visit, sharing a late-night whiskey with my dad, discussing boats and horsepower and having boring technical conversations to do with the engine on the yacht. So Conleth was already one of the family and, as Max's crew, he was bathed in the same golden light anyway.

And no one thought anything when Conleth came to find me in the den, saying he'd play a game of pool with me. Or he'd meet me on my way home from school and we'd use the lane behind the boat yard, or the rocks on the far side of the pier – anywhere we weren't seen.

Before we left for Lanzarote, Conleth whispered, 'I want you,' in my ear, and I felt a flood of heat sweep my body, like a wave rolling down, down from my brain that heard the words, to my crotch, which understood them. And every time I recalled those words, the wave swept through me.

I was fourteen – I thought I understood what was happening. I thought it was simple. That one day you lived in the land of Barbies and sleepovers, and then you got a boyfriend and moved into the world of parties and kisses and drink. I thought I was so cool. And so I led him on. That's what he said. And I imagined him like a cartoon bull and the ring through his nose. All I had to do was tug on it. Because, back then, I still had the power. Or I thought I did.

I was wearing the dress with the cut-outs – it was raspberry-coloured with black zebra stripes and these two big cut-out circles at the waist. And it was a Lanzarote warm night, but with that breeze that disguised sound. The breeze that made the sailing so great. And so, when he grasped my face and kissed me and his tongue stabbed mine like an angry creature, I tried to relax my jaw, to breathe evenly, though a part of me was frightened. I'd expected butterfly kisses alighting on my face, skimming my collarbones and the top of my breasts.

And I'd pushed him off – very gently, because even then I knew how angry Conleth could get, and how quickly.

'Don't you dare,' he said. 'You're not getting away that easy.' And the lights from the party in the distance glowed in his pupils and he pushed me down on to the sand and his hands roved over me like minesweepers. Into the cut-outs of the dress and under my bra, squeezing and scrabbling over my skin, and I tried not to push him away, but he was scaring me.

'Oh, for Christ's sake,' he said. And he flipped me over, shoving me on to my face in the sand, and it was as though his rage was a living thing and I was being punished for something I didn't know I'd done. Beach stones pressed into my hip bones and I couldn't understand that people did this and called it beautiful. And I felt broken and dirty and sullied.

'You'll get better at it,' he said afterwards.

And soon I learned how to please him – and I didn't dare displease him. If I stepped out of line, if I was needy or whiny. If I looked for more – more affection, more time, just more – he shut down. Or he said cruel things. One time, in the treehouse, he pulled away from me in disgust, telling me he couldn't go through with it because I stank. I gargled with saltwater and mouthwash for weeks. Another time he studied me in the daylight and told me I had acne. From that day I never went out without make-up.

He didn't contact me for weeks, but when he showed up I dropped everything to be his personal groupie for over two years. Nola and I drifted apart. I don't even know where she lives now. I heard she became a solicitor. I gave up the drama club and my after-school art classes. I ate nothing. I didn't study. I made no plans for the future. I existed only for him. There was no Gemma without him. And somehow, my brother became my love rival.

*

And maybe Dad does remember about the medal, but he says nothing. And I don't tell him about Conleth. No one ever knew our secret. As far as Mum and Dad were concerned, Conleth and I only got together after Max disappeared. Anything was forgivable by then. No one cared about the five-year age gap – you're not going to care about something like that when your son has gone missing. If anything, maybe they thought we comforted each other.

The irony.

Dad is completely silent.

'They should've beaten the Austrians,' I say.

He nods – barely perceptible. But I see it.

Tuesday

29

Niamb

'God love her.' I nod towards the tribe of journalists and onlookers milling on to the road. 'At the school pick-up, for pity's sake! Should we clear them?'

We're parked in an unmarked car on the residential square nearest to the Gaelscoil. We'd been on our way to collect Gemma for interview when we got stuck in this mayhem. Parents and childminders are spread out along the footpath nearest to the entrance, standing in clusters like granola, eyeing up the media. It's like a bloody cocktail party. Gemma is standing a little way apart, dappled light from the trees gleaming on her blonde hair. She's beside a short woman with wavy dark hair who has one hand protectively on Gemma's forearm and the other raised in a kind of 'stop' gesture towards a small group of reporters.

'Hmm, let's wait a minute. The friend – that must be Penny, do you think? Looks like she has it under control.'

'Yeah, fair play to her,' I answer, watching as Penny shoos the reporters away with both hands like they're a clutch of hens.

As I speak, a ripple of action surges through the waiting crowd in response to the opening of the main school door. Chatting pairs separate and a navy-tracksuited river of three-foot-high children trickles across the yard and up to the tall gate. Teachers stand guard, ensuring the correct pairing of child and minder.

We watch as the kids find their adults. Two sturdy boys with dark blond curls barrel through the others and stake their claim on Penny, who begins admonishing them immediately for the trail of destruction in their wake – a little boy who tripped and another who wanted to join them but wasn't fast enough.

Ferdia comes out last, struggling with a lopsided school-bag and the digger toy clutched awkwardly under one arm. It seems to be held together with ragged bits of ribbon. He has a turned-in walk and a way of peering upwards through the glasses as though they're not strong enough.

'Ah, God love the little maneen.' I smile. 'Jaysus, that's a tragic sight.'

When he spots his mother, his pace quickens and then he breaks into a trot. The strap of the giant schoolbag dangles around one knee.

'Christ! Is he wearing the schoolbag?'

Gemma bursts into action and runs to him, catching him just before he falls. She lifts him up, burying her face in his neck and holding him close.

'There's your answer,' says Laura. 'Needs her fix.'

'No kidding,' I say, holding her gaze.

The crowd melts apart quickly and the river is dispersed. Gemma turns back towards Penny, but someone has come between them. I glance at Laura.

'Where did he appear from?'

Conleth looks like a giant beside Penny, who couldn't be more than five foot tall. His back is towards Gemma.

By unspoken agreement, Laura and I get out of the car and cross over towards them. Gemma is almost as pale as the hoody she's wearing. Ferdia is clinging to her leg, looking up at her, begging to be lifted.

I catch the tail end of the exchange between Conleth and Penny, neither of whom has noticed our arrival.

'So, you'll give her some space?' He's smiling, but something about it sounds like an instruction. Immediately, my radar is pinging. Strange that he's asking her friend to give her space, not the gang of reporters who are, even now, scrambling to get photos of her. Penny bends to referee between her boys, who are literally chasing around her as though she was a tree. Her face is flushed – even the tip of her ear, which I can see emerging from the curls, is bright red. Anger? Embarrassment?

She straightens.

'Come on, boys, we'll see Ferdia another day,' she says, turning to leave. 'Bye, Gem.' She smiles at her friend. 'Here for whatever you need.'

We've obviously just missed something important, but when he turns towards us, Conleth's expression is pleasant. Jaysus. If he was an ice-cream he'd lick himself.

'Ladies.' He smiles. 'Good timing.' He turns to Gemma. 'You head on with the officers, I'll bring Ferdia home.'

'Can I come, Mummy?' whines Ferdia, clinging on to her so tightly his kneecaps whiten. His right hand is buried in a bunch of Gemma's long hair and, from the left, his knackered digger toy dangles.

'No, love,' Gemma soothes, motioning to lift him down. 'I'll be back in a little while. You go on home with Daddy.'

The child makes no move to get down. Conleth swoops in and plucks him off Gemma's hip, holding him high in the air.

'Come on, Ferdia! Be brave now. We'll see Mummy in—'

'Nooo!' screams Ferdia as the digger tumbles on to the pavement and a wheel falls off.

Conleth sets the child down on the path and takes a firm hold of his hand.

'I'll take it from here,' he says. 'Call me if you need a lift home.'

30

Niamh

I reckon Laura knows – or suspects. She's kind of watching me. But now is not the time. We have about an hour to get this done with Gemma and she's already looking antsy. I busy myself getting the video tape set up while Laura chats to her, trying to put her at ease.

'Would you like a coffee or anything?' she says, unpacking her briefcase and putting out her notebook and pens. 'They have an actual coffee machine here, I believe. Don't they?'

This is addressed to me.

'Sure they'd have to, in fairness,' I quip. 'We're practically in Dalkey.'

This lands flat. Not a smile. Nothing.

'No, thanks,' Gemma whispers. 'Just, em, water would be great. I forgot—'

I get her a bottle of water and a paper cup and the second interview gets underway. And it's like pulling teeth – with nothing new being added. Just the version of Max's last night, as she had outlined before.

Laura ramps it up a notch.

'What was it like for you, growing up with such an accomplished older sibling?' she says, her head tilted in that way she has which signifies how closely she's listening. Gemma gives a whisper of a shrug of her shoulders. 'Did people compare you?'

'I don't really remember,' says Gemma, pushing her hair

back behind her ear. 'Not that I recall. I mean, I was in Sancta Teresa's, you know? The girls' school in Sandycove. So obviously, that wouldn't be a problem.'

'Yes,' says Laura. 'But I presume people would have heard of him? I mean, Dún Laoghaire is a small place.'

'Well, yeah. I suppose. But I didn't – I mean, I wasn't involved in the sailing. So, I mean, everyone in the sailing world would know Max, obviously. But I – I hung out with some of the girls. I had a good friend, Nola.'

She looks across at me then back to Laura.

'Why?' She's frowning. Suspicious.

Laura smooths the front of the file before opening it.

'Nothing – no particular reason,' she soothes. 'I'm just trying to get a picture of you as a person, and the family dynamics. The more we know about you and Max – your family and friends – everything helps us, you see? Literally, every fact we find gets us closer to knowing what happened. And you want that, don't you? You want to find out what happened to Max?'

'Of course.' Gemma sighs in frustration. 'Of course I do.' She has her hands clasped together on her lap, like the nuns told you to sit. And her thumbs are circling each other, around and around.

'Good. Good. Okay. And can you think of anyone who might have wished him harm, Gemma?'

'Of course not.' She shakes her head. Laura doesn't add anything. The silence lengthens.

'That's the whole point!' snaps Gemma, a flush appearing high up on her cheekbones. 'That's what you're meant to be finding out.'

'That's why I'm asking you,' says Laura, calmly. 'I'm starting with you, because he was your brother. So, you of all people might be close enough—'

163

'We weren't close! There was a huge age gap – he's five years older than me. He – he was away at school and he was away sailing. I—'

'You're married to his best friend, who is, presumably, also five years older than you,' Laura says simply. 'So, you and Conleth and Max – you must have all been close?'

Laura's taking a risk, needling her. Sometimes it works as a technique, but other times it can make the witness clam up entirely. But we don't need to check in with each other to know that it's having an effect. Gemma swallows. The skin on her neck is so thin you can count three little ridges along her throat.

'Conleth and I, we only got together after – after Max.' She takes a deep breath. 'Conleth was – he was very good to me – to all of us. Mum and Dad too.'

She gives a little nod, and I feel like she's stepped back from the brink of something.

'Did you know – did you ever see Max involved in drugs?' Laura says in a sweet voice, as if asking if he enjoyed tennis.

'Drugs? What drugs?'

'We were hoping you could tell us,' says Laura, opening her folder and running her pen across a paragraph.

'And I was wondering where you got the banned substance that was found in your possession in' – she pauses and looks at Gemma – 'October of 2007. Four months after your brother died.'

Now Laura shrugs and adds a little shake of her head.

'I just thought there might be a connection?'

Gemma seems to deflate.

'I was in a bad way,' she whispers. 'Yes. Okay. I did drugs for – it was only a short while. I—'

She lifts her head, her eyes brimming with tears.

164

'Max hated drugs,' she says. 'He'd never— I – I got them from a guy in the town. Not Max. Never Max.'

'Okay,' I say, taking over from Laura. Not so much good cop bad cop, as cop other cop. 'Thank you. So, what can you remember about the last time you saw Max? Tell us again about that night.'

Gemma takes a tissue from her sleeve, expertly pressing it just below her eyelids to catch the tears without smudging the make-up. She's wearing a pale lilac hoody and track bottoms from that new Irish gym-gear brand. They're everywhere. Yummy-mummy gear.

Suddenly, a huge sob bursts from her.

'I was such an idiot,' she blurts, shaking her head from side to side. 'I was sixteen. I was drunk. I thought I – I thought I knew it all.'

She blows her nose, her face caving in on itself with grief. 'If I'd known I was never going to see him again – oh!'

Then her mouth clamps shut, and she swallows. The three ridges doing their up-and-down motion.

'I got blind drunk,' she repeats. 'Even before the speeches and the dancing. I don't remember – honestly! You expect me to remember? All I know is that I was drunk. I felt sick and I must have gone outside. I – I remember going out through the little half-door. It's behind the bar. And I was outside when Conleth found me, and he walked me home.'

I don't make eye contact with Laura, but we both clock that change of story. They've clearly discussed this recently. Their stories tally.

'He – he knew I'd be in trouble if my dad found out. I'm sorry. Christ! How can you expect me to remember after all this time? That night – it was the worst night of my life.'

She balls the tissue and looks for somewhere to put it. Laura passes her the bin.

'Okay,' says Laura kindly. 'Thank you. That's interesting – and it ties in with what Conleth told us. That he walked you home.'

She looks relieved.

'Because in your original statement, you said you walked home alone. Did you know that?'

'Oh, no – I, well, I must have been – I got it wrong. Or maybe—' She's speaking faster, like she's worked out something. 'That was – I was with my mum that time when I made the statement. I – I probably didn't want to get in trouble – or get him in trouble.'

'Because your mum wouldn't want Conleth to walk you home?' Laura says, her tone gentle. 'Is that – I don't know. It seems strange. Would your mum not have been happy that someone was looking after you? Is there some reason she wouldn't have wanted you to be alone with Conleth?'

She flushes.

'No. I mean, yes, if she knew that he was just being nice, it would have been fine, and he was. He just walked me home. But, look, I was sixteen. I'd a bad relationship with her at the time. We were always arguing.'

She stops suddenly, pressing her lips together as an expression of pure pain seeps across her features, moistening her eyes, crumpling that pale skin like a tissue.

'I'm sorry,' she whispers. 'Even now, I miss Mum so much.'

I feel Laura's eyes on me and I know we're on the same page. We've just witnessed something actually real. In the midst of the shite, that was real.

'Okay. I'm sure you do. Just a couple of final questions for now. What do you remember from the speeches? Did Max speak?'

She pauses. Nods.

'Yes, a bit. He did a speech, and he thanked everyone, you

166

know – like, everyone, and Mum and Dad and – and me.' Another hiccupping sob bursts out. 'And he – I just remembered – he thanked me for being a great little sister.'

'And then?' I probe, needing her to keep at this.

'Then, I don't know, there was cheering and clapping and' – the tears start again – 'and I hung around a bit. And I – I just felt so bad. I needed air, so I ran outside.'

Laura jots down something, then looks up.

'So, okay, thank you for that, Gemma. You ran outside. Did Max see you? Can you remember what happened then?' Laura leans closer, trying to keep eye contact.

'You're outside the club, yeah? What can you see?' I add, but it's no use. She's shaking her head, her eyes scrunched shut.

'I—' A little sob bursts from her. 'I never saw him again. I never – never.'

Laura and I exchange a nod without even looking at each other. We've pushed that as far as we can.

'Now,' Laura says, in a brighter tone. 'We're trying to go through some of the items which were recovered. As you know, we have the belt and a cufflink. Does this ring a bell? It all helps, you know. It helps us build a picture.'

She hesitates, glancing at me. And I know she's wondering about whether or not to show her. Simultaneously, we both give the tiniest of nods. Laura places the photos in front of her. A small tear trickles down Gemma's cheek as she studies them.

'Well, the cufflinks were a twenty-first present from Mum and Dad,' she says in a small voice. 'Them and the boat – the new 49er was his proper birthday present. That and the party at the club.' A frown. And something is bubbling up, because the memory stalls her momentarily. Fresh tears build and shimmer.

'And yes, that's his belt, of course. He – he had to wear it because the suit trousers were too big. He wouldn't wear braces.'

Laura is nodding.

'Okay, great. Thank you.' She slides the photos back into the folder without taking her eyes off Gemma's grief-stricken face. 'You must miss him terribly,' she says softly.

Gemma's body jerks with silent sobs and she presses her fist to her mouth as though she's terrified of the noise escaping. Laura catches my eye. Time to shift a gear. She seems to be on the brink of a meltdown.

'He sounds like a wonderful person,' I say, moving in to pass her fresh tissues and taking the opportunity to pat her shoulders. A bit of physical reassurance is sometimes necessary. I put on the GAA team-talk voice.

'And how great that you have little Ferdia – he's a dote!'

She blows her nose and takes some shaky breaths. I repeat the pats and Laura passes her the cup of water. She gulps it down.

'Look,' Laura says. 'We're going to leave it there for today. You've been very helpful.' She moves towards the camera, ready to switch it off, then turns back.

'Tell me,' she says. 'It's not important, just for a broader picture, but can you remember if you gave Max something for his birthday? Your parents gave him the cufflinks and the boat, yes? What did you give him?'

She closes her eyes, inhaling deeply. We wait for her to exhale.

'I – I gave him a penknife,' she says, the words barely audible. 'One he'd wanted for ages. I got his name engraved on it.'

She lifts her head to look directly at Laura and tears spill down her cheeks.

'He loved it.'

31

Gemma

Somehow, he's heard about Max. I don't know if it was one of the older kids in school or if he heard something on TV, or maybe Conleth had been talking to him about it, but when I get back from the station, Ferdia is full of questions.

'Did Uncle Max know how to swim?' was the opener as soon as I walked in the door. I tell him Uncle Max was a great swimmer. Conleth looks up from his phone, his expression unreadable, and I gather Ferdia into my arms, willing him to calm down before Conleth gets annoyed. I scour his face, searching for signs of tears.

'But did he forget? Maybe he forgot and that's why he drownded.'

I feel my gaze slide away from Conleth's – though I want to scream at him. What has he said? What new terrors has he put in Ferdia's brain?

'Well, sometimes the sea is just too strong,' I say, hugging him even closer. 'And even really good swimmers can have accidents.'

'I'm going to learn to swim really good,' he glances over at his father for approval, 'so I don't never, ever have an accident.'

'That's right,' says Conleth. 'And there'll be no more non-sense about not wanting to get in the pool for your swimming lessons.'

Later, I bring Ferdia to bed and I steer the talk away from

Max and accidents and swimming. I try to channel something of Penny's calm. So we talk about Eli and Jude, and the Lego fortress and the stunt car with the giant tyres and the raptor which you put on your finger. It takes more than an hour to get him to sleep and, finally, I close the bedroom door and stand outside with my forehead resting against the smooth wood. I don't want to go back into the sitting room, where I know he's waiting.

But this is my fate and this is my punishment. If I could change that night – like in those stories where the hero changes one tiny detail in the past, and the whole future is reshaped – oh my God, I would give anything to change it. I wouldn't fight with my mother over what to wear – she wanted me to wear the pale pink dress. It was – I mean, now I realize it was a classic: boat-necked raw silk with cap sleeves and a full skirt. Perfect for a family party, for a skinny sixteen-year-old – now I know that. But then, I thought I'd never seen anything so ugly in my life. It was a dress for a child.

I'd got a ruched black velvet number in the market in Dún Laoghaire which clung to me, making me look – I believed – sophisticated. French. And that's what I wore, teaming it with massive heels and about five inches of eyeliner. I had half a naggin of vodka even before the dinner, and I poured in about three glasses of champagne on top of that because when I got there, Conleth and Max were besieged, it seemed to me, by women – grown-up women from the club, and college girls, shiny and polished – sailors and rowers, hockey players and skiers. They glowed with a kind of strength and assurance, with the sheen of money and physical health, while I stumbled around in the heels, sidling up to Conleth at what felt like elbow height, trying to sneak one hand into his pocket or up the back of his shirt.

I was so desperate for his attention, for any affection – I

had no shame. And he kept shaking me off, saying he had to mingle, telling me to sober up. He said if I behaved myself he'd meet me on the boat after the speeches and he'd make it up to me. And I hid his keycard down my bra because there were no pockets in the ridiculous dress, and I plonked myself on one of the velvet banquettes in the bar, so I could watch him flirt and laugh with the college girls and the sailing gang. And I hugged my triumph to myself, that later, he'd be mine. All mine.

If I hadn't been so drunk that night, maybe I'd have joined the dancing in the clubhouse, the music blasting into the orange-and-gold-speckled Dún Laoghaire night sky.

If I hadn't been so obsessed with Conleth, maybe I'd have sat with Mum for a little while and let her put my hair behind my ears and said nothing when she shook her head in sorrow at the state of my make-up. Her sister – my auntie Jayne – had only been gone six weeks. I remember that now. How sad she was. How disappointed in me. And I was about to rend her life asunder.

If I hadn't been so stupid – such a stupid, selfish, self-centred little madam – I would have danced with my dad and laughed at his dad-dance moves, the way he mimed 'stacking the boxes' accompanied by a little 'chu-chu-chuh' sound.

If

If

Yeah, Gemma. One thing you have learned is that you can't rewrite history, can you?

'You baby him far too much,' says Conleth when I walk in. 'You're doing him no favours.' He fixes me with a stare, waiting for me to disagree. As if I actually would. But I nod.

'Sorry,' I say. 'You're right.'

I walk past him, intending to sit on the end of the couch.

Because this man – I know he has the potential for kindness – I know it. He must have.

And so, when he points at the floor, the part in front of the windows, I freeze. He nods with impatience, and I know that the faster I accede, the faster it will be over.

For this one, he doesn't want to see my face. This is the one part of the room not tiled in smooth marble. There's a narrow strip of ridged concrete where the marble ends and the window area begins.

'Now.'

The cold in his voice turns my hands to ice and my stomach to a swirl of acid, but I know not to keep him waiting. It will be over soon. He'll get it out of his system. He shoves me between the shoulder blades.

'Down.'

I can see us both in the glass, me kneeling up with my hands on my head like I'm awaiting execution. I see him raise his knee and, even though I see it before it happens, the kick that lands in the small of my back forcing me face down into the musty fabric of the beanbag is as shocking as it was the first time. It's like my bones shudder.

I try to breathe, and I press my fingers against my head as he presses his heel into my back, shoving me lower into the fabric, my knees scraping against the floor. He won't be able to do this for long, I think. There'll be marks on my knees and shins. He's careful not to leave marks. That's one thing to be grateful for. Especially when I'll be modelling the summer gear in a few days. If that happens.

And I don't even cry, because what's the point? I think someone said that the saddest words in the whole of the English language are these two – *if only.*

If only.

Wednesday

32

Laura

We're back in the incident room with O'Riordan, Stephen, Tara and a couple of others from the team. And a very tired-looking Senan. He's probably been here since daybreak. We used to joke that he slept in the cells because, no matter how early Niamh and I got in, he'd be at his desk ahead of us.

'She's fragile,' I'm saying. 'Gemma, I mean. And there's definitely something weighing on her mind. I mean, apart from the tragedy itself, and—'

'People, especially family members, they always blame themselves, don't they?' Senan interrupts, with his trademark stating the obvious.

'But there's more.' I keep going. 'We got some interesting, if conflicting, information. First off, Conleth told us that Max had been using cocaine recreationally, and that a possible motive for his so-called suicide was that he knew he couldn't provide a clean sample when the Olympic Committee came looking for it.'

'But?' O'Riordan looks up. 'Who says otherwise?'

'Gemma. She was adamant that Max hated anything to do with drugs. She admitted her own drug use, said she'd got weed from someone in town, but she was absolutely certain that Max disapproved.'

'Right.' O'Riordan nods. 'What did we get from Skehan, the coach? Did she mention anything more on the Olympics?'

No one answers, and I catch eyes with Niamh, biting back

175

my frustration. We were talking about this on Saturday – four days ago. Surely someone should have got to her by now. O'Riordan clearly thinks the same thing.

'Shaw, Darmody, can you interview her as soon as possible?' he growls. 'By which I mean today.'

We nod vigorously, familiar with the growls of cigirí. I turn to the next page of my notes.

'And more conflicting information. Now we have Gemma saying that Conleth walked her home, which was not in her original statement. And he's corroborating that, of course.'

'But basically, nobody saw them, and there's no record of them leaving,' Niamh chimes in. 'And we only have their word. Either of them – both of them together, the three of them, even – could've gone down to the boat.'

I'm distracted by her pallor. My mum's phrase *green around the gills* comes to mind. Something's up.

'Although he, Conleth, says he went back to the party and—' I stop, niggled by something, trying to focus.

'And proceeded to shift a hot young lawyer,' Niamh interrupts, grinning. 'Although that's not what he called it. "Behaved inappropriately" was the phrase. He should've seen Coppers back in the day!' Her laugh is infectious.

'And this lawyer that Conleth O'Hara proceeded to, eh, behave inappropriately with – do we have a name for her?'

'Indeed we do, Cig. He claims he got up close and personal with Fiona Cassidy.' She waits a beat.

'The eminent senior counsel?' says O'Riordan, his eyebrows somewhere near his hairline.

'The very one. Although she was presumably just a non-eminent law student then.'

'The point is that we checked this out.' I pause. 'And that's legit. Although I wouldn't think she wants it to be widely known.'

'Where was Max at this point?' O'Riordan furrows his brow.

I shake my head. 'No sightings of him at all for the later part of the night. O'Hara says he presumed he'd left to go home. Earlier, he'd seen Max deep in conversation with a girl, and he reckoned that what he'd observed might have been them breaking up.'

'Right. And do we have her name?' O'Riordan clicks the top of his pen.

Niamh nods. 'We do. Michelle Byrne.'

McCarthy nearly gives himself a whiplash. 'The former Olympian?'

'Yup. All the beautiful people. Mingling. Annieway, Conleth seemed to think that the break-up and the problems with the sample were enough to tip Max over the edge. And, erm, Shaw did an inspired bit of questioning and elicited this gem of info: guess what Gemma gave her brother for his twenty-first?'

She gets to her feet, phone in hand. 'A penknife. I've already emailed Parminter,' she says. 'Apparently, it's a type used by lots of sailors – a brand by the name of Leatherman. He's – Parminter is checking dimensions and so on, to see if it could be the one we're looking for.'

'Great work,' says O'Riordan.

Niamh is pale, I realize. I watch as she places three fingers flat against her sternum, pressing. She swallows, and it looks as though she's trying hard not to throw up.

'Right,' I say, getting up. 'We could do with a bit of air, couldn't we, Niamh? Cig, we'll go and talk to Skehan.'

Immediately she's gathering her things together.

I stride ahead of her along the corridor, out into the

parking lot. When we reach the car, I pop the locks and turn to face her.

'When were you going to tell me?' I say. 'Or was I meant to just work it out for myself?'

33

Gemma

I kneel in front of him, glad that Ferdia is safely in school. That I'll have hours to recover. Between us on the stone floor is a plastic basin of freezing-cold water into which he has poured the bleach. Both my bare hands are submerged and the pain thrums through me in waves of stinging, burning cold. I'm clutching a j-cloth because the official version of this punishment is that I didn't clean the floor properly. I count the stitches on his handmade shoes. Dangerously, I let myself imagine throwing the basin at him. In his eyes. Could I do it? Could I really do it?

'Here,' he says.

I take my hands out, squeezing out the cloth, trying not to cry as the air hits my raw skin. He taps his toe to the left. Three taps – imperious. I scrub the imagined stains he's pointing out. The heels of his shoes click as he walks across the room. Then the toe tap. 'And here,' he says.

He walks behind me and I cringe, because that's what I do.

'Then here,' he says. Another imperious tap. 'And over there by the door. How can you have let it get like this?'

I shuffle along on my hands and knees like some medieval beggarwoman and my eyes are dry, because why would I shed a tear for myself? I'm despicable and I'm weak. And I'm so self-centred my only concern is that he'll tire of this soon.

And I'm right, because I hear him walk into the kitchen

and then a large cardboard box is dropped on to the floor beside me.

'There are three dresses and a trouser suit,' he says. 'Tidy yourself up and do it soon.' He jangles the car keys with impatience. 'What are you waiting for?'

And the woman who a few hours ago was swimming – well, almost swimming, with her friend Penny – that woman is gone. She's been replaced by a cringing, shivering, weeping excuse for a human who disgusts me. If you hate yourself, it's easier for others to hate you. I've discovered that. The only thing I don't hate about myself is that, somehow, I managed to give birth to Ferdia. That woman – Ferdia's mother – is the one who braved the water today.

I run a basin of tepid water into which I pour baby oil. I can't find my eczema cream anywhere and I realize that he's taken it away too. Another punishment. But in Ferdia's swimming bag there's some E45. My hands are so red I have to rub foundation in with the E45. Then, I do my make-up – low-key, natural. I tie back my hair and I face the camera. In my hands, I hold the clothes, neatly folded.

'Hi, everyone, I want to thank you for your lovely messages. You're so kind. Now today, it's all about trying to find the right outfit for—' I freeze. What am I meant to say? I delete, smooth some stray strands of hair, and breathe. The room is stuffy. It's really a glorified cupboard, but it looks cosy in the posts. It looks like I have a walk-in wardrobe.

Three sailors went to sea, sea, sea, I think, and I'm scared, because I keep seeing the same image. Max and Ferdia and me in the bottom of the deep blue sea.

He'll be checking for a post anytime now. I shake myself out of it.

180

'It happens to us all,' I say, starting over. 'At some point, we have to go to a funeral. And in these situations, even though you might not feel like planning your outfit, trust me – it's important. It's about respect.' Yeah. The irony is not lost on me.

I show the pile of folded clothes. 'Today it's formal wear. And these outfits are from—' I stop. The company is called Blue Wave. The logo is a floral version of that famous tidal wave painting. A strange, strangled gulp emerges from my throat, like a laugh and a sob combined.

Suddenly it seems like the most outrageous thing. That I'm expected to put on this gear and try it out, three – no, four – different looks to wear to my brother's funeral. My brother who lay at the bottom of the sea under the waves – and suddenly I'm full-on hysterically laughing, gasping, crying, hiccupping. I collapse on to the carpet in my cami and briefs, clutching the pile of clothes like a life raft. I bury my face in them and I howl for my brother. I never cried for him. There was no way I could, and I know that was another thing Mum and Dad distrusted. But now I sob, and it feels like the tears are burning. Bleach tears that purify and burn.

I'm sorry I'm sorry I'm sorry. I love you, Max. I love you and I'm sorry. I'm galvanized. I jump to my feet and I press record and I stand in front of the camera, in the halo from the circular light. Tears run down my cheeks and I'm still sobbing and gulping.

'I'm so sorry, everyone. I haven't been honest with you. I haven't said a single honest word to you since the dawn of – *hiccup* – time.' Be real. Be bloody real, Gemma! 'Well, here you go. I killed my brother. I killed my own brother, who I loved, no, yes. No, let's keep saying the truth. I loved him, and I hated him too. I was jealous. And while everything he touched turned to gold, everything I touched tanked. He

181

aced exams. I failed them. He was set to represent his country in the Olympics for sailing. I couldn't even swim. When he wasn't sailing, he was studying Medicine in college. I dropped out of school before my Leaving Cert. I wanted to go to art college, but I didn't even finish school. I—

'And my parents, oh my God! They loved him! He was everything to them. And I destroyed that.

'And I wanted to die. Because after Max was gone, I realized how much I loved him. I hid from the world. I hid behind Conleth, and I let him – I hide in this world he's created and I feel so bad lying to you, to you all. I'm a useless daughter, mother, sister, friend. I can't even protect my son – and I want to be – I want to be true to you all, and I'm so tired of lying. I just want to tell the truth. And I am! I swear. I am – but I have to – I have to – that's—'

A door slams upstairs. I freeze, and it's almost comical. It's like the tears are hoovered back into my tear ducts. I stand there half naked, heart thumping. But it's probably just one of the tenants going out. We share the front entrance.

But no! No! Footsteps on the stairs. Why is he coming in that way? It's Conleth back again. Quickly, I press stop, then I throw the pile of clothes on the bed and start to get into the top outfit on the pile. I hear him hesitate outside the door. He won't want to come in while I'm filming.

'This dress has a V neck and an elasticated waist,' I say, loud enough for him to hear outside the door. 'So comfy – and it's all about comfort for me. But it still shows my shape. And, ladies, it has pockets. Gotta love the pockets. Comes in navy as well.'

I dry my tears on the inside of the dress as I take it off, then I take my hair out of the ponytail and let it hide my face. By the time he comes into the room it just looks as though I'm a bit red-faced from the heat.

'I spoke to your friend Penny,' he says, layering the word with irony. 'She's kind of nosy, isn't she? She's worried about you. She gave me a card with some counsellor's name on it. Wants me to encourage you to talk to someone.'

My hand flies to my throat.

'Conleth, I didn't—'

'You can talk to anyone you want,' he says, flicking the card on to the floor in front of me. 'But just remember that if you do anything to jeopardize this family—' He pauses, and I watch him scan the room, like a wolf sniffing a scent. His eyes stop and rest on the phone. He narrows his gaze. Oh my God! Did I actually press stop? He takes a step towards it, then changes his mind.

'Finish your post,' he says, turning to leave. 'And don't waste time. We're going to make a statement at twelve thirty – outside the club. That way they'll have it for the lunchtime news bulletin.'

Hands shaking, I make a new reel. I say nice things about each outfit, paying particular attention to stitching details, pockets, quality, comfort. I add the sticker icon and do a poll: 'The suit has it' versus 'Stick with the classic dress'. Laura said it might be another day before they release the body.

I'll be gone by then. There's no other way. We both will.

#Asafehavenformax
#Keeponsailing
#Styleitout
#Coastallife
#Comfydresses
#Casualbutsmart
#Lovemybrother

@missymurfi: I hope you're taking it easy @gemstone because you need rest. You're always cleaning your house – maybe your husband would take over for this week. You should make him stay home and clean and you can walk on the pier and get an ice-cream. That would be nice.

@annahanna: @missymurfi always looking out for @gemstone! Good idea. Or we could bring you for a coffee at the library.

@missymurfi: Just us. No husbands. I don't have one anyway.

@nolimitsgrl: No rush @missymurfi haha! A woman needs a man like a fish needs a bicycle.

@missymurfi: But fishes can't ride bicycles.

@annahanna: @nolimitsgrl you are hilarious. But the coffee idea is a good one. We should do a coffee morning.

@missymurfi: Little Ferdia is a great fella and he must be your pride and joy. @gemstone it was nice to see you on the seat all cuddled up close.

34

Laura

I'm outside Corrig Point garda station finishing up a call with Matt when Niamh gets into the car, looking pale. She clocks me about to hang up.

'Bye, honey!' she trills in a constricted Southside squawk which is meant to sound like me, presumably. 'Love you, baby. Wear your sexy gear tonight again, won't you?' The opportunity to tease now brings a flush of colour to her cheeks.

'Hi, Niamh,' Matt's voice holds his grin. 'Don't tempt me.'

'Well?' she says after I end the call. 'What are you grinning at? Did ye go out last night for the romantic dinner followed by the missionary-position mind-numbing PE that passes for sex with you old-timers?'

'Very funny,' I say, concentrating on reversing out of the parking lot, hoping she won't notice the blush which says yes, that's exactly what we did. Right down to the position. What can I say? I like it. He likes it. Though it's so rare nowadays, poor Matt would like anything that passes for sex.

Neither of us mentioned the whole scenario with Alva and my father. It's like we both knew that would mess up the whole night. We stuck to the script.

'So?' I say, glancing over at Niamh now. She's tied back her hair, and it occurs to me that perhaps she had to, if she was throwing up. 'Have you done a test yet?'

She frowns in irritation. And that's so unlike her, I reckon the pregnancy test is a foregone conclusion.

'Didn't want to jinx it,' she says, her face serious. 'They said not to test until two weeks. So I've to wait until Saturday.'

'Well, yeah,' I say, pulling into the outside lane, 'but you could buy the test to be ready, couldn't you?'

A shrug. I feel like I'm driving my teenage daughter to school. For detention.

'I'll pick one up later, will I? And keep it safe.'

She grins.

'Thanks, yeah, great. Okay. And leave it out on the bed – give Matt a heart attack. No, better yet, leave it sticking out of your handbag when Justy is over. She'll freak if you go past the 2.2 kids quota. Speaking of Justy, am I invited to the party? Surely she's doing something fab for you in the mansion? Or the tennis club – or could it be the golf club?'

I sigh. As usual, Niamh's not that far off course. Justy has been trying to persuade me – via Matt, naturally – to let her 'take the reins' and plan a fortieth-birthday party for me. She called over the other night when I was out and started making plans with him and was most put out when I arrived home with a thundering headache and basically put the kibosh on it all. She'd gathered her keys and phone together with much clanking of bracelets and metalwork – a sort of huffy jangling – then looked at me closely.

'You do too much,' she said, resting her tennis-tanned bony hand on my forearm. It's only May, and she's already mahogany. 'Do try to rest.'

'Actually, yeah, that would be brilliant if you'd buy it,' Niamh says, and for a moment I've forgotten what she means. Oh, the kit.

'Hannah from my club works in my local chemist, and I don't want word getting out.' She pauses, and a huge grin creeps across her face. 'Also, because I'm so hormonally

186

challenged I'm in danger of mortifying myself every time I step out the door.' Her shoulders shake with laughter and a little snigger bursts from her nose.

'Okay, don't tell anniewan, an' I'll tell you—'

I wait.

'Swear?'

'I swear.'

'Right, so Dorothy asked me to pick up a pint of milk on my way back last night, so I hopped into the garage to get it, and I was rummaging around in my bag looking for my purse, which I couldn't find – because of course I'd left that at home.'

'Oh wow!' I say. 'Poor you.'

'No, that's not it – whisht!' she snaps. 'So in another section of the bag, I have this little small purse – only a tiny thing, like for if you're clubbing or, well, not that you'd be clubbing, or me now either, but—' Another pause, in which I say nothing.

'An' in that purse I'd only ever keep like a folded twenty, and a credit card and a pantyliner – I mean, the essentials, you know?'

'Uh-hum,' I say, beginning to smile.

'Yeah, and the young fella on the till is cranky-looking as shite and even though I'm only buying a pint of milk I know I'll have to tap, so I put my fingers in the purse, eyeballing him like crazy because—'

'Because he's a cranky-looking shite?'

'Exactly. And as I'm eyeballing him, I go, like: "I presume I can tap," and he just stares at what's in my hand, and so I look down and we both realize that I have just tried to tap for a pint of milk with a pink pantyliner.'

She throws her head back against the seat, closing her eyes and snorting with laughter.

187

'Oh Jaysus! If you'd seen his face!'

And we're both laughing, proper giggles that last, threading from one to the other, for a full minute.

'So annieway,' she says, finally, 'you'll—'

'I'll pick up a test for you,' I say. 'And I'll pay with money rather than pantyliners.'

We're quiet for a few minutes, and as I turn off the motorway heading towards the coast she speaks in a different voice. All laughter gone.

'Do you think I'm crazy to do this? You can say it, Laura. Be honest.'

Bloody hell, I'm not used to this version of Niamh. I turn to make eye contact.

'No! Not at all! Niamh, I swear to God, I think you're brilliant. You're going to be the most amazing mum.'

'Brilliant but crazy?' she says, gesturing for me to keep an eye on the road. 'I haven't told Mam and Dad yet in case they – well, I'm not telling them till it's too late.'

I nod but say nothing.

'What? Do you think I should?'

'No – no. Actually, not at all.'

'Yeah, but you've gone all quiet,' she says. 'Are you disapproving? Seriously?'

'No – no, you've got it all wrong,' I say. 'I've gone quiet because I was remembering when I did the test and found out I was pregnant with Katie. And I couldn't wait to tell Matt, because he was so, you know, invested in the whole thing. And I did, and he was thrilled and lovely and – it's Matt. So he said all the right things. And we told his parents a couple of weeks later and of course they told all their friends. But then—'

I indicate off the roundabout and sweep into the smaller roads, the beautiful wide tree-lined roads on the outskirts of

Dalkey. Niamh waits. And I think about what she's gone through. This is her second round of IVF; she went through the whole thing once before, but the embryo didn't take.

I can't believe she kept it all secret and I can't believe I didn't notice. That we sat together, drove together, worked together and I didn't pick up a single clue. So much for my detective skills.

When she told me the whole story, I saw a Niamh – a side to her I'd never known existed. Absolute commitment, determination, resilience – all of that is a given with Niamh. But when she told me of her longing for a baby and the fact that she had decided to do this alone, I was blown away.

'Later, I wished that I'd waited before telling anyone – even Matt. I wished I'd had a bit longer when it was just me and her. I don't think I even had an hour of just me and the baby on our own. Our own world. A secret.'

'I can understand that.'

'So, what I'm saying is that whatever you want – and, you know, however you want to do this – I'm here for you.'

I blush again, because we don't usually talk like this. But Niamh doesn't laugh.

I slow as we pass Bullock Harbour, both of us looking out at the jumble of boats in and out of the water, the little row of colourful cottages, the stylish, white-stepped sweep of Pilot View – our destination – opening out in front of us.

'Jaysus,' she whispers. 'Imagine actually living here.'

I look over at her; she looks like she's drinking in the sight.

'Would you love it?'

She gives a do-you-have-to-ask shrug. 'Eh, yeah? Who wouldn't? The sea, like? I'd be swimming every day.'

I nod.

'I'll have you know that even us landlocked Tipperary

boggers learn how to swim, all right?' she snaps, as though I've accused her of something.

I hold up a hand in surrender.

'Of course you do.' I grin. 'Never thought otherwise.'

Normal service restored.

35

Niamh

I hop out and tap in the entrance code, waving Laura on to let her know I'll meet her at the door. Holy God! I watch her park, the straight back and the driving position that looks like she's literally doing her driving test and, judging by the rigid set to her, not that sure of passing. She's been like that from the day I met her – a strung-out streel – like someone's twisting a dial in her brain to the max. But then, when we met, she was already a mam – or about to be. So maybe that's it. Maybe she's wired because she cares so much.

The thought occurred to me recently that maybe we humans are okay until we decide to start making babies. Maybe the mania and the stress, it's like that's nothing until you take on the biggest risk of all. It's like this high-risk investment. An investment in life, capital L. And it's terrifying to do it alone, but so what. It's worth it.

When Amber and I broke up, I realized there was no point in waiting around for a perfect partner to have a baby with. I decided I'd go for it on my own so that, if in the future there's anyone on the horizon – if I do decide to do the whole girlfriend thing again – well, it'll already be a done deal. Me and the baby – the kid – whatever. Maybe even two of them. Why the feck not? Any prospective partner can take us as they find us. So yeah, maybe I should be thanking Amber for the rage that propelled me to do this alone. Rage, energy, whatever. Thanks, Amber.

Three months ago I lay in the clinic looking up at the screen, shivering, the gel evaporating on my skin, after the injections and the bloody harvesting of eggs, the plans and scans and months of hoping, and I heard the nurse say, 'I'm sorry. That's very disappointing – there's no heartbeat.'

But I'd already boarded this train, so I dug deep, swallowed the tears.

'Sure, haven't I two more in your freezer,' I'd said, although the tone came out kind of wrong because it sounded like I didn't care, when in actual fact I'd never cared about anything more. 'How soon can I go again?'

And here we are. I'm doing this. I'm not second-guessing myself and I'm not stopping. Decision not to be revisited. If this one doesn't work, I'm going again. End of.

I speed up to catch Laura, who has her finger poised above the intercom. She's watching me with this gentle smile and, in fairness, I have a strong desire to tell her to feck off.

'Will ye stop giving me the Holy Mary look, for pity's sake!' I snap. 'Forget I said anything.'

She smiles, leaning in towards the disembodied voice on the intercom.

'Good morning, Mrs Skehan, we're from Corrig Point garda station. Laura Shaw and Niamh Darmody. I called earlier?'

'Oh yes. Top floor – take a right.'

We're buzzed in and start making our way up the wide stairs. At the top, a tiny, tanned blonde woman who could be any age from fifty to eighty waits outside the door to her apartment. She's wearing a thick white V-neck jumper over a bright blue shirt, white tailored trousers and a pair of navy docksiders with a white trim. Her eyes dart, taking everything in, and her movements are jerky and thrumming with nervous energy, like a nautical squirrel. Is there such a thing as a sea squirrel? If there is, she's it.

Laura is pure professional as usual, but I'm finding it hard not to gasp. The flat has a view which people would kill for. Views – not just one. She brings us into the living room, which has a double-height window looking out over Bullock Harbour, and beyond, to Dún Laoghaire and Dublin Bay. Miles of sea. This room opens out into an L-shape with a kitchen in the smaller section where there's another big window – and more sea.

I think of the good room at home, always in semi-darkness. Of Mam standing at the sink in the kitchen, drinking in the pitiful square of grey light. Maybe the human race would be a whole lot kinder if we all lived somewhere as beautiful as this. And then I remember what my landlady Dorothy said, because it was Dorothy I trusted with the secret first, Dorothy who brought me home and looked after me when they did the egg collection, Dorothy who held my hand after the miscarriage. She's like a human confessional – somewhere secrets can lodge undisturbed. Maybe because of her role as village pharmacist, she's just so wise. Nothing shocks her.

'When you have the child, you're moving upstairs,' she'd said. And I tried telling her that I love my basement flat and I'm happy out, but she was having none of it. 'Nonsense. The child will need light, space and a garden. You'll move up here to the first floor. Besides, that will free up the basement for the Kovalenko family. It will all work out swimmingly.'

'Call me Carol-Ann,' says Carol-Ann, pouring a coffee for Laura and handing me a glass of chilled water. Last time, I couldn't face coffee. But it might be nothing. I sip my water.

'So, can you talk to us about the Fitzgeralds?' says Laura. 'How well did you know the family?'

She smiles, and her face creases into a million wrinkles, especially around the eyes. Hers is a face that has spent a lifetime outdoors, the kind of face you'd associate with wisdom and generosity. Which is why her next sentence is a bit of a shocker.

'Oh, very well,' she says, stirring sugar into her cup. 'Well enough to know that the golden boy Max wasn't quite as golden as he seemed.'

36

Laura

Niamh and I know enough not to show our surprise. I take a sip of coffee, waiting for Carol-Ann's next salvo.

'Oh, don't get me wrong,' she immediately backtracks. 'Vandra was a great friend and our boys were the same age. Rob was in school with Max, so we all spent a lot of time together.'

'Right,' nods Niamh, 'and you're a sailing coach in the club as well?'

'Mostly retired from that. But yes, a few hours. And I like to help out with MaxSpirit when I can. Conleth does wonderful work for the underprivileged, you know. And he only has that girl Sally to help – she's very young—' She blinks away whatever she was going to say, her eyes falling on the long sideboard on which a treasure trove of awards is laid out. Trophies, plaques, framed photos in silver and crystal, a commemorative carriage clock – it's like a shrine to sailing. In many of the photographs, a heavy-set boy with dark hair smiles self-consciously. I spot a photo which shows the same boy and, beside him, a young Max.

I leave Niamh to do the approving nods for that one.

'Is this your son?' I pick up a silver-edged framed photo. She smiles.

'That's him. Rob.' She indicates the frame. 'He was twelve when that was taken. He'd just won gold in the regatta.'

'Oh, and that's Max Fitzgerald beside him, isn't it?' I tilt the frame so Niamh can see it too.

'Did they used to sail together as well?' says Niamh.

'As well?' she replies, her lips pursing. 'They were partners first. Before Max and Conleth, the boys – it was Rob and Max who were a little dream team. I used to call them the terrible two.'

'I see.' Niamh nods, gesturing for me to hand her the photo and then passing it into Carol-Ann's hand. 'So, this is the pair just after they won?'

Carol-Ann shakes her head then looks up, her eyes focusing at some distant point on the horizon.

'I took them out – I brought Max and Rob out for their first ever trip in a dinghy. They were in First Class, so they can't have been more than seven years old. I showed them the ropes – literally. Put them through their exams – there are exams, you know? I mean, it's hard to believe now, but at one time my Rob was the better sailor. He was bigger – or at least, he was until Max had a growth spurt in his teens.'

She places the photo on her lap, facing up. 'Sorry. That's not what you asked me. What did you say?'

Niamh gestures towards the photo.

'I was wondering if that's – was that picture taken after they'd won a race together?'

Carol-Ann presses her lips together.

'Actually, no. Rob won the gold that time. They'd been competing in – they were sailing Topazes. Individually. And well, as I say, Rob was such a sturdy lad and, at that point, he had the upper hand. Max got the bronze.'

She looks up. In her eyes, a slim layer of tears reflects the white glare from outside. She passes the photo back to me with a little nod, and the gesture shows me something of the teacher. It's an instruction.

'And who got the silver?' Niamh probes.

'Oh, Conleth, of course,' she says. 'Sorry, I should have explained all of this to start off with. You see, as their coach, I was in a position to – let's just say, I understood the dynamics of the situation. Yes. Conleth appeared on the scene – at the sailing club, rather – for the very first time that summer. It was the year they all were starting secondary school. And Conleth – I mean, well, he didn't come from a sailing family, if you get me.'

She frowns.

'I don't mean – sorry. That sounds like I'm saying you have to, you know, have sailing in your blood. And I'm not. Not at all. Plenty of people do a course or go out with a friend and they're bitten by the bug. It's a passion.'

She tilts her palm upwards, does a little sweep of the view, the room full of photos and memorabilia.

'Sailing people literally live for the next event, for the next time they go out on the water. Petey – my late husband – and I, we met through sailing. We were married in the yacht club. And the Fitzgeralds were the same – Max and Rob, all of us, we literally spent every weekend and the long summers together, sailing.'

'And Conleth?' says Niamh, with a little side-eye at me. There's something not exactly right here.

'Conleth was, ah – less fortunate. He – he appeared one summer for a month-long sailing camp. I think John – Max's father – had arranged it as a favour, because Conleth's dad had been doing some work on the engine of the boat. Lovely people, the O'Haras. Salt of the earth, you know?'

The phrase gleams between us like a beacon. It's like something Justy would say, and I know exactly what she's telling me. Conleth was from a different social class – well, in her book anyway.

197

'But he was instantly – I mean, he was a natural. And of course, you've seen him? I mean, even now, he's a terrific athlete. And so, when we started training the kids for racing the Lazers, suddenly Conleth was in demand. They race the Lazers and 49ers in pairs, you know?'

We both murmur our agreement.

'And at that point, you see – well, it could have been a different story, is all I'll say. Because straightaway it was Rob and Conleth who were paired together. Whereas Max – I mean, he hadn't had his growth spurt, so I don't think he could have expected any different. I don't think he was upset or anything. You have to choose your teams according to talent, after all. But what I'm saying is that for almost three years, Rob and Conleth were the ones sailing together. But the Fitzgeralds—' She breaks off, and it's as if she wakes from a bit of a trance. She shakes her head.

'What about the Fitzgeralds?' says Niamh, her earlier patience forgotten.

'Look, Vandra was a dear friend,' she says, 'and I really don't want to speak ill of the dead, but—'

'Are you saying that Max's mum interfered—'

A new burst of energy and a kind of righteous indignation comes over Carol-Ann.

'I don't know if either of you has children,' she says, with a little shuffling movement of her shoulders like a laying hen, 'but if and when you do, you'll understand – look. You'd do anything to make them happy. That's what I'm saying. And Vandra—'

We both wait. Niamh is nodding and keeping a quiet chorus of uh-huhs going.

'Oh, I completely understand,' I chip in. 'I have two at home. You'd – you're right. You'd literally do anything to keep the peace, wouldn't you?'

'You're only as happy as your unhappiest child,' Niamh trots out, and it's all I can do not to stare at her. But it works.

Carol-Ann relaxes.

'Exactly. And look – I don't blame her. And they were in a position to do this for Conleth – well, for Max really. And later, when we heard about the tragedy – well, you know his parents died in a fire, don't you? Well, afterwards, Vandra and John, they were wonderful. It was a very kind thing to do.'

'What did they do?' I say, wishing she'd spell it out.

'Oh, sorry. I thought you'd know this. It was an open secret. The Fitzgeralds became like a second family to Conleth. They – when his parents died, it was like they adopted him, and they bought a brand-new 49er for Max. Conleth changed schools. The school offered him a full scholarship, which I know for certain would have been funded by John Fitzgerald, so that he could be in the same form as Max. He stayed with them at weekends and during the holidays and then, later, when they went to college, they shared a flat in Rathmines.'

'And they did this because—' Niamh lets the question hang in the air.

'Look, I'm not saying that Max wasn't a brilliant sailor. He was. But so was Rob. And competitive sailing is pretty cut-throat, especially if you have any ambition for the Olympics. Conleth's loyalties shifted to the Fitzgerald family. We couldn't – we couldn't compete financially.' She pauses, and I wonder just how much money the Fitzgeralds must have had if she considers herself poor by comparison.

'And – oh, I don't know,' she continues. 'It seems so obvious now. Those Fitzgerald children got everything they ever wanted. Conleth and Max dropped Rob like a hot brick in Third Year. Rob still sailed, and he crewed with a cousin, but they didn't have the same bond. Plus, it was just so difficult for him to watch what was happening for Conleth and Max. It was almost like the end of a love affair. In a few months, it went from being Rob and Conleth to Conleth and Max. Rob was broken-hearted.'

She shifts in her seat, doing a little shake of her shoulders. The body language tells me there's something more. A pronouncement.

'In the end, mind you, they did him a favour. He didn't need any favours from the golden boy. He's an ENT consultant now,' she adds. 'Rob gave up the sailing and threw himself into his studies. So, you see, it wasn't the worst thing to happen for him.'

She sits back in her chair, tilting her chin upwards as she fishes in her sleeve for a hanky. She dabs at her eyes, though the tears have long dried.

'So, I suppose Rob didn't attend the party that night?' says Niamh, not looking up from her notebook, and I know it's so that I'll study the effect of the question. 'Max's twenty-first?'

She sits very still then reaches for her cup, taking a sip of what must be, by now, cold coffee. She frowns.

'Of course he went to the party. We all did. You can't let these things take over your life, you know.' Again, that little shoulder shrug. 'They were never as close, the boys, and yes, I suppose things were perhaps a bit stilted between our families, but, as I say – look at him now.'

She points to the far wall, to the graduation photo. Then she seems to debate something. She has a finisher.

'And at least it meant he never got mixed up in all the—'

We wait. She's dying to say it. With a sigh, she speaks.

'The drug-taking. I know – I know you'll say it's everywhere, and maybe it is now. But you can take my word for it, back then Corrig Point was a wonderful, wholesome club. A family club. And it gives me no pleasure to speak ill of the dead, I promise you, but when I heard about Max, about his drug *habit*' – she stresses the word, as though it's alien to her – 'I wasn't the least bit surprised.'

'And where or who did you hear that from?'

She bristles. 'Well, of course I kept it completely quiet at the time – confidentiality is a vital aspect of the club secretary's job – but it was only natural that letters from the Olympic Committee would first pass through my hands. I was the first to know that they were withdrawing their offer because of failure to produce.'

She draws her neat brows together in a frown. 'And I had the unhappy task of breaking it to them.'

@missymurfi: How r you bearing up, Gem? It must be desperate raking up all this pain again. Would you like any help at all with the funeral? I can make sandwiches. Did you not get your online shopping delivery this week?
@nolimitsgrl: Can you talk to anyone? A professional?
@theirishmammy: I can post names of therapists – someone you can talk to.
@missymurfi: The gemstones are here for you @gem-stone. I lit a candle for you and one for your brother.
@unatracey5: Managed to bag the last two skincare sets. Tks, Gemma. Great discount!
@missymurfi: I'm sure she's too busy for this now.
@unatracey5 presume you've heard the news?
@unatracey5: Of course. Just saying thanks.

37

Gemma

Conleth's arm is around my shoulders, and he keeps pressing me against him and I know what that means. Another code. I can gauge the level of his anger, or the intensity of the warning I'm being given, by the pressure of the squeeze. I reckon the pressure is about ninety per cent. Maybe more. We stand on the steps of the yacht club and it's like being in ancient Rome in the arena. The reporters and photographers and passers-by form a semicircle, like they're the gladiators and we're the prisoners. Above us the gulls wheel and cry. One bird spots a half-eaten sandwich in the gutter and it swoops to grab it, skimming the railings, startling a reporter into dropping her phone.

I hold Ferdia's hand – we collected him early from school; Conleth insisted – while Conleth's squeezes my shoulders, and it looks like a cosy photo of the strong man comforting the little woman, supporting the family. Only I can feel how hard the squeeze is. Only I know what it means.

I move closer, resting my head against his chest then looking up at him – in gratitude. Because that's what it means. It means *Get on board*. He looks down at me, a sad smile like a scrape across his mouth. He's a media dream, actually. Approaching forty, but only growing more chiselled, the jawline firm, the hair still intact though sprinkled with grey. He doesn't look like a cruel man. He doesn't look like a man who locks the pantry on a whim, depriving not just his wife but his own son of access to food. If anyone opened the kitchen cupboards, they'd find them pretty much bare. He has an online shop delivered once a week. It never varies and it's not enough. He eats at the club or buys food for himself when he's out. If I've been very good, he'll bring something back. If I'm very good, I'm allowed a coffee – the ones you make with the sachet. I get an allowance and I can use my phone to tap and pay, but he keeps track of it on an app on his phone.

'When's the funeral, Gem?' The shout is friendly, almost like the reporter was asking when's the party.

'How are you holding up?' A female voice – she writes for one of the main papers.

'She's a trooper,' he says, kissing the top of my head.

He doesn't look like a man who once scraped his leftovers on to a plate and said, 'Now, come on, Mummy-dog,' click-clicking his teeth as he put the plate on the floor, Ferdia's eyes skittering left and right in panic.

'Dog mummy is so funny, isn't she?' He'd laughed as I bent to pick it up. 'I'm only joking.'

'We are hoping the coroner will release the body for burial any day now,' he says now, his tone serious. 'You'll find details on RIP.ie. Thank you.'

A squeeze.

'Thank you,' I echo.

'Why haven't you done that post yet?' says Conleth as we pull up outside the house. Automatically, I look over my shoulder to make sure Ferdia is wearing his headphones. Things can escalate quickly. He cuts the engine and turns to face me, holding his hand out for my phone.

Did I delete it? Shit – did I delete it? I think I did. I must have. There's no way I'd be careless enough to leave that on.

I pat my jeans pocket, then lean forward and reach into my handbag, my hair swinging down to hide what I'm doing. I rummage in the bag, playing for time and – thank God, thank God – he tsks in impatience and takes his own phone out, tapping into Instagram and searching the stories.

'Here,' he says, tilting it towards me. 'That's your last one. Where's the one you did earlier this morning?'

'Oh God, sorry!' I say. 'Yes – I couldn't finish it. There was a problem with one of the outfits. The trousers were way too long, even with heels, and I—'

He looks closely at me, frowning.

'You were in there for long enough, for Christ's sake. Anyway, it needs to be done today. I mean—'

We both leap at a tap on the window. It's the taller garda – Niamh. And in the rear-view mirror I spot Laura waving at Ferdia through the car window. We never even noticed them park behind us. I plaster a huge smile on my face and start getting out, ready to greet them. Before I can, Conleth hisses for me to look at him. He's smiling, but his eyes are flat. His fingers twist in a small movement, thumb and first two fingers close together. The greeting dies on my lips. That gesture means *Shut it*.

Niamh moves to hold the door to stop it swinging back against me, and it crosses my mind to grab her wrists, to whisper in her ear, *Help me. Please help me*. But I don't. Conleth gets out of the car, all bonhomie and civility.

'Ladies,' he says. He leans to open the door for Ferdia, who clambers down and moves towards me. Conleth stops him, grabbing hold of his wrist, and I wait for the tears or, worse, the brave face. But instead, his face splits into an enormous grin and he looks from me to Laura, who is carrying a large, shiny, not-broken digger, almost identical to Ferdia's, except both the bucket and the crane part are red, not yellow.

'May I?' she says to me, ignoring Conleth completely. 'Don't worry, I didn't buy it!' she says, with a laugh that sounds forced. She's watching me. She bends down so she's at Ferdia's level.

'This is for you, Ferdia,' she says, 'from my little boy. He doesn't play with it so much now, and he said you could have it. He was very sad when he heard yours got broken. Would you like it?'

Before Conleth can say anything, Ferdia pulls his hand free and grabs the digger, clutching it to his chest.

'What do you say?' says Conleth, his voice stretching to hold the smile. He's not pleased. But he's not going to say anything.

'Ah, Jaysus,' grins Niamh, watching Ferdia, who immediately starts talking to the toy. 'Let him off. He's made up.'

I catch eyes with Laura, and I feel the threat of tears in mine.

'Thank you,' I say. She nods, her face serious.

'Thought it might be a good distraction,' she says, pointing towards the house. 'While we talk. Something's come up.'

'Of course,' says Conleth, gesturing towards the path. 'Come in.'

He steps aside to let us go ahead of him and it's all I can do not to grab Ferdia and run. They know. I'm sure of it. And they don't want to arrest me outside. Will they do it? They wouldn't do it in front of Ferdia, surely? My heart — instead of thumping in panic, it feels like it's slowed to nothing. Like suspended animation. And I don't know how my legs are moving, but they keep walking. Conleth passes me the key to the front door and I know he wants us to enter that way, not through the side and into the kitchen directly. And I know why. If we come down the staircase, we go straight into the sitting room, which is immaculate. It should be. It was scrubbed with a toothbrush. I lead the way up the stone steps and, hands shaking, open the front door.

38

Laura

'Did you order for me?' I say, placing the glossy white box down on the marble tabletop and sitting beside her so we can both look at the view. I shake my head in admiration – the orderly and well-maintained gardens, the Victorian fountain, the neatly swept path leading to the seafront and beyond, the blue sea flecked with an occasional bright boat. I have the feeling that, apart from the massive cruise ship floating outside the harbour, the view is unchanged since the 1870s. We're sitting on the veranda of the pavilion-styled café in People's Park, which is all verdigris and ornate wrought-iron decoration. I'm just about to reach for the wipes – old habits – when the server comes to the table armed with the spray and a gleaming white cloth. We watch as he rearranges the condiments and table setting.

'I did – what? Oh.' Niamh looks up after picking up the box, a flush appearing on her neck. 'Oh, thanks,' she says. 'What do I owe you? You didn't have to—'

'Would you like me to hang on to it until Saturday – it's Saturday you have to test, isn't it?'

She grins an embarrassed grin.

'Jaysus, I'm not that bad. No. I'll look after it till then.'

She stuffs it into the backpack that serves as her handbag.

'So,' she says. 'What are you thinking? That was pretty weird, wasn't it? Like, what is going on there?'

I think back to the meeting we just had with Conleth and Gemma. We'd gone down on the pretext of letting them know that the body was going to be released tomorrow, but really it was so that we could ask a few questions about the Skehans – float Carol-Ann and Rob's names out there and see what happened.

'Maybe they'd just had a big fight? I have to say, I think the guy's a complete bastard.'

Niamh takes her hands away from the table to let the server place our plates. 'Thanks, mate,' she says, before tucking in. She eyes mine.

'Big day for you. Can't believe you didn't bring your packed lunch.' She looks at my spinach and ricotta quiche. 'Can't believe you trusted me to order.'

I smile. Time was, there was no way I ate anything I hadn't prepared myself. But—

'People change,' I say, biting into a forkful of flaky pastry and tangy cheese. 'I'm laid-back now.'

'Yeah, right.' She laughs, rolling her eyes. 'But yes, I'm starting to agree about O'Hara. And she is falling apart. I mean, she's worse each time we see her, isn't she?'

Gemma had sat on the sofa beside Conleth, her hands pressed between her knees to stop the trembling. She fought tears the whole time we were there.

'Maybe it's only really hitting her now. Maybe as long as there was no body, she still had hope?'

'Well, yeah.' Niamh nods in sympathy. 'I suppose she never really accepted his death as a real possibility.'

Neither of us speaks.

'But annieway, let's go back to what Conleth was saying about interfering busybody Carol-Ann. Certainly no love lost there, was there?'

'No. And the way he tells it, Rob is a mummy's boy who

never got over not being selected for the team.' I take a sip of my water. Niamh is nodding.

'Exactly! A raging mammy's boy could want revenge? Or Mammy's raging at Max for not being Rob's partner and for ruining the club or the Olympics or whatever, so on the night of the party, she lures him outside and down on to the pontoon, and she takes out her knife—'

'Which she's hidden in her ballgown?' I say drily. We'd seen a photo of a trim and glittery Carol-Ann at the party. 'No room in that dress for a weapon.'

'True – unless she had it in an evening bag. Anyway, never mind that yet. Let's think – she's bitter and jealous. The two boys have teamed up and left her lad out of everything, his big dreams dashed.'

'And you reckon, as outraged mother, she takes matters into her own hands, kills Max and what – pushes him into the harbour? They searched the harbour the very next morning – even weighed down the way he was, they said the body would have been found if it was in there.'

Niamh tilts her head, considering.

'I have it. She kills Max with his own knife! That's it, Laura! The one Gemma gave him – and then hides the body until – until she's able to go out in a dinghy or whatever and dump him in the bay.'

'First off, Gemma said she gave him the knife two days *before* the party – on his actual birthday. And it's just a little sailing knife. So why would he have it with him at his twenty-first? Second: how does she lift him? She's tiny.'

'Fecking wiry, though.'

'Yeah, but he was six foot something and a dead weight. And more importantly, I refer you to my earlier point. Didn't Gemma say he'd probably already lost it – before the party? He was always losing stuff.'

'True,' Niamh says, deflated, dusting crumbs off her shirt with her hands, managing to streak grease marks across her boobs as she does so. I say nothing.

'Okay, let's say it's Rob. He bumps off Max with a different knife, hides the body in the boot of his car. Realizes what he's let himself in for and calls his mam to help. She obliges. He swears her to secrecy and they dump the body, then he fecks off to – where is he working?'

'Limerick.'

'Sorry, yeah, Limerick.'

I think about it. It's part of the job. No matter what Cig says, you have to theorize. Every contact leaves a trace, I think, eyeing the traces of butter across Niamh's chest.

'Well, first off, let's talk to him. Will you call this afternoon?' She nods. 'And second – evidence-wise, what have we got? A stab wound inflicted by a knife which may or may not be similar to the knife that Gemma gave Max for his birthday. We don't even know if you could kill someone with one of those, do we? What does Parminter say?'

'Hasn't got back to me yet. And – but—' Niamh points at the table in front of her. 'First off, you don't need a big knife to kill someone, and then, apparently everyone – half the yacht club – has those knives. So, going back to the bold Carol-Ann, or Rob, they're familiar with how to use the knives and, I don't know, let's say she says to Max that she has something to show him, maybe at her car – yes! She tells him she has something for him in the car, they meet in the car park. She stabs him with her own knife or maybe with Rob's, and then she shoves him in the boot, then, the next day, when everyone is out looking for him, she and Rob drive to Howth or somewhere and dump the body there? Or – or – they hire a boat and dump the body—'

'Maybe,' I say. 'It's a stretch, but maybe it's worth considering.'

'Feck it.' Niamh sighs, sitting back in the seat. 'Cig is right. Too much speculation.'

'It's not a bad theory. And we have one if not two people with motives that we didn't have before. There was certainly no love lost between Carol-Ann and Max.'

'Each crow thinks her own the fairest,' says Niamh. 'That's what my da would say.'

'Enough to kill though?' I'm shaking my head, answering my own question. 'And she's too slight – definitely.'

'Yeah,' agrees Niamh. 'I don't know how they didn't bump *her* off! I mean, she took one hell of a risk doing what she did.'

I think of the scene Carol-Ann had conjured for us in which she starred as a kind of avenging angel, marching into the locker room, confronting the lads and basically telling them to withdraw their application.

'I mean, seriously, what if they'd decided to get rid of her?' says Niamh. 'These are high stakes.'

'She said Max denied it,' I remind her.

'Yes, and he was dead twenty-four hours later,' says Niamh, taking out her phone. She reads a text then looks at me. 'Excellent! Parminter has something for us. I'll pick it up. And I'll make the call to Rob. See you at Corrig Point.'

39

Laura

'Sarge.' Niamh does a little salute as we enter the incident room in Corrig Point station. McCarthy sits up straighter and gives a terse little nod. The crowds have thinned out. There's only four other guards in the room. He sees me noticing.

'An attempted robbery at the Centra last night, and a nuisance complaint in People's Park,' he shrugs. 'Garda Bourke said to give this to you,' he says, passing over a plastic pocket containing some scanned pages. 'He's looked into the original searches done at the time of the disappearance, and basically he says that there's absolutely no way the body was in the harbour. Someone had to have brought him out into the bay and got rid of him there. And he's got copies made of the visitors' book for the night of the party. The comings and goings. He's planning on visiting Emily Nolan, the widow of Gerard, who—'

'Was SIO at the time, yeah, thanks,' interrupts Niamh.

'Great, thanks,' I say, taking the book from him and immediately scanning to see if I find entries for the Skehans.

O'Riordan enters the room like a raincloud.

'Jaysus,' he snaps, to no one in particular. 'What have you got for me then, Shaw? Darmody?'

Niamh gets to her feet.

'We have another possible suspect – Rob Skehan – and/or his mother, Carol-Ann. A bit of a long shot, but there's not much love lost there. I called to speak to him – he's based in

Limerick. Got the secretary. He's away at a medical conference.' Niamh stands by the computer, loading the images. 'So watch this space.'

She clicks to start the photos scrolling on the screen.

'Right, Cig, we know Gemma gave Max a penknife for his birthday, two days before the party. Here, you'll see the Leatherman penknife,' she says. 'Favourite tool used by the sailing community. I googled it and got this.' She clicks to a second image, showing all the parts extended. 'The Leatherman Wave. It has a needle-nose pliers, an electrical crimper, a serrated knife, a spring-action scissors, a diamond-coated file, a large and small bit driver, and here, a rather short but bloody sharp blade.'

I grin. Even hormonal and tired, she's always ahead of the game.

'But, hold on, lads. I sent the image to Parminter and he said, "It is unlikely but not beyond the bounds of probability" that this type of blade could be, you know, the weapon.'

She clicks back to the first picture. 'Even though it's a bit like, hold on, let me file my nails and then I'll stab you, isn't it? Like, it'd hardly be your first choice of weapon. The killer can hardly argue a crime of passion, can he?' She mimes struggling to open the instrument. 'Oh no, that's the bottle opener, sorry. Give me a minute.'

I say nothing. She's right, but at the same time we both know that almost anything can be turned into a weapon.

'Now what's interesting here is that I did another search under *Leatherman knives 2005–2007*. Because some of these are new models.' She thumbs impatiently through more photos of pocket-knives. 'And some that were made in 2006 and 2007 have now been discontinued.'

Finding the image she's been looking for, she does a little nod of satisfaction.

'Look at these. They're hunting knives which were in production with Leatherman around that time – 2005 onwards. There's a couple of series of them: the E series and K series.' She turns the screen so we can see, and we find ourselves looking at an array of gleaming, deadly looking chunks of steel designed to kill.

'See? Any of these bad boys would be capable of doing that damage, wouldn't they?' she says.

'Did you show these to Parminter?' O'Riordan peers at the screen.

'I did. Parminter saw them and said yeh, a knife like that could do it.'

I shiver. 'We're not – you're not saying that half of Corrig Point yacht club are wandering around with one of those in their pockets, for God's sake?'

'No, they're more likely to have the one with the spare champagne cork. I mean, come on.' Then, as if realizing she'd been flippant, her face falls.

'But no, all I'm saying is that we'll need to show these to Gemma – see if she recognizes the model she gave her brother.'

O'Riordan inhales noisily, then blows out a long exhale.

'Get hold of Skehan. Start there. But whatever way you look at this, it's a strong possibility that it's someone from their own club. Many of the sailing community carry these knives. These are people who understand the tides, who would know where to dump a body. We've still got to work that out – how did he end up in the bay?'

'And the Skehans were seen leaving,' says Tara, who had come in while Niamh was speaking. 'We checked the visitors' book and the CCTV from the front of the club. They signed out together – the three of them – at 11.45 p.m. At the same time as another couple, Orla and Ian Williams.'

This earns another growl from O'Riordan. I walk over to the board. In one, the Fitzgerald family stand outside a church — maybe a wedding or a confirmation, as they're smartly dressed and the parents are smiling. Max is maybe sixteen or seventeen, and Gemma a very thin, sad-looking twelve. My eyes track the other photos: grinning lads standing on quaysides or on the decks of boats, Max receiving a trophy, Max and Conleth holding a silver cup aloft, watched by a grim-faced Rob Skehan. Nothing jumps out at me.

'Okay, we know *how*,' I muse. 'But who? Why? And how the hell did they dispose of the body?'

40

Niamh

'Niamh!' Dorothy's voice somehow manages to sound above the noise of the engine before I've switched it off. 'Niamh?' she repeats, breaking my name into two equally posh-sounding syllables – *Nee-Ov.* 'Hellooo? A moment?'

I try not to wince. I mean, I love her to bits and you couldn't ask for a better landlady, but you need to be in the whole of your health for Dorothy.

'Coming,' I reply, getting out of the car and crunching my way across the gravel, my bag slung over my back. Dorothy is leaning over the railing, seemingly determined that I won't be able to sneak unnoticed into my basement apartment. As usual, she's wearing one of her hand-knit jumpers. Today it's tucked into a long multipocketed skirt which is made of a fabric so stiff it looks like it could stand up on its own. Like a tent or something. Her cap of steel-grey hair frames that bird-like beaky face, purpled in places with the evening breeze. I inhale, summoning up a bit of energy.

'Oh hi, Dorothy.' I smile. 'I was in another world. Didn't see you—'

She holds up a hand, bruised and blackened with blood spots from either gardening or baking, both of which she performs with her trademark vigorous clumsiness.

'Oh my goodness, don't finish that sentence!' she hoots. 'You were hoping to sneak in and have a rest. I know that for a fact.'

She pats my shoulder when I draw level with her, looking closely at me. 'And I won't keep you. You look exhausted. I just thought you should meet Sarita.'

She steers me by the elbow into the large hallway, where a young woman dressed in a business casual vibe at odds with her youth and a sleek bob of dark hair is standing by the hall table arranging pages in a folder.

'Hi, Sarita,' I say, wondering why Dorothy hasn't let go of my elbow yet. Wondering why she's pinching me.

'It's fortuitous that you should arrive right now,' continues Dorothy, 'because I was just assuring Sarita that I *do* have someone to call on, you know, in case I should fall or collapse, hah hah.'

I play along. Ever since she fell and broke a bone in her ankle last autumn, which required hospitalization, Dorothy has been attending the falls clinic in St Olaf's, something she has been none too happy about as it cuts into her gardening/ baking/prison-visiting time.

Sarita smiles, opening her mouth to speak, but Dorothy is in full flow.

'Sarita is my wonderful OT from the falls clinic, you remember? I was just showing her the modifications and safety measures I've been making.' Dorothy points to the folders. 'I hope you noted everything, my dear? I had a rather sweaty man working here for almost a week, installing handrails to grab on to, seats to sit on, ramps to traverse and suchlike.'

She smiles, revealing ancient and gleaming teeth. 'I'd hate for his efforts to go unnoticed.'

'Hi,' says Sarita, reaching to shake hands with me. But as she does so, the strap of her leather briefcase slips from her shoulder on to her elbow, jerking her hand forward to knock against the edge of the marble-topped console table. There's an audible cracking sound. Sarita gasps.

'Ooow!' I flinch on her behalf. 'That sounded sore! Are you okay?'

'I'm fine – it's nothing,' she says, rubbing the side of her hand. 'Sorry, I was just leaving anyway. I'm—'

And suddenly, her face drains of blood and takes on a yellowish-grey tinge and tiny beads of sweat appear above her dark brows. Her knees crumple like an accordion.

'Whoa!' Dorothy and I both lurch forward to grab hold of her, managing to stop her hitting the floor at speed. Between us we half drag, half carry her to the bottom step of the staircase, by which time she's come back to consciousness. I sit beside her on the step, holding her upright. Dorothy regards us both, leaning against the carved newel post.

'Oh my God, I'm so sorry,' she says. 'That's mortifying. I almost fainted. Really, I—'

'You did faint,' Dorothy says, matter-of-factly. 'Actually. So, you're going nowhere until you have a strong cup of tea and something to eat.' She nods at me. 'Bring Sarita into the living room, please, Niamh. I'll be back in a moment.'

'Oh God, there's no need.'

'Save your breath to cool your porridge.' I laugh. 'There's no arguing with her.' I motion for Sarita to stay put for a moment as I collect up her briefcase and the papers which fell. Shit! The pregnancy test is right bang in the middle of the hall rug. I dropped my rucksack in all the kerfuffle and it must have slipped out. I stuff it back in and close the zip with my back to her, then I turn and extend a hand.

'We'll go inside,' I say. 'Are you okay to stand?'

Half an hour later, fortified by Dorothy's builder-strength tea and flapjacks that could double up as the foundations of a detached house, Sarita is about to be sent on her merry way. Dorothy can barely contain her delight.

'So you've absolutely no need to be concerned for my welfare,' she trills, patting Sarita's shoulder. 'Niamh is always on hand and—'

'And you'll consider a panic button as well?' interrupts Sarita, grasping at straws. 'For when Niamh is working?'

'Oh yes, I will, of course,' says Dorothy. 'I'll get on to that immediately. One can't be too careful. Anyone could have a fainting spell. Not just the octogenarians.'

She pauses. It seems an innocent comment. Sarita and I make eye contact. She thinks we're laughing at her.

'Mind the hand,' I say, nodding at where she's still kind of cradling it in the other. She lets go, shaking her head.

'Oh, it's nothing. Honestly. Thanks so much for the tea and the biscuits, Mrs – I mean, Dorothy.'

'My pleasure,' says Dorothy, opening the hall door. 'See you again when you next need to check up on me, hah. And maybe check your iron levels?'

Dorothy nods, and I take the hint, following Sarita down the steps.

'Are you on foot? I can give you a lift?' I begin taking my keys out of my pocket. She's a tiny scrap of a thing, now that I see her upright and outdoors. Somehow she looked more substantial clutching her folders inside. Patches of dappled light from the tall beech trees dance across her shiny dark hair, shift over her smooth cheek. God, she's pretty.

'Oh, not at all. Thanks, Niamh. I'll get the Luas,' she says, lifting the strap of her briefcase so it's across the body rather than the shoulder this time. The bag is way too big for her. I tilt my head towards it.

'Are you sure? Mind yourself now,' I say, then I wince. What class of an eejit says that? What am I – her granny?

'Thanks, Niamh, I will.'

I like how my name sounds when she says it.

Back in the house, Dorothy can't hide her grin.

'So did you slip tranquillizers into her or what?' I say, following her to the kitchen with the empty cups. 'Lucky I came back when I did.'

She takes the cups from me, putting them into the small plastic basin in the sink. Dorothy doesn't use a dishwasher. She'll wash the dishes by hand each evening, in about four centimetres of hot water.

'Oh, for goodness' sake! You shouldn't joke about things like that – you of all people!' she scolds, wiping the tray and tucking it against the bread bin. 'I didn't do anything wrong – I was eminently cooperative.' She's nodding. 'Even though I told them there was no need and that I'd complied with all the recommendations. But they insisted on sending her out. Well.' She tosses her head. 'Ridiculous. This is what annoys me so much about ageing – not the ageing itself, rather people's expectations. Just because I've passed a certain number of years on the planet, I'm expected to tolerate – even welcome – the interference of do-gooders—'

'It's her job.' I tilt my head, lips pursed. 'And you did have a fall.'

'Heavens above!' she tsks. 'Fine. I fell. I did not *have a* fall. And you're right, she's a lovely girl.'

The word sounds like 'gahl'.

'She is—' I start to say, thinking of the look we'd exchanged, like conspirators. Allies.

'And she was most relieved to hear that you've – ah – moved upstairs,' she says quietly, turning to look out the window into the back garden. 'To keep me company.'

'I see,' I say, prolonging the 'ee' sound. 'When did that happen? When did I move in?'

She has the decency to look embarrassed.

'Well, it has to happen this evening – now,' she says, 'so

that I haven't fabricated any falsehoods. The bed is made up and I've cleared all the cupboards. I'll be in there.' She points to what used to be called the breakfast room. I walk over and peer inside. The oak table has been cleared away and a large hospital-type bed now dominates the room.

'They insisted,' she says. 'Though I'm perfectly able to get in and out of bed and to manage the stairs.' *Stahrs.*

'Fair enough,' I say. 'I'll go get my stuff. We'd better keep Sarita happy.'

I like to think of her happy.

41

Laura

'Are you tired, Mummy?' Noah's tone is uncertain. It's seven thirty and Alva has him already in the pjs. I muster a smile. I've just come in. I insisted that Niamh left early – it seemed the least I could do. She looked shattered.

'Hang on, pet,' I say, my hand going to my hip. I need to put the Sig in the gun safe. 'I just need to do something, then we'll have a snuggle. Where's Katie? Where's Dad?'

'Dad is on a run. Katie's upstairs with Alva cos she's crying.' I pause.

'Why is Katie crying?'

'Not Katie. Alva. She's making Alva better. She drawed a picture to make her better.'

'Oh.' I hurry into the hall and lock the gun away, coming back to take Noah's hand.

'Poor Alva. Come on, we'll go upstairs and help Katie.'

'Yes,' he says, stoutly. 'I can tell jokes.' He looks up at me. That's his latest thing. My youngest – always trying to find something his sister hasn't already done better, faster, earlier. It was magic tricks last month. Just for a second, I think of Gemma, only emerging from Max's shadow after his death.

'Can't I, Mummy?'

'You sure can.'

'An' if you're cranky, I can tell you jokes too,' he continues, letting go of my hand to hold on to the rail of the narrow attic staircase.

'I'm never cranky,' I say, stung. He turns, holding the banister with both hands and looking at me in surprise.

'You are, Muma. But it's not your fault. Daddy says it's work – hiya!'

Spotting Alva and Katie, his tone changes to a shriek and he bounds into the room. They're snuggled under the duvet looking at a photo album. Alva's eyes are red-rimmed from crying and Katie is like a miniature therapist, complete with professional smile. She's working hard, but cracks when Noah leaps on to the bed and starts burrowing under the covers too. A feeling too complicated to unpack in the instant takes hold of me. I'm angry and sad and sorry for Alva and profoundly, disgustingly – jealous, I realize. And then I catch myself with a lurch, as I consider the possibility that her dad – our dad – may have died and she had no one to—

'Oh! Hi' – Alva hiccups – 'I'm sorry for—'

'What happened?'

'Alva says I can sleep here tonight,' announces Katie, in triumph. She's been asking for ages, and I always say no.

'We'll have to see—' I begin, before being interrupted by a wail from Noah.

'That's not fair! I want to sleep in Alva's bed too!'

They start shouting over each other and it occurs to me, not for the first time, that Niamh's whistle from GAA refereeing might be a useful parenting tool. I hold up both hands.

'Sssh! Indoor voices!' Nothing. I clap my hands. Nothing. 'Quiet!' I yell.

'You *are* cranky,' sobs Noah, bursting into tears.

I remember a tip from Niamh with the coaching: Tell them what's going to happen, then make it happen.

'Now, you two are going to be quiet and let me talk to Alva for five minutes on our own. On. Our. Own. And if – if – you're really quiet and if Alva says it's okay, you can sleep in here on the air mattress.'

I look at Alva. '*If* Alva would like some company. But she's not going to want fighting children for company, is she?'

Noah shakes his head. Katie is holding her finger to her lips. There's complete silence. How they adore her.

'So you're going to creep downstairs like mice, and brush your teeth—'

'I've already—' begins Noah. Katie shushes him. She takes hold of his hand. 'And if you've already brushed your teeth, then you go to the bathroom and wash your hands and get your teddies and you can creep back up again, but only if Alva says so.'

They scurry out of the room.

'Sorry—' Alva starts.

'Don't be ridiculous.' I sit on the end of the bed. 'Is – did something happen with—' I can't utter the word.

She shakes her head, and the feeling of relief that surges through me is astonishing. I don't speak to him. I haven't spoken to him or allowed him in my life since he walked out over thirty years ago. But I'm not ready for him to die.

'No,' she's saying, 'but we spoke to the palliative care team, and it – it won't be long. He' – she looks at me, but it's like she's looking through me – 'he's trying – he wants to write letters to us, you know, to say goodbye, and I – I just don't know if I'm strong enough to – he needs someone to write them, you see. He's too weak.'

She blows her nose and takes a deep breath. From the hall-way outside, we hear stage whispers of intense cooperation.

'Let's bring two teddies each,' hisses Katie. 'One for us and one for Alva.'

'Yes,' Noah hisses back. 'Then she has two, and it isn't fair but it's okay because she's sad.'

Our eyes meet, and I feel the jealousy fall away.

'He really, really wants to see you,' she whispers. 'I'm sorry. He made me promise to tell you that.'

I don't have a sister. Niamh is the closest friend I've ever known, and she's sister, brother and sometimes mother to me. With Alva, I've been paying lip service to the whole idea of family, I realize. I've let her live with us, but I've never really accepted her. She's never moved beyond the polite layer. Niamh's right. I'm closed off.

Alva is my little sister. Can I do this for her? Even if I can't do it for him?

'I – I—' I'm struggling to find the words, and then my work phone buzzes.

'I have to take this.' I point at the phone, stepping out of the room. 'I'm sorry.'

Katie and Noah take this as the green light, and they barrel past me and start clambering on to Alva's lap. As I go to close the door I pause to look at the image, framed in a narrow rectangle by the doorjamb. Alva's tears are gone and she's the centre of a triptych flanked by my children, who look up at her adoringly. I don't know what I think about that.

'Shaw? Can you hear me okay?'

'Yes, Laura Shaw here. Sorry about that. Who—'

'No worries. Yeah, it's Stephen Bourke from Corrig Point station. Look, sorry, you're probably gone home, but I wanted to tell you that Rob Skehan called back – he'll be in Dublin at the weekend and is going to come in to talk to us. He was sound – very helpful.'

My phone pings, and I move it away from my ear to look at it.

'He sent this. Have you got it?'

'I have,' I say, frowning at the image. At first glance, it's a photo of the Skehans, Carol-Ann and the husband – Petey, I think she said he was called. They're shiny and flushed – perhaps both a little worse for wear. His arm is around her shoulders and he's squeezing her against him. She has tilted her head towards his shoulder in a girlish gesture and she's smiling – but it's a kind of desperate grimace. And something is happening behind them – your eye is drawn past the smiling pair to a drama playing out in the background.

'What do you make of that?'

I zoom in as much as I can to the two faces in profile behind the Skehans. It's Max Fitzgerald and Conleth. They're squaring up to each other. Conleth is the taller man by a couple of inches and he's glaring at his friend, the strong jaw jutting forwards, shoulders set and elbows flexed as though ready to throw a punch. I can just make out the knuckles of a clenched fist behind the outline of Carol-Ann's hip.

'Well now, that's something to think about,' I say, shifting the zoom across to study Max. 'A new angle, what do you reckon?'

'You betcha,' says Stephen. He waits, and I check out Max. He too has a stubborn line to his mouth, but Max's body language is different. Both his hands are in front of his body, palms and fingers facing upwards. He's frowning, mouth slightly open, as if the camera caught him saying something. What could it be?

'Thanks for this.' I click out of the photo, hearing the front door close downstairs. There's no point in doing anything now. 'Will I meet you—'

'Yeah, great,' he interrupts. 'We'll talk in the morning. And I'll show you – I got Nolan's notes. A whole box of them. All his notebooks too. We can go through them tomorrow.'

'Thanks, Stephen,' I say, coming down the stairs into the hallway as I end the call.

Matt stands at the bottom step looking up at me – and both the aspect and the blue eyes seeking mine emphasize the similarities between him and his three-year-old son. He's flushed from his run and his hair is wet. It's not raining. He just always pours the remainder of his water over his head as he finishes his run.

'Steeephen,' he says, batting his eyelashes. 'Sergeant Stephen from the yacht club gardaí – should I be worried?'

I try not to grin, but one escapes anyway. He reaches up and grabs me into a hug.

'Ew, gross! Sweat!' I say, though a tiny thrill shivers through me at the sudden contact – and the smell of my husband's sweat. Like Niamh says, hormones are bastards. I'm too busy. On cue, I hear a wail from upstairs, and I turn, preparing to go back up. Matt sweeps his hand down the small of my back to cup my buttock. He gives a playful squeeze.

'I'll sort it,' he says. 'You're in no fit state to deal with children.'

42

Gemma

Conleth is in a good mood – the best I've seen him in for a long time. He taps a small amount of white powder from the bag on to the marble surround of the bathroom sink.

'This will get right up the nose of poor old ENT Rob,' he grins, bending to snort the first line. 'In a manner of speaking.'

He straightens up, pressing his thumb against one nostril, watching himself, watching me in the mirror. I lean forward to release the bathwater, bracing myself for his cold, appraising stare, for a cutting comment. I'd hoped to finish before he got back, but I wasn't fast enough. I'm not allowed to lock the door.

Avoiding his eyes, I step out of the bath and reach for the towel on the rail. Conleth pulls it so it drops to the floor, and he laughs. At this point, he's still having fun. It's a game. I have to bend – shivering – to pick it up. Conleth smiles with satisfaction and does another line. He quotes statistics about the number of killings having doubled or something since 2021 and all the while his eyes stay on me in the mirror and the smirk stays on his mouth. He knows I want privacy. We both know I can't have it. There is nowhere he won't spy on me. There's nothing he won't watch. I'm his property and his plaything.

He thumbs his nostrils together, then brushes the last traces of white powder off his upper lip, watching me.

'You're getting flabby,' he says, while I struggle to cover myself with the towel. 'Which is quite an achievement. How does someone with no muscle tone whatsoever manage to look both too fat and too thin?'

I don't answer. That's not a question I'm meant to answer. I wait, clutching the fabric against my chest, breathing in the scent of fabric softener. Trying to concentrate on that.

'Have you been doing the sit-ups? You haven't, have you?'

'I—'

'I went to the trouble of writing you your own personal schedule, didn't I?' he says, taking up his phone. 'Wait. Let me see,' he goes on, moving his thumb across the screen, searching for—

'Here,' he says, turning the phone so I can see the photograph. It's me, standing on this same spot a few months ago. Naked. 'This was meant to be the Before shot, Gemm–a.' He emphasizes the syllables of my name slowly as his smile stretches.

I remain shivering on the bathmat, my toes whitening as they clench the soft fabric. As if the action of touching something soft can calm me. Why don't I just walk away? I could just—

'But it's not like we got to where we were going, is it?'

Exaggerated head movements as he looks from the screen back to me, back to the screen.

'Saggy and baggy,' he says, with a weary regret in his voice. 'Then and now. Even though I wrote out a whole programme for you. Ten minutes twice a day, that's all it would have taken you – but oh no. You're too lazy for that. I don't know why I bother.'

'Conleth, I did – I do – I've been walking, and I—'

He holds up a hand.

'Don't bother.' He sighs. 'You're just going to lie and go

for sympathy and tell me that it's loose skin after pregnancy and you're so busy with the child and the job and blah blah blah. Excuse after excuse. It's important for your career, Gemma. This is not me being cruel or unkind. I'm thinking of your career.'

He glances at himself in the mirror once more, and the sight seems to perk him up. He's wired. I reach to get my silk kimono, which is, thank Christ, hanging by the door. Without meeting his eyes, I tie it around myself and step towards him.

I think I can salvage this. He bought me this. He loves the silk.

'I'm sorry,' I whisper, leaning against him. 'I'll try harder.' A beat. Then he pockets his phone and begins sweeping his hands over the smoothness of the fabric.

'You'd better,' he says. 'Show me.'

Afterwards, I lie awake, remembering. Thinking about Ferdia – about giving over my body to my baby and giving it to a man – to my husband. How different it is – but how both can take what they want unless – yeah. Unless I can find a way not to let him. With Ferdia, the pregnancy ended before I was ready – before he was ready. And I know it sounds crazy, but I wish I could have had more time sharing my body with my baby. That was a takeover I wholeheartedly welcomed. When our hearts beat together. When he was safe. But Ferdia was born ten weeks early. And when I saw his little body in the neonatal ICU, strips of narrow tape holding naso-gastric tubes in place, monitors attached to his blue-veined taut flesh, huge eyes taped closed against the heated lamp – like an incubator chick – I vowed I would do anything for him. Anything. I will tolerate all of this – all of it, it's nothing – if his life is spared. Putting up with Conleth is part of it.

I thought I'd lost him. We were hosting a MaxSpirit dinner dance at the club – Conleth reckoned we'd easily pull in over €150,000 if it all went to plan. Tickets were €250 a head, but that hadn't put anyone off. We'd been turning people away for a month. Someone had spread the rumour that Bono was going to be there – it was only a rumour, but let's say Conleth was happy to spread it.

I was exhausted. I was just over seven months pregnant and, even though my bump was small – way smaller than normal – I felt like someone had attached lead weights to my body. My hands and feet were swollen, my face puffy. Conleth had told me to wear the champagne sequinned dress – my least favourite of all the ones he'd got in. It was full length and fully lined with a gathered knot at the bust, long chiffon sleeves – the pale pink satin was completely covered in silver sequins. Like someone's idea of a pregnant princess.

'Megan wore one of hers,' he'd said, 'so I don't want to hear any whingeing.' That figured. It was so heavy, like wearing chainmail, but I was glad of the sleeves to hide the bruising. Pregnancy hadn't granted me immunity. In fact, the sight of my growing belly seemed to enrage him further. Like I was beyond his control.

And so I stood beside him in the foyer of the club greeting people as they arrived, ignoring the throb of my swollen feet and the nausea and the dull, deep backache. My hands pulsed too, the fingers so swollen that none of my rings fit – ugly and red.

'Put one hand around my waist for the photos,' Conleth had said. 'And hide the other in the dress.' His nose and cheeks pinched together, like he smelled something bad. 'They look gross.'

We were at the top table with Rick and Xandra – the music producer and singer he was most hoping to impress. During the meal, he drank steadily and fielded questions like the pro he was. It was all jokes about how he'd have to hang up his lifejacket once the baby arrived, though he hadn't done any real sailing in over a year. I felt dreadful. Waves of pain rolled across my lower back, and I'd a terrible feeling of pressure in my groin. I felt like I needed to pee, though I'd barely drunk anything.

'I'll be back in a minute,' I whispered into his ear, longing for the cool of the bathroom, fantasizing about taking off my shoes even for a couple of minutes. Under the table he grabbed my knee and squeezed so hard I almost gasped out loud.

'Wait,' he hissed through gritted teeth. 'After the speeches.'

The commodore of the yacht club spoke. Rick spoke. There was a raffle, where the prize was a trip to the Canaries. And sweat rolled down my back and between my buttocks and countless times I thought I'd just get up. Just stand up and smile and apologize and leave the room. But I couldn't do it. A spasm rolled through me, and I felt a wetness in my groin and I wondered if I'd – could I have actually lost control of my bladder? And just when I thought I would pass out, Conleth stood up.

In his speech – hilarious and charming, naturally – he thanked me for leading him over the rapids of family life. He said I was the captain of the family ship, the lighthouse in the dark and the glimmer of bright hope after Max disappeared.

There were cheers and tears for that one.

And then I staggered to my feet, hoping to get to the bathroom. The last thing I saw before I blacked out was the drenched seat of the chair. My waters had broken.

There are nanny-cams all over the house – hidden, not hidden, it doesn't matter. I don't know where he watches those – in the office, I suppose. And then the other stuff, like this – the Before and After photos, the punishments, when he makes me clean things and fetch things on my hands and knees, he films that too, saves it all up on a memory card. And then he sits on the sofa and watches, a towel across his lap. Sometimes he makes me sit through them too.

I long to escape. And I know I never will. On Friday, we will turn my brother to ash, and the guards will lose interest and even Penny will tire of me and my lies. And Ferdia will never be what his father wants him to be and that will be my fault too.

I could creep into Ferdia's room now and I could end this pain for both of us. He cried himself to sleep – huge sobs that tore jagged strips off my heart because I couldn't go to him. Conleth found him in bed with the new digger tucked in beside him, under the duvet. He snatched the toy out of Ferdia's hands and jammed it on top of the wardrobe. There was scolding and laughter. He laughed when he told me, but his eyes contained a warning.

I could go into Ferdia's room now and bring him the digger. I'd get into bed beside him and we'd snuggle together and then quickly, I could do it, when he's asleep, I will get the pillow and hold it tight, tight over his face. And it will be quick.

And then I will end my life – I just need to find a way to do that quickly. Finally and with no room for error.

Thursday

43

Gemma

I wake before six, lying painfully on my right hip, a shaft of sunlight filling my palm like a promise. For a few moments I just stare at it, feeling the warmth – a kind warmth – enjoying the image. It would make a beautiful photograph. I lift my gaze to follow the trajectory of the beam. It's a bright morning. The kind of morning I would enjoy posting about – simple pleasures, a beautiful view, a bright flower, light reflected on water. I get so many likes just for those types of things. My followers are interested in more than just stuff.

And it feels good to still be able to notice beauty. Even now, I see these things. I've always noticed them. There was a time, before Max's death, before Conleth – I suppose it was before I became who I am – a time when there was a possibility of a different future. The only subject I liked in school was art; it was the only time I was completely engaged. I remember we had a student teacher – well, a young teacher, I suppose: she can't have been a student because we had her for our Junior Cert year. She was called Ms Green – and we used to tease her about being named after a colour. We teased her, but kindly, because we all loved her. She let us play music while we worked. She even hummed along. The art room was a place of refuge and she let us hang out there for hours after school, working on our Junior Cert projects. She encouraged me, praised my work. I remember when Mum came home from the parent–teacher meeting; it was one of the first times I can ever remember her being proud of me.

'Well, that's something to aim for, isn't it? Art college? Your teacher says you'd have no problem getting a place.'

She'd stepped towards me and opened her arms ready for a hug. And I know now – now that I'm a mother, I understand what she was trying to do. To close that gap. We both felt it. A chasm had opened up between us, filled with secrets. All the stuff I couldn't tell her – the things that were happening with Conleth, which I believed were my fault just as much as his, and my old resentments – the strain of being Max's imperfect sister. The food restrictions. The self-harm. And behind it – always – Conleth.

Now, I feel the strength of the bond between me and Ferd – and it's like he's still a part of me, almost as much as when he was in my womb. He clambers over me, clings to me, sits on my lap and snuggles into me. The bond is still there, but already it's under attack.

Stop babying him. Don't encourage him. Put him down.

I think of Eli and Jude, Penny's boys, and I don't think I've seen them sit still for more than a second. Have I seen her carry them or sit with them on her lap? They're always bombing around the place on scooters or clambering up walls. Maybe Conleth's right. Another thing I've messed up. Already.

The thought of Penny gives me strength. I'd told her that I wouldn't make the swim this morning – but now I want to do it. I know she'll be there. I'll bring my phone and do some posts – he was saying I need to do more. And he needn't know about the swim – anyway, it's like a valve with him. For a few hours afterwards, something has been released. The beast has been fed.

I draw my knees up carefully, so as not to wake him, and

sit cross-legged, the sunbeam cupped in my hand. Maybe I – maybe there's another way.

The familiar trepidation – Penny says just call it excitement, but it's not, it's a kind of dread – takes hold of me as I approach the steps. Penny is already in the water, a small distance away from a group of swimmers. More are clustered around piles of clothes and towels at varying stages of getting dressed or undressed. It's unbelievably perfect – chips of fractured light are scattered across the moving blue water. The sun has already climbed high above the old stone of the Martello tower on my left and the path sweeps down into the little bay. A line of Prussian blue marks the horizon and, above it, that clear Virgin Mary blue of an Irish summer sky. I take some live footage, and a few shots of the new flats I'm wearing – and one of my sunglasses. I'm supposed to be launching my own brand in June. They're in production.

I sit on a pile of warm, smooth stones taking photos: the edge of a bright red spade half buried in pink-tinged seaweed, the meeting point of sea and slipway, a zoomed-in shot of one of the square hollows in the tower, the bobbing bright bodies of swimmers.

'Gemma!' Penny spots me and begins swimming, then wading, ashore. 'I didn't think you were coming! I'd have waited.'

She draws level with me, water trickling from her sodden curls on to the tight tanned skin of her chest and arms. She grabs my shoulders with both hands – freezing hands.

'Come on! You're getting in, right?' She nods and steps back, clearly waiting for me to get ready. 'Today's the day. We'll swim to the buoy and back.'

There's no arguing with her and, anyway, this is why I came. And I realize now, I don't care and I'm not scared.

I want this — the shock of the cold water and the way it squeezes the air from your lungs and the thoughts from your brain simultaneously. I want the freezing crash of a wave over my face and the chill it brings. A line from a poem we did in school comes into my head, surprising me, because I don't remember learning it and I don't remember who wrote it. I think it was religious, and for that reason I would have discounted it. But it must have stayed with me. *Batter my heart*, that's how it began, and there was a line about *break, blow, burn and make me new.*

I shrug off my coat and track bottoms and I kick off the shoes. Penny is looking at me curiously.

'Okay. You're on.'

I see her check out the bruises on my knees, then the one on my forehead. She presses her lips into a line. And before she can say anything, I start running, half stumbling on the sharp stones, towards the ocean.

Break, blow, burn and make me new. Or kill me. I don't care.

'Brilliant!' screams Penny. 'Keep going!'

A shiver rips through my body as I plunge into the water, waves breaking over my knees and splashing my stomach. I keep running, the water now above my waist, then my chest and then — whoosh — I'm in. I thrust face in and down, feeling the chill grab my neck and shoulders. My legs float upwards, and I'm moving my arms in big circular sweeps and from somewhere behind me, Penny is squealing.

'That's it! That's it!'

She draws alongside me, her face split by a grin, treading water. She points out to sea.

'Come on, it's not far.'

And it's not far, but to get there we have to swim out of the clear sandy shallows and over a massive bed of seaweed.

And it's too late to change my mind – I know that if I stop moving, I sink. I don't want to look down. I don't want to think of what's underneath. My courage wasn't courage – it was a kind of madness. And so I follow Penny's bobbing head in desperation, my arms lurching and splashing from side to side in an ugly front-crawl stroke, trying to stop my legs and bare feet touching the hideous black plants.

My mind whirls, memories surging to the surface like air bubbles from the bladderwrack. The slither of brown weeds tangles my legs and I'm trying not to scream. Because the memory surfaces.

I was seven or eight. We were – I don't know where Mum was. Max and Conleth were there and we were at some beach and Max was doing something with the kayak. They had an inflatable kayak, that's it. And Max was getting it ready. I was in the water, sitting up to my waist in a deep rock pool. It was before the real fear began. And I remember my togs – God! I loved them. It was a set – top and bottoms in a pink and orange shiny fabric – like fish scales. Conleth calls me over to look at something. He's at the far side, hidden by a big outcrop of barnacled rock, and I can just see his face. He's grinning. I go over, intrigued. Usually, he never bothers with me. Nor does Max. They're always too busy.

The water is deeper, but I can still stand – just about. I reach him, out of sight of Max, of the people on the shore.

'Look,' he says, nodding at where he's pointing at a red anemone. 'You can only do it a bit before they realize. It thinks I'm food.'

I watch as he pokes his finger into the centre of the tiny red tentacles. They clasp on to his finger as one.

'Does it hurt?'

'Of course not. You can do it.' He pulls his hand back and

241

the sea anemone shrinks into a blob of red. I wonder if it's angry.

'Wait. I can't.'

'Don't be a baby,' he says. 'Here, I'll help you.' And he grabs me so I'm standing in front of him, held in place by one arm around my waist, him holding my right arm in his other hand.

'Put out your finger,' he says. 'Do it. Go on.'

I extend my finger, my hand clasped inside his, and he pulls it closer, closer to the sea anemone, whose tentacles have extended once more. And I don't want to hurt it. I don't want to disappoint this creature, expecting food. But Conleth's grip is strong and, anyway, something else is happening.

Even as my finger touches the soft redness of the anemone, Conleth's left hand snakes down and down, across the front of my sparkly togs, and his finger pushes underneath the seam of the bikini bottom and down – a sea creature looking for somewhere dark to hide. And when I wriggle and try to pull away, he pulls me back and down under the water, into the strands of seaweed, and he holds me there. Not for long. But for ever. And inside my head is roaring, screaming, rushing – water and bubbles and weeds.

'Oopsy!' he says, lifting me out. 'Mind out.'

And I'm thrashing in the water, panicked. I'm going under. Penny is calling my name and I feel her strong arm around my ribs and she's hauling me up and up.

'This way,' she gasps, trying to keep me upright, treading water. She turns her head, then looks back to me. She's panting. 'Trust your body to float, Gem,' she says, and I feel her hand underneath my shoulders, pushing me upwards. 'Let your head tilt back – go on. Trust the water to hold you up. Keep calm. Follow me.'

44

Niamh

Cig is hunched over, looking at his phone. I don't think he heard me coming in. I clear my throat and he bolts upright, slamming the phone face down on the desk.

'Ever hear of knocking, Darmody?' he blusters, his face blotchy, eyes red-rimmed. Holy Christ! Is Cig *crying*?

'Sorry, Cig. I—' I want to tell him that I did knock, but yeah – the sight of him would discourage any disagreement. 'Is – is everything okay?' I look towards the chair in the corner, half expecting to see Laura there. Did he only summon me?

'Okay?' He makes the word sound ridiculous. I say nothing. 'Okay? No, everything is not okay, Darmody.'

I'm tempted to sit down, bone-weary after a poor night's sleep in the narrow creaky metal bed which Dorothy has slept in for the best part of eighty years. And me wondering at every twinge if it was a sign.

'I'll be getting a new bed delivered,' I'd told her this morning as she scraped the burnt bits off her toast into the sink. I would have brought her breakfast in bed, but she was up and dressed and burning her toast as usual by six thirty.

'Really?' she'd said, like it was an outrageous extravagance. Before she could tell me how perfectly good the bed was, I leapt in.

'Did you buy that off the monks in Glenstal or something? Jaysus, it was like sleeping on a steel cable.'

At least I can get a bit of cooperation from her now, a few

luxuries for herself. Or I'll threaten to call Sarita. The thought bolsters me. Distracts me from the waiting – always with IVF it's a game of patience and resilience more than anything else. You need to develop a talent for waiting. And the courage to hope.

'Are you listening, Darmody?' Cig's voice cuts through the image that's playing on a loop in my brain. I'm picturing the test kit, the longed-for line in the little plastic window.

'Sorry, Cig. Yep, I'm listening.'

'Really?' he says, in a sarcastic tone. God, I hate when he's like this. What the hell is wrong with him? 'I was on to that fisherman boyo – O'Riordan, asking him what's taking ye all so long? Ye know we're fecking short-staffed here, I says to him. You think crime stops in Seskin West because you're busy in Dún Laoghaire?'

I shake my head. Then nod. Not sure which is better.

'No – I mean, yeah, I know – he knows you're under pressure here. It's—' I start to tell him about the waiting game, but he holds up a leathery red palm to stop me.

'Bollocks to that.' He moves to look at one of the photos behind his desk, one of those black-and-white family portraits that people get done for big birthdays. Cig, Linda and Leonie are all in white T-shirts and faded jeans, Linda and Leonie barefoot, playing with the dog – Ziggy, I think its name is – and Cig stands behind the three of them with, thanks be to Christ, his runners on. I don't even want to imagine what a barefoot Cig would look like.

Absent-mindedly, Cig adjusts the frame, his fingers resting on it for longer than necessary.

'Never mind the yachting yahoos, I said to him. It's a cold case. And you've feck-all evidence. Isn't that right?'

He carries on without waiting for my reply. 'Which means you might have to accept that you'll never work out the truth.

So' – he turns to look at me, his face pained – 'I told O'Riordan that ye can have twenty-four more hours at this lark – at the detective frigging yacht club malarkey, but if nothing's doing, you're both back here whip-smart. After the funeral.'

'Right, Cig. Gotcha.' A part of me is relieved. We're on a losing streak. We're going round in circles, and it's too long ago, and he's right, there's the small matter that we have no evidence. And while I don't want to be mollycoddling myself – I promised myself that I would go after this baby with all that I had, but I wasn't going to wrap myself in cotton wool in the process – but still and all, it wouldn't hurt to be based here for the next few weeks. A couple of easy cases. Job satisfaction.

'And, Darmody' – he sits back down, a long sigh escaping him like air leaving a balloon – 'what was the point of doing your sergeant exam if you're doing nada about it?' He waits. 'Are you taking it further? You know you – you know it only lasts five—'

'Five years, I know. Thanks, Cig,' I stammer, worried he'll murder me for cutting him off. 'I – I'm still, you know – thinking. You see—'

There's a knock on the door before I can answer – thank Christ. I open it and stand back, because a plate of brownies – brownies? – is coming through first. The hands holding the plate belong to Sarge – Declan.

'How're you, Darmody?' he says, flushing.

'Did I miss – is there, like, a special occasion?' I'm too mystified to answer Dec. He strides past me, head down, and places the plate on Cig's desk, like some class of high priest at an Egyptian temple.

'Thought these might go down well – at home,' he says shyly, scuttling back towards the door. Passing me, he turns his head like a swimmer, mouths something I can't work out.

245

'Ah, Jaysus!' says Cig, looking like he might be about to cry again. 'You're too good. Thanks.'

'I'll leave you to it,' I say, seizing the opportunity to get out. In the corridor, I grab Declan's sleeve.

'What the hell? Did I miss something?'

'His dog died.'

'Ziggy?' I say. 'Ah, that's—'

'Siggy – as in Sig Sauer,' he corrects me. 'He was fifteen.'

I shake my head, not sure what's making me sadder. The fact that the dog is dead, or the fact that, all this time, I'd got its name wrong. Cig had called his dog after one of the most popular Garda guns and I hadn't realized it. Or the fact that it took desk sarge Declan to step up with a random act of kindness.

I can't work this job out, sometimes. I fecking can't.

45

Laura

Stephen hands me the coffee and I smile my thanks. *The cup is clean, Laura. They're stored in long tubes wrapped in plastic. Nobody touches inside the cup.* I do the tapping sequence, or the start of it, as Jackie taught me.

'Flat white, right?' He waits for me to sit before pulling a chair over for himself and sitting down. Nice manners, Detective Bourke. I find myself wondering if it's Mammy Bourke or Daddy Bourke we've to thank for the charm. I shake my head as if that'll stop the irrelevant thoughts. We're in Corrig Point in the incident room. No sign of Senan this morning.

'Right, thanks,' I say, lifting the lid and checking. A small compulsion that I regret as soon as I give in to it. He grins.

'Do you not trust me?'

'Something like that.' I smile back. 'Not used to this posh Southside coffee.'

'Haha! I know! If someone told teenage me that I'd be asking for a freaking low-fat oatmilk matcha latte—' He breaks off, shaking his head. Then he shrugs. 'But it tastes great.' He opens the file and starts spreading pages out.

'So look, there's a couple of things going on here.' He passes me the photo of Conleth and Max head to head, glaring at each other. 'There's this – the photo – and then this.' He opens a dog-eared folder in which lie pages of blue-biroed notes in a sprawling cursive script that I don't recognize.

'What's this?'

'Detective Inspector Gerard Nolan's retirement project, it seems,' he says, frowning. 'Unfinished business. I haven't had time to go through the notebooks, but there's a fecking mountain of stuff here. And all – well, most of it is focused on one guy. The best friend – Conleth O'Hara.'

He shuffles the pages, some of which have Post-its curling in various degrees of tackiness from the edges.

'Apparently he was doing this on his own time after he retired. And he was the perfect guy to do it – he even took part in the search for Max, back in the day. He was an RNLI volunteer and he'd do stints in the lifeboat. But this case for him, it was, you know, *the case I can't forget* kind of thing. So from this' – he points at the photo of Conleth – 'I reckon this puts O'Hara firmly in the frame.

'And these,' he adds, before I can answer, tapping the bag of notebooks, Garda-issued sturdy reliables. 'I'm going to have to do a lot of reading.'

I nod.

'The best friend,' I say, walking over to study the wall of photographs pinned on the board.

'And Nolan had been looking at the finances as well,' he says. 'O'Hara's personal accounts and later, info on MaxSpirit.'

He runs a palm from eyebrow to jaw and leaves his hand half splayed across his mouth, as though not wanting the wrong words to escape.

'I asked Mrs Nolan if he'd spoken to her about it, and she said no, but that he was always working on it. That he never actually retired properly. He just exchanged one office for another, closer to home. All this was in a shed in the garden, along with all his fishing stuff. It's sad, isn't it? When you can see, like, the whole person, just from the contents of a shed?'

He suddenly looks old. Weary.

'She said her husband didn't believe for a second that Max drowned in the harbour – or they'd have found him. It was a still night, apparently, and a full moon. Someone would've seen him going in. And sure, they'd everyone on the search – the inshore lifeboat, the coastguard, the sub-aqua team – everyone.'

'And what did he think really happened? Did she say?'

He shrugs, tipping his palms upwards in a who-knows gesture.

'Not suicide, anyway. Someone killed Max – maybe on the boat – and disposed of the body later, plain and simple. And then Nolan, poor fecker, didn't even get two months' full retirement, you know? Before he's found floating off the coast.'

I think of Mum – dead before she could retire. And then an image of my father comes to mind and I feel a lurch of guilt. I picture him as Alva described it: in his hospice bed, too weak to write a letter of farewell. I see him shrunken into the pillows and – how come life is so short? I never set out – it's not as if I made a vow never to speak to him after he left. It just happened that way. And now, it's too late.

'It has a dodgy bang off it, wouldn't you say?' Stephen sighs. He's looking at the stack of pages.

I slide the photograph into the clear space at the front of the desk, then I tap the sheet of figures. Get a grip, Laura.

'Have you had time to look at these? Monies in?'

'Yeah. He had it registered as a charity in jig-time. Max-Spirit was bringing in cash from the get-go. And you know they don't own the whole house?'

I shake my head. 'Well, I thought – I mean, I knew that they rented out apartments upstairs?'

'No, no,' he's saying, leafing through a series of pages.

'The house was sold to a consortium way back – over ten years ago – and it's Conleth and Gemma who are renting.'

It's not theirs. Interesting. He takes a slug of his coffee, wincing at the heat.

'Not as glamorous a life as they'd have you believe.'

I sip my coffee, thinking.

'Do you know what?' He sits forward, energized. 'It makes me so sad to think of Nolan working all those years and never even getting to enjoy the fecking pension. You'd need to have seen the shed. Wall-to-wall shelving stacked with fishing tackle – flies and spinning whatchamacallits and rods and, I don't know what half of the stuff is, but it's all like for deep sea fishing – and the empty desk and this lone box. She said – Mrs Nolan said – she hadn't the heart to clear it away.'

'And she didn't hand it – this – into the station when he died?' I say, gesturing at the file. 'Because it shouldn't really have been taken away. I'm surprised it wasn't handed over to MisPer.'

We exchange a look, both of us knowing that the missing persons unit does not have the manpower or authority to investigate something like this. He pushes his chair back, sliding it across the floor with a clatter, and gets to his feet. I stand as well.

'Right,' he says in a brisk tone. 'I'll start going through the notebooks. This definitely puts the focus firmly on Conleth O'Hara. Let's get him back in. Time for a proper interview. Then we need to look again for any witnesses – anyone who saw Max or Conleth outside the club. Someone's got to have seen Max on his way to the boat. And the weapon – we're still looking for the knife.'

46

Gemma

Ferdia is lying on the flagstones beneath Dad's wooden bench, whispering to his digger, one arm slung over it like they're sleepover buddies. I take a photo and post.

@gemstone: This little guy keeps me going. Best friends with a JCB. #simplethings #kidsdocrazieststuff #familylove #cutekidsinsta #hugyourkids

Straightaway, the messages start to come in.

@missymurfi: Ferdia is a lovely little boy. Thinking of you, Gemma.
@theirishmammy: The worst is over. May your brother rest in peace.
@marymary2: Hope the funeral goes well tomorrow. The dress looked great.
@nolimitsgrl: Love and sympathy.

There are heart emojis and hugs. No matter what Conleth says, they do care. It's genuine. I click on the 'Thanks' emoji and then switch it to silent, putting the phone away. I feel Dad watching me, and I hang my head.

'You know I really love you, Dad, don't you?' I whisper, sitting as close as I can to his chair while still keeping an eye on Ferdia.

Dad doesn't reply. He's distant today, which is maybe for

the best. Because I can't keep doing this. He deserves better. I can't keep doing this, but I don't know how to escape. It's like that cube puzzle; Max had one, we both did. Rubik's cube. I would twist and click the plastic toy, my movements increasingly impatient as I got closer and closer to having one whole side of it the same colour. Then I'd show it to him, carefully hiding the remaining faces, the jumble of colours incorrectly aligned.

'Great,' he'd grin, before knocking it out of my hands with a little upward tap and catching it on the upswing. 'What about the rest?' And he'd show me the other sides, with all their mixed-up squares of colour.

'Loser.'

'Pig.'

'Baby.'

'Bully.'

Even when he was calling me names, I loved him. Even when he was being mean or teasing me for being too scared to climb out of the treehouse by the rope ladder or threatening to throw me in the sea, I still loved him.

But that night, when he came down to the boat, I hated him with a roaring red hatred for what he was saying, for every prize and every award and every *well done* from Mum and Dad, who barely noticed me – and it seemed to me that he was jealous. That he wouldn't tolerate me taking the tiniest step into his world. And I hated him for interfering and for coming between me and Conleth. And for being a killjoy, because I knew even then what the drugs could do and where they bring you.

How is it possible to hate someone – and love them too? That night I hated my brother. Though I loved him too.

How can I still be alive when Max is dead? How can I have continued living, lying, hiding the truth? I should have confessed that night. No. I should have killed myself that night.

'Can he have a Jammie Dodger?' Ferdia says in a stage whisper, eyeing the plate of biscuits they gave us with the cup of tea. They're so kind – after all this time, they'll still offer us tea when we arrive. The hissing whisper is because I've told him he has to be quiet and not disturb the Seaview residents, although I know they really don't mind. They love it when I bring him along to visit.

'You mean, can you have one,' I say, handing him a biscuit and, when no one is looking, pocketing the remaining three. 'Okay, because you're a very good boy.'

He blinks that near-sighted smile at me, takes hold of the biscuit and starts trying to snap it in half. When he can't do it, he immediately hands it back to me for me to do it. I know him well enough that he'll have a freak if it's messily done, and there's no way of pulling apart a Jammie Dodger tidily, so I rummage for my keys. I've a miniature blade on my keyring, which I pull out and use to cut a neat line through the biscuit. And that's when I think of it. Max's knife. I can picture it so clearly – and the engraving on it. I brought it to the jewellers in Dún Laoghaire to get it engraved. *Maxattacks*. Our joke.

They asked me what happened to it.

Ferdia rolls back under the bench and starts feeding one half of the biscuit into the front-loading part of the toy. I love him so much I would die for him. And I love him so much that, if I had to, I could kill him. I love him so much I will bring him with me when I leave this life.

How can I consider something so against nature? I'm his mother. My job is to protect him. But that just shifts colours around the cube – because if I confess, they'll take me away from him and send me to prison. If I tell them about Conleth, what he did to me, what he still does, Conleth will deny it. And even if they get him, he'll tell them what I did. And they'll take Ferdia away, maybe put him into care. But is that

253

the solution? To protect Ferdia from Conleth, I have to keep the lie. To save myself, I have to keep the lie. Round and round it goes.

Ferdia is still lying under the bench, his feet pressed against the seat.

'Don't kick Grandad's bench, please, love,' I say. 'It's too noisy.' He drops his feet immediately, watchful.

'Sorry, Mummy,' he whispers. 'Don't tell on me, okay?' And we both know who he means. I smile at him.

'You're a great boy,' I say. 'That's all I'll ever say about you. I'm just telling Grandad how great you are.'

His smile cracks another fissure in my heart.

'Dad, I can't stay long—' I start, then close my mouth. I try again. 'Max is coming home, Dad.'

Nothing.

His body will be released this evening. I've called the undertakers and they're picking him up at seven thirty and he will repose – their word – in their chapel until the cremation on Friday. Tomorrow. I asked if I needed to find something for him to wear. I don't know what I was thinking of. The guy – he was so kind – if he was shocked at my stupidity, he didn't show it. How could they put clothes on him? For once, the phrase 'human remains' describes exactly what it is.

'Not in cases like these,' he said, and I felt better, thinking that there's a little club somewhere of girls like me, burying their brothers' remains after eighteen years underwater. It's an exclusive club. A club with a membership of one where the girl in question killed her brother.

'The casket will be closed, as requested,' he said. 'And the body wrapped in linen. We have beautiful linen shrouds.'

'I'm going away, Dad,' I say. 'With Ferdia and Max. You – you won't see us for a while.'

Because this is the only answer.

47

Niamh

Stephen shows Conleth into the interview room. He waits for a moment, raised eyebrows signalling that he'll hang on if needed, but Laura just nods. We've got this.

Conleth is spitting feathers, though hiding it well. I glance at Laura. She's in full-on armour mode, the sharp edges of her suit mirroring her set jawline, the high cheekbones. She'd added a layer of make-up when she nipped to the bathroom a short while ago, and not a soft, smoky-eyed touch-up – it's like she put on a layer of frost. She's a marble statue of tension. I know what it takes out of her to confront these guys. So I won't be slagging. Not now.

He pulls out the chair and sits without waiting to be asked. Laura is still eyeballing him, so I do the friendly-cop schtick.

'Thanks for coming in at short notice,' I say. 'Would you like a cup of tea, glass of water?'

He attempts the charming smile, but trapped energy radiates off him, like he's dying to smash something.

'Before we start—' Laura uses the side of both palms to align the pages in front of her and gives the voluntary caution statement. 'So, to clarify, this is a voluntary statement. It's being recorded, but you are not under arrest and you're free to leave at any time.'

He swallows and clears his throat, waiting as she finishes the caution, informing him that he does not need a solicitor, but that he can have one if he wants. I start the audio, knowing that both cameras are already rolling.

'No, thank you, ladies – officers, rather.' He slaps his thighs in a 'let's do this' motion. 'Happy to help, though I've told you everything I know already. And I don't know if you realize this, but I should be with my wife and family at the moment. So let's keep it brief.'

He shrugs his arm with a violent jerk so that his chunky gold watch flips out from under his sleeve. 'The, ah, remains are being brought to the removal chapel, right about now? So, I'm not sure how much more I can be of assistance.'

His teeth clamp together on the word 'assistance', a muscle twitching in his cheek.

Laura smooths a fresh sheet of paper and removes the lid of her pen. The corners of her mouth tilt upwards in the 'gloves off' smile.

'This is now a murder investigation,' she says in a pleasant voice.

He sits back, folding his arms across his chest, shaking his head in bafflement.

'Jesus! That's – that's—'

We wait. I know Laura, like me, is watching him, hoping that he'll betray something, anything.

'But Max was suicidal. I mean, everyone knew it. He, like, how on earth can you be certain? After all this time? The body must have been—' His mouth closes, and his expression changes.

'Our forensic experts are just that,' says Laura. 'Experts. You don't need to know the details, but suffice to say that, due to certain conditions, the state pathologist was able to determine that Max was murdered. It was only afterwards that his body was dumped in the sea.'

'But he – I'm telling you – I've told you already, he was depressed.'

We've definitely rattled him.

'He was about to be exposed. He'd just been dumped by Michelle – that's why he – he – well, I – I mean, it's obvious.' His words dry up and he drifts into silence. He still hasn't asked how Max died.

'He was about to be exposed by who?' Laura's voice is steady. 'Were you about to expose him?'

'Of course not! I didn't – I didn't mean that – I just meant that it would have to come out. When we weren't going to be eligible for the Olympics, people would ask. That's all.' His expression darkens. We wait. He begins nodding, calmer.

'Murder,' he says in a whisper. 'Right. Christ! That's a shocker all right. So, how can I help?'

Laura removes the photograph of the two young men arguing and slides it towards him.

'You can help by telling us what's going on here,' she says. 'Tell me what you remember about this.'

He peers at the photograph. It looks like he's genuinely never seen it before. He shakes his head.

'Christ!' he breathes. Then he sits back. 'Well, there you are then,' he says.

'What?' I blurt.

'Well, it doesn't reflect well on me, I suppose. But that's – someone has managed to get a shot of the two of us arguing, haven't they? And I'm not going to lie, I was furious with him about the sample. He'd ruined things for both of us.'

He looks into the middle distance.

'I've forgotten so much about that night – deliberately. Okay?' He shifts in his chair, flexes muscles. 'But that's not a crime. Who would want to remember a fight with their best friend on the night – on the night he later went on to kill himself?'

'Except he didn't kill himself,' says Laura. 'Someone murdered him. So tell me, what way did you leave it? After this argument? I mean, you're both clearly very het up.'

She tilts her head to one side. 'What happened next?'

'Again?' he says, with a swift glance at his watch.

Laura's reply is a terse nod. And he goes through it, and it tallies with Gemma's version and his own.

'So, you escorted Gemma home,' Laura emphasizes the word 'escorted', 'although no one saw you because you went out the back way. And then what?'

'Well, like I said – I went back to the party. And I had a few drinks – and, you know, partied. Ask Fiona.' He leans forward, both hands spread in supplication.

'We did.' Laura smiles. 'And she says this is true. So, to clarify, you went back to the yacht club after you escorted Gemma home, but no one saw you re-enter, because you—' she waits.

He presses his fingers into his thighs. 'Yes. Correct. I went back that way as well. And ask Fiona. She – she was with me all night, or – till it ended. When I went home.'

'Did anyone see you leave? Were you with anyone?' Laura asks mildly. 'What about Fiona Cassidy?'

He presses his lips together. Adds a head shake.

'Fiona left with – ah – her boyfriend, Sam.'

'Sam – what's his surname?' Laura looks up.

'Kirwan,' he says. 'They – he's now her husband.' We let that sit, but I make a note to check him out later. Laura turns to a new page.

'And I think I know what the answer is here, but help me out. You were alone when you left, but nobody saw you.

There's nobody who might recall seeing you because—' She leaves it hanging, and I try not to snigger.

'Very funny,' he says.

He nods, as though setting something down, and sits back. The chair creaks under his weight. We already know that there's no record of him at the final stages of the night and no footage of him leaving from the front of the building.

Laura waits, looks down at the page.

'So you and Max didn't go down to the boat, that night? To – perhaps – clear the air?'

'What? Why would we do that? Why would you think that?' He raises his palm to the back of his neck, as though easing tension.

'We have records for the keycards, for the gate that accesses the marina.' She smiles. 'And they record two entries that night, one just after 10.15 p.m. and the other at 10.42 p.m. Did you go down with Max to the boat? Did you argue, perhaps?'

'Jesus! No!' He's spluttering. 'No, I didn't. You couldn't have a record of my keycard – I'd lost mine earlier that season. I remember because it was a bloody pain in the arse getting people to tap me in for weeks. It wasn't me on the boat and it wasn't my keycard. So whose was it?'

Laura writes something.

'Thank you. We can check that out. But as you say, it's possible, or it was back then, to get people to let you in. Perhaps you and Max were alone on the boat and—'

'I see,' he says slowly. 'It was Max's keycard.' He seems calmer. 'What you seem to forget is that I brought Gemma home, after the speeches. I escorted her home, and I went back to the club, where I – where there were plenty of witnesses, if that's what you're looking for. I did not go down to the boat with Max. And I – in fact—' His mouth closes.

'In fact what, Mr O'Hara?'

'And okay, well, I may as well tell you, I suppose. Gemma knew. She would have known all about Max – about the drugs.' He shakes his head sadly. 'Because she was taking a lot of pills and stuff at the time. They both were. The Gemma you know now – I mean, she's nothing like that troubled girl. I' – he turns his palms over, as if looking for stains – 'I've worked very hard with her, I really have, to leave all that behind.'

He tilts forward in his seat, his body humming with energy. He's decided something.

Again, the glance at the watch.

'Perhaps it's my wife you should be speaking to. But not now. He – the body is arriving at the chapel in less than an hour for the removal. I mean, your timing is – could you not show a bit of respect? The service is tomorrow. Seriously, Gemma will be frantic by this stage. Actually' – he stands – 'I'm leaving.'

'Of course. One final question before you leave,' says Laura, getting to her feet as well. 'What kind of knife do you use for sailing, when you're out in the boat?'

He sighs a long-suffering sigh.

'Oh, for Christ's sake!' He whispers it as if to himself, but loud enough for us to hear. 'A Leatherman, actually. I've had it for years.'

'Thank you,' says Laura. 'Could you drop it into the station, please? As soon as you get a chance? We need to look at it.'

He pauses.

'Of course.' He musters a smile. 'No problem.'

The door slams and we hear him being buzzed out into the foyer and the slam of the door.

'What do you make of that for a shitshow?' I say,

straightening my shoulders. There's a heaviness across my chest, like my boobs are weighing me down. I adjust my bra to make a bit of space. I know it's a good sign. But we've been here before, so I damp down the hope. Laura clocks it and opens her mouth to speak.

'Well, you've shaken things up a bit,' I say, not wanting her to mention it. Not able for her hope or sympathy. 'Let's see what happens next.'

48

Laura

I take a sip of my coffee. Bad idea at a quarter to seven in the evening – my tolerance for caffeine is waning as I approach forty. Matt thinks I'm making it up, but Christine said it happened to her too. 'We're peri-menopausal,' she'd barked, her voice way too loud for the tiny restaurant where we were having a catch-up meal on her last visit home. 'Stuff like this happens.'

Niamh is speaking. I shake my head to clear the random thoughts.

'This is not ideal,' she's saying. 'We've nothing firm, no weapon and no witnesses. He and Gemma back each other up on the walking-home story, and later – well, the times don't tally for him to have gone down to the boat afterwards. The keycard is telling us that whatever happened to Max was earlier. While O'Hara was bringing Gemma home.'

She pauses. 'Did Stephen find anything at all on the CCTV?'

I make a face.

'Not Stephen. Senan got one of the rookies to trawl through the footage. Very poor quality – you can just about make out who's who from the front of the club. People leaving, taxis drawing up and people who should have been getting taxis staggering to their cars, but where the club backs on to the quayside, nothing. There's a grainy bit showing people dancing when the party spilled outside, and then it's all a huge white blur because of the full moon shining on the water. Basically, there's nothing to show us who was outside on the pontoon. Just shadows and blurs.'

She considers this as she cuts into her panini. We're in a different café on the seafront. Niamh had to have a tomato panini. Now, she tilts her phone towards me, open on the home page for Hannigan's Funeral Home, where the removal for Max is being held.

I frown.

'We could go on the way home?' I say, without much enthusiasm. I'm dying to get some silence and a chance to think about what we've just heard from Conleth.

'Yeah – nah. Forget that.' Niamh is wolfing into her panini, face flushed. She picks up a sun-dried tomato that has fallen and pops it in her mouth. With her other hand she thumbs buttons on her phone, checking information.

'Service of commemoration tomorrow morning at eleven at the crematorium. Let's swing by that instead?'

She takes a gulp of tea. 'But if you did want to go to the removal, they're letting people in to sign the book of condolence till eleven thirty.'

'So late?'

'Yeah, apparently people from the yacht club volunteered to do a rota, to cut down on the crowds. They've arranged for the book to be kept in the lobby of Hannigan's. You'll be able to sign anytime tonight up till then.'

She looks up.

'Popular family. Have you seen Gemma's Instagram feed?' A low whistle. 'Look at this, wouldja?' Again, she turns her phone so I can see the screen. A fragile-looking Gemma – immaculate as ever, manicured nails, freshly blow-dried hair – addresses the camera straight on. The skin over her high cheekbones is stretched tight, shadows beneath those blue eyes hinting at the emotional pain underneath.

The background noise in the café makes it impossible for me to hear what she's saying.

'She's deciding what necklace to wear,' says Niamh. 'From her own jewellery line.' I watch her trail a strand of knotted silver through her slim fingers, holding the piece up to the camera, then placing it out of sight on her right. She then repeats the action with a different necklace – a gold version of the same piece.

'May I?' Niamh hands me the phone, and I hold it up beside my ear.

'My favourite is actually the silver,' she's saying. 'I get more wear out of it, you know? And it suits my skin tone. But loads of you have been messaging me about the gold, and I think – sorry, I have to check, but it may be sold out. All you darker-haired girls must be going mad for the gold.'

I freeze the feed by pressing on it. Her sweet smile. Her frank way of leaning right up to the camera.

'God, she's good!' I hand the phone back. 'Already I want one. The gold would be useful.'

Niamh grins.

'You could wear it at your party.' She holds up a hand to stop me answering. 'Christ! I was fair hungry and I'd no idea! What the hell is in tomatoes anyway? I'm craving them – I was like that before.'

I reach as though to touch her arm, then pull my hand back. She's smiling.

'Niamh, I – I'm so sorry.'

'Don't start this again,' she says, her voice firm. 'I didn't tell you. I didn't tell anyone.' Anniewan. 'For exactly the reason – for exactly – because of exactly what you are doing now.' Her face folds inwards like a crumpled tissue in a parody of sympathy. 'I'm doing this for me. And I'm doing this by myself. And mostly it's not too bad, apart from the hormones.'

264

'Bastards,' we both say together. She grins.

'And the egg retrieval wasn't fun. But I didn't have to do it again for this round.'

'But when you miscarried – I mean – I'm so sorry that I didn't know. I don't know what I was even doing then. You should have had time off! If you'd told me, I'd have covered.' I sigh. 'If I'd known – I just wanted to be there for you.'

She's still shaking her head.

'Look, I know all this. I know you're there for me. That's how we work, you and me. We don't have to be crying on one another's shoulders or having long, meaningful conversations. Even if I'm not telling you something, it's enough to know that I could, you know?'

My eyes prick with tears and I look down at the plate to hide them. But she's seen. She puts down the panini, places both hands on the table edges, leaning towards me.

'You're a freaking legend, Laura. Remember? You and McArsey both! Boom!' She grins. She mimes shooting a pistol, tilting it sideways like a gangster. 'The Clonchapel siege, as McArsey insists on calling it.' She sits back into the seat, folding her arms. 'You saved me. So in my book, like, not that we're keeping score, but you're right up there. Hundred per cent.'

A pause.

'Look, the worst part is the waiting and the hoping. This bit – you're here for me now, aren't you? The fourteen-day wait from when they transfer the embryo to being able to test, it's tough. You've got to keep a lid on the hope. And that's hard. Well, it's hard for me anyway. Cos you know me, I've always got a fecking full jar of hope – not like certain people.'

She finishes her panini then reaches across the table to take the remainder of the flapjack I'd bought but not finished.

'Okay?' she says, popping that in her mouth where I think she is still chewing the panini. 'Okay?' she repeats. And I don't know what she's asking. 'Can we leave it on the understanding that I have, like, a blank cheque of sympathy and hand-holding available from you at any time. And I can cash it in anytime. Anytime at all. But it's unspoken. It – it's just a thing. Our thing.'

'Okay,' I say. 'And I—'

'C'mon,' she says, getting up to leave. 'We've worse things to be worrying about – McArsey's on *Crime Call* after the nine o'clock news! His finest hour.'

@nolimitsgrl: Thinking of you this evening.
@gemstone: You're very kind. Thank you.
@marymary2: We'll be praying for you.
@nolimitsgrl: We will. And tomorrow too. Keep strong.
@missymurfi: Hope himself your husband is looking after you @gemstone. Am just around the corner if you need me.

49

Gemma

I click out of Instagram and place the phone face down on the table. Lesley is so sweet. I think she resents Conleth's nearness to me, but she needn't worry, because he's in overdrive. He's fussing around, barking orders at people. He made them set up chairs and a table for us – though he's not sitting – and the line of people calling to pay their respects snakes around two sides of the room, past the coffin, out the door and halfway down the street. People enter the room trying not to look at the coffin, or giving it sympathetic looks, and they wait in line, whispering, until they reach the table.

I'm sorry for your loss.

Rest in peace.

God love you.

At least you can have peace now.

So many kindnesses – faces I recognize from the town and the club, women who introduce themselves – 'You don't know me, I'm' – and they say their Instagram title. And Lesley herself of course, bless her. Her face was all red from crying. And through it all my shame burns and I hate myself even more. I'm not worthy of this sympathy.

Behind me, I can feel Conleth's presence. He's on edge, shifting from foot to foot. My heart lurches at every sudden movement. From the moment he came home from the guards, he's been acting weird. I was expecting him to be fuming, so I'd everything ready. I put on the black dress – the one he told me I should wear – and I'd put my hair up in a chignon so that the pearl earrings he gave me are on full show. I'd got a fresh shirt and tie ready for him, just in case he needed to change.

'Where's Ferd?' he'd said, coming into the bedroom and shrugging off his jacket. I'd thought that odd. He normally calls Ferdia by his full name.

'Penny's minding him,' I'd told him. 'She says she'll meet us there or, if we'd rather he didn't go, she'll mind him for the evening.'

'Of course he's going,' was the response. 'He has to be there.'

'How – how did it go with the guards?' My voice was faltering, but I'd chanced it. 'What did they want?' I watched him behind me in the mirror. He'd stripped off his shirt, his back to the window so I couldn't see the scar. Back when I thought I loved him – before he'd destroyed that part of me – I used to feel sympathy for the boy, the boy who tried to save his parents and almost died in the process. The image of him frantically trying to unlock their bedroom door while smoke filled the house – it's like that image almost – it almost allowed me to forgive. Almost.

He'd felt my eyes on him and he'd straightened up, filling his chest with air. And as he breathed in, I'd held my breath.

'Just a fishing expedition,' he'd said, locking eyes with me, and I'd felt a trembling in my lower spine. He'd walked over to where I was standing at the chest of drawers and I'd tried not to flinch, mentally cataloguing what could be used to hurt me here. Every movement he makes sets up an involuntary one in my body.

My mind was frantic. It was twenty minutes till we had to be at the funeral home for the removal. He'd just come back from the garda station. He could hardly be looking for sex. Could he? And he hadn't time to take anything – unless he did a line on the way home in the car? I looked at his eyes, gauging whether or not they were dilated. Because this is the reality of my life – always trying to read him.

But he'd moved to one side of me, opening the top drawer of the chest of drawers. *He's just choosing a tie*, I'd told myself, though the panic in my chest fluttered, a bird flailing against a window. Throwing itself over and over against the glass. *Or maybe he needs a money clip.* The fluttering turned into thumping. Because as well as ties and cufflinks and bits and bobs, he keeps his belts in that drawer.

'I think they're going to have to drop it,' he'd said, choosing a black tie and closing the drawer. He'd sighed, as though deciding something. 'They have absolutely nothing. They'll drop the investigation. And when they do, we should go away for a few days, to recover from all this stress.'

He'd taken hold of my shoulders and spun me around so I could do his tie. Above me, his breath rolled over me in moist waves. Why was he so calm? I'd reached up to do the knot of his tie, my chilled hands shaking.

'The three of us,' he'd said, over the top of my head, addressing his reflection. 'It's about time we had a little holiday. We'll go away for a week – even a few days. Let's head off on Saturday. Get the funeral out of the way first, then off we go.'

He'd placed his hands on my shoulders and I was pinned in place. If I stepped backwards, it would be seen as a betrayal. My mind raced with questions. Why now?

'I –' I'd swallowed. 'B—but what about school? Ferdia can't miss school, can he?'

And I'd hated myself then. For my itty-bitty baby voice and the fact that I'd turned it into a question.

And usually, that insurrection would have been enough to ensure a punishment. But his mood held.

'You're such a stickler for the rules, aren't you?'

He'd pulled me towards him, pressing my head against his chest, his palm holding the back of my head. With his other hand he traced a line from my buttocks, up my back and shoulder, coming to rest on my neck, his fingers loosely curled around it.

'Let's get all this out of the way. Then we'll leave lunchtime Saturday, when I get back from the office. I'm trying to do something nice here. Of course he can miss a few days.'

Father Joe, the priest who leads the prayers that now close the removal service, is the same priest who called regularly to the house in the months after Max's disappearance, and who later married us. A kind man, with the bright eyes of a blackbird set in skin so wrinkled and shiny it looks like it's covered in a layer of cling film. He steps forward now and raises his hands, and when he looks at me I have to look away. The honesty of his gaze.

'May Christ grant him safe harbour, a holy rest, and peace at the last,' he says, bringing his hands together in front of his chest.

A safe harbour for Max.

I want to die.

50

Laura

'I'll bring you in something to eat,' says Matt, nodding in the direction of the front room. 'Will you talk to her?'

He watches as I lock away the Sig and throw my jacket over the banister, hesitating in the hallway. He's in jeans and an old T-shirt and bare feet. I say nothing. Now is not the time to nag him about the Lego that lurks in every corner. He's trying.

'They told her it won't be long. She's' – he reaches to pull me into a hug, speaking into my hair – 'she's going to sleep for a few hours and go back in first thing tomorrow. And—'

He plants a kiss on the top of my head. 'Go on. Whatever you need.'

Alva is sitting on the end of the couch, her legs tucked up underneath her, scrolling through her phone. She lifts a red-eyed face to smile at me.

'How are you doing?' I say. 'Shove up.'

'Okay,' she whispers, shifting over. 'Just, you know – memories.'

She moves as if to turn the phone off, as if I might not want to see the photos. And usually I wouldn't. In the years after Dad left, I'd stalk his new wife and family on Facebook, fuming over the family photos: birthday parties for the twins, Alva and Áine, photos of Charlie, always busty and beaming, and their youngest, Seán. What annoyed me most was that it looked fun. The whole package. It seemed to me that our dad moved on without a care – like he left behind something shabby and broken and moved on to a more perfect life.

'Let's see,' I say now, steeling myself.

And she scrolls through the years, and I find myself crying. Not for me and what we lost – for Alva and her mum and her siblings. Because the parties segue into holidays and graduations and meals out and family hikes. And I can't deny that, second time around, Dad had clearly got the hang of this fatherhood thing.

'And this is him the other day,' she says, her voice a whisper. 'I thought you might like to see it.'

Dad is sitting up in a chair in the hospital room with Noah perched on his knee and Katie on the chair arm. She's holding a picture up to the camera. She's drawn a hospital ward with animal patients. She's beaming. So are Dad and Noah. I suddenly realize that Katie is almost the same age I was when Dad left. She looks like me.

'But I'm sorry. I understand now that I should have got your permission before I brought them in,' she says. I shake my head, not trusting myself to speak. From the kitchen, I hear a curse and a clatter.

'Nothing to worry about,' he yells. 'Just stood on something.'

Alva grins at me, her eyes shining with tears.

'You're always telling him,' she says.

'Yeah.'

We say nothing for a few moments as Matt limps in, carrying a plate of cheese on toast slathered in Ballymaloe relish, and two mugs of tea. Decaffeinated for me – in deference to perimenopause. He reads the room, deciding to leave us to it.

'You're right,' he calls from the hallway in a weary voice. 'I should wear slippers.'

'You two are so cute,' says Alva. 'As a couple, I mean.' She hesitates. 'And I can't tell you, it's been – you've been so brilliant to me. It's so kind of you to let me be here, these past months.' She shakes her head. 'I mean, Áine is here now, and Seán too, and I watch them, and they're – it's like they're trying to get up to speed with the whole thing. But I've been with him every day for months. And that – like when he, when he dies – I mean, thanks to you guys, when he dies, I'll be able to say that I was there for him. I've no guilt – none. I've been able to see him every day and we've had such a great time and—' She stops. Shrugs. 'Thanks to you,' she whispers.

'I never thought of it like that,' I say, truthfully. 'It's sweet of you to say that.'

She clicks the phone again and the screen lights up. She opens a voice memo app.

'And because of this – just bear with me, okay? Trust me. Let me play you this.'

She presses play and my father's voice rises between us.

'Laura – I just want to say a little word to you. I hope you're okay with this, but sure, sometimes when – at times like this when you know the end is nigh, so to speak – I reckon I'm allowed to send a message. Your mother, God be good to her, always said I had to have the last word. And maybe she was right.'

There's a pause and something clicks.

'That was when someone tried to come in,' says Alva. 'We shooed them out.'

'And I want to say, well, well – goodbye, I suppose. And you know, I'm – I'm sorry for the way things worked out for yourself and Cian. It wasn't – it wasn't something I'd planned' – I hear him sigh – 'but look, it was a long time ago and—'

I hear a click, as though the recording was paused. Then it begins again.

'Well, that was then, I suppose. Can't be helped. But now – Alva

274

tells me all about you, and the other day, when she brought in the kids, sure I thought to myself, well, isn't that great now? Grandchildren and all! And they're lovely kids. A credit to you.'

There's another pause and he clears his throat, then sniffs. Then nothing.

Alva is watching me closely. I swallow the sob which is lodged in my throat – a razor shell. A boulder.

'I told him that'd be easier than writing a letter,' she says softly. 'He – he was delighted with that. Cian phoned him yesterday morning – did he tell you?'

I nod, not trusting myself to speak. My older brother had WhatsApped me last week, saying he wouldn't be able to come over and that he was going to call. Natalie's MS is bad at the moment. He'd urged me to visit. **If Mum could forgive him, so can you**, was the last line of the text.

Alva bites her bottom lip as though stopping herself from saying something. A beat.

'If you wanted,' she says, her voice barely audible. 'If, you know, you don't have time to visit, you could – you could just record a message?'

I know I should try. It seems all I'm capable of right now. I think of little Ferdia and the fear in his eyes – that combination of fear and wanting – and I think of Conleth's stony face. Dad wasn't like that. That's something. I squash down the voice that wonders why he – he didn't mention my children's names. Why he didn't simply say two words – *I'm sorry*.

He's dying, Laura. He's on medication. He did his best.

'I'll – I'll see what I can do,' I say. 'Thanks.'

51

Gemma

They know. I'm sure of it. And if they don't know yet, they will soon. It's after midnight and we're back at the house. It took me nearly an hour to settle Ferdia. I hadn't wanted him to come to the removal, but Conleth insisted. And the whole way home, it was more questions about Max. Like he was summoning him back to life. *Was he like Daddy? Was he a champion swimmer too? How many medals did he win – was it more than a hundred? Did he win a hundred gold cups? Do I really look like him?* It's like Max has come alive for him, only to be snatched away. Finally, sleep took over, and I made my way back to our room.

Conleth is lying on the bed when I come in, his legs spread so they take up the whole space, phone in his hand. Mine is charging on the locker, so I know he's already checked it. His left hand is down his shorts – moving.

'Get into bed,' he says, not looking up.

So I'm sleeping in the bed again tonight. Oh God. How can he even think of it at a time like this? He nudges his foot against a pile of clothes on the end of the bed and utters a sort of muffled grunt. I clock the nightdress, the satin one with the hibiscus flowers, one from my line of nightwear that's sold out countless times over, and I know that's what he's chosen for me to wear. I know what is required.

My throat begins to constrict, and it's like, somewhere inside me, the girl that I used to be – Max's little sister – is sobbing. Not now. Too late, I tell her. In the bathroom I clean my teeth and wash myself, my eyes roving the surface of the marble looking for any tell-tale signs that he's taken something, snorted something. In the bathroom mirror I see my reflection, the tendons in my neck standing out, my face tightened by invisible strings. That's what I am. I'm the puppet. I know I'll go in now and do whatever he wants – move my little hands up and down, turn my head, nod my head, kneel, twist, bend, open, close, lie, stand – I am nothing. I'm a doll and I can be used for whatever he wants. And it's my own fault and I can't expect any sympathy and I have only myself to blame.

'Get in.'

'Coming,' I say, walking over to the dresser and opening the drawer to find the lighter I'd spotted earlier buried in all the bits and pieces of junk. 'I'm going to light a candle. Atmosphere,' I say, despising myself. I'll light the sandal-wood candle – the smell will distract. In the candlelight, it can't be so bad, and the smell is comforting. He's not even listening.

And I walk to the bed because I'm a plastic doll. I feel nothing. The real girl is buried deep, and tomorrow she will be free. After all this.

He doesn't even put down his phone. I climb between his legs as he keeps scrolling, and from the phone I can hear grunts and moans. With the heel of his free hand, he pushes me downwards and I do what he wants. And I'm glad that it's only this. I'm glad that it will be over soon. And I despise myself for being glad.

He lies back afterwards, pushing me off him, but not roughly. And I wonder again at his mood – his strange calmness.

'I'm just going to the kitchen?' I whisper afterwards. 'Okay?'

He humphs assent and does the little flip of his fingers which means I'm dismissed. I've pleased him. And I'm allowed to help myself if I've pleased him like this. 'Okay?'

Okay? What have I become? I have no memory – not a single memory of when I used to be different. Conleth has been controlling me – I've been ruled by his wants, his commands, since I was barely a teenager. I cannot imagine life without him. I cannot think of what I would be – who I would be without him.

I tiptoe into the kitchen, where bright moonlight slices through the trees, illuminating the shining work surfaces. I stare at it, remembering the night of the party and the same huge moon. So big, so round – like a painting or a stage set. It lit Max in the cabin, silvering his smooth skin, his fair hair, spinning bright discs in his pupils. I stare at it now and wait for the kettle to boil.

If I ever paint again, this is what I'd paint. The cold, shining beauty of the moon.

In the semi-darkness, across the table, I imagine I see my father in his favourite spot – the leather armchair by the window. It used to be a shabby wreck, but I got it reupholstered by a local firm and we documented the whole process on Insta. Even now, sometimes, I imagine I can still get his scent of cinnamon and pepper from the soft leather and, sometimes, only when the house is quiet, I can 'see' him here. Though usually I prefer to go and sit in the garden at Seaview. He had a special corner there too.

'Don't cry, love,' he says.

I run my palm down my cheeks, feeling the wetness. Though I know he's not real and that he's long gone – dead for over three years now – I stretch my hand out towards him across the cool marble.

He's leaning back in the chair, watching me, his hands

steepled, resting on his abdomen. And he's wearing the clothes he used to wear in the boat – an ancient navy cotton jumper and faded cords. And it's so long since I've seen him here, in the house. The home where I grew up. I think it's been easier to cut off those memories of the four of us, because there were good memories. Mum and Dad and Max and me. Just the four of us. Before Conleth.

I hadn't wanted Dad to go into Seaview, but Conleth insisted. He was incontinent and he had trouble walking. He couldn't manage the shower and he couldn't manage the stairs down to us.

And it was easier to override my father's wishes than my husband's. Easier for me. Because I'm weak and self-serving. And Dad made no fuss – not really. And Seaview is a great place with brilliant carers. He had a lovely room, and I visited him as much as I could. And it freed me up to build up the brand.

This apartment is for me a prison. The house bears no relation to the family home it had been. It's more like a studio – all for show, all fake. It's why I've kept visiting Seaview all these years, to sit in the memorial garden in the spot Dad loved.

I tell him about the pillow. The knife. Pillow for Ferdia. Knife for me. He shakes his head slowly from side to side, and it's like a pendulum of No. No, no. No, no.

'Don't do this, Gem.'

'I have to. They're going to find out what I did.'

In the cupboard in Penny's bathroom, there's a box of medicines, including a cough syrup with a stronger sedative than the one I have. I took it – stole it, yes, because that's another thing I'll stoop to. Stealing from friends. Ferdia won't suffer even for a second. He'll be asleep, and then he won't wake up. That's all. Pillow. Knife.

Dad hangs his head and, when he lifts it again, I see the film of tears threatening to spill.

'Gemma, no. How can you even think of something like this?'

'There's no other way, Dad. There's no escape. I – I'll make it quick. He won't suffer, and I—'

No. No. No. No.

'Find another way,' Dad says. 'Please.'

Pillow. Knife. Over.

Friday

52

Niamh

I spot Laura on the far side. She's sort of hemmed in near the wall as people continue to file in and bunch up closer and closer together. All very gently done – nobody wants to start shoving at a funeral. She sees me watching her. A tilt of the head means *catch you outside after.* The place is rammed.

Ahead of me, people are stopping to sign the condolence book in the porch, and still more file past them to fill up the aisles. I sigh and take out my phone. We could be half an hour getting in.

It's still open on the contacts page, and I smirk like a teenager. Sarita's name and number are entered and saved. She was crossing the road near the Luas when I was stopped at the lights this morning. We caught eyes, and I lowered the window.

'Quick coffee?' I'd said, nodding my head in the direction of the coffee hatch, conveniently located right beside the station. 'I'm buying.' In the nano-second that she hesitated, I'd pulled into Dunville Avenue and parked up.

'So, how are things?' we'd both gone with as an opener, at the same time.

'You first,' from me.

'No, you – okay, sure.' A grin. 'Things are fine, thanks. I'm on my way to work – I'm late.' She'd relented then: 'Well, I'm not late yet. But I will be if I don't—'

'Ah no, you're grand. Sure, look, I don't want to make you late.'

'How's Dorothy?' from her, at the same time as 'How's your wrist?' from me.

'You this time.' She'd lifted the coffee to her mouth, looking up at me. *How can anyone have such dark eyes?*

'Fit as a fiddle,' I'd said. Then, 'But she's – she'd love a visit.' A nod. 'To advise her on, you know, safety in the home.'

She wasn't buying it. I thought of the posters I'd seen. 'Yeah, you know, when she's preparing food and stuff, she – she's sort of lurching around the place,' I'd lied. 'She probably needs a whatchacallit – zimmer frame.'

'I see.' She'd nodded. 'Really? So, she's not using the walking aid which I had delivered, oh, when was it? That's right. Yesterday. Gosh, that's a shame!'

Feck it to hell! I'd been caught rapid.

'Oh, yeah, I mean, she is, yeah. Brilliant. It's a great yoke. It's just she needs, like, a driving lesson on it.'

I had busied myself taking the lid off my coffee and blowing on it. A short distance from us the gates of the level crossing clattered in place and the Luas arrived, with a rush of air and an electric whooshing sound.

I'd asked her about her wrist. Told her that Dorothy and I were worried she'd broken it.

She'd looked up at me through those dark lashes and blinked a very slow blink, as though deciding something.

'Oh, that?' she'd said. 'It's grand. I kind of hammed it up a bit.'

'Oh,' I'd said. And then, 'Why?'

'I think you know why.'

I look up now to find the queue has moved again and there's a bit of space to stand near the pillar. I nip in, and glance back at Laura, who's also checking her phone. Clicking out of mine, I control my smirk as much as I can. She's something else, Sarita.

53

Gemma

Father Joe gives his sad smile as Conleth takes his seat beside me. He'd read a piece that Father Joe had chosen for him, and Sally has already posted it on the website. It was sailing-themed – the last line was something about sailing away into infinity. His voice cracked on that line and, beside me, I saw people nod, or dab their eyes. But beneath the sadness ran a current of strange excitement. Murder. It was all over the news last night.

And as Conleth walked back to his seat, he wiped a tear. And I doubted myself – again. Maybe that wasn't an act. Max was his best friend. All of this – this darkness inside him – maybe it *is* all my fault. When I think of him as a boy – the two of them, Conleth and Max. Max and Con. They had such unadulterated fun together. They were a team. I came between them. I destroyed them. And I forced him to keep this secret for almost twenty years. How can he forgive me, when I can't forgive myself? I don't deserve to be forgiven.

I turn to him and whisper a 'thank you'.

He smiles and shifts in his seat so he can reach an arm around my shoulders. The happy couple. And little Ferdia sitting inside, against the wall. And my heart breaks, because even this false life is at least a life for Ferdia. It's all he's ever known. And if – if I don't choose to end our lives – if I choose instead to do this, to confess, then both his parents will still go to prison and the bright world we've created will be smashed apart in the storm of publicity and shock. I'd be exposed – everything, the whole world I've created, will be exposed as fake. I'd be dropped by every brand, and it'll taint Conleth too. There'd be nothing left for Ferdia.

The decision has been made and unmade a thousand times in the past twenty-four hours. And the thought of confessing and everyone knowing who I really am – how could I live with the shame?

I had over two hundred DMs this morning – my followers wishing me well. Missymurfi – Lesley – is in overdrive. She's been following me for almost six years, and literally following me for most of that time too. I spotted her among the wall of women outside the crematorium, brightly dressed. Many of them wearing outfits I've featured in the last months: the linen trouser suit, the Phoebe dress with pockets, the long, belted mac. What will they think when I – when it all falls apart? When they find out what I did? The thought of their disappointment in me is crushing.

I try to gather my thoughts together. I have to do the eulogy. The last bars of 'Chasing Cars' fade, and that's my cue. I walk to the front of the chapel, smoothing the sides of the dress. She's a young Irish designer, so it's only fair to show the garment properly. I'm aware of Max's coffin, just visible behind the soft, draped fabric.

The building is jammed tight with people. They're standing in the side aisles and in four or five rows at the back. Sally is luminous in a long, embroidered coat of crushed velvet. It occurs to me to wonder if Conleth gave it to her, but almost as soon as I have the thought, I let it drift away. I don't care. It doesn't matter.

I spot the tall guard – Niamh – near the pillar. That's kind of her. I didn't know they went to the funerals. She gives me a little nod, her face so open, so genuine, I immediately smile

286

back. And maybe that's all it takes – that combination. Sally and the sham that is my marriage against the honesty of Niamh's smile – because suddenly I know what I have to do. It doesn't matter if he's chosen the next – there's always another one. And it doesn't matter what happens to the Gemma of Gemstone the brand. It doesn't matter if it all implodes. Gemma is a lie. I've been lying to myself for so long I don't even know who I am.

I make a note of what Niamh's wearing, so I'll be able to spot her after. I know what I have to do.

Ferdia is staring at me, his eyes magnified and shimmering behind the thick glasses. I give him a smile, and there's a ripple of understanding in the congregation.

'Max attacked life with one hundred per cent of his energy,' I begin. 'We used to have this saying – *Maxattacks* – and it sums him up so well.'

And people's faces are tilted up towards me like flowers – even Conleth's. And I think, *I could tell them now. Get it over with.* Instead, for the last time, I suppose, I conjure up the young man who was really still a boy. I describe a final scene, before it's ruined. And they smile – why wouldn't they? The world I'm speaking about is a happy one: sparkling seas, frilly waves breaking over the gleaming bowlines of sleek boats – blue skies and trophies and dinners and galas and college escapades and suntanned skin. Flags flapping in the breeze and the clink of spinnakers. Laughter, sunshine, security. I give them the memory of my beautiful, talented, kind brother and my innocent, trusting parents, who only ever wanted the best for us. I give them this truth, aware that by this time tomorrow, it will all be shattered.

'Well done,' says Conleth when I take my seat beside him. He plants a kiss on my cheek and I suppress the urge to scream.

*

Outside, we stand in yet another reception line, and there's more pressing of the hands, comforting pats on the shoulder, whispered messages and memories. People are getting hungry – it's well past twelve o'clock. Beside me, Conleth is now all affable charm, thanking people for coming, reminding them to head to the club for lunch. Penny has gone ahead with Ferdia and the twins, so it's just the two of us in a tide of well-wishers and the curious.

A tall guy with dark hair draws level with us. He's young – early twenties – tanned and fit-looking in a sharp suit.

'Gemma,' he says softly, taking my hand in both of his. He leans forward to kiss the side of my cheek.

He's familiar – the smile, the green eyes – but I can't place him.

'I'm sorry, I—'

'Beach barista,' he grins. 'Tom.'

'Oh! Tom! Sorry – thanks so much for coming. I didn't recognize you. Are you a member of Corrig Point too?'

'Naturally,' he quips. 'The best one.'

He turns to Conleth, hand extended.

'Tom Flaherty,' he says. 'I've met Gemma on the beach a few times.'

'Really?' says Conleth, with a smile that barely lifts the edges of his mouth.

'Thanks for coming,' I repeat, willing him to move on.

Thank goodness he gets the hint and moves along, but I know that whatever fragile peace was in place, it's gone now. Beside me, anger rises from Conleth like a heat haze.

'That was a lovely service,' says a voice. I turn, or rather am pulled into a hug by Carol-Ann Skehan. She smells of bleach – that locker-room smell she always had – mixed with a floral scent. She releases me, pressing my shoulders together and holding me in place, as though I'm a doll.

'It's just so heartbreaking – all of it. That your darling parents never got closure, they never got to say goodbye to Max. It's tragic – their darling boy.'

I watch her walk away, her words drifting in a mist behind her. Darling boy. Max. Maxattacks.

Conleth's hand presses my lower back as the people file past. I shake hands, lean in and out for embraces, my mind floating free. It doesn't matter any more. None of it matters. Dad, I choose your way. I'll turn myself in. One more night. Tomorrow.

54

Laura

I watch Conleth herd his family out of the chapel and every instinct I have tells me not to trust this man. He's charming and he talks the talk, but underneath there's an arrogance, that sense of entitlement. I need to talk to Stephen and see what else has turned up. The info on the retired SIO is a start, but it's not enough. Maybe O'Riordan can get someone else to help him go through the notebooks and the bank accounts. Before our Cig pulls us out of Corrig Point.

We're going to be another half-hour at least getting out of here. More people are stopping to sign the book of condolences on their way out, and stopping in front of the family to pay their respects. Why did I come? I could've nipped into the hospice first. Niamh would have been fine here on her own.

Christ! I'm so torn. I'm second-guessing every decision I make. You're here now, Laura. Stop it. I still myself for less than a minute, before checking my phone discreetly to see if Alva has replied, or even seen my message. Although 'Thinking of you all' hardly warrants a response.

Alva has her settings private, so I don't know when she was last online. I presume – I mean, of course she's not going to be checking her phone now. They're pretty much doing a vigil.

'Just so you know – I mean, no pressure or anything, okay?' she'd said last night on her way to bed. 'But my mum, you know, she's – she'd be so happy if you wanted to visit him. She's not – she says herself that she's not good with this kind of thing. So – just, if you did decide to eh, go in – it's' – she nodded to herself – 'it'd be cool.'

It's not good enough, I think. That can't be my last inter-action. I look up, waiting for Niamh to draw level. We still have about ten people ahead of us in the line of those offer-ing sympathies. I take a breath. The sight of her galvanizes me, as it always does. I make a decision.

'Are you okay if I take off for a bit later?' I wait. 'If I head off for the afternoon,' I amend.

Her brows knit together.

'Of course? Are you okay?'

'Yes. Thanks. No – it's just that I've decided: I will do it. I'm going to go and visit my father,' I say, and it comes out in a rush. 'To say—' I feel my throat constrict and I know I can't finish the sentence. Niamh's eyes immediately swim with tears on my behalf. She leans towards me, grabbing my wrist.

'Of course!' she repeats. 'Definitely you should do that. You'll be glad.' More nodding.

I feel myself stiffen at her touch, and she takes her hand away. God! She's infuriating. She's too much – I mean, I can't fault her in any way. She's so kind. But this—

I glance over my shoulder to see if anyone has noticed.

'I'm absolutely fine,' I say. 'I just want to do this right. Don't make a – production out of it.'

She gives a little head tilt.

'Gotcha,' she says. 'Boss.'

We draw level with Gemma and Conleth. He's standing in a wide-legged stance which emphasizes his bulk. He's alternat-ing between a handshake accompanied by a clap on the shoulder for male well-wishers while, for women, he leans down and clasps their hands between his two large palms, holding them in place for two or three shakes. He straightens up when he sees me and offers a perfunctory single-handed shake.

'My deepest sympathies,' I say.

'Thank you.'

Beside me, Niamh has clearly not been observing any of this, and she lurches forward to Gemma, grabbing her in a hug. What on earth? Conleth frowns but says nothing.

I wait for Niamh to finish the hug then shake hands with Conleth.

'Sorry for your loss,' she says. 'Desperately sad.'

We're carried along in the tide of people which then dissipates across the wide expanse in front of the building. The crowd separates into clusters of two or three, dressed in smart jackets and suits or blazers – the striped jackets that I think signify the wearer is on a varsity rowing team. Justy and Dermot would fit right in. In fact, there's a woman wearing a long silk jacket identical to one my mother-in-law wears. I'm surprised they don't know the Fitzgeralds. Though I recall the Thompsons are members of one of the other yacht clubs. I know there's a hierarchy between them but am not sure which one is the 'right' one to belong to.

'Something to tell you,' says Niamh, already walking towards the car park. I follow her, aware that I'll have to run if I want to catch up.

She's parked close to the gate, waiting for me.

'Sorry I snapped,' I begin.

She rolls her eyes. Clearly that's not worthy of a response.

'So Gemma wants to come in and give a statement. Tomorrow morning. First thing. She asked us to send a car and' – she lowers her voice, though we're not in any danger of being overheard – 'she wants us to make it look like we're arresting her. And we've to bring someone to look after Ferdia. He'll be with her.'

'Christ!' I breathe. 'What do you think she's got?'

Niamh gives a one-shouldered shrug, her face scrunched in confusion.

'Evidence? Or a confession? Who knows?'

'What did she say exactly? I mean, why tomorrow? Maybe we should—'

'She said, "Can you send a car to pick me up tomorrow morning? I have to talk to you." And when I said yes, she said it had to be at eight – exactly then.'

'Right,' I say.

'It'll be something on him,' she says. 'Got to be.'

She takes a step backwards, grins. 'And there's you thinking I was just being an idiot bogger going in for the hug.'

'Not at all,' I lie.

'Yeah, right.'

55

Gemma

'When I'm six, will I be a really good swimmer?' Ferdia is sitting on the bed, watching me throw clothes into a suitcase, the furrow in his brow tilting his glasses skew-ways above his eyebrows. 'Will there be a pool for little kids? I don't want to do big-boy swimming like Daddy. I want to stay with you. I'll swim with Daddy when I'm six.' Six is obviously the dream number.

I'm barely aware of what I'm packing – there's no holiday going to happen. No hotel. No pool. If everything goes according to plan, by this time tomorrow he'll be with Penny. And I'll be in custody. The familiar ache pushes its way from my stomach into my chest, building panic. How will I cope without him? All the things I'll miss. He'll be—

'Mummy! You're not listening.' He frowns.

'I am – I am now, pet. Sorry,' I say, sitting down on the edge of the bed and pulling him towards me, into my lap. I wrap my arms around him, resting my forehead on the top of his head. His hair smells of burnt sugar and shampoo, and that little-boy outdoor smell of smoke and salt. His bony limbs are tangled, all sharp edges digging into me. *This time tomorrow it'll all be over. You can do it, Gemma.*

'What was it?'

He kneels to whisper in my ear, his knee digging into the tender skin of my inner thigh.

'I said can we bring my arm bands?' he hisses urgently. 'Cos I'm not big yet. Okay? Just till I'm big.'

I hug him. 'Of course,' I whisper back. 'I'll pack them now. And look—' I check the hallway in case Conleth is in the shadows, then turn so my body blocks the camera, lifting the layers of clothing to expose the bright plastic body of the toy digger.

Ferdia's eyes grow round and huge, his face a pantomime of joy.

'Ssh,' I mime, my finger against my lips.

'Can I have him now?' he pleads, reaching for the toy. I shake my head.

'No, be brave now. He's in here waiting for you. You'll get him tomorrow.' I wait, my heart twisting at the emotions working on his face.

'Can you be a brave boy for me?'

'Like Maxattacks?' He reaches for my wrist, beginning to twist the silver bangle around and around. 'You said you played Maxattacks with your big brother. Was it a good game? Can I play Maxattacks? Why don't I have a big brother?'

I say nothing for a couple of seconds, concentrating on the feeling of his small, sticky fingers working the bracelet.

'That's right,' I say, my voice a whisper. 'Be brave like Max.'

He watches me cover his digger with folded clothing, leaning across to pat it with the air of a cowboy burying his favourite horse. I pull him into a big hug.

'Okay,' he says, resting against me, tired. It's after eight, and he's been up since the crack of dawn.

Conleth's heavy step in the corridor gives us both a fright.

'Are you packed?' he says, a wide smile stapled to his face. Ferdia leaps off the bed guiltily and stands to attention beside my leg, gripping the fabric of my jeans so tightly I can feel his fingernails.

'Hmm?'

'Yes – yes, almost,' I say. 'I haven't finished – I haven't packed for you though—'

I flinch, waiting for his displeasure. But the smile holds.

'Oh, don't worry about that, I – I'm sorted. Right,' he says, moving to take hold of Ferdia's hand and pulling him away from me. 'Come on then, sailor. Ready for the big adventure?'

A whamming in my chest. I take a step towards my son.

'Conleth, I was just – I'm going to put him to bed now,' I stutter.

'Oh no, you're not,' he chimes in a pantomime voice. 'Because our holiday starts now. Surprise!'

He's already in the hallway, and Ferdia is staring up at him.

'Are you really Daddy?' He blinks. And I'd laugh, except I'm terrified, because this is an Oscar-winning performance of a jolly dad.

'Haha! I am indeed,' he says. 'Come on, Mummy! Good girl.' He makes the summoning noises that you'd make to call a dog. 'Surprise! We're going early! We're sailing away to our holiday.'

'Now?' I whisper. 'We're sailing? On the boat?' *Keep calm. You can still do this. The phone – where's my phone?*

'Yes to all three. Right now.' He beams, with a weird smile. 'I've the boat all ready – with snacks and drinks and all sorts of treats you wouldn't believe. We're going to sleep on board tonight and tomorrow we'll sail down the coast to our hotel. What a treat!'

@marymary2: You gave him a lovely send-off 💝 Hope you're resting up this evening, Gemma.

@becka98: Rest in peace.

@unatracey5: Lovely seeing ye all there. The Gemstones are right behind you.

@missymurfi: We absolutely are. Is there anything we can do?

@theirishmammy: You should rest now @gemstone.

@looptheloop: We were rocking the place in our suits lol!

@unatracey5: We must have cleared out the entire stock! 😂

@marymary2: You did! There were none left in the 14 when I went on. Thanks, girls. Tryin to make my way into an 8 lol!

@looptheloop: She might be getting more in. Huge demand there, Gem. For when you're feeling up to it.

@nolimitsgrl: You going to take a break now, Gemma?

@theirishmammy: You should. Good plan.

@unatracey5: Agree. Definitely you're due a rest, Gemma. ♡

@theirishmammy: Deffo agree. Here for you when you get back. 😘

@missymurfi: We're here for you @gemstone.

56

Gemma

I think I'm going to throw up. What's he thinking? I follow him into the hall, barely able to keep up with his strides. He's holding Ferdia's hand, dragging him along. What's he planning? What – how will I be able to turn myself in? Maybe I can call the guards . . . Christ. Why am I so slow?

'I'll just – I need to get my bag,' I say, turning back towards the bedroom. 'And my phone – so I can post?'

'Yes, you get the bags. We'll wait here.' He's still holding Ferdia tightly. 'Won't we, little man?'

Ferdia nods, his eyes huge behind the glasses, hope and fear vying with each other across his face.

I all but sprint back to the bedroom and, when I get there, I grab the suitcase and start looking for my phone. Spotting it on top of the chest, I reach for it and, as I do so, something catches my eye in the half-open top drawer. In the jumble of keyrings and old ties and wallets, I spot a penknife, half hidden. I grab it and stuff it in the pocket of my jacket.

This is not good. What's he doing? I've got to call someone – think! Think! I click my phone on and start thumbing through Contacts to find Niamh. If I can just tell—

'I'll take that,' says Conleth, his voice loud in my ear as he snatches the phone from me. 'No work for you – no posting for a whole week. It's a holiday.'

He shoves the phone deep in his pocket and strides to the door, Ferdia stumbling in an effort to keep up. It's not dark, but it's been raining for the past half-hour, and there's no one outside – no photographers, no strollers, nobody. He manoeuvres Ferdia into his car seat and slams the door shut.

'Get in.' He smiles.

And I'm sort of stumbling, my body betraying its terror. He's taking us away. I trip on the kerb and land heavily, stuck between the car door and the footpath. I feel the burning sting of skinned knees, but it barely registers. It's all happening too fast for me to take it in – to come up with a plan.

'Mummy!' shouts Ferdia. His eyes flicker like a startled foal's.

'It's okay,' I soothe, righting myself and climbing into the car. 'I'm coming.'

Because I can't think what else to do. There's literally no one watching. He pulls out of the terrace and on to the main road and I think I see – is that Lesley under the awning of the shop?

In a couple of minutes, we're parked outside the club and he's striding ahead and Ferdia's still stumbling trying to keep up. What is he planning? I'm half sprinting to stay close by Ferdia.

The pontoon area will be locked at this hour. Thank God – we'll have to go through the club. There's a function – or maybe it's just dinner – and I'm praying that we meet someone, anyone – someone to witness what's happening. But there's nobody in the foyer, just voices from the bar and the dining room. The clink of glasses and bursts of laughter.

Conleth drags Ferdia down the corridor and stairs to the basement, where the locker room is. My heart sinks. The pontoon can be accessed from the locker room.

'I just need to use the bathroom,' I say in desperation, pointing towards the ladies. He turns, still grinning that big fake smile.

299

'On the boat,' he says, swinging Ferdia's hand in his. 'Silly Mummy should have gone before we left, shouldn't she?'

Ferdia looks at me, blinking. I try to smile.

'Oh, okay. Conleth, it's just – don't you think it'd be better to sail in daylight? I – you know I'm still—'

'Absolutely agree,' he says. 'We're not sailing off anywhere yet. We're going to have a little sleepover, isn't that right?'

Now Ferdia is grinning too. He's heard about the boat sleepovers on *MaxSpirit*. Groups of four to six kids go out in it for trips. They board the boat the night before and set off at first light. It's like scout camp or something – a rite of passage.

'We're taking *MaxSpirit*?' I whisper. 'But – b— who will crew? I—' My feet stop walking. We're standing at the gate to the pontoon. Behind me, light and noise from the club spill out on to the quayside. I could run. I could scream.

'Stop fussing,' he says, placing his thumb on the screen to release the gate lock. 'It's not exactly my first rodeo. And what you'd know, if you ever bothered to find out, silly Mummy, is that *MaxSpirit* is a Hallberg-Rassy – the perfect husband-and-wife boat, they call it in the advertising brochures. So we'll be well able to manage. And if you can't do it, my little man here can, can't you?'

Ferdia is nodding fiercely, looking up at Conleth. The rain has settled into a misty drizzle and tiny drops catch in his curls.

'Come on, Mummy,' says Conleth, in a voice that's almost kind.

'Come on, Mummy,' echoes Ferdia.

I walk behind them, weaving our way along the wooden pontoon. It's calm, and the clinks of halberds merge with the gentle wash of water in and out of air pockets under the deck. We reach the boat, my heart thudding. And even through my fear, I can see how beautiful she is – the long, sweeping line of the wedge-shaped hull with two stripes of blue swooshing along to emphasize the length of the craft. A sleek central cockpit is elevated, with a windscreen for shelter, and everywhere little examples of craftsmanship and expertise. Brass and steel, shining wood and chrome, bright white ropes and neatly furled sails.

Conleth lifts Ferdia and sets him down on board, then he turns and offers me his hand.

'Now, Mummy.'

Feeling my stomach lurch upwards as I leave the solidity of land, I take his hand and step on to the boat. I've never seen him so happy. He claps his hands.

'Look in the cabin,' he says.

'First, lifejackets,' I say, casting around to see where they might be.

'Of course. But we're not going anywhere yet.'

From the cabin a shout of joy from Ferdia.

'A party, Mummy! A party!'

I hurry along the deck and step down into the cabin. Ferdia is scrambling up on to the seat already, reaching for the crisps.

'I – when – when did you do all this?' I whisper, gesturing to the spread. He's set out a plate of biscuits, bags of crisps, cans of soft drinks and even an ice bucket in which a bottle of wine sits, laced with condensation.

Conleth smiles. He takes my phone out of his pocket and opens the camera app, pointing it towards me.

'I know we said no posting,' he says, 'but we should certainly get some nice photos for when we're back. Wait a sec.'

He takes a step towards the pedestal table, clearing away the foil top of the wine bottle and an empty plastic wrapper. Then he pours white wine into a glass and passes it to me.

'Smile.'

I think of the knife in my pocket. If I had to – could I? I shape my lips into a smile.

57

Gemma

I can hear the notifications coming in. They're so good, the girls. From the forward cabin, I can hear the beeps of Ferdia's iPad. He's stuffed full of food and will probably fall asleep before he can finish the game.

'I should probably post something,' I say, reaching my hand out for the phone. Conleth's lips compress and he frowns.

'You're taking a break,' he says. 'I said I'll take care of it.'

I watch him as he takes the phone from his pocket and begins scrolling. 'Interesting,' he says, thumbing a message and then switching off the phone entirely. 'Nothing from your loverboy – unless he has a code name I don't recognize.'

Oh God. The guy – Tom – from the beach.

'Conleth, I swear to God, I barely know him! I've – I've seen him on the beach is all. I met him with Penny, when we were walking—'

'I bet you did. Penny – I should have known. Penny would put you up to it all right.'

He takes a swig of his beer, and I watch the swallowing action of his throat, the bob barely discernible in the thick cords of muscle that wrap his neck. I don't understand. My eyes dart around the cabin, looking for the ways in which he might be going to hurt me. I've – it's so many years since I stepped in a boat, it's—

'Did you think I wouldn't find out?' he says, leaning over to grab the wine bottle and refill my glass. He nods and, like the puppet I am, I take a gulp of wine, trying to buy time by pretending this is normal.

'What? Find out what? Conleth—'

'Your beach bum is at Blackhall Place, training to be a solicitor, but of course, you knew that.'

'I – I swear to God. I swear, Conleth. I didn't know that, and – and what does it matter? And – and anyway, I'm not doing anything. I haven't done anything wrong. I haven't been disloyal.' I take another slug of wine. I've got to control this. Tomorrow – if I can – I've just got to make it till tomorrow. So they can find me. If I can get through tonight, then find a way to get a message to Niamh. I swallow my wine. Already, my head is spinning, the edges blurred. I can do this.

'Con.' I stand unsteadily, unzipping my jacket and allowing my shirt to slip off my shoulder.

His head tilts to one side, and he looks at me with something complicated. There's sexual desire – but there's a kind of scornful pity too. Like he's watching a puppy whimpering. Big, strong man. Baby doll. He likes that. Broken doll – he likes that even better.

'You have to believe me, Con,' I whisper, climbing on top of him, my legs either side of his hips, knees pressing into the seat. He makes a kind of sighing noise. A soft movement of water beneath the boat unsteadies me, and I grab hold of the rail above his head to steady myself.

'So you're not getting free legal advice from a baby solicitor?' he says, putting his hands under my shirt and grabbing my waist. He squeezes, and I feel his thumbs pressing along my stomach, up my sternum and outwards until he's holding my breasts. 'Not plotting with that witch Penny? Hmm?'

His fingers hurt, they press into my tender skin, but I've

got to do this. I struggle to focus, realizing I'm somehow drunk already, even though I only had a single glass of wine. Think, Gemma. Think. I can do this. I can do this, and then after – I have the knife. I lean towards him, and he thinks it's desire – or maybe he doesn't. It doesn't matter to him. Don't think, Gemma.

'Hmm?' he says, bending his head and biting – small, painful bites across my chest and along my collar bones. And I try not to cry out, because Ferdia is only a few feet away. I can do this.

'Of course not,' I whisper. 'There's only you.' I put my arms around his neck, hiding my face. All of a sudden, he pushes me off him.

'You're drunk,' he says, disgust lacing his voice. 'And what did I tell you about getting in shape?'

He moves to stand without waiting for me to get off his lap and I slip down on to the floor, my spine banging against the edge of the table. My shirt is open, both breasts exposed beneath the twisted fabric of the bra. I cover myself, but my hands are clumsy. How am I so drunk? And I turn my back and feel in the pocket for the knife.

'I don't know why I bother.' He fixes his hair, adjusts the crease of his trousers and walks to the sink, where he washes his hands. 'Go to bed,' he snaps, in the dog-Mummy voice. 'Now!'

And the pocket is empty. Both pockets. There's no knife. And so, like a beaten dog, that's what I do.

Saturday

58

Gemma

I wake with a sickening lurch, realizing that the boat is moving. I'm somewhere dark. Where am I? What time is it? Where's Conleth? We're moving? What the hell?

'Wakey-wakey!' A yell from above, from on deck. A sing-song teasing voice. 'Get up, Mummy!'

'Conleth?'

I try to sit up and I bang my head. Everything spins. I'm in the forward cabin, lying in the bunk. Hauling myself to the far end of the bed, where it opens out, I reach for the edge of the doorway and pull myself upright. I'm standing, but oh my God, I feel so sick and so weak, like every muscle is slackened. Like my legs are made of wool. I try to swallow, my tongue thick and a bitter taste in my mouth. The wine? How much wine did I have? I can't remember anything after the wine.

'Conleth?' My voice doesn't sound right either. I'm slurring. The drone of the engine drowns me out and I lurch sideways, banging against the tiny handbasin. I stagger from one foot to another, grabbing hold of the fixtures to keep me steady.

Passing through the saloon part of the cabin, I see the table strewn with the remnants of the party we – there was a party, wasn't there? There are crisp packets and an open can of Coke, and smashed biscuits and – there's the bottle of wine upside down in the ice bucket. Oh my God, did I drink the whole bottle? Why can't I remember? And it's mixed up in my head with the night Max died. The table littered with drugs and wrappers and beer cans. And I see it all spread out – the penknife Conleth had been using earlier to cut the stash. Max's shocked face when he saw me.

And now I'm seeing Max. I see my brother as if he's standing right in front of me. He's barefoot, which looks strange with the dinner jacket and the formal trousers. And his face is shocked shell-white.

And I don't understand, but I know there's something huge to understand. I feel it waiting for me. But I don't have time to chase it down because Conleth's shouting.

And I stagger through the cabin, shivering in the chill, making my way up on deck. What time is it? Through the portholes, a line of palest blue against the navy sea. Is it dawn? Already? How long have I slept? The wind has picked up, and I don't know what speed we're doing, but there's a sickening rise and fall.

Grasping the stair rail and the edge of the doorway, I haul myself up the steps and on to the deck. Oh my God! We're in the bay.

Sitting right in front of me is Conleth, legs spread wide and one hand on the wheel.

'Good morning,' he shouts above the whoosh of the breeze.

'What are you doing?' My voice is whipped away by the wind. Conleth shakes his head, mimes the words *I can't hear you*.

'Why didn't you wait? What—'

And there's something about his face – there's a kind of nervous smirk. And my body knows. Because I know that smirk. It's when something bad is going to happen. I feel my mouth drop open, my breath coming in shallow little puffs. He's done something bad.

'Where's Ferdie? Conleth! Where's Ferdia?'

59

Niamh

It's only six in the morning and the forum group is hopping already. I suppose it's good news – mammies are up early with babies. SMBC – Solo Mums By Choice – it's been my lifeline and, in fairness, a bit of an obsession. I feel guilty too, kind of stalking them and never putting a reply on the boards, never saying anything about myself. I find myself wanting to befriend them – the girl who posted:

Hi! I took the plunge and opted for a kind Danish donor. It worked first time!!!!!!

I count her exclamation marks. Six of them. And another woman talks about the loneliness.

I think I felt more lonely leading up to actually making the decision to become pregnant in this way. Now, with my lovely little girl, the loneliness comes and goes but guess what – it is a billion per cent worth it.

And the Instagrammers too – they're all so brave, the way they document the journey, the hopes, and the heartbreak when it doesn't take and you have to start over. I told Laura I didn't let it get to me, and that was more or less true – but it took guts not to sink into self-pity. And a lot of scrolling through Lisa's feed – right back to her first post, where she said something like **Never give up on something you can't go a day without thinking about.**

So, fecking own it, Niamh. Just own this. It took me so long to recover from Amber – to find my backbone. But in the end, Amber did me a favour, breaking up with me. There's no way I'd have pursued something like this if I'd still been with her. Amber required a hundred and ten per cent commitment.

This is my dream. No, it's not a dream. Dreams are fluffy and insubstantial. This is a blood-and-guts mission. Maybe mission fecking impossible. But own it. A mission.

I think about the shiny box sitting in my handbag. I could test now. I mean, I should actually wait until Monday and go into the clinic for the blood test which measures the amount of HCG in the bloodstream. But that's Monday.

I cross the room quietly, aware that the creaking floorboards could wake Dorothy, they're so bloody loud, and I take my bag off the back of the chair, but then I put it back. I tiptoe to the bathroom. Not going to test now – not with so much on today. I mean, it's an either/or situation. Either I am pregnant, in which case I'll be fair giddy like an eejit and not ready for the interview with Gemma, my brain skittering all over the place. Or the other scenario is I'm not pregnant. And I'll be disappointed – yeah, I may as well own that one – I'll be bitterly disappointed and I'll need to regroup and gather myself and find a way to give myself a kick up the arse in order to come up with the strength to go again. Because I will go again. I've got to. I can't go a day without thinking about it.

When I'm dressed, I grab the bag, after first taking the pregnancy test out and leaving it on the locker. Too tempting. Tonight, when all this is over, because I've a feeling that whatever Gemma has for us, it's big – tonight I'll test. Dorothy might even hold my hand. She's great that way.

'Although you do know I think you're absolutely crackers,' she'd huffed when I first told her about the fertility clinic. 'You may find that motherhood is a tad overrated, dear. Ask your own mother.'

I'm just stirring my cuppa when a text comes in from Laura.

Can you take over this morning if I'm not back? Going into the hospice. End game.

I blink, like I can't believe it. Fair play to her – that's not going to be easy. She literally hasn't seen him since she was a little kid. And she's well able to hold a grudge is Laura.

Of course, no bother. Thinking of you. Will sort.

I tip the tea down the sink. I'll need to call to Corrig Point first and get hold of someone. The tea tasted all wrong anyway.

I'm in the car when the phone starts hopping. At first, I'm confused – I'd been expecting Laura's voice on the line – but it's Stephen. Detective Bourke.

'Whoa, slow down,' I tell him, he's talking so fast. 'Say that again.'

'Where are you now, Darmody?'

'I'm on my way to Nelson Terrace. I'm picking up Gemma and the kid – it's all arranged. She says he'll be out.'

Stephen cuts across me. 'Okay. Me too. What's your ETA?'

'Ten minutes tops,' I say. 'What's—'

'The husband, Conleth – we need to bring him in now.' Stephen's voice is hoarse. It sounds like he hasn't slept. 'Yeah, we got a call from Carol-Ann last night and she's saying that she saw him – O'Hara – that night after the party, down near the boat. And it all fits with the cards – you know, the key-cards? She says Conleth and Max were always using each other's card, that people lost cards all the time and she handled the reordering.'

'Jaysus, yeah, actually, O'Hara told us—'

But Stephen is in full flow. He carries on. 'And get this – the other thing is you could prop the gate open, so not only did it not record you leaving, but you could go through it with the keycard and leave it open for someone else. They even kicked a kid out for doing that before the new system came in. He was charging people. But anyway, thing is, Conleth or Rob or anyone, they could have followed Max or killed him somewhere else and used his card to stage the scene.'

'Whoa.' I breathe, concentrating on turning on to the terrace. 'Hold on. So, we've a witness placing him at the scene, and we—'

'Right.' Stephen sounds like he's indicating. 'She saw him there – after midnight.'

'But I thought she'd left?'

'Left her bag behind,' he says. 'Went back down to get it, saw something or someone on the pontoon. It was empty by then and everyone was inside. And it was bright because of the full moon. She went to investigate. Anyway, she'll swear to it.'

'Jesus! Okay, great. But why now? Why didn't she say anything about this before?'

'She says at the time she'd thought nothing of it. And when Max disappeared, she reckoned that what she saw was Conleth looking for him. She presumed he would have told the police at the time. It was Cig's stint on *Crime Call* made her start to wonder.'

'Wait – what?' The signal drops. The static crackle breaks apart his words.

I check the clock on the dash: 07:43.

'I'm almost there.'

'Is Shaw with you?'

'No, but I—'

'Do not – repeat: Niamh, don't go in there on your own. Wait till we get there. McCarthy and I are on our way. Wait for us.'

60

Gemma

He sits at the tiller and it's like he's in an ad. The breeze whips his hair across his face, his eyes hidden by sunglasses. Above them, his brow creases into a frown of concern.

'Still asleep?' he says, pointing down below deck. 'I haven't seen him. Didn't want to wake him.'

And I start to panic because that's not like Ferdia. And if he's still asleep it means he hasn't put his lifejacket on. I start backing down the steps and, when I reach the bottom, I sort of stumble into the cabin and start looking for my boy.

'Ferdia! Ferdia!'

I run into the forward cabin where I found myself when I woke, thinking he must be in the other bed. He'll be under the covers.

He's not. I run the length of the boat, banging open the door of the first cabin to see the two untouched berths. Nothing. Nobody. Staggering against the opposite doorway, I push the door open and stand there, staring at two more empty berths. He's not there either. Where is he? And I keep standing upright as though, if I stay there long enough, he'll appear in front of me.

'Ferdia?' I yell. 'Ferdia! Ferdia!'

But all I hear is the boat's engine and a roaring sound in my ears which could be the wind and it could be terror. I check under the table, behind the door.

'Where is he?' And now I'm screaming. 'Conleth! Where is he?'

Another lurch of the boat sends me crashing into the table and I'm bent over it, hanging on to it as though I'm drowning. I'm drowning.

'Conleth! Stop the boat! You have to stop the boat!' I yell, sprinting up on deck again. Conleth turns to look at me, his movements slow. Why is he doing everything so slowly? I spin round in circles, scanning the length of the boat, the roiling sea. I can see Dún Laoghaire harbour in the distance, the streetlights still on, though it's just getting light. With every second, we're moving further away from the harbour.

Conleth is frowning, cupping his hand behind his ear.

'Conleth!!!!'

The terror in my own voice sends a shiver like a splinter of glass through me. At last, he cuts the engine and we drift.

I'm sobbing, gulping in great bursts of air.

'He's not below! He's not – not there! He's not anywhere! Is he – did you see him since last night? Was he up here with you? Oh my God! Where is he?'

Conleth stands, keeping one hand on the wheel. Why is he so calm?

'No, of course he's not up here. I haven't seen him – he must be down below. He's got to be. Have you looked in the cabins? All the cabins?'

I'm shaking all over.

'I've looked. I've searched everywhere – all the cabins, the toilet – there's nowhere he can be! Oh Christ – oh my God! Where is he? Call the search and rescue—'

He steps away from the wheel and immediately the boat is lurched to one side.

'Go back down, one more time. He must be asleep or something.'

317

And I do what he says, though it wastes more time, though I know something bad has happened. My body knows it. My legs are weak and my mouth is dry. I'm dreaming. I must be dreaming. I stagger back down the steps into the cabin, run through the saloon and the bathroom to the front berth, where he was. There's his iPad, his jumper – the runners he was wearing. On the floor by the bed is the case I'd packed, half unzipped, contents spilling out of it. And time stands still.

I lift the case on to the bed and unzip it completely, my fingers shaking uncontrollably. Everything is all jumbled together. But something is missing.

No digger.

And something else – the armbands are gone.

61

Laura

After I text Niamh, I bury my face in Matt's chest and he strokes the back of my head, the way he does with the kids when they're crying.

'Sssh. It's all right,' he says softly.

'I don't know if I can do this, Matt,' I whisper. 'Yesterday, I – God! With all of them there together – it's – it's – I'm just in the way. There's no point.'

His hand curves under my jaw and he lifts my face, tilting it towards him gently. He puts his head on one side, saying nothing. A shaft of early-morning sunlight catches his cheek, silvering the stubble along his jaw. When did his beard start going silver, I wonder? I look up at him in his old-man stripey pyjamas, and his expression is so familiar – that patient kindness. Like he's waiting for me to be the best version of myself. And sometimes that's infuriating. Today though, it's okay.

We're whispering so as not to wake the kids and, just for a second, I'm back, remembering us sneaking through his parents' hallway after nights out, Matt trying to smuggle me into his room. Even though we were in our twenties and could have been living together if we wanted. Justy and Dermot always wanting things done properly.

'They called you,' he says. 'Go on.' He places his hands on my shoulders and gently moves me away from him. 'Don't overthink it. Go.'

He's right. It was the overthinking that finished me

yesterday. I'd arrived at the hospice in the early evening. I'd even got as far as the corridor outside his room. They have an end-of-life suite and it's so beautiful. There's such a comforting, homely feel to the whole place. But, as I approached the door, through the side panel of glass, I saw so many legs and feet. They must have all been in there – Charlie, the girls and Seán were all in the room. I pictured myself opening the door and – and I just couldn't do it.

I backed up the hallway, then turned and almost sprinted into one of the little sitting rooms, trying to control my breathing, to drown out the thoughts. In the end, I just came home. Maybe it's too late. There's too much to do in work, with the Fitzgerald case.

Matt sees me hesitate. He turns to the table behind him and grabs my car keys, presses them into my hand.

'You've got this, okay?'

'But Niamh's on her way to – maybe I—'

He plants a kiss on my forehead and I know he's treating me like one of the kids, but this time it works. I feel commissioned. Strengthened.

'I should just go up and get my stuff for work. I'll go straight to work after.'

'One thing at a time,' says Matt. 'Go on.'

He's right. Niamh's got this. She's always two steps ahead. It's time to face my father.

@nolimitsgrl: Just checking in – how's it going?
@annahanna: I thought we were giving her a night off! Although sure, look – while we're at it. Is it too late to order the sunglasses? Looking for a pair in the silver.
@theirishmammy: I bought a pair last night! Go for it. Now's good probably. Not much traffic on the site. The code is Gemm15.
@nolimitsgrl: Anyone else think it's weird that she hasn't replied in over 18 hours?
@annahanna: @theirishmammy thanks! @gemstone we're thinking of you.
@missymurfi: You okay, Gemma?
@missymurfi: I thought I saw them last night in their car – the whole family.
@theirishmammy: Stalker much? You'll give us a bad name.
@missymurfi: It's not being a stalker to worry about her. I noticed because it was late. Ferdia would usually be in bed. Kids should be in bed by 8.

62

Gemma

'He's not here!' I'm screaming. 'He's not here – he's not any-where and his digger's gone, and his armbands. I—'

My breath is coming too fast. I'm hyperventilating. I grab hold of the rails and scramble up the steps.

'Where's my phone? Conleth!'

Why isn't he doing something?

'Where's my phone? Your phone! Call the guards! Call the rescue – the R L – R—' I can't even remember the initials for the rescue boat.

Conleth is standing in the prow of the boat looking out to sea. He's as calm as I've ever seen him. We're drifting.

'Conleth!' I think I'm going to pass out.

And it's like slow motion. He turns to face me, his hand stretched out behind him, pointing. His mouth moves, but the wind roars and I hear nothing. He turns away again, then back.

'Look,' he's saying.

And I don't want to look, but I do. I look where he's point-ing. He's pointing at a dark bundle bobbing in the water. A misshapen blob, not a boy. Definitely not a little boy with gangly arms and glasses and curly hair. This is a black, shiny blob – a bundle that looks as though it's wearing my boy's jacket. It looks like this blob is wearing armbands.

63

Niamh

I pull up at the house. That's good. Conleth's car is not there. She said he'd be out till at least twelve. Even so, I want to get them out of the house as soon as possible. Especially now. I will Stephen to hurry up, pulling into a parking space and killing the engine. There's no one about, which is also good. We want to keep this low-key. The fewer journalists that find out the better. In fact, it'd be great to get her into the station with no witnesses at all. But that's got a freaking snowball's chance in hell of happening, the later it gets. Someone will leak it. I get out of the car and click the door closed quietly. *Come on, come on, lads.*

Suddenly, I'm aware of a loud rapping sound. Really loud. What the hell? I run down the short path towards the side door of the house, where the noise is coming from. A bulky form – she: it's a woman – dressed entirely in pink, is alternately rapping on the side door and peering in the kitchen window, her hands drawn up to the side of her cheeks, forming a rectangular shape, like a pair of goggles, so she can look in.

'What's going on?'

Hearing me, she lurches backwards, looking around guiltily.

'Sorry – it's – it's not what it looks like,' she's stuttering. 'I didn't mean – I wasn't spying.'

'Well, if that's not spying, I don't know what is,' I say. 'What are you doing?'

She hesitates. I flash the ID, grabbing her elbow and trying to steer her away from the house.

'This is a Garda matter,' I snap. 'I need you to move along.'

'I'm a friend of Gemma's,' she blurts, grabbing my wrists. The hood of her jacket slips backwards, revealing a fancy-looking pair of sunglasses perched on top of her head. It's a dull morning. There's not likely to be much call for shades. The glasses are two-toned, a kind of bronze shade that fades into black. Gemma's logo – the lozenge-shaped diamond – winks, and it clicks suddenly that I'm looking at a major fan, dressed head to toe in Gemma's products. The windproof zippy jacket with the hood, the cargo pants, and now the sunglasses – all in a shade of baby pink which looks a bit strange on this woman, who has easily twenty years and as many kilos on the designer.

'I'm – I'm a gemstone. A follower. My name's Lesley Murphy.' She keeps glancing over my shoulder, trying to look in the window even as I manoeuvre her towards the gate. 'No – no, sorry. I was just – I was out doing, you know – we do our eight by eight, like Gemma.'

'Eight by eight?'

'Eight thousand steps by eight in the morning,' she says. 'All her gemstones – that's what she calls us, the fans. Her followers. We all do it – for our fitness. Gemma says it's really important. Or you can do ten by ten, or—'

'Got it. Thanks. But you need to leave now, Lesley. Like I said, this is a Garda matter.' I gesture towards the path. It's all quiet, not a sound from the house, no activity.

A sheen of sweat glistens on her smooth forehead. Her cheeks are pink. I move my attention to her hands. The knuckles of her right hand are grazed. She sees me looking and pulls down her sleeve to cover it.

'That's – I'm really worried about her. I've been knocking

on the door for ages. There's no one in there. Can't you, you know, break down the door or something? She's – I think she could be in trouble!'

'Why would you think that, Lesley?'

'Can we not break it down?' she says now, letting go of my arm and trying to get back to the house.

'There's no "we", Lesley,' I say. She's obviously deranged. 'Now, I need you to step aside and, like I said, you need to move along.'

Where the hell is Stephen? I know Gemma said that Conleth would be out, but still, Lesley banging on the door would have woken the dead.

'How long were you knocking for?'

'Erm, maybe a minute?' she says, and I know by her guilty expression that I can multiply that by five. Shit.

'Lesley, I need you to leave,' I say, shooing her away with hand gestures. 'Right now!' I bark, when she doesn't move. She retreats a few steps.

I peer in the window myself, not sure what I'm looking for, shading my eyes exactly as Lesley did. The kitchen is empty. I can see clear from the front window almost all the way to the beanbag that blocks the French windows that lead into the garden. Opposite, the door into the stairwell is half open and I can see what looks like clothes or bundles of washing or something on the floor. The kitchen table is completely clear – nobody has had a cup of tea or a bite of breakfast. Or if they did, they've cleared it away already. No sign of the kid. And kids get up early – in Siobhán's house, there'd already be about five half-finished bowls of cereal by eight in the morning. I don't like this at all.

'Move, please,' I snap, pushing past Lesley. 'I'm going to need you to leave this property. Leave!' I point towards the road. 'Out!'

Lesley heads slowly towards the gate as I grab hold of the iron stair rail and start running up the main steps. I bang on the front door and ring the bell simultaneously.

'Eh, Garda?' says Lesley, watching me from the path. She's literally only a single step outside on the road.

'What?' I turn away from her. Is that footsteps from inside the house? I ring the bell again.

'Eh – can I just?' She motions a scissors movement with her fingers.

'What?'

Needing no further encouragement, she trots back to the steps of the front entrance, stands looking up at me with her phone in her hand.

'We were messaging her, you see? Her – her friends on Instagram. We're her friends – well, followers, I suppose, really. And I look out for her – we all do. And there's something you should know—'

The front door is opened by a tall, sleepy-looking guy in what are clearly his pyjamas.

'Thanks,' I say. 'Gardaí.' I push past him, dimly aware that Lesley's saying something.

'Stay there!' I yell, ready to check out the flat. 'Wait there and don't move.'

64

Laura

Alva spots me through the panel of glass in the door and comes out, arms wide to hug. Her hair is gathered in a messy ponytail and her face is streaked with dried tears. I switch my work phone to vibrate and pocket it.

'You made it,' she says. Her chin trembles. We hold each other for a moment and I smell the clean scent of her shampoo layered over a toasty smell – the smell of hospital breakfasts.

'Is he –' I'm the first to end the embrace. 'Sorry. I – I couldn't find parking and it's—' A part of me – a part of me that I hate – hopes I'm too late.

She grasps my shoulders and squeezes. She's shaking her head.

'No – he's – he's still with us. Come on,' she says, holding me against her with one hand and pushing the door open with the other. 'It's okay.'

Charlie is sitting in the armchair near the head of the bed, her face creased with tiredness. One hand rests on top of my father's, the other is folded protectively across her stomach. She looks old. Áine is perched on the deep windowsill, her legs dangling against the wall. She's put a deep red colour in her hair since I'd last seen photos of her, and she looks nothing like her twin. In fact, I realize with a start, that if you had to choose which one of us was Alva's sister, you'd probably pick me. I'm trying to process everything at once – the

327

people, the thin man on the bed who looks nothing like the dad I remember, the machines beeping, the music playing softly. What is that song?

I'm grateful for the gravity of the situation – that it renders introductions irrelevant. We all know who each other is. Even if we've never met properly. Now Charlie smiles at me. She clicks her phone and the music stops.

'We have his playlist on Spotify,' she says. 'He was the one who chose Fleetwood Mac. Wouldn't be my first choice.'

'The Chain', I realize. That's the song. Charlie beckons me to the bedside, turning to speak to him.

'Look who's here, love. It's Laura.'

The man who used to be Dad lies propped up on the pillows, a thin, dark stick against the white of hospital sheets. His hair has thinned and someone has cropped it close against his skull. There are purple shadows under his closed eyes.

'Look, love,' says Charlie again. 'You need to see her.'

'It's okay – don't – he doesn't have to—' I say, feeling a lurching in my stomach, like when a lift starts its ascent. I don't know if I want him to open his eyes. I – what will I say?

I'm aware of movement behind me as Alva comes to stand at the other side of him. She reaches past me to rub his head, then smooths his forehead, the way I'd comfort Noah or Katie if they were upset.

'Of course he does,' she says, and there's such kindness in her voice. It's the way she is with the kids. 'Dad,' she says, louder. 'Dad. Open your eyes, okay? Just for a minute. Your three girls are here.'

A smile – I think it's a smile – hovers at the corner of his lips, and Alva nods. She steps back and ushers me closer to him.

'He knows we're here,' she says. 'Go on.'

And I silence the voice in my head, the one with all the questions. The eight-year-old's voice that asks, *Why did you go? Why did you leave us? How could you do it? What about Mum and Cian and me? What about me?* I copy Alva and I place my hand against his cheek and the other on his shoulder, and I can feel the bones under both. And I kiss his cheek and rest my head on his chest, lightly, for fear I'd crush it. And I close my eyes.

08:15

@missymurfi: Anyone know what's going on with Gemma? Anyone heard or seen anything? Still no posts?
@theirishmammy: Nope. Heard nothing. Maybe she's taking a day or two off.
@missymurfi: She'd have told us. It's like she just vanished. @nolimitsgrl?
@theirishmammy: Having a lie-in? It's Saturday.
@missymurfi: I'm at the house right now. She's definitely not here. The guards are though.
@theirishmammy: What the? What do they say? Why are they at the house?
@nolimitsgrl: Wait there @missymurfi. I'm on my way.

65

Gemma

I'm grabbing on to the rail at the front of the boat, and I don't know what I'm screaming. All I know is that I'm trying to keep it in my sight – the bundle – the dreadful shape, the blob that can't – it can't be Ferdia! It can't be! But where is he?

The wind has picked up and the water is navy and black and splashes of white, and the – the thing – it keeps disappearing. And I'm grasping the rail and already my body is – I'm starting to climb it, and then I realize I'm not wearing a lifejacket. I turn back to look at Conleth. He'll know what to do. He'll – he's fixing this. He'll save him. He'll dive in.

But Conleth turns and begins walking away. This has got to be a nightmare. I smack my palm against my cheek, feeling the damp and the cold. It's real. It's really happening.

'Conleth!' My voice is a scream of agony. Why is he doing nothing? 'Is it – is that Ferdia? Oh my God! Oh my God!'

Conleth is moving about the boat, his back to me. Maybe he's getting – could we reach him with the boat-hook thing? Another big wave comes – it's like we're sideways in a current. I can see the town in the distance and I think of all the people just walking around, shopping or visiting the library, and – and they – if they look out they won't see anything to worry about. Just a boat bobbing in the waves.

Oh, thank Christ! Conleth turns, and I see that he's holding – it looks like he's got something – there's a coil of rope and a float thing in his hands. I turn back to the spot where I saw the bundle, squinting. Maybe – the water drops once more, and I catch a glimpse of yellow. A single armband.

'Get him, Conleth!' I yell over the noise of the wind. In slow motion I watch Conleth's movements – they're slow, unhurried. He begins winding the remaining rope in a figure-of-eight motion around two metal prongs.

'No can do.' His voice is flat. He shakes his head.

'Please! Please! Get him – Conleth, why – what are you doing? CONLETH!' I scream, and the shriek is tangled with the noise of wind and wheeling gulls.

And still he does nothing. I can't bear it. I jump into the navy water.

66

Niamh

Thank Christ! I hear a car door slam and the sound of running footsteps. I sprint up the path to where McCarthy and Stephen are trying to make their way past Lesley and nosy onlookers blocking the gate.

I brief them, as quick as I can. A second Garda car arrives and two lads in full body armour emerge, one of them clutching the battering ram.

What the hell? I stare at McCarthy. He tilts his head towards the door, motioning for me to join him.

'We've a warrant?' I say, hoping to feck that we do.

'We have reason to fear for the safety of the wife and child,' he replies, his face taut with strain.

Up on the top step, neighbours are gathered, tutting, whispering, some of them already filming on their phones.

'Through here,' McCarthy instructs the lads, pointing towards the door.

'Clear the scene!' Stephen yells up the stairs. 'And stop filming!'

Lesley has burst through the makeshift barrier yet again.

'You've got to leave, Lesley,' I say, shepherding her past the officer manning the gate. I give him a look. 'Keep everyone out, okay?'

'But I just need to—'

'No, Lesley.'

From the side passage, a splintering sound tells me that

the door has finally given way. I sprint back down the path, pausing to shoo the residents on the steps.

On the threshold, McArsey is issuing orders, explaining the plan for a search sequence. It's just the three of us on the step. Stephen and I exchange a look. It's so still. A part of me dreads the thought of going in. That horrific recent case in Wicklow – a whole family. Neighbours had alerted the guards after a few days without seeing the family – and when the officers got in, just bodies – three kids, the mam and an auntie.

He nods, and I know he's thinking the same thing.

'I know the layout,' I say, stepping ahead of him and McCarthy. 'I'll lead.'

67

Gemma

I jump. It's only a couple of metres into the water but, even so, my legs and feet and body are jarred with the impact. I feel it judder through me. I feel it seize my heart and steal my breath and I'm going down, down, down. Penny says trust. Penny says I can do this. She says you'll float, but you have to trust, and I close my eyes and oh-my-God-oh-my-God-oh-my-God. It's so cold. And I still haven't breathed. And I'm still going down.

It roars. The water scalds and screams in my eardrums and I think of Penny and I think of Max and I think of Ferdia. My boy. And I stop sinking and I begin to rise. My lungs are screaming to breathe, but not yet, not yet. I have to get to Ferdia.

I break the surface of the water and gasp. It's black and freezing cold, but my body demands oxygen and I take in a huge breath. My clothes feel heavy and clumsy and I'm pedalling my legs as I turn and turn, trying to get my bearings. I'm on the far side of the boat – I can't see the harbour. The boat is blocking my view. And my neck muscles are seizing up rigid in the cold, but I keep circling my hands. I've made them into paddles and I'm circling. Circling.

Where is he? Ferdie – Ferdie – I'm coming! Hold on. Hold on.

And the waves are choppy like peaks of icing on a

cake – those Christmas cakes where you can snap off the little points of sugar – and I'm up and down, craning my neck.

I'm screaming for Conleth. I scream his name over the noise of the wind. Did I hear something? I heard him – I think I heard him jump in – he must have jumped in.

And then I see Ferdia.

And he's – but that can't be right – he's in the water and he's clutching the digger and he's got one armband on and his head is dipping, dipping. He's all lopsided – but it's him. I can't see his face. My baby!

'Ferdie!' I scream, trying not to gulp saltwater. 'Hold on! Oh my God! Hold on! Wait!'

68

Laura

I hold my father's hand in both of mine, trying to ignore the pulse of a message landing in my phone, trying to push Niamh, Gemma – Max – all of them, pushing them out of my mind. Charlie is sitting opposite, her head resting on his shoulder, and beside her Alva and Áine mirror my pose, clutching his hand.

'Thanks,' says Seán, shutting the door after the nurse. She'd closed his eyes and done something with the sheets and a plastic thing, so his mouth didn't hang open.

'Take as long as you like,' she'd said. 'Just ring the bell when you need me.'

Fleetwood Mac sing on.

'Thanks, Seán, can you turn that off now?' Charlie sniffs.

Seán clicks his phone and the room is silent. Out in the car park, a car alarm bleats six, seven times before someone turns it off.

His hand is already cool – already it feels like the hand of a corpse. I let go of it then lay it straight alongside his body. Charlie watches me. She looks so desperately tired, her curly hair dishevelled and dry-looking. She nods.

'I'm glad – I'm glad you made it,' she says. And I wonder if she's serious, or if there's something sarcastic in her words. My confusion must show in my face, because she smiles.

'Honestly.' She's crying again. 'It doesn't matter, does it? Not when you're staring death in the face.' She blows her nose noisily into a tissue then crumples it into a ball in her fist.

337

'It means so much to him that you forgave him in the end. Forgiveness is so important.'

I return her smile, wanting so much to be the person she thinks I am. I adored him with that absolute devotion of a little girl, but still he walked out of our lives without a backwards glance. I couldn't have loved him more, but it wasn't enough for him. And to see him today, it's like – I mean, it's desperately sad. I feel sad for him. But I'm not sure if I've forgiven him. Niamh says I've a gold medal in grudge-holding. And she's right.

'Thanks for – thanks for letting me be here,' I say instead.

'And he forgave you too. It hurt him so much when you cut him out of your life,' she says, her lips pressing together as though to stop worse words emerging. 'And he tried so many times to reach out. I'm just glad you were able to be here for the end.'

My mouth opens, and I know I'm staring. My eyes begin to sting with tears. My heart pounds.

'He loved you,' she says. 'He dearly loved all his children.' She nods. A satisfied little nod.

'He forgave you, Laura. Bless him.'

He forgave me. *He* forgave *me?* I'm on my feet in an instant and my heart is hammering in my chest. I look at Alva. She looks back, her head tilted to one side, face twisted with emotion.

'I'm – I'm sorry,' I stammer, 'I have to go. I—'

Oh my God. I've got to get out of this room – away from Charlie, from this family. They're not mine. They're nothing to do with me. All I can think of at this moment is Matt, the kids, Niamh. Niamh who I've left to deal with a crucial morning on her own. My pulse thrums. I'm aware that I'm frozen upright, kind of looming over the deathbed.

I scan the room, their faces, their eyes, and now I see they all look alike – they have Charlie's eyes and her broad cheek-bones. They're nothing like me. They're strangers. You choose your family.

I should never have come. I should have been with Niamh. My phone has been hopping, and I ignored it. Or I could have been at home with Matt and the kids doing Saturday-morning things. Why did I think I could do anything here? Why did I think I could fix this now, after all this time?

He was – and I don't let myself go there. Not now. I'm in the doorway and my hand is grasping the handle, white bones of knuckles stark against the paintwork. Keep it together.

'I've got to go,' I say.

And I close down the hatch where I loved my dad and where I thought he'd love me again. And I put Ice Laura back in place because she's got a job to do.

'I'm so sorry for your loss,' I say, looking right through them.

69

Niamh

An eerie-sounding whistle of wind howls through the doorway we've just battered, but inside the apartment the silence is complete. It's like a showhouse – polished marble surfaces, gleaming chrome, glossy banks of cupboards and everything in its place in the kitchen and the small pantry beside it. I follow McArsey through to the next room, a TV den of some sort. Again, it's tidy. The only sign of a four-year-old living in the house is a large basket at the end of the sofa in which various toys are placed, neatly. We pass a bathroom on the right – glass tiles, marble, shining clean – and beyond that there's a small room which I recognize from her Instagram, though it's much smaller in real life. A full-size mirror takes up the corner, a large built-in wardrobe along the opposite wall, and a rail of clothes – bright and garish in the midst of all the white and cream. I catch sight of myself in the mirror: my face is white.

'In here.' I follow the sound of Stephen's voice, dreading what I might be about to see.

We're in the main bedroom, and it's the only room that looks messy. The bed is crumpled and there's a rectangular crease set into the duvet where clearly a suitcase had been placed. To the right of that, a small pile of children's clothes has toppled over on its side. On the cream carpet, a child's sandal.

From the en suite bathroom I hear McCarthy.

'Reckon we need a sweep for drugs. It looks as though someone's using.'

Stephen turns to me. 'Everything in here suggests a rapid exit.'

'Looks like it,' I agree, turning back to look at the chest of drawers beside the doorway. It looks a bit cock-eyed, the top-left drawer half hanging out and the lower drawers not completely closed. I pop gloves on and get out evidence bags.

'What've we got?' Stephen frowns.

I lay the stuff out along the plastic. It's like one of those memory games you play with kids: what goes with what? Who owns this?

There's a wallet with an old twenty note in it, from when we had púnts. And a business card – *Patrick O'Hara, Marine Engineer*. I tilt it so McArsey can read it.

'The father, I presume?'

'And look at all this,' I say, pulling out a brooch tangled with a large fishing hook which itself has become embedded in a tie. I recognize the Corrig Point crest. Stephen is shaking his head.

'The bastard,' he breathes. 'You know what this is, don't you? A stash of trophies.'

'Darmody? Darmody! Can you come here, please! Darmody!' A yell from the doorway. I whirl around.

'She says she needs to tell you something important,' says the young guard who's been put manning the doorway. 'Sorry, she won't—'

He jerks his thumb outside and I follow his gaze, to see Lesley hopping from foot to foot.

'Oh Christ!' I curse, before remembering his bodycam.

He colours. 'She said it's really important.'

'Of course,' I say, locking eyes with Stephen. 'Can you—' Carefully, I hand him the evidence bag.

'Sure.'

I make my way out of the room and outside, running down the path, ready to give Lesley, and the woman who has joined her, a piece of my mind and a lecture to the uniform in When Not to Disturb the Detectives.

'Garda! I've been trying to tell you,' Lesley shouts in a panicked voice. 'I saw her last night – I saw Gemma last night.'

'When? Do you know where she was headed? Where was this?'

'I was – it was just – kind of near here,' Lesley murmurs, looking ashamed. 'In the car. I—'

I'm on the phone straightaway to McArsey. I hold up a finger.

'Hang on, Lesley, you've been— Senan – Sarge – we need to run a check on the family car. Reg number—' I flip back to the page where I'd noted the registration number, what now seems like weeks ago, and call it out to him, then end the call.

'Can you give your contact details to the uniformed officer there?' I point to where the rookie, Hugo, is standing near the gate.

Lesley's cheeks redden.

'Did I do something wrong?'

'Not at all.' I shake my head. 'You've been really helpful, Lesley.'

I take a few steps away from them to make another call to Laura.

70

Laura

Matt answers on the first ring, and I nearly lose it at the kindness in his voice – the concern. He always sounds so good on the phone. In the background I can hear the kids chattering. I tell him about Dad.

'You okay? Where are you now? Do you want me to come and pick you up?'

I tell him no, that I'm fine.

'I'm in the car heading to Dún Laoghaire.'

'And he's – you saw him before he died?' he says.

'Yeah – I – it was—' I break off, distracted by the sound of the kids. 'What are they watching?'

He laughs. 'They're not watching anything, chief. Believe it or not, they're looking at a book. But it's good to know you're not so distressed by the death of your father that you don't have time for a bit of micro-managing.' His voice is gentle. 'That's my girl.'

'Sorry,' I sigh, taking the exit off the motorway. 'Thanks.'

'So what's the plan? Are you driving?'

'Yeah, sorry—' I break off, realizing that Niamh is trying to get through.

'Bye. Tell the kids – will you do that? And I'm okay. I'm fine. See you later.'

I end the call and Niamh's voice, urgent, distorted by the wind, comes on the line.

'It's him – it's Conleth. No doubt about it. And she's not in the house, Laura. He's taken them. Get here now!'

I blue-light it, and the lyrics to 'The Chain' repeat on a loop in my brain.

71

Gemma

I can't scream – I can't even wave. If I open my mouth, the water sloshes and I'm gulping, and I know Penny said trust and just let go and you'll float – but my boy! He's over there – I saw him! I know I saw him and now I can't see anything. Where's Conleth? I tread water and I try to turn, and why's Conleth not helping? And I hear the engine, and Conleth – oh no, oh God! He's going away! And I – I tread and pedal my legs faster, faster, and where is he? Oh my God! Is that a flash of yellow?

The water is fighting me like a – like a wild creature. The wild horses. They call the waves wild horses and I know that's right. They're trampling me down like wild horses. The sea pulls me down and it slaps me in my eyes, across my face. And Conleth is gone. The boat is gone, and I know then. I know something deep in my brain. He hates us. Max and Ferdie and me. We three. He wants us dead.

And I let my head tilt back because my neck is so tired and it's frozen rigid. But I'm so close – I can almost touch him. I'm so cold. And the bottom of the deep blue sea is waiting for me. Max and me and Ferdie three. And I'm skimming my hands like paddles, trying to turn. Where is he? Where's my boy? And I try to turn in the water, but it's so cold. I'm so cold. And I want to lie back and I want to sleep, but no. No. Penny says trust. Penny says keep moving. And there's shouting – see me! Ferdie! Hold on, Ferdie!

I can't. Cold.

72

Niamh

'So, Lesley. Tell me a bit more about where exactly you saw Gemma. Are you sure it was her?' I'm trying not to panic Lesley, but everything about her delivery – everything – is like in slow motion. A buzzing in my pocket alerts me to an incoming text. While Lesley assembles herself, I glance at the phone.

Please call me.

From Sarita. Can't deal with that now.

'Out on the main road, you know? Just down there.'

She points over the small, grassed area towards the pedestrian gate.

'And which way was she headed?'

'It's one-way,' says the woman with her, who gave her name as Nola Shanley, said she was a childhood friend of Gemma's. 'They'd have to head up towards Blackrock before going anywhere.'

'Thanks,' I say, though really I'm thinking, hell – we've no idea where they went. They've had hours to get away. 'And this was—'

'About half eight or nine last night,' says Lesley. 'And he was driving. Ferdie was in the back in his car seat. And that's not right, is it? Because children should be in bed by eight.'

She nods, and then her features seem suddenly to loosen. Tears surge in her eyes.

'Should I have called you last night?' Her voice is choked with emotion. She grabs Nola's forearms. 'I should have. Shouldn't I? I just didn't think anything was wrong – though I hate how she always does what he says. Like she always – don't you think – don't you think she always looks so sad, Nola? Even in her posts? I'm always saying that. Oh my God, maybe there's something else, like—'

Nola hugs the larger woman, patting her back.

'Lesley's what you might call a superfan, Detective,' she says.

'Not a stalker.' Lesley's voice is muffled.

'Certainly not,' replies Nola.

My phone rings again and McArsey's voice comes back, distorted by movement. I've no idea what he's saying, but before I head back into the building he comes running up the path.

'I'll head to the station. You and – where's Shaw?'

'On her way,' I say. 'We'll meet you at—'

'Wait!' A cry from Nola, who is still embracing a sobbing Lesley, her shoulders shaking, clutching her phone like a talisman. 'Lesley's got something else for you!' Lesley shuffles towards me, holding out her hand.

'It was on the ground over there.' She turns, pointing to the footpath outside the gate. 'On the ground beside where her car – the car is parked. There.' She points to their parking space.

I reach to take it. A Leatherman knife. I brush the specks of dirt off and turn it over to read the inscription.

Maxattacks

Love Gem

30/05/07

'Go on,' nods Stephen, drawing level with me. Our eyes lock – waiting. I click the blade out. It's shiny, sharp. But it's not as sharp as it should be.

347

Stephen bags it and turns to the rookie guard.

'Hugo? Get this to FSI straightaway. And alert Parminter, right? Could be the murder weapon.'

The lad's eyes widen. 'Will do.'

I'm just about to call Laura again when Nola comes running over.

'Guard! A message has just come in from another follower – Úna. *MaxSpirit* is not in the harbour,' she says, shaking her head. 'Could they be out in the boat?'

'Right, I'll contact the LOM,' says McCarthy, who has just reached us. 'And the Water Unit. You—'

'Heading to the harbour,' I finish, sprinting to the car.

73

Laura

'Should be there in a couple,' I tell her. 'I'm just at—'

'No, wait, come straight to the harbour.' Niamh's voice is strained. 'They're in the yacht. Mc— Senan's contacted Marine Patrol and the Lifeboat Operations Manager, and there's a satnav-type thing in boats. They're going to try and trace it.'

'Oh hell!' I snap, annoyed at the timing, as I've just turned down towards the seafront. 'Sorry, I'm on – what's it called? – Albany Avenue. I'd turned off already. I'll be there as soon as I can. It's one-way.'

I inhale, trying to ease the clenched feeling in my stomach. We should have pushed it with him yesterday, rattled him more. Instead, I just let him walk out the door. I realize I'm shaking my head, like it's all over already. *There's a little thing called evidence*, I hear, in Cig's voice. We couldn't take him in without evidence. And we don't know for sure that—

My thoughts are interrupted by the sight of a small group of women on the steps leading to Seapoint Beach. A few are in dryrobes, others in track gear or outdoor clothes – pinks and bright colours. They're clustered together, gesticulating, checking phones, pointing out to sea. What the hell?

I pull in and park near the walkway, leaving the lights flashing. Before I reach them, I recognize Penny, her wet hair leaving a shining trail down her jacket, running towards me. She's clutching her phone, her fingertips white with the cold.

'T—Tom is out there,' she points to a tiny speck in the

distance in the bay. 'With Alex. They've been out since, I don't know – just before eight. They go out most mornings when they're training. But it doesn't look right – there's something wrong. They haven't moved.'

She presses the phone into my hand.

'I took a photo – I mean, it's miles away. They're never out that far unless it's a race or something. So it's out of focus, but look.' She points at a blur in the middle of blurred blue water. 'Like, that's not the position they're in when they're sailing. It's all wrong. They're not capsized, but they're not moving either. Something's wrong.'

74

Niamb

Stephen's wearing the bright yellow jacket and red life vest of the RNLI, adjusting his helmet when I arrive. The two other crew members are already here: a short girl, who introduces herself as Izzy, and a rangy bearded guy – Paul. Everything seems to be happening at once.

'Well.' Stephen nods. 'What have we got?'

'Their berth is empty, that's confirmed,' says Paul, 'and we have a possible sighting, about a mile out, south of the pier.'

The bright orange and black of the rescue boat is stark against the grey stone of the pier. Along the side it reads D – 865.

'This is *Réaltín*,' says Izzy, throwing gear into the boat. 'She's brilliant.' She grasps the handle. 'Absolutely solid – a pocket rocket.'

A few metres away, McCarthy is in full flight on the phone, gesticulating. He ends the call.

'We'll follow you,' he says, nodding at Stephen. 'Nothing at all on the AIS?'

'Deactivated. They – he – must have switched it off,' says Paul.

McCarthy turns to me. 'The automatic identification system – AIS. All boats have it, but it can be deactivated. Come on,' he says, beckoning me.

I look down at my phone – nothing from Laura. She should be here by now. But I see a missed call from Sarita. I frown, like I can squeeze the thoughts out of my brain. I can't think of her now. McArsey strides along the slipway, away from the RNLI boat.

'Come on,' he says, breaking into a run. 'They've got a rib ready for us in the club.'

He points towards the yacht club, where a large number of boats are assembled behind blue wrought-iron gates.

The red light starts blinking and there's a beeping sound as the lifeboat gets ready to launch. Izzy takes a call on the radio, confers with Stephen and Paul, then shouts over to us.

'Change of plan. We've reports of a body in the water, beyond Seapoint. We're taking that.'

The boat begins moving, Izzy jogging to keep up.

'You head out of the harbour and then basically turn right – that's south – towards the sighting,' she shouts over the noise of the beeping. 'We're heading the other way, towards Seapoint. Keep the radio on our channel, yeah?'

75

Niamh

A body in the water? I swallow down the nausea. Bouncing over the waves is not recommended, but it's not that making me sick. *Body in the water. No. Please.* I'm sick at the thought of them alone with him – the fear that we might be too late. What if the body in the water is – stop. I stop. No point in *what if*. Deal with what's here and now.

I look over at McCarthy. He's in his element manning the rib. It's a glarey morning, the white of the sky refracting off the water with an almost painful strobe effect. He has his shades on, the wind whipping his hair in little tufts around the side of his helmet because, naturally, he found time to put on a safety helmet. I'm not knocking it – he gave me one too. It's just he's so methodical, whereas I'm panicking – my heart in my throat with the terror that we're too late. I'm sitting in the front of the boat, grabbing on to the handle with one hand, clutching the VHF radio to my ear with the other, trying to make out the info coming in from the control room. Which is not easy, because every time we bounce over a wave, I levitate, then crash back down on to the seat with a thump. Maybe it's called a rib because it breaks your ribs. Christ's sake!

We parted ways with the lifeboat a couple of minutes ago, and now we're exiting the safety of Dún Laoghaire harbour, turning out beyond the West Pier, heading into the wide expanse beyond.

'They say do a loop along the coastline, heading south,' I shout back to McArsey, miming a looping motion with my free hand. 'Towards Greystones. Do you know what we're looking for?' I yell, the wind whipping my words away. He nods.

'Roger that. A Hallberg-Rassy!' he shouts back, the words distorted by the wind. 'It's big.'

'I mean, if they set sail last night, how far could they be by now?'

He's shaking his head.

'Don't know,' he yells. 'No idea. We're alerting the nearest harbours. He's not in Greystones harbour, or we'd have heard.'

I raise my gaze to the fast-receding seafront of Dún Laoghaire: the spires, the higgledy-piggledy buildings, the stunning modernity of the Lexicon. Why does it feel like we're leaving civilization behind? I turn around again to face forwards, feeling the wind blasting my face. We pass Bullock Harbour and, beside us, Dalkey Island seems to be tagging alongside, lurking on my peripheral vision. The radio buzzes again.

'We've just had a distress call,' the voice crackles on the line. 'Sending you the coordinates. We have it at just beyond Coliemore Harbour – about half a kilometre south.'

I relay the message, yelling over the noise of the boat.

'Come on, come on!' I'm shouting over the wind, jaw clenched.

'Roger that,' nods Senan.

I lift my gaze to sweep the bay, straining for a sighting, for anything – anything that could be them.

76

Laura

'They're heading back.' Penny squints, shading her eyes from the glare. 'Maybe they'd just capsized or something.' She turns to me. 'But the sail—'

'The sea is really dangerous,' Lesley butts in. 'You should never take risks with the sea.'

I step away from them, trying to make out the voice of the garda on the other end of the line.

'Sorry, what?'

His words are scrambled in the poor reception and the offshore wind whipping my hair against the phone. 'What?'

He repeats himself, and the phrase sends a weight of despair crashing through me like a stone. I turn to make eye contact with Penny, who is standing a little bit away from the assembled women. There's about six or seven of them now. She and Lesley come towards me.

'They've radioed in. They found—' I start again. 'A body has been recovered from the water,' I say.

'Tom?' whispers Penny. 'Is it him? Or Alex? Oh God – but how – what?'

I hold up a hand, wait.

'No – hold on. It was the lads who found it,' I say slowly, willing her to understand. 'The boys – they found a body.'

Lesley's hand clamps over her mouth with a clapping sound and Penny holds her breath.

'No! No! Is it Gemma? Not Gemma!' Lesley wails. 'The sea is very dangerous.'

'Ssh. We don't know that. Ssh,' soothes Penny, putting her arm around Lesley, and I nod, willing her to contain the tide of emotion threatening to spill.

'The lifeboat is on the way out to them,' I say, and even as I speak, we see the flash of red skimming across the water, closing the gap between them.

'They'll bring it—'

'They'll bring it here. Corrig Point's the nearest,' Penny says. 'Oh my God, that must be why Tom had stopped – why they turned back. Who is it?'

'I need you to manage everyone here.' I make eye contact with Penny. 'We don't know who. We don't know anything yet.'

I turn away from the scene, the green water innocent-looking, bright boats and sails sprinkled across the dancing waves. I see the two boats draw together but can't make out what's happening from this distance.

'I have to get down there. Do not – do not let everyone follow, Penny. You won't get in.'

I run to the car, despairing, angry thoughts flinging themselves kamikaze-like around my brain in a storm of self-loathing. *You messed up. Again. Too late. You're too bloody late.* The siren wails and it sounds like despair, like howling heartbreak. I drive the wrong way along the seafront until I can cut up through on to the main road.

Too late. Why did you not take her in for her own safety? Whatever he's done, you're at fault. You're too late. Too late.

77

Niamh

'Can you go any faster?' I yell, though I know by the scream of the engine that he can't. We bounce along over the waves, past the point of Coliemore, the harbour a distant grey blur and, beyond us, a vast expanse of sea. And suddenly, I spot her.

'There! Look!' I yell. 'Is that them? That's them!' Senan nods, bringing the rib in a wide sweep, slowing the boat so we approach alongside the craft. It rears up out of the water, steel and chrome, rocking at an angle, waves slapping it broadside. McCarthy cuts the engine, manoeuvring us closer to the boat, our inflatable sides bumping against the side of the larger vessel in rhythmical thumps.

O'Hara stands in a central cockpit. He's pale. He's alone. No Gemma. No kid.

'Thank God!' he shouts. 'Where is she? Have you found her?'

Have we found her? We? What the hell?

He steps up out of the cockpit and on to the main deck, gesturing for us to move around to the rear of the boat to where there's a small wooden platform.

'Wait,' says McCarthy. 'We need to—'

While he's busy tying the smaller boat to one of the rails, I reach across and grab hold of the side rails then start clambering on board the boat.

'Where is she, Conleth?' I say, trying to peer around him to the cabin below. 'And Ferdia? Where is he?'

So much for playing it smoothly. I try to calm myself.

'What do you mean? I radioed you! That's what – that's why I just radioed in! She – oh my God! I don't know what happened – I don't know how it – how she just ran past me. I—'

He's blocking my line of vision. I look over my shoulder as McCarthy steps on to the main deck.

'Step aside, please,' he says. 'We need to search the boat.'

'You don't understand!' says Conleth, his eyes fixed on mine. McCarthy begins making his way down below deck.

'Oh my God! Please tell me you found her. Did you find her?'

He looks all around him, lines of concern etched in his face.

'No,' I say. 'We're looking for her – for both of them. What happened?'

'Jesus!'

He groans – and if he's acting, then it's good. 'Oh Christ.'

He takes a couple of steps along the side deck, looking back towards Dún Laoghaire, then turns to me.

'It was meant to be a surprise,' he says. 'I got up early and started sailing – she was asleep. She was asleep, for God's sake. It was meant to be a surprise. After—'

'What happened?' I snap. We don't have time for this. 'She was with you. They both were. Where is she?'

'That's what I'm trying to tell you! That's why I radioed for help.'

He puts his hands either side of his face.

'She came up from below deck – I don't know when – how long ago it was – five – a few minutes. I stopped the boat, I—'

McCarthy emerges from beneath the deck. He shakes his head.

'Where are they, O'Hara?' I'm rapidly running out of patience.

358

'It was maybe twenty – no, less, ten, fifteen minutes ago. Gemma came up on deck and she was yelling, screaming. Screaming our son's name. And before I – I mean, I thought maybe she was having a nightmare or she – I don't know. It was like she'd lost her mind. She was screaming Ferdia's name and – and I couldn't get to her in time. She ran down—' His arm lifts slowly, a finger pointing towards the bow of the boat, towards the way we've just come. He frowns.

'Before I could stop her, she just jumped right in,' he whispers, shaking his head.

'You said that was fifteen minutes ago?' I'm yelling, grabbing one of the handrails to steady myself. 'Are you kidding?'

The boat is bobbing in the most puke-making motion possible. McCarthy scans the water on all sides. There's no sign of anyone, of anything, in the dark depths.

'Why did you only just radio in?'

'Because I was trying to get to her!' His voice is strident. 'I tried to reverse. I cut the engine and lowered the anchor. But the tide – it's a spring tide and she can't swim. You know that, don't you? And I couldn't even see her.'

He scans the horizon, and he looks like an ad, or maybe it's a still from an old movie. His craggy face is lit by the morning glare and a tear – maybe it really is a tear – snakes down his cheek.

'I tried to reach her, but—'

'Was she wearing a flotation device?' McArsey's face is set in stone and I'm scanning the water, my head wheeling like I'm watching a tennis match.

'She jumped in?' I yell. 'Why would she do that?'

'I don't know!' He shakes his head. 'No. She didn't have a life vest. Oh my God,' he breathes. 'She's gone.'

And I can't believe it, but Senan is taking notes. 'No flotation device,' he repeats.

I whirl back around to face Conleth. 'What about Ferdia?'

He turns to look at me, his face blank.

'Ferdia! Your son? Where is he?'

Conleth sinks on to his knees on the deck, his head in his hands. I feel like punching him.

'Where's the child, Conleth, for Christ's sake?! Where is he?'

78

Laura

I abandon the car at the pier and sprint down the slipway. An ambulance and its crew are waiting beside the open door of the vehicle a few metres from the water's edge. Two of them – a heavy-set man and a woman – are making ready the equipment in the vehicle. The other guy is speaking on the radio.

'Have they picked up the body?' I say to the pair, flashing my ID badge. They nod.

'And? Male or female?' Please God not the child.

'Affirmative,' says the woman. 'A female. Apparently, the two lads had pulled her out of the water and they'd already begun sailing in with her when they radioed for help.'

'Is she – do we know if she's—'

The heavy-set man interrupts.

'We don't know,' he says. 'No idea how long she was in the water, and, well, it's not warmed up yet, this time of year.'

He exchanges another look with the woman.

'Exposure would get you in about maybe fifteen minutes, depending on body size.'

My face must show my feelings, because he fixes me with a brown-eyed stare, his eyebrows pulling down like curtains.

'But, Jaysus, those RNLI lads, if anyone can save the day, it's them. They're unreal. And they've the full resuss equipment in the bow pod of that boat, the responder bag – even an ambulance pouch. So like, whatever needs to be done, you can be sure they're already doing it.'

I turn to look out to sea, adrenalin surging uselessly through my body like fizzing electricity. Because there's nothing I can do at this point. I can't save her. Just beyond the mouth of the harbour, by the East Pier, the lifeboat craft is beginning its approach. A short distance behind the lifeboat, I spot the boat – Tom's 49er – following. If I prayed, I'd pray now.

More squad cars arrive, and uniformed officers begin clearing the quayside of onlookers, pushing everyone back behind a cordon. One starts directing the traffic above on the main road, where people have begun to slow.

I put a call into the incident room, and Tara updates me.

'Sarge and Detective Darmody are on the yacht. Due west of the harbour – they located the boat.'

'And the husband? The child?'

'O'Hara was on board,' she says. 'Negative for the mother and child.'

79

Niamh

His shoulders are shaking and he's full-on sobbing. Behind me, I hear McCarthy relaying the information over the radio.

'I – I—' I lean forward to hear Conleth.

'What about Ferdia? Where did you last see him?' I feel like shaking him. This is all an act. He won't look at me.

'Get up,' I snap. 'Get up – we need to coordinate the search. Where did you – where were you when Gemma jumped? Was Ferdia with her or with you?'

I catch Senan's eye, and he's still speaking to the team. I catch the words 'surface operation' and I hear him giving coordinates. At last Conleth staggers to his feet, then he seems to think of something.

'Maybe – oh please Jesus—' he says, lurching towards the steps below deck. I race after him, finding myself in a low-ceilinged room, everything clad in smooth oak. The walls are lined with small cupboards and lockers, their handles inset into the wood. Beyond the central table, which is littered with wrappers, I can just see a narrow short corridor leading through to a cabin at the front of the boat. Behind me on the right is a galley kitchen. Again, it's more luxurious and spacious than I expected, though it's cluttered with empty glasses and bottles. I feel the contents of my stomach begin to roil dangerously. Conleth is looking wildly around him.

'Was the child on the boat, Conleth? Answer me.' My voice

is harsh and I'm hard on his heels, worried about what he's going to do. He nods without turning around.

'He – he was asleep – we put him to bed.' He stands blocking my view of the forward cabin, gesturing to the bed as though expecting to see him there. 'There. Or maybe—' He breaks off, pushing past me and running a few steps along the right-hand corridor underneath the main deck, opening out into another wide cabin, in the middle of which is an unmade double bed. In the centre of the bed sits a pair of child's glasses. Ferdia's sturdy little plastic glasses.

'He's not here, Conleth. Are you saying – are you telling me Gemma jumped in the water?' I'm shaking my head, like I don't want to say the words, but I have to. 'Did she take the child? Is he—' I break off at the sound of whimpering, and a kind of dull thumping noise. I step back a few feet, turning to where the sound is coming from – a double-height locker on the left-hand side of the corridor, opposite the table.

'Stand back.' I open the door. It's a narrow locker, less than a metre wide but about two metres tall. Cramped in the base of the locker, curled like a prawn, is a small body.

80

Laura

Tom's face is blanched white. Both he and Alex are draped in survival blankets over their wetsuits. Someone from the club has given them hot drinks and the smell of coffee on the pier brings a weird thread of Southside weekends to an unreal situation. In the distance, the ambulance wails its siren, taking Gemma away. I'd watched the handover as they stretchered her from the lifeboat to the ambulance, then the doors slammed and the engine revved off.

'I'm so sorry.' Tom is frowning. 'We – I – I – Alex started doing chest compressions; I thought the best thing was to just start bringing her in, you know? Just get her to the nearest shore as fast as possible and radio for help on the way? Should we – maybe if we'd . . .' His voice trails off. 'Maybe we should have stopped and done the CPR?' Both of them are clearly in shock still.

'I ' Alex shakes his head. 'I really hope she's okay. I couldn't feel a pulse – nothing. She was so cold.'

'You did the right thing,' I tell them. 'Both of you. Absolutely the right thing.' I pause, not wanting to ask more of them when they've already been through so much. But it can't be helped.

'Did you see any sign of the little boy?'

Tom's expression pales further, if that's possible.

'A boy?' says Alex, his voice low, looking towards Tom with that easy communication of people who work together. They're both shaking their heads.

'We don't know for sure if he – if the child was in the water as well,' I amend. 'Her son, Ferdia. He's four.'

The three of us are silent, and it feels like my words brought ice to the windchill.

Stephen jogs up the slipway towards the bench, long strides shredding the distance in a few steps. He nods at the lads, then turns to me.

'McCarthy and Niamh are – you heard they've located the boat?'

'Yeah. But not Ferdia?'

He shakes his head. 'No. We're going back out now. I just—'

He reaches over to shake first Tom's, then Alex's hands.

'You two were unreal,' he says. 'If she – if she survives, and please God she makes it – if she does, it's down to the pair of ye. How did you' – he turns to Tom – 'how did you sail at that speed with no crew, with Alex doing CPR in – in the middle of the boat? Like, how did you even hold her on the deck? I thought there's no room for anything in the middle of a 49er?'

'Alex is pretty handy with the knots,' says Tom. 'We had to tie her in place, and she had—' He pauses, allowing Alex to take over.

'She was holding a weird – like a home-made float thing,' he says. 'She had it wedged under her chin and it was all tangled around her hands. It just about kept her mouth and nose above water.'

'I don't suppose you still have it?' I say, a tiny flare of hope rising in my chest.

'Sure,' says Tom. 'It's in the boat. I'll get it now.'

81

Niamh

Ferdia! I start hauling him out before Conleth can get to him.

'Mummy, Mum-meeee,' he's whimpering, barely awake, his small body heavy and strangely limp. He's wearing a red T-shirt that's too big for him, no trousers, and a pair of blue wellies with sharks on the sides. 'Want Mummy.'

'Sssh,' I say, taking hold of him under the oxters, pulling him close. 'You're okay. It's okay.'

'Ferdie!' breathes Conleth, moving to take him from me. 'Oh my God! What happened? Did Mummy—'

'Get him some water – now!'

I hoist him on to my hip and step into the cabin, holding him on my lap. His eyes are closing again. I lift the eyelids to look at his pupils. They're massively dilated. I scan the room, but it's impossible to see anything that points to drugs or poison.

'Where's the water? Hurry!' I yell, and Conleth hands me a bottle from the fridge. I shake the child, patting his back sharply.

'Wake up. Ferdia. Wake up! You have to drink some water.' I tilt the bottle into his mouth. Much of it trickles out, but he swallows. 'And again.' I repeat the action. He takes more, and then the thirst seems to take him over and he gulps the rest.

'Come on.' I lift him back on to my hip and get to my feet. I use my elbow to squeeze his legs against me. 'Hold on,' I say. 'Tighter. We're going on deck. Let's get you some air.'

Senan is at the top of the steps, radio clutched against his chest. Immediately, he starts talking into it, requesting assistance. I lean in to whisper.

'I think he's been drugged. He's improving, but I don't want to let go of him. Can you—'

I'm frowning at him, willing him either to arrest Conleth or take the kid so I can do it. He's not reading me. Instead, he turns to Conleth, all officious.

'That child should be wearing a flotation device,' he says. 'Under maritime law, all passengers on board a boat or watercraft of less than seven metres in length must wear a lifejacket.' Conleth stares at him. And for a second, I think Senan's lost the plot. Then I realize he's trying to buy us some time.

'Get him a lifejacket, now,' I snap at Conleth, turning back to the child, who is now clutching the water bottle himself. 'Drink more, pet, come on.'

Conleth steps down into the galley.

'They're on their way,' whispers McCarthy, pulling my arm and steering us over to the seating, which is arranged on either side of the main wheel. 'They've an ambulance on standby.'

'I found this,' says Conleth, his voice strange, coming up from below. He drops the lifejacket on to the seat and, with his other hand, thrusts a white flip-top phone towards me. 'She – this is her phone,' he says, and behind the large arrow I see Gemma's pale, tear-streaked face.

Senan takes the phone, moving away to look at it. He frowns.

'It's a confession,' says Conleth. 'Oh, Gemma!'

He moves towards the control panel of the boat, shaking his head. 'Don't you see? This explains everything. She must have – she couldn't live with the guilt any longer and she – she filmed this confession—'

A side-eye look, measuring how this is going down. His hands grip the wheel of the boat, knuckles white.

'It's too late,' he whispers. 'We're not going to find her alive.'

He turns to look at Ferdia. Takes a few steps closer and bends on his hunkers so his face is level with the child's. I feel the flinch rather than see it and, behind my back, where Ferdia's little hand is clutching my jacket, I feel the fabric tighten as he grasps it more firmly.

'It's just you and me, little man,' says Conleth, tears glinting in the corners of his eyes.

'Want Mummy,' whispers Ferdia. 'Where is she? I want her.'

Conleth straightens up, rubs both his palms over his face and back, into his hair. Overcome with emotion is the vibe.

'Why don't I just bring us back to shore?' he says, pressing a button on the control panel. 'Get treatment for Ferdia, and then I – I'll help with the search for the body—' He breaks off as another call comes in on McCarthy's radio, straining to hear what's being said. Meanwhile, there's a rumbling noise and the boat begins moving in a new way. We're drifting.

'What did you do?' I say.

McCarthy holds the receiver to his ear, his shoulders hunched, listening. He straightens up, catches my eye. Some kind of warning in his expression.

'Reactivate the anchor,' he says.

'We should go back,' Conleth blusters, ready to press buttons.

'Negative. I need you to stay where you are,' says McCarthy. 'The rescue boat is on its way,' he repeats.

'It's too late,' Conleth replies, misinterpreting. 'They'll never find her now. And she – she couldn't have survived this length of time.' He looks at his control panel, readying himself to start the engine.

'Leave it!' barks Senan. 'We're going back in with the rescue team. They've found her.'

82

Niamh

That stops Conleth in his tracks. He freezes. I look at Mc-
Carthy, trying to read him. Something about the tone of his
voice doesn't ring true, but he's not known for his ability to
lie. I frown at him, wondering what he's at. He nods in the
direction of my holster, and my heart begins thumping.

'Is she – is she alive?' Conleth steps back from the wheel,
his face pale.

'She's in ICU,' says McCarthy. 'They're working on her.'

'Oh my God!' breathes Conleth. 'So she might live? Oh,
that's amazing!' His expression belies the words. He looks
stricken.

Senan lurches forwards, holding out the handcuffs.

'Hands out,' he says. 'Keep your hands where I can see
them.'

'What on earth?' Conleth says, raising his hands slowly. He
steps around the steering wheel, so now it's between him and
McCarthy and he's in front of me. Carefully, I slide Ferdia off
my lap, reaching with my free hand towards my holster. I'm
just out of his line of sight, slightly behind him.

'What do you think you're doing, man?' Conleth is all
bluster. 'What the hell? You can't arrest me! What are you
arresting me for? I've done nothing!'

'I'm going to need you to put these on,' McCarthy continues, taking a step closer. He throws a glance at me and I step
closer as well, like we're doing a pincer movement.

'I'm arresting you on suspicion of the murder of Max Fitzgerald. Now, slowly lower your hands and—'

'You're mad! He was my friend! She – she did it! Gemma! Jesus Christ! You've got her confession there!'

'Lower your hands, slowly,' repeats McCarthy.

Conleth begins lowering his hands, his face frozen. McCarthy steps closer with the cuffs. I reach for Conleth's forearm with my free hand, but before we can cuff him, before I can train the gun on any part of him, he lurches to one side and, grabbing Ferdia by the fabric of his shirt, hauls him like a puppy up over the edge of the cockpit area and on to the deck, the heels of the little boy's welly boots bouncing with the movement. He begins backing away towards the rear edge of the boat – to the fold-down step from which we had boarded the boat.

Ferdia's face is blanched almond-white, his eyes enormous, panicked. 'No! No! Want Mummy! Mummy!' he starts screaming. His father grasps him even more tightly, thrusting him across the front of his own body, using the boy as a shield. I'm training the gun on his chest, but the boat is rocking and there's no way I'd have a clear shot.

McCarthy too has his weapon drawn.

'Don't do this,' he says. 'Don't make – this is a mistake. Just hand over the child. Hand him over.'

Conleth doesn't respond. He takes another step back, clutching Ferdia against his chest with his right hand, holding on to the rail with his left. And then he's got one foot on the ladder, lowering himself down to the platform, to where our rib is waiting. I shoot a look at McCarthy, and he frowns, shakes his head. I can't fire.

'Ferdia!' I shout. 'It's going to be okay. Just keep still.'

'Don't come any closer!' yells Conleth, reaching the platform and checking behind him quickly. 'I mean it.'

'There's nowhere for you to go,' I yell. 'You're not thinking straight! Let Ferdia go, for Christ's sake!'

I break off at the sound of a high-powered engine. The rescue boat. Thank God! They're rounding the corner – no more than three hundred metres away. I look back at Conleth, in time to see him jump down into the rib, still clutching Ferdia to his chest. They stagger backwards, but somehow Conleth manages not to fall. Our boat is drifting wildly, moving backwards. Below us, Conleth undoes the knot which had tethered the rib to the larger boat and in two strides is at the tiller and the outboard engine. A wave catches us broadside, and I stagger.

'The anchor!' I yell.

McCarthy whirls around to the control panel. I try to keep the gun trained on Conleth, but it's no use, we're lurching, and below us, the engine of the rib roars into life. I can't believe McCarthy left the keys in the ignition. Conleth has spent a lifetime around boats and it shows, because, using one hand only to steer, the other still clutching the child as a shield, he unleashes the throttle and the rib bursts forward at a crazy angle, its nose clear out of the water.

Two hundred metres away now, the rescue boat alters course in pursuit. They'll catch him within seconds, I think. The RNLI boat must be the more powerful craft. It's got to be. And then – then I watch in horror as Conleth does the unthinkable. He hauls his little boy on to the edge of the boat, and the small figure – his face a thumbnail of glistening white, arms and legs spinning in their sockets, welly-clad feet flailing – is suspended momentarily in the air – before landing with a sickening splash in the inky blue water.

83

Laura

No! No! Oh my God! He's thrown the child in the water! I leap to my feet, mouth gaping. I look wildly at the team in the boat – at Paul and Stephen. White, shocked faces. I look back at the boat – to the little space in the sky where the boy was suspended. To the dark depths into which he plummeted. To the horizon, where already that bastard is making his escape.

Why is there no splashing? A hand – a flash of something? Where has he gone? Nothing. I hear the engine surge to the maximum throttle possible, but we're not there yet. We're nowhere near where he went in.

And then a scream. A bloodcurdling scream with a Tipperary edge. If you can hear a Tipp accent in a scream, that was it – and then I'm screaming, 'No! Wait!'

But it's too late.

Niamh dives from the deck of the yacht.

84

Niamh

No, Jesus, please! No!

The child drops like a stone, weighted by the boots. And there's shouts and a scream, but that's me. McCarthy's on the radio, and the boat – the rescue boat is almost there, but still I'm closer, and I try to keep my eyes on him – his red T-shirt, his pale arms – but they went down. And I wait for him to bob up. He doesn't.

I rip off my lifejacket and I'm at the edge of the boat and then I breathe. Siobhán was a lifeguard at Mercy Convent and she drilled me to breathe in always before the dive. And then I'm in the air and bam! I'm in the water, going down, down.

It's burning in my lungs and I'm still going down and the salt is stinging my eyes and I blink them again and I level out and I'm looking.

And the water is cloudy and grey green, except when I look up and there's a wide circle of white and, centred in it, the dark hull of the boat. No fish. No rocks and no weeds, but dark, cloudy water.

Where is he?

Burning breath, and I long to power up towards the white circle and gasp, but I can't. I can't. Not.

Yet.

85

Laura

Oh my God! Why hasn't she surfaced? Senan is on the radio, his back to us, yelling something I can't hear, then he turns, jumping from the cockpit up on to the deck and making his way to the stern of the boat, peering at the space where Niamh disappeared. The larger boat is broadsided by waves powerful enough to make it seem like they're shoving it out of the way, and the boat rises, drops, rises, drops as the waves smack against the side.

Réaltín blasts along the water and I grip the handles with all my strength so as not to be thrown over. It seems we'll never make it – the distance doesn't get any less. Where is she? Why isn't she – why hasn't she surfaced yet?

At last the engine slows and the boat curves inwards towards the site where we saw the child drop into the water. We're lurching too, waves breaking over the side of the boat. Paul gives a yell, and I look back in time to see him launch himself into the water, wearing a mask and fins. The radio crackles.

'Air rescue is on its way.' Senan's voice on the radio.

'Hurry!' I yell. 'Get them here! Here! For Niamh!' I'm screaming, worried they'll search for Conleth. 'Tell them here, Senan! Now!'

Stephen controls the boat so we do a sweeping circle. I stare into the depths, trying to see. Thirty seconds more. It's so dark, the water. You can maybe see down about a metre – and then nothing but shadow, dark depths. Another thirty seconds pass. *Oh God. No. No no no.*

There's a sudden splash and my heart lurches, but it's just Paul breaking the surface. He shakes his head, then turns and dives again.

'No, no, no, no, no.'

I'm aware of someone crying. Maybe it's me. We circle, looking down.

Another thirty seconds. Senan on the radio, his words lost on the wind and water.

No, no. Please, no. And then, something.

Sunday

86

Gemma

A giant hand is crushing my chest like I'm a can. A beeping can with beeping sounds. Like I'm a can of Coke, but I hardly ever let him have Coke, it's too much sugar and it will make him – and that's not – it's not it's not Ferdie it's me. It's crushing me and it's when I breathe the inward breath and it goes in and a thousand million tons of pressure but I have to breathe it in. And where – I have to breathe it in and it's so burning heavy burning sore and softly, ssh, now it's out. And a rest before it starts again but I can't not do it I have to . . .

'You're okay, Gem.' A voice. 'It's going to be okay. I'm here.'

And the voice puts a soft cool hand on my forehead and she leaves it there and it's a girl I love and she says, 'Sssh, just relax,' and it's – it's Penny. She's the voice. And I – I have to open my eyes and I have to breathe and I have to know – I have to know the thing. There's a terrible thing I have to know and—

'It's all going to be okay. Ferdia's okay. And you're okay. You're both going to be fine.'

And the cool hand moves down my cheek and the cool hand leaves my cheek and I'm crying but I can't do it because of the pain in my chest and my heart is breaking too. And Penny swims in shimmering tears in front of me, and her face is wet but in her hand is a white tissue. She sweeps the tissue in gentle soft circles of care across my cheek and under my eyes and she smiles and then she laughs a little laugh and takes the tissue up to dry her own face.

'It's all going to be okay.' She smiles. 'You and Ferdia, you're going to be grand. Both of you.'

And I know this must be true because Penny wouldn't lie.

Monday

@missymurfi: They say she's out of danger. But no visitors yet. They wouldn't let me in. We are not allowed.

@nolimitsgrl: Thanks @missymurfi. You are amazing – it's thanks to you, you know.

@missymurfi: Ah no – friends should look out for each other. That's what real friends do.

@nolimitsgrl: You got that right. You're a great friend @missymurfi. Gemma is lucky to have you. And that guard should get a medal. Unreal.

@unatracey5: I couldn't believe it.

@becka98: I lit a candle for her. The garda. Niamh Darmody.

@nolimitsgrl: Beautiful thought. She was so brave to do what she did.

@marymary2: God love the pair of them. And the garda.

@missymurfi: The gardaí are our friends. They help us. She was so brave to do it. I'm going to light a candle for her as well.

Six Days Later

87

Laura

In the week since I've seen him, Cig's face has been scored by a new batch of creases – lines of grief and worry gouged into the leathery skin. These aren't wrinkles – they're not something you get from smiling. There's a twitch at the corner of his mouth, as if he's thinking he should attempt a greeting, but no words emerge. He nods for me to close the door. To sit. I do both, returning his nod, which he doesn't see, because he's already back looking down at the pages in front of him.

I should speak first but, like him, I don't know where to start. Framed in the window behind his desk, dark clouds bloom like bloodstains against the white brutalist office buildings of Seskin West Garda Station. He taps a gnarled forefinger, which looks more arboreal than human, on the lines of type. Now we're both looking at the page. Much better.

'O'Riordan and McCarthy must be ecstatic – you'll be able to get your charges.'

'Yeh.' I cough, my voice, like his, unsteady. 'Yes, Cig. We're charging him with the murder of Max Fitzgerald, with obstructing a Garda investigation. He's still being questioned in relation to the fire that killed his parents, and of course—' I pause. Cig has looked up, and our eyes meet. Please God don't mention her. Please.

'Go on,' is all he says.

'They're pretty sure he killed Detective Nolan as well, so they're looking for witnesses, for anyone who might have seen him in the harbour on the day Nolan disappeared.'

I shake my head.

'All – for—' Again, he breaks off.

'Who knows, Cig? The usual. Power, money – plus it was his fault they were ruled out of the Olympics. It was him – Conleth was the one who couldn't give a clean sample.'

Cig nods. 'Do you know, the longer I'm at this game, the more I believe in evil.' His voice is weary. 'Evil, pure and simple.'

He sighs from the depths of his lungs. 'There was no call to do what he did, you know? Any of it. He was all set for a great life – by all accounts he came from decent people. Sound. Solid.' Cig turns his palms over, as if answers might be scored into the flesh, written on the many lines.

'And it wasn't even about money. They had enough.'

Another sigh, which lingers in his throat, almost like a growl. 'Evil incarnate. That's the only explanation. I mean, the fact that he took part in the searches – I mean, what does that tell you? He killed his friend, then hid the body on the boat, and next morning, cool as you like, he's the first one out "searching" *mar dhea*. And then he dumps his childhood friend at the bottom of the sea.'

I mirror Cig's head shake. Because I don't understand it either. What motivates someone like Conleth to do what he did. What motivates any of them.

We had some work to do with tide experts, matching up currents and ocean flora found at certain depths, but the part of Conleth's statement where he admitted to dumping the body, before the first searches had got underway, that part checked out.

'You know he's still saying she killed him, though – that she was jealous of her brother's success. That he just disposed of the body.'

Cig shrugs. He turns a page.

'I mean, there's no doubt she *thought* she killed him,' I say. 'All this time, he'd twisted the truth and manipulated her until she didn't know which way was up.'

Cig shakes his head wearily. 'They were kids – she was drunk.' He sighs. 'If it hadn't been for him, if it hadn't been for – for the sheer evil of that man, it would have been nothing. A family story – *Do you remember when I knocked you out?* – a thing ye all laugh about at Christmas.'

He stands. Neither of us wants to think about Christmas yet. 'So, get on to Parminter and get what you need. You know, the angle of the blade, the depth of the nick in the bone – whatever it takes – to show that only he could have done it. There's no way a sixteen-year-old of her size could've inflicted that injury. And ye have the witness who saw him at the scene late that night, whatshername – the coach? Get your charges, Shaw, and make them stick.'

'I will, Cig.' I nod.

'Evil will out.' Cig sighs. 'No matter how deep you try to sink it.'

In the silence, I know both of us are thinking of bodies rising to the surface. We're not going there.

'Get him. Tell O'Riordan, anything he needs from us, he's got. Just make sure you get him on all charges – everything. Get it done, Shaw.'

He sweeps his palm across his face, the branch-like fingers crumpling more creases into skin. Closes his eyes in a slow blink or a prayer.

'Do you know what, Shaw?' he says, looking up, skewering me with his gaze.

'When you start believing in evil, you know it's time to retire.'

'Cig, maybe she—'

'Don't,' he says.

88

Gemma

'You're so kind.' I smile at the care assistant holding the door open for us. 'We won't be long, but thanks.'

She's new, and I know she's already heard the story because of the way she looks at us. She shakes her head as if in wonder, ruffling Ferdia's hair.

'Great boy,' she says, accented with her soft Italian lilt.

'Say thank you.' I nudge him with my elbow, doing my best not to drop the large plant container I'm carrying.

'Thank you,' he says. She grins at him. My funny little fella. My – no. Not going there.

Ferdia squeezes my hand as we make our way down to the wooden seat where I plan on depositing the lavender plant.

'How 'bout here, Mummy?' he says, pointing to a small patch of ground. 'Beside where you put your tea?'

'Good idea,' I say, plonking it down and dusting my hands. 'Now you and Digger go and – and dig the leaves, okay? Just for a few minutes while I talk – while I think.'

He has about ten diggers now. People kept sending them, along with the bouquets. He dives into the bushes behind the bench. And I sit, imagining Dad – his big, worn hands, the cords and the old jumper, his eyes a faded grey-green sky.

'This is my last visit, Dad,' I say, imagining myself taking his hand in my lap, bending the fingers to curl around my own. I breathe a deep breath, a vestige of pain and infection lurking, but the scent of the lavender fills my head, and I say what I have to say.

'I need to say something. Max is dead. He's never coming back. And – and it's – some of it is my fault. I'm sorry. I'll regret it for the rest of my life, I'm sorry.' I shake my head, finding it difficult to go on. But I need to say the words aloud.

'But I didn't kill him – it was Conleth who – Conleth wanted him dead.'

I hesitate, heartbreak washing through me in a flood. Poor Max. Always looking out for me.

'Oh God, if I could only go back and change things!'

And now I see Mum beside Dad, her outline faint as a mirage. Dressed in her favourite cardi – the lilac one. She takes hold of his hand.

My face is wet with tears, though I thought I had no more left. I wipe them away, closing my eyes, wanting to finish this.

'I – that night, I took Max's keycard and I went down to the boat and I waited for Conleth in the cabin, but he never came. It was Max. Max was worried about me. Of course. He was so good, wasn't he? I'd left the gate open. And when he came in and saw me – I – I was drunk and – and wasted and he was shouting at me. Really shouting. He was just so angry. And so disappointed in me. And I pushed him. I meant to just push him away, you know – like, it was only meant to be a get-away-from-me push. Like a shove. It was nothing. But he fell and he – he banged his head on the table. And I thought he'd get up, but he didn't.'

'Mummy, when can we go?' Ferdia scrambles out of the hedge. 'There's only leaves in there.'

'Now, pet,' I whisper, and I take a deep, deep breath which shivers. I don't know yet if I'll be prosecuted for concealing the – the murder. Laura thinks it's unlikely – I was sixteen. And even then, he controlled my every waking thought.

'And I panicked,' I whisper. 'Max didn't get up, so I ran back to the club, and I got Conleth, and he yelled at me to go home. He said he'd sort it. And I crept home along the shore-line, hiding in the shadows. While Conleth – I thought he was taking care of it. I thought I'd killed Max and I didn't know what – I thought Conleth would know what to do. All this time, I thought it was me, but Dad, Mum, I'm so sorry.' My voice catches in a sob.

'Max wasn't dead when I left him. I didn't – I didn't kill him. Conleth did. With the knife that was on the boat. Conleth stabbed Max with his own penknife – the one I'd given him.'

I can't go on. My husband stole my brother's life and the lives of my parents – and mine – for nothing. Nothing. And he kept the knife, Max's knife, in the top drawer of the chest in our bedroom. The knife he used to stab my brother.

I scrunch my eyes closed and I feel myself fold over, collapsing from my core. Too empty even to cry. And then I feel my brother's presence. *Maxattacks*, he grins, sunlight slicing through his messy hair. I feel him take my hand in his – like the night when we camped in the tent.

I'm here, Gem.

'I'm sorry, Max,' I say. 'I will spend the rest of my life making it up to you.'

Four Days Later

89

Laura

Martina, Niamh's mum, waits until the last chord of the hymn echoes through the vaulted building before leaning into me and grabbing my elbow. Two funerals in one week. I'm turning into an expert in not falling apart.

'A lovely service,' she whispers.

'Lovely,' I agree, passing her a fresh tissue for the tears that shine on her cheeks, taking another for the ones that linger on mine.

'It's good when they make it more of a celebration, isn't it?'

'It is, for sure,' I say. 'She'd definitely have approved. She loved a celebration.'

We stand like soldiers at attention as the minister begins walking down the aisle, followed by the plain wicker coffin. It passes us, and I turn to follow its progress, smiling at Gemma and Ferdia, who are sitting in the front row of the gallery, surrounded by about sixty of her followers, who have been pretty much escorting her everywhere since she and Ferdia were given the all-clear. The press have been kept away.

The church is absolutely packed. I'd no idea she'd touched so many lives. We begin filing out, and I'm aware of Martina still sniffing behind me. I turn back to her, my hand on her sleeve.

'Are you okay?' I whisper.

She wipes her eyes fiercely, dragging the balled tissue across them.

'Of course – I am of course.' She smiles. 'It's just so much to take in, and—' I nod sympathetically, not wanting her to have to finish that sentence. If you've buried one of your children – I mean – why am I even asking her if she's okay? She'll always carry that pain with her.

A second door is opened at the side of the church, and suddenly we're outside in the bright sunshine, everyone standing around beginning to smile, casting off the shadows. Ranelagh traffic streams steadily by as usual, leaves rustling, cheerful voices, birdsong.

Niamh spots us, and she finishes up whatever she was saying to the minister and strides over. She's grinning.

'You'll be getting a fierce big head, now,' says Martina. 'I could have told Dorothy – God rest her – a few things about you. Imagine her asking for you to do the eulogy!'

She smiles, and I watch her literally drinking in the sight of her daughter. As I am – because we all know how lucky we are to have her. Still.

Niamh was underwater for almost three minutes. A full minute longer than little Ferdia because as she thrust him towards the surface, her shoelace got caught on the edge of a rock and she struggled to get free.

'And I could too.' I laugh.

'What are we all laughing at?' smiles Sarita, joining our little group.

'They're ripping the piss out of me, as usual,' grins Niamh. 'Which is not fair – in—'

'In your condition,' we chorus, and Martina's cheeks pinken.

I look from Niamh to her mum, the fire that burns between them, and I think of Katie and Noah, and of my own mum. All that love. All that energy and power. I think of Dorothy, brilliant, brave, wise and inspirational – a mother figure to

Niamh and to half of Ranelagh, it seems, who are filing out of the church gate in pairs and groups, who will always remember her kindness and professionalism.

Niamh should have drowned, but she didn't.

Instead, she's here, all guns blazing, ready for us to assemble a watertight case which will ensure that Conleth O'Hara is put away for a very long time. He was spotted by the coastguard helicopter before he'd gone any distance and picked up by the Water Unit. He'll stand trial for the murder of Max and for that of Detective Inspector Gerard Nolan as well. Nolan had been investigating Conleth in relation to the death of his parents. He believed that Conleth set the fire that killed them and locked them in their bedroom, sealing their fate, though he claimed he had been trying to open the door. Nolan suspected foul play in Max's disappearance as well but, crucially, he had kept his findings secret. After Nolan died, O'Hara, a man with no moral compass, a thief and a murderer, was able to pass undetected, hiding behind his guilt-stricken wife and her supposedly perfect world. Maybe, as Cig says, he is plain evil.

It's early days, but we're hoping that Gemma will have the courage to give evidence in court – against the man who tried to kill her, against the husband and father who betrayed his own family. When Conleth realized that he couldn't frame Gemma for the murder, he was prepared to use his own son as a decoy to buy him a bit of time. I will never forget the sight of him flinging Ferdia into the water, though later he claimed to be throwing him to the rescue boat. Because he's always got a self-serving answer.

And Niamh. Niamh leaping in after him without a thought for her own safety. I'll never forget that sight either.

I inhale, trying to shake the thought away.

She should have drowned, but she did not. That's what I

will remember. To think that even at that early stage of pregnancy – the day that Niamh dived in to save Ferdia was only the fourteenth day after implantation – to think that already her body had begun changing at a cellular level. Not just in the womb.

Already her blood carried more oxygen, her lungs had greater capacity. Her heart was working harder, with every beat. All that love. All that energy and power. I'm going to think about that. About love beating evil every time.

Women. Mothers. Sisters. Daughters. Sons and dads and brothers. Friends. The family you choose for yourself. Love.

My work phone buzzes with a message. I frown. Today is actually my fortieth, and I've taken the day off. Everyone's forgotten.

It's a WhatsApp from Cig – posted in the wrong group.

Did Matt say to arrive at the tennis club at 7.00 or 7.30? Don't want to ruin the surprise. Not going to mess up on my watch. Not in front of Justy! Lol. See ye later.

Niamh checks her phone pretty much at the same time as I do, and her eyes lock on mine. A grin creeps over her face as she steps towards me. And I feel myself filled with a burst of such happiness that I have to hide my face. I pretend to zip up my bag as I tuck the phone away, and I'm beaming. I'm beaming because Niamh did not die. She's okay, she's here. She's here.

'A surprise fortieth party?' I say, as she pulls me into a hug and pats the back of my head, messing my hair.

'Yup. With me, and all the other people you love,' she says. 'It's gonna be a tough one.'

I suppose that's okay.

That's okay.

Epilogue

LEINSTER TELEGRAPH

EMOTIONAL SCENES AS NEW LIFE-BOAT ARRIVES IN DÚN LAOGHAIRE

Dún Laoghaire RNLI's new all-weather Shannon-class lifeboat was given an emotional welcome on Saturday afternoon, having completed its week-long voyage from the charity's lifeboat centre in Poole.

The lifesaving vessel arrived into Dún Laoghaire in a flotilla made up of both the inshore and all-weather lifeboats from the harbour, along with a group of local vessels. Friends, families and supporters lined the quayside to get a glimpse of the new boat.

The lifeboat was funded through a bequest made in memory of the late Max Fitzgerald, brother of former influencer Gemma Fitzgerald. Gemma and her young son, Ferdia, were rescued by the Dún Laoghaire RNLI crew in May of last year.

Commenting on the arrival, Gemma said: 'Without the RNLI, Ferdia and I would not be here. They are a charity founded on values of selflessness and courage, the vast majority of whom are volunteers. We – and so many others – owe them our lives. Today is the realization of my long-held dream that Max should rest in peace, knowing the world is a better place because he lived among us. I am so grateful to the Gardaí, the RNLI and all the volunteers who help keep us safe, and I wish safe, speedy rescues to this wonderful vessel, *MaxAttacks*.'

Acknowledgements

To friend and agent, the wonderful Faith O'Grady, heartfelt thanks for the pep talks, the guidance and emails that arrive at exactly the right moment – I do wonder if you're psychic. You set this voyage in motion, and I'm eternally grateful. Huge thanks also to the team at Lisa Richards for their support and professional brilliance.

To Captain of Editors, Patricia Deevy of Penguin Sandycove, a thousand thanks for your sharp eyes and relentless pursuit of the best version of the story – and for (let's continue with the nautical metaphors) ensuring that I plug any leaks in the plot and batten down the hatches! The editorial team of Sarah Day, Leah Boulton and Natalie Wall have time and again saved me and basically thrown me a lifeline when I most needed it. Joyce Dignam at Penguin Sandycove, thank you for an insightful and important read; to Michael McLoughlin for encouragement and a most welcome phone call; and to the brilliant Sandycove flock – Cliona Lewis, Carrie Anderson, Louise Farrell, Leonor Pestana Araújo, Finn Roche and Lorna Browne – a thousand thanks. None of this would have happened without you. Thank you to the brilliant actors Martha Breen and Aisling Kearns who narrate the audiobooks and bring Laura and Niamh so vividly to life. Where would we writers be without the booksellers, librarians, bloggers and Instagrammers? Thank you so much for your support and for keeping the joy of reading alive.

Thank you, writer pals Clare Harlow and Gianna Pollero, for the earliest of early reads and for the ongoing friendship and support. Massive thanks to writer bestie Fiona Gartland for an emergency read at a crucial point (we were almost on the rocks . . .), and I want to thank the amazing crew of fellow crime writers who have welcomed me on board, buoyed me up and shown me the ropes. The support and friendship from the very start have been unbelievable. Cups of coffee and lunches and chats and even overnight stays away have been most gratefully enjoyed, along with encouragement and advice and the feeling that we are all in this together. I will never forget the sight of you all rocking up to my launch and I am so thankful for the fun, friendship and support – which has even extended to the sharing of precious anecdotes for Niamh to use. Thank you!

This story would not exist without the help of two brilliant young sailors. Firstly, thanks to Tom Flannery who gave me hours of his time explaining all matters related to sailing, followed by an all-access tour of the yacht club and a subsequent early-morning phone interview during his school holidays. The photos and notes I took that first day and in our subsequent conversations helped shape the story and kept me motivated. Huge thanks also to Lara MacWilliam for a fascinating discussion about the experience of preparing for sailing exams and capsizing practice, and the peaks and troughs of sailing. And to Ian MacWilliam, Commodore of Courtown Sailing Club 2021–2023 (also Lara's dad), for yet more seafaring and sailing information, which I hope has added to the realism of this book.

Likewise, there would be no story without the help of Paul Cummins – who is (wait for it) a garda AND RNLI lifeboat coxswain! Thank you, Paul, for our lengthy talk and for your patient help with subsequent questions. Thanks to you and your RNLI colleagues Laura Jackson and James Traynor for the tour of the Dún Laoghaire RNLI lifeboat hut, for explaining the launch and rescue procedure, and for basically inspiring the whole rescue scene. I even got to study the book on search patterns! The work you do is truly amazing and I was honoured to get a glimpse into this world and to write about it.

Aoife Cooney, I was blown away by your honest and inspirational account of what's involved in choosing to become a solo mum. Thank you for the long interview and for emails and messages that helped to build a realistic picture of what Niamh is embarking on in this book. Congratulations and continued joy to you and your wonderful family, living proof of how perseverance, vision and belief can bring about this happy ending.

As ever, there would be no Laura and Niamh, no Seskin West and no finished stories without the ongoing help of friend and garda Danni Cummins. Danni, your enthusiasm, patience and sense of adventure help bring these stories into being. Thank you, also, for allowing me to include a certain brilliant pair of boys who elbowed their way into the story, to my great delight.

Continuing the garda roll call, Mary Fallon and Deasún McNally continue to advise and provide answers at the right moment, and I am unendingly grateful. (Any errors are of course my own!)

I've been calling this story *the Dún Laoghaire book* since it had a word count in the double figures. My Shaw and Darmody stories are usually based in the fictional village of Clonchapel, which is basically Rathfarnham and Churchtown combined, but the genesis of this book goes way back to my childhood, and my time spent in a boarding school called Glengara Park. Glengara was situated at the crossroads just above Dún Laoghaire's main street and within sight of the seafront. On Sundays, we were marched down to the church at the end of the road wearing our blue crimplene dresses. Yes. We marched in our pairs and took our places in the pews and thought ourselves bold for swapping sweets during the sermon. Sometimes we were allowed to watch the boats bobbing in the bay before we headed back.

Our music teacher lived in a stunning seafront mansion on a terrace very like Gemma's and, once a year, we were invited over for tea. I can still remember tramping up the long flights of stairs and looking out the tall windows at the harbour and, beyond that, the bay and all the way off to Howth. You don't forget a view like that.

This Dún Laoghaire – privileged, genteel and wealthy, with echoes of Victorian seaside grandeur and whimsical, charming Dalkey where my grandmother lived – contrasted starkly with my later lived experience. I came of age in Ireland in the early 80s during a recession, in a country whose darkness was still hidden but beginning to leak out at the seams; where men were to be feared, smiled at and placated, and boys were not to be 'led on'. The glittering charm of this seaside town was layered over the myriad and complex social problems of unemployment, poverty, addiction and a generally accepted misogyny.

On the surface, Gemma is living a glamorous and enviable lifestyle that people can only dream about. But underneath, there's a tragically different story. So I knew that for this book, Laura and Niamh would be heading out along the coast, exploring Dún Laoghaire and Bullock Harbour, Pilot View and the People's Park, to do what they do best – what I constantly ask them to do for me – namely, to make sense of a confusing and sometimes cruel world while still maintaining their deep friendship, their sense of humour, and hope.

Speaking of making sense of the world, there are not enough words to thank my brilliant friends, old and new – you know who you are. Wexford besties, crime writers, choir buddies, Never2Late dancers and Wednesday Movers, book clubbers, dance pals and dog walkers.

To the sisters-in-law, the sons-in-law, the cousins, the in-laws and outlaws – your love and support is everything. To the best brothers, Keith and Con, and best sister, Adrienne, in the world – you are the ballast that keeps me steady.

Daughters Jess and Sara, you are the lighthouse beams. Thank you for more than you can ever know. To my husband who listens always – even at breakfast. A is for Anchor and Angus.

Finally, but most importantly, dear reader, thank you for reading this book. I hope you enjoyed it.